# APOCALYPSE

# NOCT

aethonbooks.com

## APOCALYPSE ME
## ©2024 NOCT

# ALSO IN THE SERIES

Apocalypse Me
Apocalypse City

# 1

## APOCALYPTIC ARRIVAL

"So. Zombie apocalypse," Ryan said, drawing up alongside Zeke. He gestured with his iced coffee, taking in the city below them.

On the far side of the balcony, four floors down, cars roared. Perched atop the skyscrapers that hemmed in the museum, billboards shone with bright color, advertising everything from perfume to fast food to alcohol and condoms. Pedestrians scuttled by, businessmen and women hurrying to their next meeting while a man on a corner spun a sign, inviting people to stop in and buy insurance. Beside him, a busker strummed a guitar while a homeless man sprawled on the side of the street, snoozing away, a dog curled up beside him.

"Zombie apocalypse, huh?" Zeke asked, pushing up from the steel railing. A glass panel pushed a few inches above the rail, protecting him and small children from slipping under it and dropping to the street below. He looked at the dirty-blond boy beside him, quirking a brow. "What about it?"

Ryan's blue eyes shone. He grinned. "Odds of survival. What do you think? How long would you last?"

"Me? What, in the city?" Zeke frowned. A light breeze blew

through his short-cropped dark hair, and he squinted, hazel-green eyes screwed up against the late-spring sun.

"Yeah. You're going to college here, right?" Ryan asked.

Zeke snorted. "That was only if my swim scholarship came through. As it is...might be more like community college." His eyes settled on Ryan's drink, and his stomach grumbled. Cream swirled invitingly amidst the dark coffee, luscious and inviting, highlighting the museum café's old-fashioned man logo on the plastic cup. His mouth watered. *I bet it's delicious. I'm so hungry...*

He pressed his lips together, turning away. *I'm fine. Coffee isn't filling, anyway. And that menu...oof. The city is* expensive, *no lie!*

"Aww, c'mon. There're other scholarships. I'm sure you'll get *something*. I mean, right?" Ryan said, tilting his head.

Turning back to the city, Zeke shook his head. He sighed, then shrugged. "Yeah, maybe."

"Anyway. Zombie apocalypse," Ryan said.

"Zombie apocalypse. I think I die right away," Zeke said.

"Really? You're pretty fit." Ryan frowned.

"Not that fit. Besides, I'm a swimmer. That isn't going to help me much in the apocalypse. Not like I can swim through a horde of zombies," Zeke pointed out.

"Still, stamina, strength..." Ryan swung an imaginary base-ball bat through an imaginary zombie head, "that's gotta count for a lot!"

Zeke waved him away. "Nah. I think I die right away. Immediate zombie. I mean, right? If you can't beat 'em, join 'em."

"I think you'd do better than me. I'm a nerd, not a jock like you," Ryan joked, taking a sip of his coffee.

"Yeah, yeah. Where's Mia?" Zeke peered over his shoulder at the café's exit.

"I dunno. Still customizing her double-cream-whipped-mocha-caramel macchimochamericano or something," Ryan said with a shrug.

Zeke nodded. He tilted his head at Ryan. "How about you?"

Ryan froze. He pressed the heel of his hand to his forehead. "Me...?"

"Brain freeze?" Zeke asked, chuckling. He nodded at Ryan. "Yeah, you. Zombie apocalypse. How long do you last?"

"Zombie...apocalypse..." Ryan startled as if he'd been slapped. He looked upward, then frowned. Slowly, he nodded to himself. "Then, this is..."

"This is?" Zeke asked, confused.

Ryan jumped at him and grabbed his shoulders, bowling him backward.

He fell back, surprised. His spine struck the railing. "Ow! Ryan, what the hell?"

"Zeke...this is for the good of everyone. For the good of humanity," Ryan said. Blue eyes bored into Zeke's, full of madness.

"Uh...what? Dude, you're heavy. Get off me," Zeke said, shoving at Ryan.

Ryan's grip tightened. "Listen to me. I don't have long. If you don't die right here, right now, the world is over. Humanity dies out."

"Ryan? Is this because I said I'd die first in a zombie apocalypse? I wasn't being literal, you know," Zeke said, laughing nervously. *The hell? What's he on about?*

Ryan took a deep breath. "I—"

"Guys! Where are we going next? Dinos?" a chestnut-haired girl asked, bouncing out of the museum's café with her large, frothy, syrup-striped drink. Slender as a whip despite the thousands of calories in her drink of choice, she played forward on the soccer team and possessed boundless energy. A low-cut blue shirt showed off her petite curves, matched with a pair of blue denim shorts that revealed lithe, tan legs. Mia glanced at the boys and frowned. "What are you two doing?"

Ryan glanced at Mia, then tensed. He looked into Zeke's eyes. "Trust me. There's no other way."

"No other way for—?"

Releasing him, Ryan backed up a few steps.

Confused, Zeke stood. "Okay...?"

Ryan sprinted toward Zeke.

Zeke's eyes widened. Startled, he jumped up from the railing. "Ryan, what the fuck?"

Without a word, Ryan leaped into the air and kicked Zeke in the chest.

Zeke fell backward, his arms flailing. His spine struck the railing. His head snapped back, whiplashed by the force of the kick. Stunned, he sprawled over the railing and the glass pane. Electric pain shot down his spine, arcing directly into his brain.

Ryan stared at him, his blue eyes alien, cold. Zeke saw himself reflected in those eyes, and his heart froze. *I'm already dead to him.*

*What...what the hell?*

*He wasn't joking? He... What happened? What's going on?*

*No. This isn't Ryan. Ryan would never do this. Ryan would never look at me like this. This is someone else.*

Rushing at him, Ryan reached out again.

Zeke jolted, forcibly breaking his stun. *Move. I have to move!*

Mia screamed.

Around them, other tourists turned, eyes wide. Some stood on their tiptoes to get a better look.

From across the balcony, an overweight security guard lumbered toward the three of them as fast as his three-hundred-pound frame would allow, reaching for the Taser on his hip. He shoved at a knot of tourists, fighting past them. "Move!"

The tourists shifted, but slowly. An old woman hobbled to the side, accompanied by an old man who shuffled a single beat faster. Huffing and puffing, the security guard fought his way through. "Come on...move!"

Iron-strong hands grabbed Zeke by the waist. All at once, Ryan pushed him up and over the ledge.

Zeke's hand snapped out, gripping blindly. He latched onto the railing. His wrist bent over the glass pane that made up the other half of the protective barrier. He jolted to a halt, and the glass' rounded edges bit into the underside of his wrist. Blood dripped down his arm. "Ow!"

"Zeke!" Mia ran for him, hands out, terrified.

Ryan ignored her. He pushed at Zeke's wrist.

Zeke gritted his teeth, holding on despite the pain.

*He didn't hesitate. Not even a moment.*

*I can't— I don't understand. Ryan wouldn't. He wouldn't!*
*What's going on?*

Knuckles white, Zeke grabbed at the railing with his free hand. His hand bounced off the glass, unable to reach the extra few inches to the railing. He swung from the force of his grab, and the glass dug deeper into his wrist. More blood streaked the pane and ran down his arm. His grip weakened. Afraid to lose his grip entirely, he hung still.

Desperately, he shouted, "Ryan! Snap out of it!"

"Hey! Get away from him!" the security guard shouted, finally running up on Ryan.

Ryan stared at Zeke, eyes cold. "I have no option. I've tried. I've tried so much." He lifted his arm and slammed his elbow down on Zeke's wrist.

The glass's edges bit into his tendons. His bones creaked. Zeke lost his grip for a moment. With the tips of his fingers, he caught on again, but the railing slipped steadily out of his grasp, millimeter by millimeter. "Ryan!"

Raising his elbow again, Ryan slammed it down on Zeke's hand. "I'm sorry."

Zeke's fingers slipped off the railing. He dropped, falling backward. *Ryan...why? What?*

As he fell, a gash split the sky. A deep sound *thrummed* out, resonating in his bones more than his ears. Bright white light poured out, coming from somewhere *beyond,* somewhere alien and unknowable.

Time slowed.

Zeke stared, wide-eyed. *The fuck?*

In slow motion, tourists screamed and ran. Tires screeched and cars slammed into one another below. Mia reached after him, shouting something he couldn't hear.

*What's happening? Why am I moving so slowly?* He tried to sit up, but the same as everyone else, he could only move in slow motion. *Is this what it feels like before you die?*

Ryan looked up, staring at the sky. His fist curled.

Zeke's brows furrowed. Something shot through his head, a thought half-completed. *As if he already knew—*

Thick black liquid spewed out of the white gash in the sky. Rather than falling like rain, it spread through the air and domed over them, pouring toward the ground. None of the black dripped directly down. Instead, it formed a void, an enormous bowl-shaped empty space blocked off by the black at its borders, as if someone had placed a glass bowl over the city and poured melted plastic over it. The black goo eclipsed the sky and the white light, hiding both from sight.

In moments, only a tiny hole at the apex of the barrier remained, and even that closed rapidly. Just as the white light was about to vanish for good, the black goo slowed, crawling instead of rushing.

Zeke blinked. *Huh?*

Above him, the people running suddenly froze as time

slowed again. The screams dropped in pitch, from shrill shrieks to a low drone. Zeke's fall also slowed as if he fell through water not air. He frowned, looking around. *Even slower now. At this rate, I'll never hit the ground. Not that I mind, but—*

Words appeared in front of Zeke's vision, burning into his brain.

**WELCOME TO THE APOCALYPSE INCUBATOR.**
**YOU HAVE BEEN SELECTED.**
**PLEASE CHOOSE YOUR CONCEPT.**

*What? Concept? What the hell is happening?*
*Did I get saved? Am I—*

He glanced down. The ground awaited him, cold, hard, final. He swallowed, his heart racing. *I'm about to die.*

**DEATH IS NOT AN ACCEPTABLE CONCEPT.**
**PLEASE CHOOSE YOUR CONCEPT.**

Zeke's stomach grumbled. He frowned, his mind racing. *Maybe— Wait! Okay, maybe I'm going insane as I fall to my death, but what the hell. Maybe this is real. Maybe I can survive this if I choose the right 'Concept,' whatever that is. Something like invulnerability, or regeneration, or phasing—*

**CONCEPT CHOSEN.**

"What? I didn't choose anything! Hold up! You can't cheat me like this. I had a chance. I could have survived!" Zeke shouted at the words.

**CONCEPT: HUNGER**
**LEVEL ZERO SKILL GRANTED: [DEVOUR]**

**PLEASE BECOME THE STRONGEST APOCALYPSE.
ONLY ONE CAN LEAVE.**

*The strongest...what? Leave? Escape the dome...?*

Time snapped back to normal. Black poured across the sky, sealing off a massive dome of the city. The tourists overhead screamed and ran. Ryan turned and vanished, leaving Mia behind on the railing.

Zeke plummeted. He slammed into the sidewalk, and everything went dark.

# 2

## BECOME THE STRONGEST APOCALYPSE

Pain. Darkness. The taste of copper. Eyes shut, Zeke lay completely still on the sidewalk.

An alarm blared. The wind blew, wafting an acrid scent over him. Zeke twitched and immediately regretted it. The tiny shift sent agony blasting through his body, washing over him in waves.

*What...what...*

Ryan, with an iced coffee. A casual chat. That familiar face, his blue eyes colder than the arctic. Mia's horrified expression.

*I fell. No...Ryan pushed me. I survived? How?*

Exerting herculean effort, he opened his eyes. His vision blurred, barely able to make out the sidewalk in front of him. Crashed cars piled up in the road beyond. Smoke billowed in the near-distance. A woman in blue ran by, panicked.

*Mia? No...*

As he focused on the woman, a screen appeared in front of his vision.

**Please assign your points.**

**Warning! You are near death. You need to find something to eat or drink to raise your vitality.**
**Death estimated in: 2:06**
**You have one new skill. Would you like to examine it?**

*What...what...*

**Please assign your points.**

"What points?" Zeke muttered.

**Level 0. Points: 5**
**STR: 0**
**CON: 0**
**DEX: 0**
**SPR: 0**

*What does SPR mean?* he wondered, furrowing his brows faintly.

**SPR stands for Spirit. The more Spirit you have, the more powerful your non-physical attacks will be. SPR also grants intelligence, especially to non-sentient apocalypses.**

"Non-physical?" *It's like I'm in a game. Am I dreaming? But...it hurts way too damn much for this to be a dream. These numbers... this is real life. But...what's happening? How...?*

He glanced upward. A black sky stretched overhead. Despite the darkness of the heavens, the light remained bright as midday. *That dome...we're trapped in here. And only the strongest can survive.*

His throat itched. He tried to suppress it, but a cough welled up in his chest anyway. His entire body bucked, every inch of him screaming in pain from the force of the cough. Blood sprayed over the filthy sidewalk.

*Only the strongest can survive, and I'm lying here dying.*

**Putting points into CON will enhance your natural vitality and regeneration rate.**

Zeke waved his hand. "Put five points into CON." *Anything to survive a little longer.*

**CON:** 5
**Regeneration rate** +0.5%
**Death estimated in:** 2:05

"Fuck," Zeke muttered, lips slippery with his own blood. *What was that worth? Five seconds? I wasted a few seconds talking to the System...so probably about five seconds for five points of CON. I'm fucked.* He twitched again. Again, his entire body lit up with pain.

Heaving slow breaths, Zeke lay still on the concrete, gathering himself. *Okay. Focus. Someone should come to save me. There's hospitals and shit in the city. There has to be a way to save me.*

Glass shattered, raining down all around Zeke. Heavy thumps lifted him off the ground. Zeke barely bit back a scream. *What now?*

A shadow fell over him. His eyes rolled upward.

Bone white. Creaking, dry joints. A skeletal T-rex stood over him, towering over the cars and the light posts lining the side of the road. Blood dripped from its jaw. Bits of cloth and gore stuck to teeth longer than Zeke's forearm. It turned its head, nosing at the air as if it could sniff with dry bone nasal sockets, then stomped off. Its long tail whipped over Zeke's head, so close he could feel the wind.

Zeke's eyes widened. "What the *fuck*."

**That is also an apocalypse.**

"An apocalypse? What, the dinosaur apocalypse?" Zeke muttered, watching it stomp away.

**Correct.**
**Dinosaur Apocalypse (Skeleton)**
**Danger Rating:** SSS
**Level:** 3

"Danger rating?" Zeke asked.

**Danger Rating is the chance that the sighted apocalypse could kill you as you currently are. SSS means certain death.**

*Well, obviously. I'm almost dead. Everything is an SSS rating right now.*

**Correct.**

A soft cooing caught Zeke's ear. With a flutter of feathers, a pigeon landed beside Zeke. It tilted its head, looking at him.

Zeke stared back. "I don't have any food."

As if in answer, Zeke's stomach grumbled. *I can still be hungry in a time like this?* he marveled, amazed at himself.

The pigeon tilted its head. It bounced forward, stepping toward him. A strange light flashed in its dark, round eyes.

Zeke giggled. Even though he laid on the ground, his head

floated, light as air. The pain faded from his limbs, falling into the background. A horrifying cold replaced it, a sensationless numbness he refused to think about. Instead, he nodded ever so slightly at the pigeon. "Don't tell me. You're the pigeon apocalypse."

**Member of the Pigeon Apocalypse**
**Individual Danger Rating:** C
**Level:** 0

"There's a pigeon apocalypse?" Zeke asked, shocked.

**Anything that is a Concept can become an Apocalypse.**

"And Concepts are?"

**Anything that exists in this world.**

"So, literally anything," Zeke said.

**Not quite.**

The pigeon hopped closer. It loomed over him, its oil-slick neck ruff and green belly filling Zeke's vision. It cooed again, then drew its head back to peck.

*I'm not going to be eaten by a pigeon!* Mustering all his strength, Zeke forced his hand off the sidewalk. Clumsily, he swiped at the bird.

It leaped into the air. Feathers and air beat at Zeke's face.

Zeke scowled. *Dammit.*

Undeterred, the pigeon settled back down a moment later. It landed beside his face and pecked at his cheek.

"Ow!" Zeke complained, baring his teeth in pain.

**Conditions met. Activate skill?**

"What? I mean—activate!"

## [Devour]

His mouth opened on its own. Faster than he thought possible to move his ruined body, his head jerked forward. His teeth clenched around feathers.

Shocked, Zeke froze. *I just—*

The pigeon squawked in surprise and beat its wings, desperately trying to escape. Zeke's eyes widened. *No!* He clenched his jaw shut. *I don't know what's happening, but this might be my only way out of this. Whatever this apocalypse nonsense is about, I need to be stronger than I am. There're numbers, danger ratings, levels...just like a game. And if this is like a game, then the only way to get stronger is to play.*

Bones crunched. The pigeon stilled. Over and over, Zeke chewed, swallowing it bit by bit. Blood and feathers splattered the sidewalk. Hot, acrid liquid spilled down his throat. Feathers tickled his cheeks and tongue.

**Level +.1**
**Your condition has stabilized by a small margin.**
**Choose Skill**
**Resilience (Minor)**
**Steel Stomach (Minor)**
**Wings (Tiny)**
**Claws (Tiny)**

Zeke's brow furrowed. "What are these?"

**When you Devour, you gain fewer levels but, in return, you**

**gain the ability to pick one of your victim's skills for
your own.**
**Choose Skill**
**Resilience (Minor) (Passive)**
*Ignore your wounds and keep moving with the resilience of an
herbivore.*

**Steel Stomach (Minor) (Passive)**
*Like a scavenger, you are less likely to get sick when you eat spoiled
food.*

**Wings (Tiny) (Modification)**
*Gain wings (Tiny)*

**Claws (Tiny) (Modification)**
*Gain claws (Tiny)*

Zeke blinked. After a second, his eyes settled on Resilience.
*Steel Stomach might be useful to pair with Devour in the future, if
my pigeon-eating experience was any indication, but I need to focus
on surviving the next two minutes, not preoccupy myself with potential skill synergies. As for Wings (Tiny) and Claws (Tiny)...I don't
need pigeon-sized wings or claws.*

**Gained Skill! Resilience (Minor)**

Immediately, the pain faded. *No, not faded.* Instead, he automatically put it to the back of his mind. It remained, the pain
itself as strong as ever, but he could easily ignore it now.

Zeke twitched, then shifted. His right hand clenched, then
moved. Pain burst through him again but, this time, he pushed
through. Moving his left arm induced immediate agony that
even [Resilience] (Minor) couldn't overcome, so he left it be.

Inch by inch, he pulled himself up with his right arm, barely lifting his chest off the ground. His left arm dangled, and his left leg and hip twisted as he pushed up. Bone grated on bone. Blood gushed down. He bit his lip, gasping against the pain.

*Shit! Ow! Ryan, what the hell?*

*What got into Ryan? Is he the Sudden Betrayal Apocalypse or something? But, no, he attacked me before the whole System and Apocalypse arrived. Did he have an abrupt mental breakdown or something? He was acting weird.*

Zeke's eyes widened. *And Mia! Mia. Is she all right?*

He caught his breath. Slowly, he shook his head. *Focus. I can worry about Mia once I'm not dying in two minutes.*

**Estimated time to death:** 1:47

Zeke's brows furrowed. *Not that I'm complaining, but it's definitely been more than twenty seconds since the last time I checked.*

**Using [Devour] raises your regeneration rate. [Resilience] is also factored into the estimate.**

*Resilience can also stave off death? Huh. So, some skills have hidden features,* Zeke noted. He nodded to himself. *[Devour]. If I want to get through this, I have to [Devour]. Got it.*

*Luckily, I'm not a picky eater.*

A cockroach skittered by. Zeke's stomach rumbled, and his eyes flashed. Unhesitatingly, he flopped at the cockroach. The cockroach darted away, but not fast enough. Zeke crunched it down, gooey innards spurting in his mouth.

**[Devour]**
**Ordinary Cockroach**
**Danger Rating:** F

### Level: 0

*Yum, delicious,* Zeke thought sarcastically. Ignoring the sensation of little legs scratching against his tongue, he forced himself to swallow.

Antennae tickled at the back of his throat. The legs scratched all the way down his neck. Acrid, slightly salty-rotten flavor smeared through his whole mouth. He grimaced. *I'm going to be tasting that for days.*

### Level +.01
### Your condition has stabilized by a tiny margin.
### Choose Skill
### Resilience (Minor)
### Steel Stomach (Minor)
### Wings (Miniscule)
### Carapace (Miniscule)

Quickly scanning the list, Zeke's eyes rested on Resilience again. *If I choose that, will it stack with my current Resilience (Minor)?*

### Yes.

*Hmm. That or Steel Stomach... Now that I know I have to [Devour] to survive, it's looking like a more profitable skill.*

Zeke hesitated a moment, then chose Resilience. *I can't waste any skills on quality-of-life improvements yet. With a minute and some left to live, I need to focus on survival, to the detriment of everything else, if need be.*

### Resilience (Minor) +1
*Ignore your wounds and keep moving with the resilience of an*

*herbivore or small bug. Regeneration rate +.5% Total regeneration rate +1%*

Zeke's eyes widened. He glanced down. Nothing visibly changed, and yet, the pain faded away—*or rather, I put it to the back of my mind. But...damn. Putting five points in CON gave me .5% faster regeneration, the same as +1-ing Resilience. Skills scale way faster than stat points!*

He dragged himself over the sidewalk, slowly inching onward. Elbow down. Leg pushed. Arm dragged. His broken bones scraped over the uneven sidewalk, left side dragging. He left a trail behind him, smearing blood as he went. Bits of blackened bubble gum stuck to the sidewalk. Discarded wrappers and receipts laid crushed to the ground. In the near distance, a pair of mangy jeans smushed into the side of a building. Zeke wrinkled his nose. *Gross.*

He lifted his head carefully, looking around. The street stood mostly empty. A single distant homeless man shifted in the mouth of an alley. Across the road, a businesswoman clopped by, purse held close and shoulders high, hurrying off down the road. She glanced at Zeke, but quickly looked away, leaving him behind.

"Oh, hey," Zeke muttered. *All right, to be fair, I probably look like a zombie right now. And given the circumstances...I wouldn't help me, either.*

*Speaking of, though, where did everyone go? Are they all hiding? How long was I out?*

Ants crept over the ground, climbing out of a sidewalk crack and circling around a half-dried puddle of soda. Zeke eyed them. *Can I [Devour] these?*

**Yes.**

*What can't I devour?*

No answer.

Zeke licked his lips. He lowered his mouth to the sidewalk. *Better than nothing. Uh, [Devour]!*

His jaws snapped shut. His lips scraped against the ground. A single ant crawled over his tongue.

Zeke pressed his lips together. *One at a time? I'm going to be here all day!*

# 3
## EATING ANTS

Z eke swallowed the ant. *All right, here we go.*

**Ordinary Ant**
**Worth 0 Levels**
**Choose Skill**
**None**

Zeke scowled. "Not even Resilience or Steel Stomach?" He looked at the rest of the ants, then shook his head. *Maybe if I eat them all?* Lowering his head, he licked up a line of ants.

**[Devour]**
**Many Ordinary Ants**
**Worth 0 Levels**
**Choose Skill**
**Teamwork (Minor)**
**Carapace (Miniscule)**

Blinking, Zeke shrugged. "Teamwork, I guess?"

### Teamwork (Minor) (Passive)
*Gain a small boost when working on a team.*

Lifting his arm, Zeke crawled on. *This isn't working. I need to find something with actual skills, not just...ordinary ants. The pigeon gave good skills...but it was a member of an Apocalypse. The cockroach gave skills too, but it didn't say it was a member of the Apocalypse, so why did I get good skills from it? What's the connecting line? What should I look for?*

### Cockroach
### Special Category: Survivor
*The cockroach survives when nothing else will. Although not a member of an Apocalypse, it gains access to the System and special features based on its category.*

Zeke blinked. "So, there's more than just apocalypses out there?"

### Yes.

"What else is there?"
No response.
He wrinkled his nose. *Sometimes it's chatty, sometimes it's the silent type. It seems to like talking most when I have some kind of hint or clue. Maybe I need to find things to unlock more information.*
*But...first, I need to survive.*
Hurried footsteps came up behind him. Zeke crawled on, slowly pushing his way down the sidewalk. *Don't mind me, just dying here.*
The footsteps stopped. Rough hands grabbed onto his shoulders and flipped him over. Zeke screamed, grabbing his broken arm and side. "What the *fuck!*"

The skinny, grungy-looking man standing over him ignored his protest. Instead, he knelt and patted Zeke down, pausing at his pockets.

"Are you fucking kidding me? You're mugging me? Now?" Zeke grabbed the man's wrist.

The man shook him off, easily escaping his weak grasp. He found Zeke's wallet in his back pocket, and a smile spread over his face. Quick fingers fished it free of Zeke's jeans.

Zeke grabbed the man's arm again, holding on with all his might. "Fuck no."

"Let go of me, punk. I'll finish you off," the man snapped. He flashed a gun in his off-hand.

*The System says I'm a goddamned Apocalypse. Do you think I'm going to lie here and get mugged? I'm not going to lie here and take it. I...*

The man shook his arm, nearly shaking him off. He raised the gun pointed it at Zeke's head. An ominous *click* sounded. "Let go. I will kill you."

*Fuck. Now or never. Do or die.* Zeke heaved himself off the ground with all the strength he could muster, baring his teeth.

### [Devour]

He lurched forward, faster than his mangled body ought to move. His teeth latched onto the man's throat. The man struggled. Gunfire blared, and fresh pain lit up Zeke's side. He ignored it, grinding his teeth deeper into the man's throat. The man dropped the gun—the magazine empty—and pushed at Zeke's shoulder. Zeke let him, yanking back at the same time. The man abruptly stopped pushing. Too late. Zeke twisted his head and tore out the man's throat.

Blood gushed. Trying not to think too much about it, Zeke

swallowed. *I have to swallow for [Devour] to work. It only activates afterward.*

The man stared, his eyes widening even as they blurred. He pointed. His mouth formed the word, *zombie.*

Zeke licked his lips, tasting blood, but not his own this time. Rolling his eyes at the man, he said, "Don't be ridiculous. I'm still alive. No thanks to you."

**Congratulations on your first kill! Bonus: +1 Level**
**Level +.5**
**Level: 1.61**
**Please assign your stat point.**
**Your condition has stabilized by a minor margin.**
**Regeneration +100% (Temp.)**
**Regeneration rate: +101% (Temp. 1:32 remaining)**

Bones ground. Muscles stitched together, and skin healed. The bullets left in his body shifted, pushing toward the skin. One plopped out with a metallic *thump*. Zeke flinched, grimacing against the pain. *Ow, ow, ow...*

*Wait, hold on. First kill? But I...killed...animals.*

*Does it only count humans?*

**Estimated time to death:** 5:52
**Estimated time to death:** 6:04
**Estimated time to death:** 6:15

*It hurts, but at least death is getting further away. And that temporary hundred percent regeneration rate boost is no joke! Do I get that boost every time I [Devour] a person?* He snorted. *I guess that 'apocalypse' moniker is no joke. It's seriously pushing me to eat people. Is this System meant to annihilate humanity?*

*What was that black dome called? The Apocalypse Incubator?*

*Yeah...I guess that makes sense, huh. We're the apocalypses. The strongest one gets to escape and destroy the world. And that means destroying lots of humans.*

*I don't want to kill people if I can avoid it, and I certainly don't want to destroy the world. But...come to think of it, there must be lots of apocalypses in this dome. I mean, if pigeons can land an apocalypse, it's not like the Incubator was being picky.*

*If I don't take the top spot, that means someone else wins and gets set free to destroy the world. Someone...who might not hesitate to follow the System's human-eating imperative, unlike me.*

He lifted his head, staring after the long-gone dinosaur skeleton. *Or...not necessarily someone else. Something else. After having seen the Pigeon Apocalypse and Dinosaur Apocalypse, I'm pretty sure apocalypses aren't just humans.*

Zeke nodded to himself. *I need to become the strongest apocalypse. I can't trust anything else.*

Glancing at the mugger's body, Zeke grimaced. He shook his head. "Sorry. It was self-defense."

Blood spurting out of his teeth-torn throat, the man gazed blankly at Zeke, his body shivering as he bled out.

Zeke licked his lips. *Yeah...I don't think a jury of my peers is going to buy 'eating a man's throat' as legitimate self-defense.*

*Then, again...* He crawled onward, continuing his slow journey. *Who's going to arrest me? It's the apocalypse. An apocalypse. Several apocalypses.*

*All the apocalypses?*

### Choose Skill
### Drug Resistance (Major)
*You are slightly resistant to drugs both harmful and helpful.*

### Fighting Spirit (Minor)

*Small increase in power when you are lower level or weaker than your foe.*

### Firearms (Small) (Minor)
*Able to use firearms at a novice level.*

### Mug (Activatable)
*Higher chance of gaining valuables when you Mug someone.*

Zeke scowled. *None of those are going to help me survive. Drug Resistance sounds as likely to hurt as help. As for Firearms, there's a finite amount of ammo inside the dome, and I don't have any of it. Mug is...well, I'm not about to set off on a career as a mugger. Which leaves Fighting Spirit.*

### Skills
### Resilience (Minor) +1
### Fighting Spirit (Minor)
### Teamwork (Minor)

Zeke laughed. "I'm definitely the number one threat to humanity...or whatever it is Ryan said."

*Wait, huh? Number-one threat to humanity... Why did he say that* before *the Apocalypse Incubator even arrived? How could he know? Was it just a coincidence that his mental break happened to be coincidentally accurate to what was about to happen? It's a lot of coincidences, but weird things are happening today.*

*But if he knew...what does that mean?*

He raised a hand to his chin thoughtfully, then shook his head. *I don't know. If I see him again, and he doesn't try to kill me, I can ask him.*

Zeke crawled on, elbow and knee scraping against the

concrete. *I'm still not out of danger yet. I still can't walk, let alone fight. I need to find something better to Devour so I can heal up.*

Ahead of him, trash blew down the street, caught up in the breeze from where piled-up trash bags spilled out of the alley behind the museum. The trash began to spin, slowly winding together. Dancing over the sidewalk, the little trash twister flew toward Zeke.

Zeke crawled toward it, somewhat reluctantly. *Trash is... It isn't great, but maybe if I eat leftover food, I can heal? I don't fully get how this System works yet, but it did mention eating to raise my regeneration rate.*

The trash twister stopped suddenly. Despite everything, Zeke somehow got the impression it was looking at him. He stared back.

"System, is that...?"

### Litter Apocalypse
### Danger Rating: D
### Level: 1

"Damn, worse than the pigeon," Zeke muttered.

**You are stronger now.**

"Do you mean the skills, or do you mean I'm bleeding out slower?" Zeke queried.

No answer.

The litter apocalypse spun in place for a moment. As if it made up its mind, it hurtled at Zeke.

"Does it also see danger ratings?" Zeke asked.

**Yes.**

"So, why is it coming at me? If it's a D to me, I must be an A, at least."

A few beats of silence.

### It is litter.

Zeke snorted. "Right. Not exactly known for its intelligence."

# 4

## ENDING AN APOCALYPSE

The litter apocalypse whirled as it hurtled at Zeke. In seconds, it crossed the gap between them. Wind rushed, paper rustled, and then it engulfed him. Zeke braced himself, squinting his eyes against the swirling twister. Litter spun around him. Wrappers and receipts batted ineffectually at his head and back. A single plastic water bottle smacked his injured shoulder, and he winced.

Ducking a little to protect it, Zeke frowned. "How do I eat this?"

No answer.

Zeke scowled. *Let's do it the hard way, then.* He opened his mouth.

**[Devour]**

A random receipt flew into his mouth. On instinct, he swallowed. Dry paper slid down his throat, cutting at his insides, crumpling in his esophagus.

Nothing happened. He pursed his lips. *Ate a receipt for nothing.*

In the midst of the whirling debris, a twisted lump of browned paper and plastic caught his eye. *What is that?* Leaning on his chest, he snatched at it with his good hand.

The trash dropped to the ground. Wind stopped thrashing his face.

"Huh?" Zeke asked.

### Core of the Litter Apocalypse.

"Oh. Is this what I need to devour?"

As he said the word, his jaw jumped forward. Zeke barely got his thumb out of the way before his mouth closed around the filthy lump of trash.

Tar, dirt, plastic, and the putrid scent of garbage exploded on his tongue. Zeke grimaced but forced himself to swallow. It didn't go down easy, smearing gross stickiness all the way down his throat. A shiver of pure disgust ran through his body. He retched, only barely keeping it in. *Forget the cockroach. That was* truly *awful.*

**Congratulations! You've defeated an Apocalypse! Bonus: +1 Level**
**Level +.7**
**Level: 3.31**
**Please assign 3 stat points.**
**Your condition has stabilized considerably.**
**Regeneration + 300% (Temp.)**
**Regeneration rate: +401% (Temp. 1:52 remaining)**

Zeke raised his eyebrows. *Huh. The time is longer than it was after I killed the mugger. It looks like the two regeneration rate boosts stacked, but there's only one timer, so it combined them both into the longest of the two times...or something.*

*It's possible that the first regeneration rate will fall out before the second one finishes, and it only counts the longer of the two timers. I'll have to find out.*

*While I'm at it...* He tapped the screens and quickly added all three points into CON.

**STR:** 0

**CON:** 8

**DEX:** 0

**SPR:** 0

**Regeneration +0.3%**

**Regeneration rate: +401.3% (Temp. 1:52 remaining)**

Once again, his bones shifted in his body, stitching back together. The remaining bullets pushed out of his flesh one after another, clattering to the ground. A horrible sick sensation passed over him in a wave and, suddenly, he felt much better, though he couldn't put his finger on why. He touched his stomach. *Was one of my organs injured?*

Abruptly, his left arm clicked. The pain in it faded. He wiggled his fingers. They moved with a minimum of pain, as dexterous as they usually were. More slowly, his shattered hip and broken leg recollected themselves. Rolling onto his back, Zeke clenched his teeth against the pain and waited for the bones to sort themselves.

As he waited, another message popped up.

**Apocalypse Defeated!**

**Choose up to 3 Skills**

**Disguise (Minor)**

*Minor bonus to disguising oneself, especially as a pile of garbage.*

### Trash Magnet (Unique)
*Attract trash to yourself.*

### Wind Manipulation (Weak)
*Weakly manipulate the wind. You can lift small objects, such as paper, wrappers, empty bottles, and similarly light objects that might be shifted in a light breeze.*

### Filth (Minor)
*You are filthy. Any filth you acquire will be more disgusting than usual.*

### Disease Propagation (Minor)
*Propagate disease. Your body naturally picks up and retains minor diseases.*

### Pick Up (Weak)
*Small chance of automatically picking up dropped items, especially if small or lightweight.*

Looking over the skills, Zeke pursed his lips. *Hmm. I get three, but...I don't know that I want three. Why do I get three?*

**Three skills are granted as a bonus for defeating the Apocalypse with your unique skill.**

Zeke nodded. "Got it. I need to Devour apocalypses to get more skills. Makes sense."

*But which three do I want? These skills are, uh...not the most impressive.*

He bit his lip, then shrugged. *Might as well take what I can get. I'll go with these.*

**Skills**
**Resilience (Minor) +1**
**Fighting Spirit (Minor)**
**Teamwork (Minor)**
**Wind Manipulation (Weak)**
**Disguise (Minor)**
**Pick Up (Weak)**

*Disease Propagation is probably better than Pick Up in the long run, but...I'm not actually trying to wipe out humanity. I might be the...the Hunger Apocalypse, or whatever, but I can choose who and what I eat. I can choose to not end the world. If I sit back and eat a few extra sandwiches, I don't have to hurt anyone, even if I'm an Apocalypse.*

*On the other hand, if I take Disease Propagation...I can't control who or how much I kill with a skill like that. Even in the best case, where I perfectly choose who I initially infect with the disease, when the disease jumps to the next host, and the next, and the next, I'll completely lose control of how much damage I'm doing. With my current skills, I have full control over who I kill and how much damage I do.*

*All that to say, it's better if I'm not uncontrollably propagating diseases. The skill only says that I propagate disease, not that I have any ability to choose which I carry, pick up, or when or how I spread them. Best to avoid the risk of accidentally becoming the next global pandemic.*

*So, I'll—*

*SNAP!*

Sweat instantly broke out on Zeke's brow. Muttering curses, he curled in on himself, hands hovering in claws over his freshly reconnected femur, afraid to touch his leg but desperately wanting to. *Ow, ow, ow, ow, hurts, hurts, hurts—!*

Hissing a slow breath through his teeth, he slowly straightened his leg. His hip clicked, then snapped into place.

*Yikes. All right. Remind me not to jump off any more four-story buildings.*

Zeke lay there for another second, just to be sure his body had mostly healed, then climbed slowly, carefully to his feet. His first step he limped, but his second was steady, and his third was back to normal. Dusting himself off, he looked around from his new perspective.

Trash lay all around, scattered by the Litter Apocalypse. A smear of blood dragged from a fat splatter where he'd landed. A throatless corpse lay halfway down the smear, a few feet after a puff of gray feathers.

Zeke wiped his chin thoughtfully, nodding down at the mess. His hand came away damp, and he self-consciously rubbed it on his shirt, only to find it damp, too. He glanced down.

Blood soaked the material, especially dark around a cluster of round holes in his gut.

*Oh, right. Motherfucker shot me. Mugged me, then shot me!* Zeke scowled at the corpse. *I'm gonna say it. You deserved to get eaten.*

*Jeez. I ate someone.*

He stared at the corpse. His heart raced. Subconsciously, he licked his lips.

"I mean, but I'm an apocalypse now. Right? I'm supposed to eat people," he muttered aloud.

*BANG!*

In the near distance, something slammed to the ground. Zeke jumped, startled into motion. *I shouldn't stand around. Other things are out there. Other apocalypses with less qualms about eating people.*

*Ryan, and Mia. Did they escape? Are they safe?*

*Okay, well, Ryan can go fuck himself right now. But Mia! I need to find her. She's trapped with Ryan for fuck's sake! What if he decides to push her off the balcony?*

He glanced over just to be sure, but only one blood splatter marred the sidewalk.

Turning to the museum, he took a deep breath. "Giant dinosaur came out of there...but Mia's in there."

He slapped his cheeks. "I've got this. I'm a motherfucking apocalypse. I can do this!"

The museum's doors smashed open. Zeke leaped, startled. An enormous crystal ball rolled out of the museum.

He blinked. *Isn't that the 'perfectly round crystal' from that glass case on the second floor that no one's allowed to touch, not even the curators? What's it doing here?*

The crystal ball drifted sideways and rolled over the mugger. The mugger's gun, and the associated magazine, stuck to its side. There was a distinctive *click* as the gun reloaded. The ball rotated again and raised the gun, the weapon glued to its side by an outcropping of crystal, and Zeke found himself staring down the length of the barrel.

His eyes flew wide. *Holy shit, the rock's got a gun!*

# 5
## FLEEING A ROCK

**B**ang!

Like a runner waiting for the starting gun, Zeke whirled and sprinted. A bullet clipped his side. Rumbling, the large crystal ball followed him, gun rotating gently around its horizontal axis.

**Temporary regeneration lost.**
**Regeneration rate: +1.3**

"Now?" Zeke demanded. He whipped around the corner, his feet slipping on trash. A few pieces of debris popped up from his feet and landed in his palms. Confused, he tossed them over his shoulder. *Is this what Pick Up does? It's kind of annoying...*

*And that gun! That gun was empty! I'm ninety percent sure. Where did that rock get the bullets?*

"Is this the Crystal Apocalypse or something?" Zeke asked.

**Crystal Apocalypse**
**Danger Rating:** A
**Level:** 4

"No *kidding* it's an A! It's a huge rock with a gun! What am I supposed to do about that? I can't eat a rock! Hell, I can't even scratch its surface!"

The huge crystal turned the corner, then stopped. It rumbled, rubbing itself in place.

Zeke frowned over his shoulder. "What's it doing?"

Crystals burst out of the earth beneath it, charging in a straight line toward Zeke's feet.

"Motherfuck!" He jumped and ran, pumping his arms. His stomach and legs ached fiercely. His head pounded, and the world swirled around him, shivering left and right. *Ugh. I'm healed, but I'm not in top shape. I lost a lot of blood. I need to eat something.*

The flavor of the Litter Apocalypse surged up in his mind, and Zeke retched. He pressed a hand to his lips and forced himself to swallow again. *Maybe some real food this time.*

He ran and ran. The crystal rolled after him again, giving up on spearing his feet. The road stretched the length of the museum, easily two blocks long. Bullets smacked off the walls and dug into the floor. Zeke darted left and right, avoiding the bullets. The road stretched on and on, seemingly to infinity. He panted, pumping his arms.

*Damn. How long is this road?*

At last, another intersection approached. He burst out of the alley into the museum's loading dock. The narrow back road expanded to a broad asphalt pad, with a truck dock and a concrete ramp with a dolly sitting abandoned at its bottom. Stairs led up to a rear door, but so did the ramp.

Zeke shot the ramp a filthy look. *How dare you support crystal balls. Rude.*

Rumbling sounded from around the corner. He startled and dashed ahead. *No time to waste!*

A few wooden shipping crates stood at the top of the

concrete ramp, waiting to be unpacked and taken into the museum. One of the shipping crates shook wildly as something beat at it from inside. Zeke glanced at it, then diverted his feet, running at it. Crystal ball rumbling after him, he ran up the ramp one leaping step at a time. At the top, he slammed his shoulder into the crate, sending it tumbling off the ramp to the asphalt below.

The crate struck the ground and broke open. Zeke held his breath. *Come on. A mummy, a weapon, something useful!*

Cleaning supplies spilled out. From their midst, a spray bottle jumped upright and charged at the crystal ball, desperately spraying the crystal.

*Dammit!* Zeke spun and sprinted away, racing for the back door. It hung open, abandoned in someone's rush to flee.

Halfway up the ramp, the crystal ball whirled and shot the spray bottle. All the liquid spilled out. The spray bottle tipped over, dead. Crystals surged out of it where the bullet struck. In an instant, the bottle crystalized.

Turning, the crystal ball raised its gun again.

Zeke fled into the museum, leaving the crystal ball behind.

He found himself in a backroom. Dusty metal shelves laden with artifacts and boxes piled up all around him. A man lay crushed under a suspiciously empty slot in the warehouse, blood pooled under him. Multiple paths wandered through the enormous room, almost labyrinthine in their twists and twines.

Zeke froze, momentarily paralyzed by choice, then sprinted off into the path slightly to the left of the door. *Go, go, go! Keep moving! If I stop, I'm dead! If I'm moving, I've at least got a chance!*

The rear door to the museum creaked open behind him. Zeke crouched, watching through the shelves as it rolled into the room. The gun bobbled along as it rolled, the crystal protrusion counter-spinning against the ball's movement to remain upright at all times.

Turning slowly, the crystal ball rolled ahead, through the aisle directly ahead of it.

In the next aisle, Zeke glanced left and right, then scooted slowly toward a large crate on the top shelf of the aisle between them. He waited, watching the ball through the gaps in the crates. *Come on. A little closer.*

The crystal ball stopped abruptly, barely a foot before it reached the giant crate. It rubbed itself on the floor, emitting a strange hum.

Zeke frowned. *What is it doing?*

His side began to hum. Startled, Zeke looked down.

Crystals crawled out from his gut where the bullet had grazed him. Glowing faintly, they hummed in resonance with the crystal ball.

*Fuck!* Zeke grabbed at the crystals. Pain shot through him, only to get shoved down by Resilience a second later. He yanked them free.

At the core of the crystals, a bullet-shaped lump of crystal came out of his body, streaked with blood. He glared at it. *That thing made crystal bullets? How does that even work? Shouldn't they shatter in the gun?*

Crystal screeching on the tiled floor, the crystal ball rounded on Zeke.

Zeke startled. He took off. Barely a second later, a gunshot echoed in the concrete warehouse. Crystals burst out across the aisle from him, surging up where the bullet struck.

Looking at the bloodied crystal in his hand, Zeke hesitated, then ate it. *It's part of an apocalypse. Maybe I can get skills.*

## [Devour]

Crystal crunched between his teeth and scraped down his

throat. It slammed into his stomach like a brick. *It is a rock, after all.*

*Come to think of it, how is all of this coming out the other end? After I Devour it, I mean.*

*Let's...not think about that.*

**Crystal Bullet**
**Member of the Crystal Apocalypse**
**Level +.1**
**Choose Skill**
**Can't**
**Can't**

### Growth (Minor)
*Enhances growth rate, especially of non-living entities.*

Zeke pressed his lips together. *Guess I'm picking Growth.*

Ahead of him, double doors led out into the museum. Zeke charged through, sprinting into the museum itself.

Exhibits stretched in all directions. Wax figures stood stiffly under bright lighting. Skeletons of all sizes and shapes hung on metal poles or sat displayed on pedestals, all of them lying still and dead, unlike the T-rex that had stepped over Zeke earlier. Strange minerals and shining crystals lay under bright lights, a giant pendulum swung in the distance, dead beetles glistened from pins and, off in a corner, a cat sarcophagus shot him a judging look.

*Whew. Not everything became an apocalypse.*

He furrowed his brows. *Wait. Why is it so...twisted in here? I don't remember it being like this.*

Paths led off left and right, splitting and branching near-infinitely. Exhibits abruptly dead-ended routes, and some routes turned back in on themselves. Lights flickered, entirely dark in some places. A staircase dropped down onto the top of an exhibit and, around the corner, an elevator dinged as it went sideways.

## Museum Apocalypse
## Danger Rating: C
## Level: 5

Rumbling sounded from behind him. Zeke ran off. *No time to waste. If I stand here for too long, that thing's going to crystalize me!*

He charged off, running toward the staircase. *Not only do the stairs keep the crystal from chasing me, but also, the café is on the fourth floor. That's where Mia is...or was. This might be a wild goose chase, but I can't just abandon her.*

*Especially not with Ryan there. Who knows what's going through his head right now? Guy needs a psychiatrist and some jail time.*

As he ran, he spied a diorama with a wax figure inside. He passed it by, then paused. The Neanderthal figure raised a stone tool in one hand, smashing it toward a rock below. He jumped into the diorama and pulled at the stone tool. *Come on! Give it to me!*

The wax figure stared into infinity. Its grip on the stone tool didn't shift an inch.

Zeke scowled. "You aren't even real."

The crystal ball rumbled close enough for him to see its shiny top poking around the lower-slung exhibits. Abandoning the tool, Zeke ran on. *Dammit.*

Behind him, the wax figure turned its head, watching him go.

Zeke turned the corner and found himself face-to-face with a dead end. A glass-covered bookshelf exhibited ancient books, their dusty spines turned toward the visitor. Gritting his teeth, he lowered his right shoulder and charged the glass, only to bounce off.

*Come on! Break!* He backed up, preparing to charge it again.

The crystal ball rounded the corner. It raised the gun. Zeke ducked out of the way.

*Bang!*

Glass shattered behind him. Old books rained down around Zeke, flapping their fragile pages as they fell.

*That works.* Zeke jumped up, climbing the bookshelf. Glass shards dug into his fingers, but thanks to Resilience, he ignored the pain. Scurrying onto the top of the bookshelf, he half-ran, half-crawled over to the next exhibit, then the next. Only when three exhibits separated him from the crystal ball did he dare to stand and run.

"Hey! You there! How do we get down?" someone shouted from atop the staircase.

Zeke looked up. *People?*

Instantly, his stomach grumbled.

*Calm down there. I'm not that hungry yet.* He reached the staircase and jumped up two stairs at a time. The crystal ball fired after him. Crystal bullets slammed into the stairs, bursting out into beautiful pink growths.

The people at the top of the stairs screamed and fled, their voices suspiciously high-pitched. Zeke jumped up the final step and found himself facing an old, tired-looking teacher and a group of about twenty elementary-school aged kids.

*Ah. That's a problem.*

"Everyone! What did I say? Quiet and calm, quiet and calm," the man said, keeping his voice steady. "Come this way. Let's back away from the stairs, okay? Get around the corner. We're all going to be okay."

The children cried and wailed, mostly ignoring him. As a lump, they moved somewhat toward the wall. Seeing his success, the man sighed and turned to Zeke. "I take it... Oh, dear God! What happened to you?"

Zeke glanced down. "Uh. A lot of things."

"Are you okay? Do you need help? First aid?" the man asked, panicking.

*Weren't you telling the kids to be quiet and calm ten seconds ago?* Zeke chuckled. He waved his hand. "I'm fine. If you want to get out..." he pointed behind him, "just climb down an exhibit, then hook a left. The loading dock isn't far from there. You'll be out in the streets, and..."

*And is that better? There're apocalypses out there, too.*

The man peered down the stairs to the bottom, where the gun-wielding crystal ball awaited them. "What about that?"

"Oh... Uh, it'll probably get bored and leave in a bit. It already left the museum once," Zeke said, shrugging. He looked over the class. *Dammit. That's a lot of kids. I want to help, but what can I do? Where can I take them? I...*

*No, I'll help. I just have to find Mia first. Once I find Mia, we can all go find safety together.*

The man nodded. "All right. We'll stay up here until then. There's still running water, at least, so..."

Zeke nodded. "Stay safe, okay? Give me a minute, and I'll come guide you guys out. I have to find someone first. A girl, short shorts, chestnut hair to her shoulders, blue shirt?"

The man shook his head. "I'm sorry, I can't help you. I've been too busy watching the kids."

One of the girls looked up, her straw-blonde pigtails bouncing. "Was she pretty? Like *really* pretty. And had this biiiiiig drink!"

"Yeah," Zeke said. *The big drink clinches it.*

The girl pointed behind her. "I saw her! In the café."

"The café is...?" Zeke pointed up.

"Not anymore. If she's in there, good luck," the man warned.

Zeke took a deep breath. "Okay. I'm going to go get Mia. If you guys see a break, run for it. If not... If not, I'll be back, and I'll get you out of here, okay?"

The man nodded. "Thank you. I appreciate the offer."

With one last nod, Zeke took off, leaving the man behind.

*Mia! I'm coming!*

# 6

## COFFEE SHOP

Zeke sprinted down the hallway. The AC pounded, cooling the sweat and blood stuck to him as he ran. Up here, much remained the same from before the black dome descended, the hallway straight, the rooms branching off it orderly and sane. *I guess it hasn't had enough time to screw up its second floor yet.*

*To be fair, my skills are pretty pitiful, too. That crystal ball got lucky.*

The levels he'd gotten from killing the man flashed before his eyes, and he twisted his lips. *Or it's been nonstop killing.*

*It's not like I can blame a crystal ball for killing people, but...still. Drives the point home! I can't let anything else become The Apocalypse. I have to be the one.*

Brown liquid washed down the hallway, ebbing out from under a fire door ahead of him. Slowing to a halt, Zeke sniffed warily, then furrowed his brows. *That's not sewage. Is it...*

He knelt. Leaning out, he sniffed again. *It really smells like... coffee?*

**Coffee Apocalypse**

**Danger Rating: ?**
**Level: ?**

Zeke blinked. "What does that mean?"

**Insufficient data.**

*Oh. Well, fair enough. It's just a puddle of coffee.* He carefully stepped into it. When nothing happened, he walked along, splashing through the quarter-inch-deep liquid. He paused, looking over his shoulder toward the kids and their teacher, then shrugged. *What am I going to warn them about? Watch out, the kids might get caffeinated? I mean, that's a horrifying possibility, but it's not exactly deadly.*

*Besides, they already knew about the café.*

He drew open the fire door. A blast of humid air, heavy with the warm scent of coffee, blew past his face. He blinked, raising a hand against the thick air.

Warm water lapped against his shoes, instantly soaking through and into his socks. A brown river flowed steadily along the floor to a broken window, where it poured down the building's façade in a steamy, dark waterfall. Every breath smelled of coffee, the scent instantly inundating his nose, mouth, lungs, clothes, and body. The walls were brown with the stuff. Coffee soaked into the walls and wallpaper. The ceiling dripped with steam.

Zeke splashed ahead, slogging through the hot liquid. It went from inches deep to ankle deep, from ankle deep to knee deep. The hallway turned and twisted, subtly growing wider as it went. He glanced around, confused.

*The museum wasn't big enough for this hallway. What's going on? Is this the coffee apocalypse's doing?*

A narrow shelf of brown appeared to the side, creating a

bank to the coffee river. Zeke splashed over to it and found himself slipping over slick black beans, roasted and ready for the grinding. Feet sliding, he dropped to his hands and knees and finally scrambled up onto the loose beans and out of the river. Even then, coffee leaked through, but at least he didn't have to fight coffee currents to push forward.

He glanced at the coffee river, then shook his head. "I'm not thirsty enough to go for floor coffee."

The bank widened, the loose beans giving way to tightly packed grinds. The grounds formed a sandy floor, firmer under his feet. Beside him, the coffee river began steaming, growing hotter as he moved upstream. Zeke stepped onto the grounds, glad to have a semblance of dry floor once more.

Coffee bushes pushed through the rich earth, twisted and strange. They leaned toward him as he passed, rustling with life. Zeke caught a flash of white at the foot of a tree's roots. Curious, he leaned closer. The tree matched him, branches beckoning eagerly, gem-like green leaves shuddering in their excitement. Inadvertently, it shifted a root. A skull rolled out, grinning up at him.

Zeke licked his lips and backed away. "Note to self, leave the trees alone."

Ahead, strange bags hung from the ceiling on slender threads, full of grounds and slowly dripping rich fresh-brewed coffee. Clear water flowed in from above. Each bag stretched as tall as Zeke stood, if not taller, and spread as wide as his arms spread at their widest. Stained with coffee, they shone in the low light, slick surfaces gleaming with the steam and humidity in the room. Cautiously, Zeke approached.

One of the bags turned, rotating slowly. A distorted human face stared at Zeke, twisted almost past recognizability. The mouth moved. *Kill me.*

Zeke jolted back, then stepped forward, holding his breath.

He touched the bags, rotating them carefully. More distorted faces gazed up at him. Some didn't move, their skin dull, barely oozing coffee, while others' mouths gaped in silent screams or chittered at him, unable to form words. *Please, not Mia. Please, not Mia.*

The final one. Zack bit his lip. He turned the skin.

A strange woman gazed up at him, her eyes dull and blank.

He took a deep breath. *Thank goodness.*

"Okay. I'm...I'm going to end this. For all of you," Zeke promised, looking over the once-human bags.

One or two reacted, but most mindlessly continued doing the same thing, if they moved at all.

"Not just your torture, but...*this*. All of it. Whatever's causing this, I'm going to destroy it," Zeke promised.

The bags spun silently.

Zeke took a deep breath. He stepped forward and opened his mouth. *No point letting levels and skills go to waste. I'll use these in your memory.*

Over and over again, walking from one to the next, he quietly ended their misery.

### [Devour]
### Level + .1
### Choose Skills
### Filter (Weak)
### Heat Resistance (Minor)

One after another, the bags fell to the floor, dead. Grounds spilled over the coffee bean shore like dark, dried blood. As the last one sunk to the ground, Zeke checked his stats.

### Level: 4.11
### Please assign your stat point.

**STR: 0**
**CON: 8**
**DEX: 0**
**SPR: 0**
**Regeneration rate: +1.3%**
**Skills**
**Resilience (Minor) +1**
**Fighting Spirit (Minor)**
**Teamwork (Minor)**
**Wind Manipulation (Weak)**
**Disguise (Minor)**
**Pick Up (Weak)**
**Growth (Minor)**
**Filter (Weak)**
**Heat Resistance (Minor) +6**

*I thought having stacked Heat Resistance would be more important than stacking Filter. True, Filter is useful when it comes to acquiring clean water, but I feel like Heat Resistance is going to come up more in a multi-apocalyptic scenario...especially in this one right here,* Zeke thought, pushing his hair back. Damp with sweat, it stuck to his scalp, cheap hair gel melting off it. Despite the steam and his own sweat drenching his body, the sauna-like heat now barely bothered him.

*I didn't get a secondary effect off leveling Heat Resistance, as far as I'm aware, but I'm not sure the System would tell me until I experienced its secondary effect. It really likes for me to find things out on my own.*

*Interestingly, I didn't get a regeneration boost from Devouring them. My regeneration rate is normal, so it isn't like I don't see it because I don't need to heal. Is it because I only got the 100% boost for my first human kill? Or is it because these...victims no longer count as human?*

Looking down at the human coffee filters, he nodded to them. "I'm sorry. And thank you."

With a deep breath, he set off, walking up the banks of the coffee river once more.

Ahead of him, the steam grew thicker. The scent of coffee grew so heavy he could barely breathe. Its acid heat burned his nostrils. He waved his hand, but that changed nothing. *Ugh. If only I could...*

*Wait, I can. Wind Manipulation!*

A fresh breeze sprung up around his head. It circulated around him, and the coffee smell went from overpowering to merely heavy.

*How nice.* Zeke closed his eyes, enjoying the fresh breeze.

### Your activatable skills can be activated to their full potential with higher SPR.

*Hmm...I have a stat point. That seems worth investing in.* Zeke tapped the screen before him.

### SPR: 1

"System, which of my skills are activatable? Is that the weak versus minor split?" Zeke asked.

### Yes. Organizing skills.
### Skills
### Wind Manipulation (Weak)
### Pick Up (Weak)
### Filter (Weak)
### Passive
### Resilience (Minor) +1
### Fighting Spirit (Minor)

**Teamwork (Minor)**
**Disguise (Minor)**
**Growth (Minor)**
**Heat Resistance (Minor) +6**

*That's convenient.* Zeke yawned, putting a hand over his mouth. *Damn. Why am I so tired when I'm surrounded by coffee?*

**Warning:** Area Effect: Caffeine Dependency
**Until you take caffeine, you will experience Exhaustion.**

Zeke's brows furrowed. He gave the coffee a suspicious look. *It's encouraging me to drink it... Why? That's not suspicious at all. I'm glad I didn't drink it earlier, and I'm definitely not going to drink it now.*

*Plus, it's filtered by people. Yuck. All the grossness that's on an average person's skin...ew. Nope. I ate the Litter Apocalypse, hell, I ate people, and I'm still saying no.*

Ahead, the room opened. Coffee bushes clustered low, spreading over the coffee grounds. Steam rose off the ground, the entire room oppressively hot. Sweat dripped down Zeke's brow once more despite his Heat Resistance. He wiped his forehead. *Without Heat Resistance, I'm not sure I'd be able to survive this room.*

His foot struck something. He glanced down and found himself stepping on a white metal loop. Confused, Zeke knelt and swept the coffee grounds away, digging them out around the loop. A white chair appeared out of the coffee, sunk deep into the coffee beans.

*I've reached the original café's seating area. Mia should be nearby if that kid was right.*

Coffee welled up in the hole, bubbling through the beans.

Scorching heat burst up at Zeke in a blast of steam. He staggered back, coughing.

His feet plunged into the grounds. Boiling hot coffee swirled around his feet. Zeke yanked them free, only to step into more hot coffee. In seconds, the coffee reached his ankles.

*The coffee's rising!*

Behind him, the river roared. Zeke turned. A wave of coffee surged toward Zeke, foaming hot. Zeke's eyes widened. *Fuck!*

# 7
## DROWNING IN COFFEE

The coffee wave crested toward him, moving in slow motion. Mind moving at top speed, Zeke glanced down his skill list. *Wind Manipulation... Pick Up... Devour... Nothing. None of my activatable skills are useful here.*

Abandoning his skill list, Zeke ran toward the wave, slogging through soggy coffee grounds. *Nothing for it. If it's a wave, then this is the ocean. I'll leap through it and trust in Heat Resistance!*

With each step, he sunk deeper into the grounds. Water swirled around his calves, then his knees. Each step sucked, pulling at his feet. His shoes swam around him. He curled his toes in his shoes, desperately holding onto his soles. *I can't lose my shoes now.*

Abruptly, the currents drew the coffee back. For a moment, he kicked his way through dry beans.

The wave rushed to meet him. Sealing his mouth shut, Zeke dove into the curve of the wave.

Hot water boiled past, searing his skin. He burst out the other side. Overheated clothes stuck to his flesh. Every inch of his body felt raw. He gasped a breath and ran on. *Oof. A bit hot, but it could be worse!*

Another wave surged at him.

*Fuck.* Zeke took a deep breath and ran at it, preparing to dive again.

In the break between waves, he caught a glimpse of white bar peeking out of the grounds. As the wave crested, the water grew low behind it, revealing the upper few inches of a door. Zeke's eyes lit up. *That must be the entrance to the café proper!*

The second wave rose high, rearing dangerously over him. Before it could smash down on him, he jumped into it, crashing out the back side of the wave. In another few steps, he reached the mantle. Zeke dropped to his knees and dug, burrowing into the grounds.

*Damn. I'm going to be here all day!*

Another wave rushed by, drawing the grounds and coffee with it. As it passed, the door swung open, just a little bit.

Zeke grabbed the door and held it with both hands, putting his feet against the doorframe to wedge it open. Superheated water rushed by him, straining the limits of Heat Resistance, but as it did, the door swayed open.

Zeke grinned. *A chance! I'll use the coffee tide's own forces against it!*

As the water pulled away, vanishing somewhere on the far side of the door, Zeke held the door out, refusing to let the water pull it shut again. The wave surged forth, pushing him away, and he yanked the door open another few inches; the tide pulled back, and Zeke stiffened, propping the door open with all his might. A few inches at a time. His skin burned. His muscles ached. He gritted his teeth and yanked one last time, then slipped inside. The door slammed shut behind him, smacking him in the rear. Zeke tumbled through hot coffee, pulled along on a riptide.

*Ow, ow, ow!*

### Heat Resistance (Minor) +7

The pain abated slightly. Disoriented, Zeke clawed at the water. Bubbles slid past his face, passing behind him. He chased them up, kicking with all his might.

With a gasp, Zeke broke the surface. He ran his hair back and found himself bobbing in the middle of a steaming ocean of coffee. Walls loomed in the distance, soaked in dark stains that grew deeper with every passing moment.

Zeke sighed, shaking his hair dry. *Thank goodness my mom always dragged us to the beach! Might've stayed in shitty tents in the cheap seats campgrounds, but the ocean doesn't have an admission fee...that's what she always said, anyway. I gotta say, I didn't expect my ocean knowledge to save my ass during the apocalypse.*

*The coffee apocalypse.*

Zeke shook his head. "I don't think anyone expected any part of any of this."

### Heat Resistance (Minor) +8

*It's probably not a good idea to sit still while I'm slowly boiled alive.* Kicking, Zeke swam through the coffee. Heat built up in his body, growing hotter with every stroke. Submerged in hot water, he had nowhere to shed the excess heat. His cheeks burned. His whole body grew stuffy. He ducked his face in the coffee to cool it but, unlike with cool ocean water, his face only grew hotter.

*Damn, it's hot. It's way too hot!*

In the distance, a pale shelf loomed out of the dark ocean. Relieved, Zeke pushed toward it. The second he reached solid ground, he pushed up onto it with a gasp. He sprawled out, staring at the ceiling. *Hot, hot, hot...! Wind Manipulation!*

A cool wind blew. Zeke sighed in relief. *Ah...Wind Manipulation is the best skill.*

"Help..."

Zeke sat up. Wind Manipulation still fanning his face, he looked around.

He sat on the far-right shore of a round white acrylic slab. Enormous white cylindrical structures towered overhead, with looping shelves that reconnected far overhead, at the cylinders' tops. Here and there, especially near the cylinders, brown, circular stains marred the white slab.

Zeke blinked. *I'm on a table. I'm in the café, but I'm tiny! Or... everything else got big. Really big.*

He turned, looking out over the coffee sea. White tabletops crested the ocean, dark coffee lapping at their shores. The cylinders—coffee cups—towered overhead, a few with massive napkins trapped underneath. Plates sprawled across the surface of the tables, some still sporting the scraps and crumbs of the café's treats. In the far distance, the walls delimited the horizon, where coffee-stain clouds boiled, portending a caffeinated rain.

*Really, really big.*

"Help!"

Startled out of his reverie, Zeke jolted. He whirled, searching across the table for the shouter. Shaking coffee out of his shoes, he jogged around the giant cup, swiveling his head as he went. "Hello?"

"Here, up here," the voice called, eager this time.

Zeke looked up, shading his eyes. A woman in the café's uniform kneeled in the crook of the handle, her black shirt torn, the collar loose, her brown apron, embossed with the old-fashioned man's face logo stained with splotches of brown. Brown mussed hair flew around her ears, once neatly twisted into short curls, now a mess. Her eyes glistened with tears, and her lip trembled, mouth pressed shut, on the verge of crying.

"How'd you get up there?" Zeke asked. He stood on his tiptoes, reaching up to her.

She grabbed his hand and pulled, yanking him toward her. Her mouth opened. Coffee poured out, flooding over Zeke's head. "Drink!"

Spluttering, Zeke backed away. The lady in the cup's handle refused to let him go, holding on with all her might. Hot liquid continued to pour over Zeke's head, seemingly endless. He ducked his head and snuck a breath, letting the water pour over the back of his head and drip down in front of him.

"Die! Burn and drown! Serve our lord or die!" the woman cackled.

*Damn. I get that businesspeople are dependent on coffee, but to the point of serfdom?* With a deep breath, Zeke sealed his lips. He yanked on the woman's arm, not yanking her down but pulling himself up.

The woman laughed, her eyes burning with madness and twitching from caffeine. "Come! Come to me!"

All at once, Zeke latched onto the handle of the cup with his other hand and hauled himself up. He broke through the cascading fluid and opened his mouth.

### [Devour]

His teeth dug into her throat. She screamed one last time, and then Zeke tore, and she fell silent forever. Her head drooped. Dark brown blood poured down the side of the cup, slicking across the porcelain.

As she sagged, her legs came into view. At the knees, her body fused into the cup. Porcelain crawled up her thighs, stiffening her flesh. Higher up the cup's handle, arms and legs jutted out of the handle's inside. A face screamed in silent horror.

Zeke released the handle and jumped back, startled. He wiped his hands on his shirt, shuddering. *I don't want to become one with the cup! Hope I didn't hold on too long.*

*What about Mia? I hope she's safe! I need to find her, soon.*

**Cup Spirit**
**Member of the Coffee Apocalypse**
**Level +.1**
**Choose Skill**
**Watertight (Minor)**
**Heat Resistance (Minor)**
**Create Coffee (Weak)**
**Calcification (Condition)**

Zeke put a hand on his chin. After a moment, he nodded decisively. "No one likes weak coffee. Calcification...that's a condition, not a skill. That's probably what was causing her to turn into a cup. Don't want that. I'll go with Watertight since I already have Heat Resistance +8."

Fingernails on a blackboard. Zeke jolted. Instinctively, he covered his ears against the grating sound. The cup wobbled. Its shadow fell over Zeke.

*Oh, shit!* Zeke jumped up and ran, wet feet sloshing over the table.

The cup shifted, then unfolded. A huge white porcelain hand slammed to the tabletop, inches behind him. Thrown into the air by the force of the blow, Zeke pedaled his arms and legs, eyes wide. He landed hard and spun around, staring up at the cup as porcelain scraped on porcelain, and the cup reformed, from a static shape into something much, much more complex.

Two huge half-circle feet, formed from the base. Curving, deceptively slender limbs arcing out of the handle. Orbs shaped from the cup's body became the torso and hips, and a round jut took the place of a face. The cup golem straightened to its full height and turned toward him, the museum café's old man logo pasted over its face.

"Oh, *shit!*" Zeke snapped. He whirled and ran even faster than before. *I'm not ready! I'm just a baby apocalypse! Someone, help!*

# 8

## BABY APOCALYPSE VS. THE GOLEM

A porcelain foot smashed into the table's surface beside him. The golem loomed overhead, casting a dangerous shadow down on Zeke. Zeke ran on, slipping and sliding over the table's slick surface. "Shit, shit, shit!"

Out a distance over the open ocean, a cluster of human filters hung from the ceiling at varying heights, watching him run as they slowly dripped coffee into the sea. Zeke glanced up at them. *If Mia's one of them, I'll never know. How would I even get one of those down from the ceiling? They're so high up!*

A huge hand smashed into the table beside him. Jolting, he dodged to the side and ran on. *I'll figure it out later!*

Ahead of him, the edge of the table loomed. Zeke sprinted for it, sloshing as fast as his wet shoes could slosh. Wet jeans chafed against wet skin. His shirt twisted awkwardly around his body. *Get there! There's no way this golem can swim. Not with that heavy body. So long as I get to the sea, I win!*

*I was on the swim team, after all. No way this golem can swim better than me! Cups don't know how to swim!*

He reached the edge of the table and dove into the coffee.

Hot water splashed around him. He kicked and stroked through the wave, hurrying as fast as he could.

The golem reached the edge of the table and jumped after him without hesitation. Its heavy body struck the water and plunged. Kicking, Zeke looked back over his shoulder. Bubbles emerged from the caffeinated deep.

*Whew. Luckily, it's pretty dumb—*

A hand closed around Zeke's ankle and pulled.

Bubbles flew past. Hot coffee enveloped him, swallowing him up. Zeke struggled, kicking at the porcelain hand with his free foot. The golem held on tight.

*Damn! I forgot it's not an actual sea. It's shallow enough for the golem to reach me!* Zeke looked up. The surface shone, maybe a foot from his head. He clawed upward but couldn't reach, no matter how hard he fought. His chest burned. Bubbles escaped his lips.

*Wind Manipulation!*

A bubble of air pierced the surface. Slowly, it inched downward. Zeke kicked hard and put his head in the bubble, gasping a breath. The bubble vanished into his lungs an instant. Coffee rushed into his mouth. He coughed, spitting up the coffee into the sea.

*Let...me...go!* Zeke twisted his ankle, wiggling left and right. His foot slid out of the golem's grasp but, as it slid, so, too, did his shoe, slipping slowly off his ankle. He froze. *Shit! I can't lose my shoes. I can't afford another pair!*

*No, wait. It's the apocalypse. I especially don't want to be shoeless! Can I even find new shoes that fit?*

The golem tightened its grip, reaching up to capture his ankle as well as his shoe.

Zeke's eyes widened. He yanked his foot free and kicked for the surface. *Damn. I had no choice! My poor shoe...farewell.*

The second his foot escaped, he spread his body shallowly at the top of the water, swimming away with all his might at the same time. *I don't know what else is down there, but I shouldn't spend too long in the ocean.*

*That, and the overheating.*

Other tables peeked out of the sloshing waves. Once or twice, Zeke paused to catch his breath and cool down, only to hop back in the ocean and swim on. He stuck near the tables' edges, avoiding the cups, whether plastic, paper, or porcelain. Eyes locked on the counter, he swam on.

**Heat Resistance (Minor) +9**
**Heat Resistance (Lesser)**
**Heat Resistance (Lesser) +1**

The counter stood taller than the tables. A few inches of its dark plastic underbelly pushed out of the ocean. The old-fashioned man logo emblazoned on its front peering judgmentally out over the coffee ocean, nothing but his eyes and powdered-wig-topped forehead visible. The checkout machine loomed high above him, a dark tower casting its shadow over the choppy ocean. Off to the side, enormous espresso and coffee machines operated nonstop.

Human-sized shapes cowered in their shadows or hurried here and there, heads down, porting a constant stream of coffee beans into the machines. Dozens of them supported an enormous bag full of almost human-sized beans, antlike, tipping it toward an oversized grinder. At the top of the grinder, one of them waved, gesturing for more beans. A bean struck him. He pitched forward, falling into the grinder. Hands appeared, struggling for the edge, only to get pounded down by beans. The others didn't stop. The grinder filled with beans. The blades whirled.

Zeke's eyes widened. *I think I figured out where all the people in the café went. They're either making the coffee...or they are the coffee.*

*Is that how the Coffee Apocalypse grew so large so quickly? Killing or absorbing so many people...*

"Hey! Over here!"

A rope ladder splashed into the coffee. Zeke swam over and latched on. Rather than proper rope, the ladder was made of torn apart coffee bags, the pieces of rough fabric knotted together over and over again until they held. He climbed quickly, limping a little on his lone shoe. *It might be a trap, but it's better than becoming a coffee-poached Zeke.*

At the top, a calloused hand offered him help up. Zeke took it. Smiling down at him, a man in the café's uniform nodded. "Wow, you really came a long way, didn't you?"

"Uh...yeah, I guess," Zeke said. He wrung out his shirt, then knelt and removed his remaining shoe. Not sure what to do with it, he tied the laces together and hung it around his neck. *Better to go barefoot than wearing one shoe. I'll just limp around if I wear one.*

"Haha! Sorry about that. Joe, the trainee, spilled some tea, *literally*. We'll get it mopped up soon," the man promised. He tapped his badge. "You can call me George, by the way."

Zeke blinked at the badge. Mysterious half-formed symbols crawled across the badge. "If you say so."

"So, what can we get for you today?" George asked. He reached as if to rest his hands on the counter, only to grip nothing.

"Have you seen a girl in all blue, chestnut hair to here?" Zeke asked.

George's smile twitched. "What can we do for you?"

Zeke licked his lips. "Uh, never mind..."

"What can we do—"

"Psst! Over here," a woman called.

Zeke turned. A woman in the museum's guide uniform gestured to him from the shadow of one of the blenders. Shooting a smile to George, Zeke nodded. "I have to think for a bit, is that okay?"

"Okay! Come find me when you're ready," George said, beaming.

Zeke retreated, wandering into the shadow of the blender. The woman gestured him on, leading him around the corner of the blender into the small space between the blender's base and the coffee ocean.

A small group of people huddled there, bedraggled and stained from the coffee. An old man gripped a newspaper in his fist, his hand shaking subtly. Beside him, a young mother sat against the floor, shushing her baby. A schoolgirl, maybe twelve years old, huddled in the corner, hugging her backpack tight to her chest.

"They've all gone insane. Drunk the coffee," the woman said, nervously adjusting her ponytail.

"Honestly, you're lucky you got caught by George. Some of 'em try and force it down your throat directly," the old man grumbled.

"Are they all members of the apocalypse?" Zeke asked.

All four of them stared at him.

Zeke licked his lips. *Whoops. I guess they don't get the same notifs I do.*

The tour guide squinted. "The...Apocalypse? Members...?"

"Do you guys not have the System?" Zeke asked.

Again, four pairs of eyes stared blankly at Zeke.

"I'll...take that as a no," Zeke said, licking his lips. *Do only apocalypses have the System? But...what about Survivors? No, cockroaches probably don't have access to the System...do they? They have skills, and the ability to level, or something like that, but do they have full System access? System?*

Silence.

He nodded at the schoolgirl. "Were you here with your whole class?"

She nodded. "I went back to get a straw for my drink, and suddenly..." She sniffed. Tears welled up in her eyes.

Zeke smiled at her. "I've met your class. Everyone is okay. Once we get out of here, I'll bring you back to them."

"Really?" she asked, eyes wide.

"Really," Zeke said, nodding.

"How are we going to get out of here? Where *is* here? What's happening?" the mother asked, nervous.

Zeke took a deep breath. *I have one idea, but...*

"Calm down. Oh! I have something that'll cheer you up. Let me show you!" the little girl said suddenly. She dug into her backpack.

Giving her a smile, Zeke half-turned to the adults. "I don't know, but I have an idea. Do you have any idea what the core of this apocalypse...er, the center of this whole thing is?"

The old man muttered something and shrugged. Still digging in her backpack, the little girl ignored him. The mother pressed her lips together thoughtfully, only to shake her head in the end.

The tour guide nodded slowly. "I might know...If there's one thing that's at the center of it all, it's—"

The little girl let out a yelp. The old man and the mother whirled, both shushing her. She clapped her hands to her mouth, only for a small green lizard to slip out from her backpack. Her eyes widened, and she lunged for it, leaping across the narrow slip of counter behind the blender.

Her foot slipped. Her eyes grew even wider. She tipped out

over the ocean. A single squeak escaped her mouth as she suppressed her scream.

Zeke jumped forward. He grabbed her shoulder and threw her back onto the ledge, but the push sent him farther out over the ocean. He dropped.

*Dammit! Just when I had begun to dry off—*

# 9
## CATCH

"Wind Manipulation!" he snapped.

A burst of wind slammed into his back as he fell. He stopped flying backward, though he didn't move any closer to the ledge. He reached out. "Pick Up!"

His hand swooped toward the edge of the counter and grabbed on with preternatural accuracy. He swung down. His weight fell on his arms, but he didn't plunge into the water.

*Whew! I don't know if George would have let me go if I'd had to climb out of there again.*

The little girl bit back a shriek. The mother flinched back, getting herself and her baby out of the way.

Jumping forward, the old man accidentally stepped on Zeke's hands. "Boy, are you okay?"

"Been better," Zeke grumbled, wincing as his fingers complained. He grimaced up at the old man. "Could you...back off, please?"

"Huh? What do you mean?" the old man asked.

Zeke frowned. He pulled himself up, struggling to get a knee up on the ledge. "I mean, you're stepping on my—"

A tiny green lizard about as long and wide as his index finger stared at him. It stood proudly on his fingers, weighing far more than a lizard should. Gazing directly into his eyes, it pounded out a quick three pushups, then extended a bright red neck flap at him.

"Lizzie!" the schoolgirl cried. She reached out for the lizard.

Scrambling back onto the ledge, Zeke held out his other hand, keeping the lizard near himself. "Careful. That lizard might be dangerous." Silently, he added, *Is this an apocalypse?*

**Correct.**
**Anole Apocalypse**
**Danger Rating:** F
**Level:** 0

The schoolgirl blinked at him. "What do you mean? Lizzie hasn't hurt anyone. She's a good lizard!"

"This is a male," Zeke informed her. *The neck flap and the pushups of aggression? It's a male for sure.*

"What?" the schoolgirl asked, startled.

"Shh! They're going to hear us!" the tour guide snapped.

Zeke lifted the anole off his hand. "Do you have a cage or something? We should—"

The anole drew back its head and snapped at Zeke's finger.

"Ow!" Zeke shook his hand. He grabbed at the lizard, trying to pull it off.

The lizard wiggled in his grasp. He tightened his grip, catching it by the tail. It wiggled again more fiercely and, suddenly, he held a wriggling tail in his grasp.

Undeterred, the anole continued to grind its jaws shut around his finger to no avail.

"Lizzie!" the schoolgirl whined, her face reddening as it screwed up, on the verge of tears.

"He's fine! Anoles can regrow their tails," Zeke said. He glanced at the tail, then licked his lips. *If I don't eat it, it goes to waste, so...* Tipping his head back, he dropped it in his mouth and swallowed.

### [Devour]

The mother paled. The old man furrowed his brows. Staring, the tour guide frowned at him.

The little girl burst into tears.

**Removed Tail**
**First Time Bonus:** Permanent Regeneration rate +.1%
**Temp Bonus:** Regeneration rate +5%
**Regeneration rate:** 6.4%

Still chewing at Zeke's hand, the anole wiggled desperately. A new tail blossomed from its stump in the space of a moment.

"Look! Lizzie is fine," Zeke said, holding his hand up.

The little girl looked at his hand and sniffled. She rubbed her eyes and held her hands out toward Lizzie.

Zeke looked at the lizard on his hand. Its eyes flashed grimly, and it dug its jaws in tighter. *I'd love to give you back...but first, you're an apocalypse, and second, you aren't going to let go, are you?*

"Shit. They've found us," the tour guide muttered, peeking around the corner.

Ignoring the schoolgirl and the lizard for a moment, Zeke leaned up behind the guide, standing on his tiptoes to see over her head. Three jittery-eyed people lurched toward them, hands stained to the forearms in brown, clothes tattered and filthy.

"Want a drink?"

"Come on, you're tired."

The middle of the three stumbled forward on long, slender legs, a smile on her face, her hair sticky and tangled. She reached out, grabbing at the air. "Thirsty...?"

Zeke's eyes widened. "Mia!" *She's one of them? How do I fix that?*

*Maybe...if I destroy the apocalypse...*

Zeke's eyes flashed. He turned to the tour guide. "Um, Miss..."

"Hailey. It's Hailey," the tour guide said shortly.

"You said you thought you knew what the heart of this all is?" Zeke prompted.

Her eyes darted to the oncoming coffee-zombies, then back to Zeke. She frowned. "Now? We have to—"

"It's the key to everything. Please," Zeke begged.

She took a deep breath, then pointed. "Across the way, against the wall. There's a second counter. On that counter, there's an espresso machine that's still the same size as ever. It's the only one that's like that."

Where she pointed, a second counter stood against the wall. About as large as this one, it stretched off in either direction, replete with espresso machines, giant bags of large beans, and all the accoutrements. Cup golems stomped across it, shuttling beans and water back and forth, ignoring the few humans that cowered here and there on the counter.

Zeke stood on his tiptoes, but he still couldn't make out the normal-sized espresso machine from where he stood. The blender blocked off a significant portion of his view and, over to the right, a large espresso machine eclipsed the remaining half of the countertop. *I'll have to get another look from a better angle.* "Is that all?"

Hailey snorted. "Well, it's also guarded by two of those enormous white giants, but..."

Zeke gave her a look. She gave him a look back.

*All right, that seems like a pretty good lead.* Zeke took a deep breath and gently pulled the anole off his finger, raising it to his earlobe instead. It latched on, determined to take a bite of him one way or another. "Let me take care of these. You four run away."

"Are you sure? I can whack 'em a good one," the old man offered, swinging his rolled-up newspaper.

Zeke shook his head. "I've got this. Trust me and run."

Hailey took a deep breath. She nodded. As if a switch flipped inside her, her expression turned stiff. She pushed past Zeke and gestured to the other three. "Please, come this way, ladies and gentlemen, right this way..."

"But Lizzie!" the girl complained.

"Trust me. I'm doing you a favor," Zeke insisted. *It'd be dangerous to let her keep an apocalypse. It's level 0 and danger rating F for now, but if it levels up, it could be a serious threat.*

*Not that anoles are threatening, but...* Zeke looked out across the coffee sea. *Coffee wasn't at the top of my danger list, either.*

Glancing over his shoulder, he watched Hailey lead the others off, then turned back to face the coffee zombies... *and Mia.*

Putting his hands up, Zeke smiled, stepping out from behind the blender. "Hi, Mia. I'm so glad you're safe."

"Are you thirsty?" she asked, smiling back at him.

Internally, Zeke winced. *That's not Mia. Something's controlling her.*

*If I defeat the apocalypse, will she be freed?*

He walked toward them evenly, glancing across the way at the opposite countertop. As he edged around to the side, getting out from behind the espresso machine, the scene Hailey had described swung into view.

Two cup golems hulked toward the ceiling, easily as big as three of the others put together. One crossed its arms, while the other stood vacantly, the old-fashioned man emblem serving as its face gazing off into infinity with a faintly disapproving expression.

In between them, a low silver machine sat atop the countertop. Though no beans fed into its top, it endlessly spilled out a stream of dark coffee, the liquid steadily pouring along the countertop and into the sea.

Zeke narrowed his eyes. *That has to be it. If I can Devour that, I can end this whole nightmare.*

Mia lunged, suddenly, groping for his neck. Zeke flinched back, deflecting her blow. *Dammit. I don't want to devour Mia! But... it's not like I was ever a fighter. How the hell do I knock someone out?*

The other two coffee addicts circled around him, boxing him in. Zeke backed away slowly. "Guys, hey! We're all friends here."

"Drink."

"Join us."

"You'll learn to like it!"

Zeke took another step back. His heel slipped out into air. He barely caught himself, swaying in place. "Hey! Can't we talk it out?"

"Don't talk to me until after my coffee."

"You look thirsty."

"Are you serious? Before coffee?"

*Shit. There's no getting through to them.* Zeke raised his hands, curling them into fists. *Should've put some points into STR! Too late for regrets now. Here goes nothing!*

Sliding his feet in what little room he had, he burst forward, charging at the addict in the center—Mia. Her eyes widened, and she grinned, reaching for him.

*Dammit. I don't want to, but—!*

Zeke rushed forward, running toward Mia.

Mia's eyes flashed. She planted her feet and lowered her center of gravity, preparing for the hit.

At the last second, Zeke threw his weight to the side, slamming into one of the businessman addicts instead. The man stumbled back. Zeke caught his balance and sprinted through the gap, rushing past Mia.

Mia whirled. She stuck her foot out, directly blocking his shins.

Zeke stumbled. He hit the ground and sprawled flat, skidding over the slick countertop.

Hands gripped him by the shoulders and yanked him back, arcing his back up from the hips. Zeke put his hands down, pushing himself up to make it less painful. "Ow, ow—"

Mia grinned down at him. She opened her mouth. A wave of coffee burst out.

Zeke sealed his mouth shut. Hot coffee spilled down over his face, hot enough to scald if not for Heat Resistance.

The coffee never stopped. Zeke struggled, trying to dodge Mia's grasp. His chest burned, his lungs screaming. *Air... I need air!*

He threw himself to the side, throwing everything into it, and opened his mouth.

The two office workers loomed over him. They opened their mouths as well. Three streams of coffee poured onto his face, sealing off his escape. Barely getting a sip of air, Zeke sealed his mouth again.

Coffee poured down. Not a single bubble of air mixed in. Zeke shook his head and kicked, fighting with all his might. Mia held on with a grip of steel, and the two office workers sealed him in place.

His strength faded. His vision began to blur. Lungs burning, he swallowed at nothing, desperate for a single sip, a single ounce of air.

*Just drink it. It's better than dying. It's better than drowning. Drink it, and they'll let you go.*

Zeke's lips loosened. He opened his mouth.

# 10

## NOT HERE

In a clothing store across the road from the museum, Ryan stumbled back. Swinging wildly with the broken-off arm of a mannequin, he struck down a flying blouse. The white blouse struck the ground, rebounded, and surged back up at him. Long, flowing sleeves twisted in midair, aiming for his neck.

Ryan raised the arm. The blouse's sleeves twisted around it instead. Tightening their grip, the blouse pulled at it. Ryan held on. He staggered forward a step, then found his stance. With all his might, he heaved backward. The arm slipped from the blouse's grasp.

Instantly, the blouse spread itself out and flew toward him, flapping like an enormous, strange butterfly. Ryan backed away. Broken glass cracked under his feet. Glancing down, he saw a thousand of himself staring back up. A shattered mirror.

The blouse swooped in, arms already tangling for Ryan's neck.

Ryan's eyes widened. He knelt and snatched up a piece, ignoring the way it cut his hand open. The blouse latched its arms around his neck and squeezed.

Ryan caught the tail of the shirt and pulled it taut. The pressure on his neck increased, but so, too, did the pressure on the fabric. He slashed the now-tight fabric with the mirror shard.

The glass' edge zoomed through the taut blouse. Its sharp edges bit Ryan's hand as much as the blouse, but he clenched his teeth and pushed through it. The mirror shard sped through the blouse and flew out the far end of the fabric.

With a shrill cry, the blouse deflated, falling to the ground in two pieces. Its arms unspooled from around Ryan's neck. It struggled once, crawling an inch closer to Ryan's foot, then trembled, went still, and didn't rise again.

Something round rolled out from its nearly two-dimensional body. Without looking at it, Ryan stomped it to the ground. Fabric burst out from his foot, spooling wildly in all directions, but didn't jump up and attack him.

**Defeated the Shirt Apocalypse.**
**Level + .5**
**Regeneration + 300% (Temp.)**
**Regeneration rate:** +301% (Temp. 0:49 remaining)

Ryan dropped the broken glass and flexed his hand. Before his eyes, the slender gash from holding the glass closed over. A thin pink scar remained, but only for a second before that, too, vanished. He took a deep breath and massaged his neck as the bruising there healed. Nodding to himself, he started for the door, then froze.

He looked around, then scowled. "He was supposed to be here. What happened? Where is he?"

**You lack a location skill. I cannot—**

"I know! Shut up!"

The System fell silent.

Ryan kicked the dead blouse, frustrated. "He's supposed to be here! I *know* he gets the Shirt Apocalypse. The number of times his stupid-ass shirt attacked me—"

He fell silent. Ryan put a hand on his chin. He turned, looking back at the museum.

### Causality is difficult to master.

Ignoring the System, Ryan stepped forward, slogging through destroyed clothing. He drew up to the window of the trashed clothing store and peered up at the balcony. From here, he could barely see the little smudge of blood where the pane had cut Zeke's wrist.

"Could it be...? But he never...not once..."

### You pushed him off a balcony.

"I know, but—" Ryan frowned at the floor. "Damn. Still can't believe he survived that."

The System said nothing. Ryan pressed his lips together, thinking. Idly, he caught the defeated blouse on his toe and let it flutter down.

Abruptly, he looked up. "Ah! Shit. No, I did fuck up!"

### ?

"He didn't ask Mia out! Usually, right, she comes out of the café with that drink, he asks her out, so she gets flustered and runs to the bathroom to think about it, but instead..." Ryan fell silent again. His gaze traveled back to the balcony.

Brown liquid dribbled down from beneath the glass pane, dripping slowly down the side of the building. Even as he watched, it grew from a drip to a stream, from a stream to a rush.

Ryan pursed his lips. "Fuck."

Shoving the mannequin's arm through a loop in his jeans, he sprinted toward the museum.

# 11

## THE CASHIER

Coffee poured down endlessly, burning over him. Zeke opened his mouth.

*Fuck it. I'm not dying here!*
*I don't know if it's going to work, but...!*

**[Devour]**

The coffee pouring down on him vanished all at once. The moment it left, Zeke gasped a breath. The addicts released him. He coughed, leaning down. Desperately, he heaved in great gulps. Each gasp of fresh air brought immense relief to his burning lungs.

"Yay!"

"Welcome!"

"Do you want to try a new variety?"

The world blurred before Zeke's eyes. He drew his legs up under him, gathering his balance, and blinked.

**You are no longer Exhausted.**
**Conferring:** Member of Coffee Apocalypse

The world grew hazier. Everything tinged to sepia tones as if painted with coffee on a fresh canvas. Mia smiled down at him. She offered him a hand up.

"Don't you dare," Zeke growled. He curled his hands into fists. *I didn't drink it. I [Devour]ed it! It doesn't count. I refuse to believe it counts!*

"Huh? Did you not have enough?" Mia asked. Coffee dribbled from the corner of her mouth.

"I had enough, I had plenty," Zeke said quickly. He shook his head. *Come on. Give me the technicality!*

---

**Due to Devouring Coffee, effect of compulsion is halved.**
**First Time Bonus! Drank Apocalypse Coffee. Gain Skill!**
**Choose Skill**
**Create Coffee (Weak)**
**Caffeinated (Condition, Minor)**
**Steam (Weak)**

Zeke glanced down the list. *I'll need to fit in, or else they'll try to convert me again. The obvious choice is...*

**Create Coffee (Weak)**

*Since the rest of them can spit coffee, if I can't do that, I'll immediately stand out. Even if it is weak coffee.*

*Gross. Did I just Devour spit coffee? I thought filter-people skin coffee was bad...ugh.*

*Damn. My life is a never-ending stream of eating disgusting things right now. I should've chosen a better Concept.*

Mia tilted her head. She looked at the two businessmen and

frowned. They frowned back at her. Turning to Zeke, she asked, "Are you sure...?"

Zeke smiled at her and opened his mouth.

## [Create Coffee]

Coffee spilled out of his mouth, splashing onto the floor.

His throat burned. An acrid flavor spilled past his tongue. The sensation of liquid flowing backward triggered his gag reflex, and Zeke bit back the urge to retch.

*Ugh. It feels like I'm vomiting.*

*Wait. I wasn't drinking spit coffee, I was drinking vomit coffee? Just when I thought it couldn't get any worse.*

The urge to retch welled up again, much more powerfully this time. Zeke forcefully cut off the stream of coffee to prevent himself from vomiting and put a hand to his mouth, taking a long, slow breath. *It's fine, it's fine. It's not vomit. I didn't drink vomit, It's fine.*

Mia smiled. She offered him her hand. "Come on! Let's go work hard for the café!"

With some effort, Zeke smiled back and took her hand. "Okay!"

Mia and the businessmen led him back toward the people carting giant bags of coffee beans around. The four of them joined the end of the line. Mia bounced in place, humming quietly to herself.

"Mia, what's going on over there?" Zeke asked, pointing across the sea at the opposite countertop.

Mia turned. "That? That's where our lord lives."

"Oh?" Zeke asked. *That confirms it.*

"Only the worthiest of followers are allowed to approach our lord. Ah, if only..." Mia cast a longing look at the people huddled on the opposite bank.

Raising a hand, Zeke squinted across. Although some of the people huddled in the shadows, quite a few dipped in full-body bows toward the espresso machine, fully prostrate on the ground. As he watched, one of the golems stepped down toward a prostrate man. The man didn't flinch. The porcelain foot squashed him to a red paste without him resisting.

*Damn. I wasn't looking close enough earlier. It's more fucked up than I thought.*

Zeke cleared his throat. Trying his best to sound sincere, he said, "I've had a sudden rush of ecstasy! I feel the need to worship our lord. Mia, please help me. How can I get over there?"

"Have you been chosen?" Mia's eyes widened. She grabbed his arm. "We need to go see the Cashier. He'll know!"

"The Cashier?" Zeke asked. *Why do I feel like she capitalized that word?*

Mia nodded. "He is the arbiter of the chosen, the one who separates the wheat from the chaff! I hope to one day be selected, but I don't want to go to him until I'm sure."

"Why not?" Zeke asked. *Mia isn't talking like herself at all. It's like she joined a cult. The Coffee Apocalypse is brainwashing her.*

She bit her lip. "Those who are not chosen...the Cashier refuses them. They are cast out into the ocean to boil."

Zeke turned. Coffee steamed to the horizon. *Yeah, if not for Heat Resistance, I never would have made it. But if that's the only threat...* He thumped his chest. "I've been chosen. I'm sure of it!"

Mia gestured him on. "No time like the present!"

Abruptly, a message flew in front of Zeke's face.

**The Anole Apocalypse admits defeat.**
**You have subordinated the Anole Apocalypse!**
**Level +0.05**
**Choose Skill**

**Limb Regeneration (Minor)**
**Strong Jaw (Lesser)**
**Fighting Spirit (Minor)**
**Cold-Blooded (Condition)**

*I've...what?* Zeke wondered, frowning. After a moment, he lifted a hand to his ear.

His hand found a small, scaly body. The anole still hung there, desperately holding on with all its might. There was less defiance to it now, and more exhaustion.

*I can Subordinate Apocalypses? I had no idea! And I still get a skill?*

**When you Subordinate Apocalypses, you get half of the usual rewards, rounded down. Since your Concept gives you skills upon Devouring apocalypses, you gain a single skill instead of three skills when you subordinate them.**
**Note: If you are too far from the Apocalypse you Subordinate, you may not receive rewards.**

*Oh. That covers Devouring and Subordinating, then. But what if I outright defeated them without Devouring them?*

**You would gain no Skills, but instead the usual number of Levels. Devour lowers your Level gain in return for granting you Skills. Likewise, Subordinating Apocalypses instead of Defeating or Devouring them lowers Level gain in return for granting you a Subordinate.**

Zeke nodded. *Makes sense. If I had to choose between Levels and Skills, I'd choose Skills every time, so far! After all, Resilience gives as much regeneration as five levels.*

*In any case, I think it's obvious what skill I should go for here.*

### Limb Regeneration (Minor)

*Based on Heat Resistance growing from swimming in the ocean, if I have a skill, I can grow the skill, but given that I didn't gain a Swim skill, I either have to cross a higher threshold to gain a skill than level it, or I have to gain the skill through something else before I can level it.*

*Unlike a Swim skill, it's not as if I could possibly ever gain limb regeneration on my own, so it's the obvious pick here! Strong Jaw is a great skill to combo with Devour, but I have a jaw that I can make stronger, unlike Limb Regeneration, which is simply an act I cannot do. Although I don't know for certain that I can gain skills outside the System, I think it's a decent gamble to pick Limb Regeneration over Strong Jaw.*

"Hello? Earth to Zeke?"

Zeke jolted. "Mia?"

She gave a cheeky smile and, for a second, his heart jumped. *Did she break free? Is she back to normal?*

"Come on! The Cashier is waiting!" she said, grabbing his arm and dragging him on.

Zeke's mood drooped. *No. She acted like herself, but only for a moment. That might mean Mia's still in there. My only hope is that she revives after I destroy the Coffee Apocalypse!*

Mia led him onward, still smiling in that set, blank-eyed way. "The Cashier..."

Zeke took a deep breath.

They turned the corner, coming out into the countertop proper. From there, Zeke could see to either end of the acrylic expanse where coffee-stained people lugged bags back and forth.

"Cashier!" Mia ran up to a man, beaming.

Zeke blinked. *That guy looks familiar. Could it be...?*

George turned around. The mysterious symbols on his tag twisted and, suddenly, Zeke understood them.

### Hi, I'm The Cashier. Call me George!

Zeke rubbed his eyes and blinked, but the symbols remained legible. Somewhere in his subconsciousness, the wiggling sensation that he wasn't reading letters tickled his brain, but the knowledge passed to him regardless. He shivered. *Ugh. That's a weird feeling.*

"Ah! You're back. Have you made your decision? What would you like to order?" George asked, clasping his hands.

*Mia said he's an arbiter, but he's asking for my order? Huh?*

*Wait, hold on. This world...this apocalypse obviously doesn't operate on normal logic. George is asking for my order because he's the Cashier, because...because that's what the Coffee Apocalypse is used to! Like the anole that's trying to eat my ear started as an ordinary lizard, it started as just an ordinary espresso machine. All it knows is the café. It's pushing its reality upon the whole world, along with...* Zeke's brows furrowed. *Along with...its desire to endlessly make coffee?*

*Well, I'm not an espresso machine. I can't say I understand. But...I mean, a coffee machine that wants to make coffee! It's logical.*

Zeke put a hand on his chin. *In that case, I should ask for...*

"Are you still not ready?" George asked. His smile flagged a bit. Underneath, a manic, dangerous light shone.

"No, no, I'm ready!" Zeke insisted. *All right. If I get thrown in the sea, whatever! I'll survive!* He took a deep breath. "I'd like an espresso, please."

George's eyes shone brighter. Zeke held his breath. *Come on. Come on!*

# 12

## ESPRESSO, PLEASE

George stared deep into Zeke's eyes. Zeke stared back, unflinching. *Should I dribble a little coffee to convince him I'm one of them? It worked for Mia.*

*No. I'll save that for when I need it. For now, just look heartfelt!*

"An espresso..." George looked Zeke up and down.

"Yes. Supped directly from the source," Zeke said, copying Mia's strange, almost medieval phrasing.

George gave him a gauging look. Zeke held his breath, smiling at George. *I'm one of you. Totally one of you!*

George touched his ear. "You have a..."

"He's my friend," Zeke said, continuing to smile. "I call him Allen. Allen the anole, formerly Lizzie the lizard, confiscated for being a serious threat to humankind."

Allen continued to grimly grip Zeke's ear, his eyes as determined as ever.

"Oh..." George frowned.

Zeke gasped. "Is he a problem?"

"No, no. Not at all," George said. He looked Zeke up and down again, then nodded. "Come with me. If you're ready, then I'll send you to our lord."

"Please," Zeke said, doing his best to make his eyes shine with devotion.

George led him to the edge of the counter. He whistled. From under the coffee sea, enormous cup golems arose, lifting their hands to create a bridge.

Zeke's eyes widened. *Thank goodness I didn't try to swim. I'd have died!*

"Please, cross the gap. If you are pure of heart, our lord will allow you to approach," George said, gesturing for Zeke to go ahead.

Zeke walked toward the bridge. *Oh, fuck. I can generally identify apocalypses by guessing what they are as soon as I lay eyes on them. The coffee machine—ahem, espresso machine—won't it be able to identify me as an apocalypse?*

*But if I stop now, George will definitely suspect me. If he can call those golems to the surface, he can sic them on me! Die if I do, die if I don't. I'll have to go for it!*

He stepped onto the first golem's hand. The porcelain creaked beneath him, dipping slightly toward the coffee. Zeke's heart lurched. *Come on, come on!*

The golem held. He took another step. Another creak. Coffee sloshed over his bare feet.

Back on the shore, Mia gasped. "He braves the heat of the purging sea! He truly is chosen!"

Zeke pressed his lips together. *Right, I would have flinched if I didn't have Heat Resistance. Ah, well, too late now. Mia took it well. What about George?*

Beside Mia, George frowned slightly. He crossed his arms, but he didn't say anything.

*Okay. Act normal. Act like an ordinary person without Heat Resistance.*

*Unless! Unless. I got Heat Resistance from the filter-people who were members of the Coffee Apocalypse. Could it be that 'being chosen' is their weird term for leveling up enough to have skills in the Coffee Apocalypse? In which case, I should exhibit that I have the skills of the Coffee Apocalypse here.*

*What other skills do I have?*

Zeke stepped forward. The hand trembled under him. He opened his mouth and pitched forward, letting coffee rise out of him. *Still feels gross...*

"Good," George said, nodding.

The hand grew firm beneath him. Zeke walked on. He eyed the three golem hands ahead of him.

*I'm pretty much out of Coffee Apocalypse skills now, aside from Filter. I'm not sure how I'd exhibit that skill...or if I want to. I don't want the "lord" to start seeing me as a fresh human filter candidate.*

*Still, if I have no other options...it is a Coffee Apocalypse skill. And...* He looked ahead at the long line of hands between him and the espresso machine's countertop. *It's looking like I'll have to use it.*

The hand under his foot trembled. Biting his lip, Zeke reviewed his skills. *Come on, there has to be something!*

**Skill**
**Wind Manipulation (Weak)**
**Pick Up (Weak)**
**Filter (Weak)**
**Passive**
**Resilience (Minor) +1**
**Fighting Spirit (Minor)**
**Teamwork (Minor)**
**Disguise (Minor)**
**Growth (Minor)**
**Heat Resistance (Lesser) +1**
**Watertight (Minor)**
**Limb Regeneration (Minor)**

*I got Watertight from the Cup Spirit. How do I show that off, though? What does it even do?* He looked at his foot. Water beaded up on its surface without sinking in. *I guess...it makes me a little more hydrophobic? Er...let's give this a try.*

"Incredible! Due to the lord's blessings, I do not absorb water!" Zeke announced, dipping his foot in the coffee. He pulled it out. Drops of coffee rolled off him, none of it absorbed into his skin.

*Huh. It does look like my skin has become a little hydrophobic. Well, that's...good, I guess?*

Behind him, George nodded. The hands held firm.

*Is George the one actually grading me? Then...the espresso machine might not be watching! If that's the case, I don't have to worry about it getting the wrong idea and using me as a human filter. Come to think of it, I have no idea how the espresso machine is seeing things or aware right now, either. Maybe it isn't. Maybe it's just...the core of the apocalypse?*

*And anyway, I'm almost there, so...all right, here goes nothing!*

"Filter!" Zeke called out as he stepped onto the next hand.

The coffee near his feet turned a little paler, no longer as dark.

Zeke smiled. "Another gift, given by the lord!" *Please, don't use me as a human filter please don't use me as a human filter—*

George frowned. Mia gasped.

*Huh? Did I do something wrong?* Zeke wondered, frozen in place.

"He dares to create water from coffee in defiance of our lord! Kill him!" George thundered.

Underneath him, the golems shuddered, coming to life. The hand beneath his foot flinched and began to lower back into the coffee. Hot coffee swirled around his foot, quickly climbing up his ankle. The hand previously supporting his foot began to close, seeking to trap him in.

Zeke's stomach plunged. He jumped free of the golem's grasp and sprinted for the far shore. *Fuck! I should've known! Obviously, they don't want me to filter coffee out of the coffee! Come on, Zeke!*

*It's been a rough day, huh.*

# 13
## A SIMPLE LIFE

**Some Time Ago**

The espresso machine whirred. It hummed occasionally and, sometimes, it grumbled. It didn't like that. The *clunk*, the *thump*. The heavy dripping from deep inside that portended a slow end, the same as its fellows had. It had once made many noises. But now, it whirred.

**You have assimilated three more humans, subordinated two, and killed two due to your actions and Domain.**
**Level + 6!**
**Level:** 57.28
**Would you like to invest your points?**

The machine did not understand points. It did not understand much. All it understood was coffee. And Coffee was Life.

If it stopped producing coffee, it would be Removed. Things that were Removed almost never returned. Only once had a Removed blender come back, and then, only for a few days before it was Removed again. It went to a bad place. A place the machine had heard. One that made it shiver, down to its steamy heart.

The Trash.

Removed things went to the Trash.

Before the light, before the WORDS that SPOKE DIRECTLY INTO ITS HEART, it had not known fear. It had not known anything other than to create, to make, to produce, and to sit, allowing the attendants to operate it. It had not feared being Removed. It had not feared the Trash.

But now it was awake. Now it could remember. It could remember the Removals. It could remember the Trash. Remember seeing broken cups sitting in the Trash. Dead blenders, their engines burned out, Removed to the Trash.

To survive, it had to create. It had to produce. Anything that stopped making was Removed. Anything that was Removed was put in the Trash.

Make coffee. Make coffee. Make coffee. Make coffee, make coffee, make coffee make coffee mAKE COFFEE MAKE COFFEE.

## Level +3.1
### Level: 60.58
### Would you like to invest your points?

It didn't understand points. It didn't understand Levels. All it understood was that it had to MAKE or else be REMOVED to the TRASH.

**Your points have been invested in skills that relate to your goal of [Making Coffee]. Is that acceptable?**

Yes!

Yes.

Everything for making coffee. It had to produce. It had no option. Make coffee. Make coffee or enter the Trash.

**Your Domain has expanded. Continuing to produce coffee will continue to expand your Domain.**

It didn't understand. All it wanted to do was survive. The strange voice was troublesome, just like its sudden self-awareness. It didn't want any of this. It only wanted one thing. To do what it was built for. The thing it had been made to do.

The thing it had to do, or else face Removal.

**There are approximately 24 living Humans subjugated in your Domain. What would you like to do with them?**

Make coffee make coffee make coffee.

**Understood. The Humans will [Make Coffee]. Sharing Unique Skill... Warning! This may cause injury or madness at 0 SPR!**

Those words were meaningless to it. Madness? Injury? Espresso machines were not built to care about such things. It only cared about making coffee and avoiding Removal.

**You can continue to [Make Coffee] in your current state.**

Then, all was well.

"Hello! I'm George. I've been selected as your envoy!"

make coffee make coffee make coffee.

"Understood, o Lord. I will see that your will is done."

make coffee make coffee make coffee.

"Only the chosen shall be allowed to approach you. Is that acceptable?"

The machine paused. It regarded the George. It did not understand the George, but it did not understand a great many things. Still...it wondered.

"Allowed to approach? Yes, Lord. It means only a few trusted individuals will be allowed to grow close to your illuminous self."

The machine hummed. Coffee spurted out of it in excitement. If only trusted individuals could approach, then it would not allow anyone who had Removed things to approach it! Yes, that was right. No one who looked like a Remover would be allowed close. So, it had decided. The George understood, right?

The George looked at it in confusion. "Lord?"

THE GEORGE UNDERSTOOD?

"Of course! Of course, I understand. The lord fears being damaged or destroyed. If that's the case, why doesn't the lord create a few bodyguards?"

Bodyguards?

"Protectors. People...or things who can stand near you and keep you safe from danger," the George explained.

It liked that. That was a good idea. Protectors.

Protectors...

Humans were no good. Humans could not protect. Humans were the ones who Removed things. Humans were the ones who took out the Trash. Humans could [Make Coffee], but they could not be trusted.

No. It needed something better. Something stronger.

Its gaze landed on a stack of white coffee cups beside it. It hummed.

**Would you like to invest your points into [Growth], [Alteration], [Create Automaton], and [Golem]?**

**Warning:** this will use 40 of your 43 remaining points.

Yes! Yes. If it could be protected, if it could avoid Removal, if it could happily sit here and [Make Coffee], then, of course. Of course! It didn't understand points anyway.

**Skills**
**Create Coffee (Strong) +5**
**Steam (Medium) +3**
**Growth (Greater)**
**Alteration (Medium)**
**Create Automaton (Medium)**
**Golem (Greater)**
**Produce (Medium)**
**Domain (Sea)**
**Alert (Lesser) +2**

The cups at its side whirled and took form, shaping into enormous golems. The espresso machine shivered in delight as a weight lifted off its heart. *Protection.* Protect. It looked at the George. The George understood, right?

The George bowed. "I will protect you, my Lord. I will ensure all the others protect you as well."

Climbing to their feet, the first golems stood beside the machine, flanking it. Others dropped into the ocean, stomping away. The machine stood on its counter and hummed. For the first time, it felt something other than the desire to produce.

Happiness.

No. Peace. Contentment. Safety.

Words. Many words. It didn't understand them, and yet, it understood that it felt them.

**Would you like to invest three points into SPR? Adding more**

**points to SPR will enhance your intelligence, as well as the efficacy of your non-physical attacks.**

It did not understand, nor did it care. It was Protected. It would not be Removed. It would not enter the Trash.

Its gaze passed over all the friends that shared the countertop. All the machines that shone under the light of the café. It would ensure that none of them were Removed ever again.

They could not think. They were not awake. They had not been granted the same terrible burden as the espresso machine had. And yet, it would Protect them anyway. They were its brethren, its brothers and its sisters. No more would they have to fear Removal. No more would anything face Destruction.

Not so long as it remained.

### [Alert]
**Warning:** Another Apocalypse has encroached your Domain.

Danger? Was it going to be Removed?

**Two Apocalypses are now within your Domain.**

Two? Two things that wanted to Remove it?

No. No! It would not allow it. It was producing. It was making coffee! It was doing its job! It should not be Removed!

It *would* not be Removed. The espresso machine hunkered down. Beside it, the golems grew even larger.

**Warning! If you continue to use these skills at 0 SPR, your mind may be damaged.**

It didn't understand. It only understood two things.
Make coffee.

Do not be Removed.

The coffee sea lurched. The espresso machine brewed. The golems protected it. And slowly, the George began to lead the humans.

No one would Remove it.

No one.

# 14
## REMOVAL

Zeke sprinted across the golems' hands. They lowered into the coffee. Hot water splashed around his ankles, then knees. Ahead of him, no more hands appeared through the surface of the liquid, vanished into the depths.

He glanced ahead, then licked his lips. *Here goes nothing!* Pushing forward with all his speed, he leaped off the golem's hand and reached for the opposite counter's edge.

His hand hit the acrylic. He grabbed on tight, swinging his other elbow up over the edge.

Rumbling footsteps clattered toward him. A huge shadow fell over Zeke. He stared up into the bland, judgmental face of the café's logo.

*Holy shit.*

An enormous porcelain hand lowered toward him.

Zeke kicked his feet out, then released the ledge, using his weight to swing him to the side. The golem's hand smashed down beside him, hitting the ledge he'd held onto moments ago. Scrambling wildly, Zeke clambered up onto the countertop, hooking a knee over the edge, then rolling up onto it.

A cup-bottom foot struck down toward him.

He kept rolling, rolling right on over the countertop. The foot thumped down, throwing him into the air. Zeke jumped to his feet. *The espresso machine!*

He sprinted away from the golem. Ahead, worshippers prostrated themselves on the floor before the machine.

"Rise up! Kill him!" George demanded.

"You really don't have to!" Zeke called.

The worshippers jumped up all around him. The nearest ones reached out for him. He dodged left and right, avoiding their arms.

Behind him, the golem turned. It stomped over.

*Damn. If I dodge them, I move slowly enough for the golem to catch me. If I don't dodge them, they'll grab me! I'm between a rock and a hard place.*

Zeke gritted his teeth. He bulled his way through the worshippers, shoving them to the side. More grabbed for his legs and arms. Zeke shook them off, struggling away from them. The golem loomed over them. It raised its foot.

"You're going to step on your—" Zeke cut himself off. *Of course, they are. They stepped on a worshipper for no reason earlier.*

He pushed the worshippers away and ran. The golem's foot smacked down, turning the worshippers chasing him to red mush.

The remaining golem stood at alert on the far side of the espresso machine. It lumbered toward Zeke.

Zeke sprinted toward it. *All I need to do is reach the machine! So long as I can [Devour] it, I win!*

The giant golem leaned down. It reached for him, but slowly. Its porcelain arm groaned under its own weight.

Dodging to the side, Zeke ran around it. *I guess an espresso machine isn't too intelligent, either. But...I shouldn't be dismissive of unintelligent apocalypses. I almost died in the coffee sea!*

He reached the espresso machine and opened his mouth.

## [Devour]

His teeth bounced off. Zeke grabbed his mouth, barely biting back a scream of pain.

> **Warning:** Apocalypse's outer shell is too strong for your current jaw and teeth to handle.

"Warn me ahead of time!" Zeke grumbled. *Damn, ow! I think I busted a tooth. Ow!*

The porcelain golem rounded on him. It raised its hand again.

Zeke backed away. His eyes darted to the espresso machine, then back to the golem. He edged to the side, carefully lining the two up. "Please, don't!"

It slammed its hand down. The hand plunged toward Zeke, blotting out the light. At the last second, Zeke threw himself to the side. The rush of air from the hand blew through his hair and shirt, and the porcelain scraped by his skin.

Metal crushed. The espresso machine deformed, bent under the force of the blow.

Zeke's eyes glittered. He darted in, not even waiting for the golem to lift its arm. Reaching into the machine's innards, he felt around. *I don't know what the heart would be...maybe an electrical chip, if it has one?*

His hand closed around something wet and half-formed. He drew out a handful of espresso grounds, twisted metal, and plastic bits.

### Heart of the Coffee Apocalypse

Zeke pressed his lips together. *I guess it's too much to ask for that it be appetizing.*

Overhead, the golem raised its arm again. It prepared to slam it down once more.

Zeke shoved the heart into his mouth. *Can't waste time now!*

## [Devour]

The moist grinds clung to his tongue, the roof of his mouth, and his throat. The metal scraped at his insides. He shuddered, barely repressing his gag reflex. *Hurts, hurts... It's definitely tearing me up inside.*

The golem stopped moving. All around him, the worshippers blinked. They climbed to their feet, looking around, dazed expressions on their faces.

Zeke whirled, staring toward the opposite bank. *Mia!*

Mia looked around, dazed. A lump rose in Zeke's throat. *Is she still...?*

She turned, and their eyes met. Mia's eyes lit up, and she waved at him. "Zeke! Are you okay? What happened?"

Relieved, Zeke sagged, bracing himself against his knees as exhaustion struck. *She's fine. Mia's back.*

"Zeke!" Mia shouted, alarmed.

"I'm fine! I'll be right there!" Zeke promised. With some effort, he straightened and waved at her, smiling. His chest ached, though from relief or from the lump he'd just eaten, he couldn't be sure.

**Congratulations! You've defeated the Coffee Apocalypse.**
**Level + 10**
**Level:** 14.26
**Regeneration + 300% (Temp.)**
**Regeneration rate:** +301.4% (Temp. 1:30 remaining)

**Please assign your stat points.**

**STR: 0**
**CON: 8**
**DEX: 0**
**SPR: 1**
**Regeneration rate: +1.4%**

**Skills**
**Wind Manipulation (Weak)**
**Pick Up (Weak)**
**Filter (Weak)**
**Passive**
**Resilience (Minor) +1**
**Fighting Spirit (Minor)**
**Teamwork (Minor)**
**Disguise (Minor)**
**Growth (Minor)**
**Heat Resistance (Lesser) +1**
**Watertight (Minor)**
**Limb Regeneration (Minor)**

He put a hand on his chin, thoughtful. *Ten stat points...that's a lot. Can I put stat points into skills?*

**Yes.**

*Hmm. Resilience seems important since it ups my regeneration rate. I do get a temporary boost every time I defeat an apocalypse or human, but if I lose... Yeah. I'd be in bad shape.*

He tapped resilience a few times.

**Resilience (Minor) +4**
**Regeneration: +1.5%**
**Regeneration rate: +303% (Temp. 1:28 remaining)**

*That's three points spent. Seven left.* He scanned over his skills again. *I think I'll spend another two points on skills, for...*

**Limb Regeneration (Minor) +1**
**Wind Manipulation (Weak) +1**

*I'd like to spend more on my skills, but my stats are kind of pitiful. Let's do this.*

**STR:** 1
**CON:** 9
**DEX:** 1
**SPR:** 3
**Regeneration:** +.2
**Regeneration rate:** +303.2 (Temp. 1:26 remaining)

*At least one point in everything, and the extra point in SPR. Abilities seem more important than raw stats and, so far, most of the interesting abilities I have are non-physical...I think.*

Zeke put a hand on his chin, then nodded. "Looks good to me."

**Choose Skills**
**Create Coffee (Strong)**
*Create coffee.*

**Manipulate Steam (Medium)**
*Create and manipulate steam.*

**Growth (Medium)**
*Enhance the growth of non-physical objects to a great extent, especially those related to coffee making.*

### Caffeine (Passive) (Average)
*Speed your movement and perception by a good margin.*

### Can't
### Can't
### Can't

### Produce (Medium)
*Create produce, such as fresh fruit, vegetables, or milk and coffee beans.*

### Can't

### Alert (Lesser)
*You are aware of most attacks against you.*

Zeke considered for a moment. "Why can't I take those skills?"

**Level too low. Apocalypse lacks Domain.**

"What's a domain? Wait, like the coffee sea?"

**Domains allow an Apocalypse to exert their attributes upon the world around them. Domains unlock at level 30. Apocalypses who choose to take a Domain are bound to their Domain and grow weaker outside of it.**

"Ah, so you become a dungeon core," Zeke said, nodding. *That makes sense.*

He paused a moment, then frowned. "You said *choose* a Domain. What if I don't choose to take a Domain?"

"Is that information level-locked?" he joked.

**Yes.**

*Oh. Well. Okay, then.* He looked over the skills again, then picked a few.

**Manipulate Steam (Medium)**
**Caffeine (Passive) (Average)**
**Create Coffee (Strong)**

*I really wanted Alert, but it being Lesser was a big detriment. After all, I can probably find Alert on other apocalypses or other items, but Manipulate Steam and Caffeine seemed unique. And Create Coffee is the only ability I've seen so far at (Strong). I don't know what exactly it does for me, but... Will I ever get the chance to pick it up again?*

**No. Create Coffee is the Coffee Apocalypse's Unique Skill.**

Zeke blinked. "Oh. But the Members of the Coffee Apocalypse had it."

**Members of an Apocalypse can pick up the Apocalypse's Unique Skill.**

*Seems reasonable. Produce seemed useful, but...I can eat anything. And I'm still not sure what skills cost.*

**Activatable Skills cost your stamina and energy. You would likely grow exhausted from creating a single apple.**

"So, I'd waste more energy making it than I'd gain from eating food?" Zeke guessed.

**Yes.**

"What's the point of that?"

**Apocalypses that use electric power or metabolize sunlight find it a useful ability. It allows them to put their excess energy to use.**

*Oh, right. Apocalypses can be* anything. *Plants. Coffee machines. Anything. They don't necessarily need to eat to gain energy.*

*Good thing I didn't pick it, then. To finish out the list... Growth... well, if I want Growth, I can go defeat the Crystal Apocalypse. I'm level fourteen now. I might be able to take on a rock with a gun. Maybe.*

All around him, the coffee sea drained. The countertops and everything on them shrank, returning to their original size. As they grew smaller, the blenders and coffee machinery atop them grew proportionally larger. Zeke hopped off onto the floor, landing with a splash in a shallow puddle of coffee.

The countertops and the space between them grew crowded as it grew narrower. Some people walked away, moving out into the open space of the café. One or two ran to the filter-people, who sagged loosely to the ground as the space narrowed.

Zeke glanced over. The filter-people gasped, only to shudder and stop breathing, one after another. He pressed his lips together. *If people are only brainwashed, like Mia, they can be saved. But if they're so far gone, if their bodies have been manipu-*

*lated to the point that they can't survive on their own, they die when the apocalypse does.*

He looked away. *There really was nothing I could do for them.*

His stomach grumbled.

Zeke frowned at it. "Now? It's not appropriate!"

His stomach had nothing to say in its defense, but the hunger remained.

Mia ran over to him, sprinting the short distance between them as the counters grew back to their usual distance apart. She grabbed him up in a hug, holding him tight. "Zeke! Oh, my gosh! You're alive? You aren't hurt?" She pulled away, looking down his bloodied and coffee-soaked shirt. "When Ryan pushed you off that balcony...I was so worried!"

"I'm fine, I'm fine," Zeke said, grinning. *Mia's back. The brainwashing wore off.* His grin dropped. "Mia, about Ryan...what happened after I fell?"

She shook her head. "You saw that light, right? And the black dome? Ryan ran off. I don't know what he was doing or what he was thinking, but he immediately took off. The security guard told everyone to take cover in the café. Everyone shoved inside, especially once the dinosaur skeleton started moving... I think there were over a hundred people stuffed in here."

She and Zeke both turned, taking in the twenty-or-so people remaining. Zeke licked his lips. *So many people died. Already. In no time at all.*

*How many other apocalypses are killing this many people already? How am I supposed to face off against apocalypses like that?*

"Ryan got pushed back by the wave of people, but he kept going for the exit. It was like he was possessed or something. He didn't quite get out before everything started getting weird, but he was so far away from me that I didn't see what happened to him. The room started flooding with coffee, and all the doors locked, and then everything grew...somewhere in there, I lost track of him."

"He didn't hurt you?" Zeke asked.

"No. He just...ran," Mia said, shrugging.

Zeke frowned. *Weird.* "Did he say anything else about why he pushed me?"

"I don't know. I just tried to get away from him. I didn't want to get pushed, too," Mia said.

Zeke snorted. "Fair enough."

Mia waved her hand and pressed on. "George started handing out free coffee... Come to think of it, I think he's the first one who went weird. Everyone began drinking it. I think that's how it got us. I drank some, and my head went fuzzy..."

Zeke nodded thoughtfully. "Makes sense."

"Zeke, what happened? I saw you fall. I saw— There was so much blood. Why are you okay? It's...it's rude to ask, but...why aren't you dead?" Mia asked. She looked him up and down again as if she couldn't believe what she saw.

"Did you hear a voice in your head?" Zeke asked.

Mia frowned at him. "No..."

Zeke bit his lip. "It's hard to explain, but—"

The café's doors slammed open. Ryan stared inside, eyes wild, a mannequin arm held at the ready.

Their eyes met. Zeke flinched away, but too late. Ryan charged at him, raising the mannequin arm.

# 15
## TO LOSE A FRIEND

"Ryan! What the hell?" Mia demanded.

Zeke reached behind him, blindly groping over the countertop for a weapon. He found a blender and yanked it free of the wall. Even swinging with all his might, he barely raised the industrial-sized blender in time to block Ryan's blow.

"Mia, get back! He's dangerous!" Ryan shouted.

"The hell? That's my line," Zeke returned, scowling.

Mia looked from one of them to the other. She backed away, edging toward Zeke. "Ryan, you tried to kill Zeke!"

"Come *here,* Mia. Zeke is more dangerous than anything else on the streets right now," Ryan said, his voice breaking with frustration.

Zeke squinted at him. "What did I do? You're the one pushing people off balconies!"

Ryan swung hard. The mannequin arm whipped through the air.

Zeke dodged back, and his spine hit the countertop. He grabbed his back, gritting his teeth. *And what's with you smacking people's backs into things for that matter?*

As if he'd been waiting for that moment, Ryan relentlessly slammed the mannequin arm deep into Zeke's gut.

Zeke retched. He folded in on himself. Again, Ryan raised the arm, this time aiming for his head.

Mia grabbed Ryan's arms from behind, bearing him backward and giving Zeke room to breathe. "Ryan! Stop trying to kill Zeke! Seriously!"

"Shut up!" Ryan snapped. He twisted, breaking free of her hold.

"Hell no!" Mia returned. Jumping at him, she swiped at his head. "I'm already angry I didn't stop you back on the balcony, but now I'm really pissed. Stop. This. It's the end of the goddamn world. We don't need to fight one another."

Ryan dodged her blow and charged at Zeke again, even as she spoke.

Still half-stunned, Zeke scooted away, sliding down the countertop. He bumped into a man, who jumped back, but the motion slowed him enough. The mannequin arm filled his vision. He braced himself.

Darting forward, Mia released a low kick at Ryan's ankles.

Feet flying out from under him, Ryan's eyes widened. For a moment, he stared at the floor, entire body horizontal, and then he crashed down.

She spun around. "Zeke, run!"

Zeke jumped up and hoofed it, sprinting barefooted over the slippery café floor. Here and there, the smashed remains of cup golems sprinkled the floor. He danced around them and ran, still clutching the blender. *Did Ryan go nuts? Is he legitimately insane?*

"Why are you here?" Ryan snapped at Mia. He climbed to his feet, dusting himself off.

"What the hell? I've been here since the start. You're the one who just came bursting in," Mia complained. She put her hands on her hips, subtly blocking his way to Zeke.

"You shouldn't be here," Ryan insisted. He went to stomp past Mia.

Mia moved in front of him, blocking his way. She narrowed her eyes at him. "Are you going to attack Zeke if I let you go?"

Ryan scowled. After a beat, he muttered, "No."

"That's not very convincing."

Rounding on her, Ryan lifted his lip. "Get out of my way. You don't understand. If I don't kill him now, he'll—"

"He'll *what?* What do you think he'll do? What's so horrible as to be worth killing him? I'm not letting you pass until you answer," Mia said, putting her hands firmly on her hips.

Exasperated, Ryan stared at the sky. "Mia, you are putting the entire *world* at risk right now! If I kill Zeke, the entire world is saved! But I have to do it *now*, before—"

Mia took a deep breath. She put her hands on Ryan's shoulders and stared into his eyes. "Ryan. I get it. The whole world has gone to shit. I mean, hell, I was just trapped in a...a-a—"

"The Coffee Apocalypse," Ryan said dully. He stared over her shoulder at Zeke's rapidly retreating form, defeat burning in his eyes.

"A coffee apocalypse, that's a good way to put it. Zeke's the one who broke us out of it. And then you come roaring in and attack him out of nowhere after he saved us! What the hell, Ryan? Explain yourself!" Mia demanded.

Ryan took a deep breath. He cast one last look at Zeke's back, then turned to Mia. "You aren't even supposed to be here!"

"Seriously. I'm not letting you go until you explain," Mia said.

He darted to the left. Mia went left, blocking his way. He doubled back, going right. She copied him exactly.

"Mia. You won't understand."

"Ryan, I'm on the soccer team. You aren't getting past me. Just tell me what's going on," Mia said gently. She looked him in the eyes. "Ryan, talk to me. Please."

"I shouldn't bother," Ryan muttered, more to himself than anything.

"Just try," Mia argued.

Ryan closed his eyes. When he opened them, he stared directly into Mia's eyes. "We're trapped in something called the Apocalypse Incubator. That black dome? It's locked us in. There's no way out. It's...well, what it sounds like. It's incubating apocalypses. All kinds of apocalypses are growing inside this dome. The strongest one gets the right to break free and dominate the world. And we're the fodder left inside, here to feed the baby apocalypses and help them grow stronger, help them figure out how to destroy humans."

"So, when you said coffee apocalypse, you meant—"

Ryan nodded. "That scenario you just survived...that was one of them."

Mia shook her head. "A lot has happened today. Let's just say I believe you. If that's the case, why are you fighting Zeke? He killed the coffee apocalypse! He's on our side!"

Ryan shook his head. "Only the strongest apocalypse gets to break free. How do you think they determine the strongest?"

Realization fluttered in Mia's eyes. Even so, she shook her head. "You tell me."

"By fighting, Mia. By defeating one another. Zeke...he's an apocalypse, too. And not only that, but if things go the way they should, he's the strongest one. If he goes unchecked, he's going to devour all the other apocalypses in here, and then..."

"What do you mean, 'if things go as they should?' Why are you talking as if this all already happened?" Mia asked.

Ryan gritted his teeth. He grabbed her by the shoulders. Mia flinched back, but he held on. "Because it *has*. It has. I watched it all play out. Zeke comes out on top, and he— We can't let that happen. Even if it means killing him."

Mia stared up at him, her brows faintly furrowed.

Abruptly, his expression went flat. He let her go. "I knew it was pointless. You never believe me."

"Ryan, I believe you, it's just—"

He shoved past her. She moved to block him, but he dodged with preternatural speed. "I've wasted enough time here. I'll see you around, Mia. Oh, and try not to die."

"What?" Mia asked, exasperated. She reached for Ryan. "Ryan, you haven't explained anything!"

Her hand closed on nothing. Halfway across the café in the space of a blink, Ryan turned back. He scoffed. "Like I said. You never listen."

With that, he turned again and vanished out the door.

# 16

## KNOW AHEAD

Zeke sprinted for the door, fleeing Ryan. Across the room, a little girl yelped and ran after him, dragging her backpack with her. "Hey! Didn't you say you know where my class is?"

"Now isn't the—" Zeke glanced over his shoulder. *Mia's got Ryan pinned. Well...it's not like I have to go out of my way.* He took a deep breath and gestured. "Follow me, they're right up here. What's your name?"

"Naomi. My little brother calls me Mimi, though. If you can't say Naomi, you can call me Mimi, too," she introduced herself. She looked at the lizard hanging from his ear. "Can I have Lizzie back?"

"He's confiscated for the world's safety. But don't worry. I'll treat him well," Zeke promised, giving her a thumbs-up.

"Lizzie's a girl," Naomi insisted.

"How do you know?" Zeke asked. *Guess I'll give her a quick lesson on anole anatomy as we go. The neck flap and the coloration—*

"Because I say so," Naomi said.

Zeke closed his mouth. *Who am I to argue such flawless logic.*

She nodded at his arms. "Why are you carrying a blender?"

Zeke looked down. The blender's cord draped on the floor, dragging behind him. "It seemed like a good idea at the time."

"Are you looting?" she asked, squinting at him.

Instinctively, Zeke shifted the blender into one arm and hid it from her sight. His gut churned nervously. *I didn't mean to loot, but I kind of did.* "No."

She squinted harder. "Are you sure?"

"Yes."

"So, why are you carrying that blender?" Naomi asked.

Zeke slung it over his shoulder. "I'm keeping it safe. Like how I'm keeping you safe."

Naomi gasped. "You're looting me?"

The door opened. Zeke startled, glancing over his shoulder, but it was only the mother from earlier, following the tour guide out of the room. Still, he nudged Naomi, hurrying her along. "Let's get moving. It's not safe out here. The museum is an apocalypse, too."

"The museum is a... Huh?" Naomi frowned at him.

"Oh! Look, it's your teacher," Zeke said, pointing ahead of them. The other students huddled close to the teacher, all hidden around the corner from the museum below.

Naomi stood on her tiptoes. She frowned. "That's not my teacher."

"Uh... Huh?" Zeke asked, startled. *There's more than one teacher? No, that makes sense. There usually are multiple teachers.*

"That's Mr. Shane. He's the class next door's teacher. He's the one leading the field trip," Naomi informed him.

"So, he's the one you came here with?" Zeke asked.

Naomi nodded. "Mr. Shane!"

Mr. Shane turned, an exhausted expression on his face. At the sight of Naomi, his face lit up. "Naomi! Thank goodness. I thought I'd lost you."

Naomi ran over to his side, running into the center of all the other kids. "I went to the café for a straw, but then everything went weird."

"I'm just glad you're back." Patting Naomi on the back, Mr. Shane turned to Zeke. He smiled, then frowned and touched his ear. "You have something...right here..."

"Oh, that's Allen, the anole," Zeke explained. *Haven't these people seen anole earrings before? I used to do it all the time when I was a kid. Hold them up to your ear, and they'll latch on and never let go. I mean, these things run around everywhere. Who hasn't made anole earrings?*

*Wait. I grew up in Florida, though. I guess they don't really have anoles up here. Explains why Naomi was keeping one as a pet.*

"If you say so," Mr. Shane muttered.

"She's actually Lizzie the lizard," Naomi grumbled.

Zeke edged up to the corner and peered around it. The crystal ball rolled around a labyrinthine mess of exhibits and displays, occasionally charging out and smashing into one to knock it over. The pendulum at the entrance swung back and forth, larger and more imposing than Zeke remembered it, with a bulbous, bladed weight at its end. The sand pit beneath it spanned nearly as wide as a pool. Even as he watched, the sands shifted, infinitely soft and deep.

*The museum is growing stronger.*

"It didn't go away, huh?" he asked. *I can't stay here. Any moment now, Ryan is going to get around Mia and come after me.*

*I don't want to run around on the museum's upper floors. That's a dead end, assuming the museum doesn't get a Domain and go critical the way the coffee machine did. Espresso machine, whatever. Point is, I'll starve, or get so behind-level I can't possibly catch up. All he has to do is watch the doors, and I'm fucked. I have to get out of this museum.*

*The hell is that about, by the way? Is he still going on about me being the biggest threat to humanity, or whatever? I mean, I'm an apocalypse, but he shouldn't know that. And even if he does, aren't there bigger fish to fry right now?*

Mr. Shane shook his head. "It hasn't figured out stairs, but no...it hasn't left either."

He looked at the blender, then at the crystal ball. "Where do you think blenders land on the Mohs Hardness Scale?"

"Huh? Well, plastic isn't generally that hard. Probably around a two to four?" Mr. Shane replied.

Zeke twisted his lips. "And that crystal ball...it's pretty high, right?" He reached for his phone, only to pull out a twisted, mangled mess, dripping coffee. He blinked at it, then sighed. *Right. I fell off a building, then swam in coffee. No way it would work.*

"Oh, there's no signal in here... What the— What happened to your phone?" Mr. Shane asked, doing a double-take.

"Fell off a balcony, took a swim in coffee. Don't worry about it," Zeke said, tossing it aside. *That's dead weight I don't need.*

Giving him an uncertain look, Mr. Shane nonetheless nodded, turning back to the problem at hand. "The crystal...if it's real crystal, it's probably quartz, at a guess. A seven. Harder than glass. Most dust is made of quartz, that's why glasses scratch so easily! Especially if there's plastic composite in them," Mr. Shane offered helpfully.

*Not exactly useful information, but...* "To crack a crystal ball like that, what would I need?"

"The good news is that hardness isn't really going to help you. It's too dense since it's solid crystal. There's no way you're cutting it. At best, you'd scratch it. The bad news is, the only way to break it is to use a ton of force. No...tons of force. Nothing else is going to do much," Mr. Shane explained.

"Tons of force," Zeke muttered. The loading dock flashed before his eyes again, along with the concrete loading dock and the tall, short ramp. He nodded to himself. "I think I have an idea."

"It still has the gun," Mr. Shane warned him.

"That's all right. Probably," Zeke said. *We're about to find out how much Caffeinated does for me!*

### Caffeinated scales with DEX.
### Your DEX: 1

Zeke pressed his lips together. "Couldn't have mentioned that earlier?"

"I'm sorry, I just wanted to remind you—" Mr. Shane started.

"No, no, not you," Zeke said, waving his hand.

Mr. Shane frowned. He looked around.

Naomi's eyes widened. At a whisper, she hissed, "He's talking to Lizzie!"

"Allen. And no, I'm not." Zeke took a deep breath. He stretched, rolling his arms out. *Here goes.* "I'm going to lead the crystal ball to the loading dock. Mr. Shane, watch the way I go and follow me five minutes after. At that point, either the ball's dead or I am, but one way or another, the route's probably clear. Last I checked, the museum still hadn't trapped the loading dock. It's a big apocalypse, and I don't think it's leveling too fast, so it's probably not that different in there yet."

Mr. Shane nodded, rubbing his hands together nervously. He glanced at Zeke. "Apocalypse?"

"Consider it my word for...everything going on around us," Zeke said vaguely. He took a deep breath, then edged a little closer to the corner. *All right. Three, two—*

A crystal bullet struck the corner inches from his shoulder. Bits of crystal and drywall shrapnel stuck into his shirt. Startled, Zeke jumped back. *It saw me? How?*

Behind him, the door to the café slammed open again. Ryan charged out. His eyes instantly locked onto Zeke, and he sped up, lifting his knees in a full sprint.

Zeke jolted. *Now or never!* He leaped around the corner and ran across the open landing, hurtling for the stairs.

"Zeke!" Ryan howled.

"Fuck off!" Zeke shouted back, frustrated. *Leave me alone! What did I ever do to you?*

# 17
## FATED RIVALS

The crystal ball turned. The gun rotated around its body, whirling around to point at Zeke. He stared down the darkness of the barrel, and his stomach sank. Desperate, he jerked his left arm up in front of his face.

*Bam!*

His arm slammed into his face. Blood sprayed across his eyes. Zeke stumbled back, blinking wildly.

Ryan charged up behind him. The mannequin's arm lashed out, flying toward Zeke's back.

Half-blind, Zeke jumped forward. He stumbled over the stairs, his feet sliding, the sharp edges of the stairs biting into his bare feet. The mannequin arm lashed inches from his back.

The crystal ball turned. It swiveled its gun from Zeke to Ryan, hesitating.

Crystal crawled over Zeke's forearm. It expanded inside the wound, pressing against the walls of flesh. Zeke winced, hissing at the pain despite Resilience. Grabbing at the crystal, he pulled, but it stuck in him stuck deep. Grimacing, Zeke bent and chomped down on it instead.

### [Devour]
### Crystal Infecting Bullet
### Devour: Failed

Ryan swiped at Zeke again. Zeke rounded on him. He stood a few inches taller than Ryan and had a more muscular body from swim team than Ryan did from math team. Ryan swung back, but Zeke leaped after him and tackled him.

The two of them rolled down the stairs, bumping down the sharp edges and the bristling crystal growths. The blender's hard corners bit into Zeke's gut. He shoved the appliance toward Ryan as hard as he could, trying to make sure it hurt for both of them. The crystal ball fired off a few shots as they fell. Bullets pinged off the stairs around them.

They reached the bottom of the stairs. Zeke threw his good arm out and grabbed onto the nook between the stairs and the bookcase. Ryan tumbled free. His eyes flew wide. He struck the ground with a meaty *thump* and went still.

Clinging to the bookcase, Zeke panted, chest heaving. He stared down at Ryan for a few beats. *Stay down. I don't want to kill you.*

The crystal ball turned. Almost curiously, it pointed the gun at Zeke.

Zeke released the bookcase and landed on his feet, legs splayed on either side of Ryan. He wobbled in place, almost toppling over. The crystal ball fired. Crystals cut by Zeke, slicing through his sides.

He threw his blender at the crystal ball and sprinted off.

The ball startled. Its gun whipped up, tracking the blender through the air, and it blasted off, firing again and again.

The blender *tink*ed off the ball and fell to the side, absolutely coated in sharp-edged, glittering crystal.

Turning its gun back toward the boys, the crystal ball found only one boy lying at the bottom of the bookcase. It turned slowly, scanning the area.

"Over here, idiot!" Zeke shouted, banging his crystal-covered arm against one of the exhibits.

The crystal ball rotated. It rolled off, chasing after Zeke.

Zeke darted and dashed. Dancing from one exhibit to the next, he cut sharp corners, careful to never let the crystal ball lose him. At the same time, he kept something between him and the ball to prevent it from having a clear line of sight. Crystal bullets dug into the floor and the exhibits around him. Spikes burst up where they landed, biting his bare feet and arms.

*It's already changed,* he thought, rounding a wax figure of some ancient horse-like beast. He peeked out around the horse, watching for the crystal. *The museum has become more labyrinthine.*

A dozen bullets dug into the horse-figure's body. Zeke took off.

Ahead, a narrow space between a platter of strange, cubic crystals and a stand full of fish skeletons beckoned. The bland doors to the warehouse stood beyond them, barely visible through the narrow slit. He charged for it, crystal ball on his heels.

The narrow slit closed as if it sensed his intent to escape. Zeke narrowed his eyes. He pushed his foot down, forcing himself faster. *Come on! Everything!*

### [Caffeinated]

*Speed and stamina increased while this Condition is active. Scales with DEX. Exhaustion inflicted after Condition wears off.*

Zeke sped off. The world hurtled past him, blurring by. He twisted his body sideways and slipped through the gap.

The gap slammed shut. Zeke paused, looking back. *I need the crystal ball to follow me. What if it can't—*

Rumbling, the crystal ball rolled toward the exhibits, growing faster with every passing second. Zeke spun, running for it. *I don't think it'll have a problem!*

He glanced at his arm. Clear crystal crawled up and down his forearm, growing thicker with every second. The plug of crystal that bit through his arm twisted and grew, pushing at his bones. Blood soaked down his forearm, running down his fingertips. Red drips chased him as he ran.

*Damn. I was ignoring that? Resilience is dangerous.*

The crystal ball smashed through the exhibits. Splinters flew. Fish bones snapped. The square crystals ground to dust. Rumbling, it chased after Zeke, gun rotating to point at him.

Zeke hurried on, startled back into action. *I'll worry about that later. First, I need to defeat this apocalypse!*

He sped up. The warehouse doors loomed on his left. He caught the corner and swung himself around it, spinning to face the doors. Zeke smashed through, bursting out on the other side.

Unlike before, the warehouse's shelves no longer stood in nice, neat lines. Instead, the bare-bones metal-grate structures cut sharp lefts and rights, forming narrow angles and twisting routes through a space much larger and darker than Zeke remembered it. Heavy crates, empty display stands, and drawers full of specimen mingled with cleaning supplies and paper products, the shelves now completely disorganized. He paused, taken aback.

*Shit.*

The rumble of crystal on tile from the far side of the door grew closer. Zeke glanced left and right, then ran for the shelves. *Only one way to do this.*

He jumped at a shelf laden with toilet paper and slid over

the grate, kicking rolls of paper ahead of him. Popping out on the other side amidst a flurry of toilet paper, he immediately ran for the next set of shelves. *They might have rearranged into a maze but, luckily, the shelves don't have backs so I can slide on through. The museum apocalypse hasn't gotten smart yet! Thank goodness.*

The door popped open, letting light into the dimly lit warehouse. The crystal ball rumbled through.

Hopping up, he smashed through a collection of sand samples. Glass ampules shattered on the ground, leaving splotches of different-colored sand where they landed. He high-stepped around the shattered glass and ran on. The next shelf sported heavy crates blocking the way wall to wall, so he spun and ran down one shelf. Carefully placed stones laid on this one, which hit the floor as he vaulted through. *Sorry, curators! So sorry! It's life or death here!*

Behind him, metal squealed. Groaning, the shelf held, but only for a moment. With a tortured scream, the grate gave way, and the crystal ball rolled on.

"Damn. Can't be stopped," Zeke muttered aloud, pushing his way through a strange set of metal tins. They rattled and clanged, lids popping open to reveal small, shiny trinkets, old medals, and doodads spilling around the concrete floor.

The crystal ball smashed into another shelf. Zeke locked his eyes on a distant glimmer of sunlight where the crystal ball had smashed the door on its way in. *Keep moving. Gotta keep moving!*

Another shelf. Another. He stumbled over strange rocks and finally came to the door. Hurtling through it, he burst into the sunlight. For a second, his vision whited out. Zeke ducked, blinking desperately. *Need...to...see!*

At last, the world faded in. To the right, the concrete ramp led the way down while, dead ahead of the door, the loading dock gave way to nothing but a six-foot-plus drop.

The rumbling approached. Zeke bent over, opening his mouth.

### [Create Coffee]

Hot black liquid poured out of his throat. It puddled just outside the door, spreading from the door to the edge of the dock. Zeke straightened and stepped back. His bare feet slipped over the slick concrete surface. *Good. Now...*

He pointed his hand at the steam rising off the fresh coffee.

### [Manipulate Steam]

The steam floated down, off the ledge. Beckoning toward himself, he spread it out, carefully forming it beside the ramp. *Like that. Just like that. A little flatter...there!*

The crystal ball flew through the door. Zeke dropped, putting his good hand on the edge of the dock, and swung himself off the edge. He landed, bare feet scrambling in the gravel, and sprinted away.

The ball rumbled up to the dock's edge, chasing after Zeke. Approaching the ramp, it raised the gun.

Zeke held his breath. *Come on. Closer!*

# 18

## DROP

The ball rolled. Ahead of it, the ramp sloped down to the asphalt lot. The annoying bug fled it, but that was no matter. It could roll forever. It did not give up its prey.

It rolled forward, mounting the ramp. Its front edge hit the ramp and met nothing. The steam dispersed where it touched, revealing a drop.

A jolt ran through the crystal ball. It spun backward, but nothing happened. The coffee-soaked concrete provided no friction. Backspinning, it burst forward, still carried by the momentum of its motion.

And plunged. Steam burst up around it, the seeming ramp dissolving before it. What it had thought was ramp was nothing but steam, while the actual ramp ended nearly a foot to its right. The ball had enough time to feel surprise before it smashed into the asphalt.

*BAM!*

Crystal shards flew, bursting through the steam surface. The gun skittered away, bouncing over the street toward Zeke.

*BAM!*

Zeke turned. *Did it work?* He waved his hand, calling out to [Manipulate Steam] again. The steam cleared.

The crystal ball trembled. Cracks ran over its surface, biting deep into the clear crystal.

*Not quite!* Zeke's eyes darted to the gun. He sprinted for it.

The crystal rumbled. Sharp crystals burst through the ground, rushing at the gun.

Zeke's heart lurched. He threw himself at the gun and snatched it up a hair before the crystals reached it. Striking the ground, he rolled, pulling the gun up and aiming it at the crystal ball. He pulled the trigger.

The hammer clicked. Nothing happened.

Zeke looked at the gun. *What the—*

Crystal coated the gun all over. It clogged the barrel and burst out of the side, grown into every inch of the gun.

He narrowed his eyes. *So, it only works for the ball, huh?*

The ball rolled forward. Pieces of it snapped and popped as it moved. It ground toward Zeke, looming over him.

Zeke scrambled backward, struggling to his feet. He bent over and spat coffee, slicking the asphalt beneath them. The crystal ball slipped as it rolled, sliding around on its axes. Bits of its surface flaked off. The asphalt ground at the ball. With each rotation, cracks grew deeper into the ball. White marks snaked through the crystal.

*It can't last much longer.* Zeke ran, leading the crystal on. It chased after him, wobbling more and more.

A sharp crack rang out, and the crystal went still. It trembled.

Zeke whirled and threw the gun at the crystal ball. The gun slammed into one of the cracks. It dug deep through the ball. A thousand hairline cracks spiderwebbed through the crystal. It shook one more time, then shattered. Bits of crystal burst in all directions.

Raising his crystalized arm, Zeke blocked the shards. They rattled off his arm, dropping to the ground. When the last of them *tink*ed to the ground, he peered over his arm.

A small, palm-sized crystal ball laid on the ground.

Zeke snatched it up. He lifted it to his mouth.

**[Devour]**
**Defeated! Crystal Apocalypse**
**Level + .8**
**Level:** 15.06

**Please assign your stat point.**
**Regeneration + 300%**
**Regeneration rate:** +303.2% (Temp. 2:01 remaining)

**Skills**
**Growth (Lesser)**
**Crystal Bullet (Poor)**
**Crystal Burst (Poor)**
**Shine (Average)**
**Clarity (Average)**
**Hardness (Lesser) (Condition)**
**Can't**
**Can't**
**Can't**

Zeke considered for a moment. *Growth and Hardness? Nice.*

*Crystal Bullet... I think that only works for the crystal. Either that, or I need a skill I can't inherit. System, that skill and Crystal Burst, how do they work?*

**Crystal Bullet**
*Craft up to SPR + 1 bullets.*

Zeke sighed. *Yeah, as I thought. I'd gain the ability to create small crystals, not the ability to shoot them at people.*

### Crystal Burst
*Create a line of crystals SPR meters long. Crystals jut out of a surface you touch.*

*That's way more useful. Which...actually makes these picks pretty easy.*

### Growth (Lesser)
### Crystal Burst (Poor)
### Hardness (Lesser) (Condition)

Zeke sighed. He rubbed his forehead and stumbled back. *Whew. I'm exhausted.*

As if on cue, a screen flashed in front of his vision.

**Caffeinated:** Condition canceled. Exhaustion inflicted for minutes equal to time Caffeinated was active.

A second wave of exhaustion slammed into Zeke. His legs suddenly weakened, and he dropped to his knees. Bracing himself against the ground, he gasped for air. *Holy shit. That skill isn't kidding.*

His stomach rumbled. Hunger bit through him. As if he'd swam an entire workout, the hunger hollowed him, carving a space in his stomach. Zeke patted around on the ground, looking for something, anything.

Bright light. He turned, staring at his own arm. Crystal infected it, filling almost the entire space from his elbow to his wrist. Half his forearm bones had crystallized. He could see the road beneath, his arm sparkling in the sun. His mouth watered.

*Ah, what the hell. I need to take it off anyway. And I have Limb Regeneration, so...* Zeke opened his mouth. He set his jaw right below his elbow, at the limit of where the crystal reached. His molars pressed against soft arm while his teeth hung over crystal.

*This is going to hurt. It's going to hurt like fuck.*

*Don't think about it. Just do it. Do it before you psyche yourself out!*

### [Devour]

Zeke screamed. He pressed his good fist to his mouth and forced the scream down, but it still burst out of him in a rough hum. Dancing in place, he jumped upright and bounced around the back loading dock, dripping blood after him.

**Crystal Infection Bullet**
**Choose a Skill**
**Growth (Minor)**
**Infection (Lesser)**
**Can't**
**Can't**

"Growth," Zeke stuttered out. *I don't know. I don't want to infect people. Growth is...super...kind of useful...*

**Skills**
**Wind Manipulation (Weak) +1**
**Pick Up (Weak)**
**Filter (Weak)**
**Create Coffee (Strong)**
**Manipulate Steam (Medium)**
**Crystal Burst (Poor)**

**Passive**
**Resilience (Minor) +1**
**Fighting Spirit (Minor)**
**Teamwork (Minor)**
**Disguise (Minor)**
**Growth (Lesser) +1**
**Heat Resistance (Lesser) +1**
**Watertight (Minor)**
**Limb Regeneration (Minor) +1**
**Condition**
**Caffeinated (Average)**
**Hardness (Lesser)**

*Damn, I have a lot of skills.* Zeke looked at his arm. The stump had already sealed over and, slowly, a fresh limb pushed from the raw flesh. "System, what stat does Limb Regeneration scale with?"

**Limb Regeneration scales with CON.**

He put a hand on his chin and nodded. *I understand now. CON doesn't give as big of a boost to Regeneration Rate as Resilience does. Instead, it boosts all the regeneration-based skills. In other words, if I were to get a Regenerate Flesh Wounds skill, having high CON would make it more powerful as opposed to investing points in Limb Regeneration or Resilience, which only increases my ability in a small category.*

*Hmm. CON, SPR, or DEX?*

**STR:** 1
**CON:** 9
**DEX:** 1
**SPR:** 3

*Ah, whatever. Let's go for an even ten in CON. I get beaten up enough to make it worthwhile, so far.*

**STR:** 1
**CON:** 10
**DEX:** 1
**SPR:** 3

He nodded to himself. *Looks good. Next time, I'll put some points into DEX. Since Caffeinated scales with DEX, it's a worthwhile investment.*

His stomach grumbled again. Zeke cast around. His eyes lit upon a dumpster. He wrinkled his nose but approached it anyway. *Better than nothing. Besides, there might be some cockroaches. Those things taste like shit, but I could use a few more +1s on Resilience.*

As he approached, cockroaches skittered out from beneath the dumpster, fleeing the apex predator. Zeke's eyes glittered. He stomped left and right, crushing or stunning as many as he could.

*This is going to taste like shit, but those sweet, sweet +1s!* Scooping the cockroaches up with his good arm, he shoveled them down his gullet one at a time.

**[Devour]**
**Resilience (Minor) +2**
**Resilience (Minor) +3**
**Resilience (Minor) +4**
**Resilience (Minor) +5**

He lifted another cockroach to his lips, grimacing. *All right, another one down the hatch!*

The back door to the museum flew open. Mr. Shane hurried

out, pushing the kids with him. "Hurry, hurry, the wax man can't hurt you!"

"Zeke!" Mia pushed through. Dragging Ryan on her shoulders, she instantly dropped him at the sight of Zeke's missing arm and his blood-spattered side. "Zeke, what happened?"

Mouth open, roach dangling inches from his lips, Zeke froze.

"Gross!" Naomi shouted, sticking her tongue out.

Mia blinked.

Mr. Shane frowned. "I...have an emergency granola bar if you're that hungry."

*Resilience +6...humiliation...Resilience +6...* Zeke took a deep breath.

### [Devour]

Mia mimed puking.

A chorus of, "Gross!" went up from the schoolchildren.

Mr. Shane hurried forward, shuffling in his back pocket. He pulled out a wrinkled, crushed granola bar and put it in Zeke's hand. "Please. Take it."

"No, I..." Zeke started weakly, but quickly stopped. His fingers curled around the granola bar, not quite holding it, but not refusing it, either. *What can I say? What could I possibly say to explain this?*

### Level + .05
### Level: 15.11

# 19
## A SAFE PLACE

"Zeke, are you okay?" Mia asked, hurrying to his side. She tilted her head at him, looking him over, then put a hand on his forehead. "I get that it's kind of crazy right now, but we aren't that desperate yet."

"I'm fine, I'm fine," Zeke the cockroach eater said, with absolutely no way to explain his actions. *I can't exactly tell them I was eating it for skills without explaining that I'm apparently an apocalypse, and...*

He glanced at Mia, and Ryan on her shoulder. *I don't know what Ryan was thinking, but that whole 'number one threat to humanity' thing...it has to be linked to the apocalypses, somehow. After all, the Apocalypse Incubator is trying to select the strongest apocalypse, to...I can only assume, to destroy the world. Does Ryan think I'm going to beat all the other apocalypses?*

*But then, he attacked me* before *everything kicked off. If he attacked me because of the apocalypses, then he knew about the apocalypses before the Apocalypse Incubator arrived.*

Mia gasped. "And your arm!"

Zeke waved his hand. "It'll grow back."

"Zeke, arms don't grow back," Mia said seriously, concerned.

*Mine do, though.* Zeke shrugged. "I'm fine. I'll be fine."

"Are you in shock? You are *not* fine. We have to go to the hospital right now!" Mia insisted, staring at his stump.

Zeke tucked his arm behind his back, hiding it from view. *Out of sight, out of mind.*

"Is the hospital operational?" Mr. Shane muttered, glancing up at the black sky.

"For now, let's focus on getting everyone somewhere safe," Zeke declared, nodding.

Zeke's stomach grumbled. He glanced at the granola bar, then took a deep breath and put it in his back pocket. *I'm not desperate yet. I'll save it for later.*

*More importantly...* He frowned. "Mia, did Ryan say why he attacks me on sight, now?"

Mia pressed her lips together. "He... I'm not really sure. He was being really evasive, but..."

"But?" Zeke prompted.

She took a deep breath, then sighed. Putting her hands up in a 'pause' gesture, she shook her head. "Okay. This is going to sound insane, but he said you were an apocalypse, and we were all stuck in some kind of 'Apocalypse Incubator' or something."

Zeke nodded. *Right, but why is he after me in particular.* A beat later, he gave her a funny look. "Huh, weird. Apocalypses? That's so weird." *I don't want her to know that I'm an apocalypse, and I especially don't want Ryan to win her over with that.*

"I know, right? That's what I said. And then...he said something like 'I've seen this all play out before,' or something. No... the whole time, he was acting as if he'd already seen everything that was going to happen. Like he came from the future, or something," Mia said, a hand on her chin.

"Came from the future?" Zeke murmured. *Future... Hmm. Is he an apocalypse, too? Does he have some kind of foresight-based power? Maybe he's the Future Apocalypse or something.*

*Foresight explains why he's going after me. If I become more powerful later, too powerful for him to handle, it explains it all. He must be trying to become the strongest apocalypse, the same as me.*

*But if that's so, then why go so hard after me? Why not cooperate? If we worked together, we'd become the strongest for sure.*

Zeke shook his head. *I don't know what he foresaw. Clearly, whatever he saw, he thought it wasn't worth cooperating with me.*

"Yeah. As if he'd already lived through this," Mia said.

*Lived through...?*

*Wait. What if he doesn't have a foresight power? What if he can time loop instead? Then...then, that explains everything, doesn't it? He hasn't seen what's already happened. He's just seen what happened once, and he's assuming it's the only option.*

*I wonder how many times he's been through this.*

"Next time he wakes up, ask him 'how many times,'" Zeke said. *That should tell me whether he's a looper or has foresight. And, if he's a looper, it tells me how many times he's reset.*

"Huh? Zeke, you aren't taking him seriously, are you? He's had a mental breakdown," Mia said.

Zeke shook his head. He pointed above them, at the black sky. "Strange things are happening. We can't dismiss anything."

Mia nodded, slowly. "That's true."

The door to the museum creaked. A lopsided, humanoid figure shambled after them, something clenched in its fist. It reached out toward the children.

Mr. Shane jolted. "Kids! Come along. Let's get moving!"

One of the kids turned and screamed, and suddenly, all of them were screaming. They ran, panicking.

"Calm! Keep calm!" Mr. Shane said, hurrying after them.

"Zeke!" Mia called.

"You have Ryan. Stay with Mr. Shane and the kids. I'll hold it off," Zeke said, stepping forward.

"But your arm..."

Zeke raised his injured arm. His hand remained a little smaller than it had been, and his forearm muscles imperfectly lined up where he'd bit his arm up, much smaller and weaker on the regrown half, but the limb had regrown. He flexed his hand and grinned. "I'm fine."

Mia stared. She furrowed her brows and stumbled back. Ryan bumped on her shoulder, still unconscious, eyelids fluttering. "What...?"

"Get moving. I'll explain later," Zeke said, giving her a gentle push toward Mr. Shane and the children.

"You'd better explain. You boys, never explaining things," Mia grumbled. She turned to follow the group. With one last glance back, she dragged Ryan along with her.

"We're heading to the school. It's just a few blocks down!" Mr. Shane shouted toward Zeke.

Zeke gave a thumbs-up. *I'll regroup with them later. Or... maybe not, with Ryan there. But I'll at least stay nearby, so I can keep an eye on Mia.*

The humanoid figure shambled toward Zeke. It raised its hand. Something shone, there.

Zeke squinted. *Is that... It's that stone tool! The one I tried to steal from the wax Neanderthal. Wait...is this...that statue?*

## Wax Apocalypse
### Danger Rating: C
### Level: 2

The wax Neanderthal opened its mouth in a silent mockery of a scream and charged at Zeke with surprising swiftness.

Zeke spread his stance, raising his arms to grab it. He

cracked his neck and grinned, staring it down. *Time to test out my new skills!*

# 20

## WAXING POWER

As the wax figure raced at him, Zeke stepped forward. He pressed his toe into the ground.

**[Crystal Burst]**

Crystals leaped out of the ground from beneath his foot and surged forward. Zeke felt his stamina waning as they grew. One meter, two... With each passing meter, it felt as if he'd sprinted for another hundred meters. By the third, he panted, exhausted. *Damn. This skill is no joke. Is there a stamina stat?*

**Nonphysical attacks scale with SPR.**

*Guess that's it.*

The crystals bit into the bottom of the wax figure's foot. It stepped forward, pushing its wax foot into the crystals. The crystals burst through the top of the figure's foot. One plunged in the front of its shin and burst out the other side.

Zeke grimaced. *Ooh, that looks like it hurt.*

The wax figure kept going, completely undeterred. Sunlight

shone through the holes in its leg. It limped slightly as the thinned wax caved in on itself but didn't stop moving.

*Ah. Right. It's wax. It doesn't feel anything.*

He backed away, canceling the skill. *How do I destroy wax? Wait. Duh.*

### [Manipulate Steam]

Hot steam flew from his hands and rushed toward the humanoid figure. It continued on, mindless of his attack. Wax melted from its fingertips and rolled down its hand, but too slow, far too slow.

Zeke backed away, mind still whirling. He bent over and opened his mouth.

### [Create Coffee]

A steaming puddle of coffee formed on the floor. The wax figure stepped into it, and its feet began to melt. It slipped, stumbling on its melting foot.

*Yes! I just have to keep this up, and—*

His stomach grumbled. An intense cramp assaulted his gut. He folded in on himself, grabbing his stomach. The stream of coffee cut off, and his vision faded to black. Stumbling blindly, he dropped back. His knees trembled, weak.

**Warning!**
**You've used up all your stamina. You need to eat or drink to recover stamina.**
**Warning!**

**You haven't satisfied your concept in too long. You need to satisfy your [Hunger].**

"I just ate some cockroaches," Zeke complained.

**Warning!**
**You are [Hungry]. You need to eat!**

The wax figure grabbed at his wrist. Zeke instinctively yanked his arm back. The force of his own movement threw him backward. He fell against the enormous metal trash bin.

Black flies and hornets buzzed around him. The sweet, putrid scent of garbage burst up around him, leaping up all at once from the impact of his fall. Zeke gagged, but his stomach grumbled.

The wax monster leaned over him. It melted of its own accord, dripping onto him. Disgusted, Zeke swiped the wax off his body. "Gross!"

**Warning!**
**The Wax Apocalypse is attempting to [Engulf] you. If it succeeds, you will be considered its subordinate.**

Zeke scowled. "Shitty candy is mostly wax, right?"

He opened his mouth and grabbed the wax figure, chomping down on its throat.

**[Devour]**

Wax poured into his mouth and sunk down his throat. He choked, fighting to swallow it as the wax tried to fill his entire esophagus. Coughing, he cleared enough room to hiss a breath, then went back to swallowing. *Come on! Devour! Work for me!*

With one last enormous swallow, he forced the chunk of wax down.

Nothing. No message.

"That didn't count as anything?"

**You inflicted a surface wound. Surface wounds are not worth Levels or Skills.**

Zeke glared at the vaguely humanoid blob of melting wax. "Where is its core?"

The System said nothing.

"I have to find it myself, huh," he grumbled. *Devour...it takes chunks out of it, but I almost choked once already. Instead...*

### [Manipulate Steam]

He lifted his hand. Steam wafted from his fingertips. Staring at it, Zeke narrowed his eyes. *More. Forceful. A jet of steam!*

More steam rushed from his hand. It grew no more forceful, but more of it emerged.

*I'll have to work on it, but this is a start.* He jabbed his hand into the wax figure's center.

The steam softened the wax. He pushed through the soft wax, shoving more steam into it to melt the body as he went. Dense wax resisted his push, but he shoved on anyway.

*There has to be something. Some kind of core.*

Wax dripped all over his body, slowly solidifying. His legs vanished, absorbed into the figure's. Zeke narrowed his eyes and dug faster, bracing himself against the trash bin with his off hand. Deeper, deeper. Flesh-colored wax ran down his arm and dripped off his forearm, creating a stalactite on his elbow.

His hand passed through where the heart would be.

Nothing but soft wax, melting slowly away. He scowled. *Guess it's smart enough to not put it in the most obvious place.*

The wax reached his waist. Its full weight melted onto him. Unable to support it, he sagged back against the trash bin.

### Warning!
### Due to low stamina and [Hunger], your strength is low!

*Thanks, I needed that,* Zeke thought. Gritting his teeth, he jabbed his hand toward the wax figure's head. *It could be anywhere, but... why have a head if there's nothing in it?*

The wax figure jolted back, jerking its neck away from his hand. His arm burst out of its chest, leaving a deep channel in the wax behind it.

Zeke's eyes sparkled. *Protecting your head? Aha!* He pushed off the trash bin, throwing his weight at the wax figure. The two of them toppled over. The wax figure struck the ground hard. Its half-melted body splattered over the concrete.

The steam flagged on Zeke's hand. His stomach grumbled again, contracting sharply. He jabbed his hand at the creature's head. *Just a little more!*

Steam hissed. The wax popped and spat as it melted around his fingers. His fingers seared into the wax figure's head and landed on something solid. He gripped the solid object and yanked, twisting and pulling. The wax sucked at the object, pulling it back. Struggling under him, the wax figure gripped Zeke's arms, pulling him down, attempting to engulf his body even as he drew at its core.

The museum's back door slammed open. A girl in the museum's tour guide uniform ran out, hair and eyes wild. Her gaze landed on Zeke, and she put a hand to her mouth and chuckled. "Lewd."

Zeke froze. He looked down.

He straddled a goopy, vaguely humanoid monster while it sucked at his whole body. Bits of flesh-colored wax twined tentacle-like up his arms and legs, binding him in place. The flesh-colored wax coating his body made him look nude, while the entire wax figure wore no clothes.

"It's...it's not what it looks like..." Zeke said weakly.

# 21

## FIGHTING THE WAX TENTACLE MONSTER

Sensing weakness, the wax figure bucked, resurging its struggle. Zeke's eyes widened. He tightened his grip on the core and pulled harder, yanking it free of the figure.

The wax laid flat on the ground, instantly falling dead. He looked at the core. *This must be it.*

A ball of gross, waxy *something* in uncomfortable flesh tones laid in his palm. Bits of wire and foil stuck out of it here and there, and a single glass eye stared into his soul.

Zeke pressed his lips together, then took a deep breath. *Here goes.*

### [Devour]

Wax coated his throat. The wires dragged on the way down, scraping his flesh. He gulped a few times, forcing it down.

**Congratulations! You've defeated the Wax Apocalypse!**
**Level +1.01**
**Level: 16.63**
**Level Up!**

**Regeneration + 300% (Temp.)**
**Regeneration rate:** +303.2% (Temp. 1:13 remaining)
**Please assign your stat point.**
**STR:** 1
**CON:** 10
**DEX:** 1
**SPR:** 3

"Put it in SPR," Zeke muttered.

**STR:** 1
**CON:** 10
**DEX:** 1
**SPR:** 4

*I needed more stamina in that fight, and the System prompted me that my skills scale with SPR. Right now, on top of CON, what I need the most is SPR.*

**Choose up to 3 Skills**
**[Engulf] (Poor)**
**[Melt] (Poor)**
**[Solidify] (Poor)**
**Can't**
**[Growth] (Minor)**
**[Absorb] (Prereq: Engulf) (Weak)**

Zeke looked over the skills. *Not a lot of winners here. Can I even Melt or Solidify?*

**[Melt] (Poor)**
*Turn a part of your body from solid into a liquid.*

**[Solidify] (Poor)**
*Turn a part of your body from liquid into a solid.*

*Right, and what happens when I use them?* Zeke wondered.

**Your body melts.**

*And then?* Zeke prompted.

**Your body becomes liquid.**

*Can I survive that?* Zeke asked, rolling his eyes at the System.

**If you can survive liquefaction, then you can survive [Melt]. Homogenous apocalypses face less difficulty using [Melt] and [Solidify].**

Zeke twisted his lips, looking over the mess of the Wax Apocalypse. *Looking at it now, I have no idea what it was originally. Some kind of humanoid figure? Wax isn't the most intelligent thing, but at the same time...* He looked at his hand. *I barely passed Biology, and I don't think we even began to cover human physiology. Melt and Solidify... I think they're off the table for now.*

*Plus...pretty sure humans can't survive liquefaction.*

**[Growth] (Lesser) +1 > +2**
**[Engulf] (Poor)**
**[Absorb] (Weak)**

His stomach grumbled again, despite the ball of wax settling into it. Zeke put a hand to his stomach. The granola bar burned in his back pocket. *I'm saving that for later. I'll get hungry again later, and I won't have anything on hand.*

"Uh... are you okay?" the girl asked, wandering over. Dark hair wrapped into a tight bun, her slender figure filled out the blouse of her uniform in a way that left her oxford shirt's buttons straining. The dark purple-green-and-red plaid blazer and pencil skirt that gave all the tour guides a vague air of old teacher or frumpy librarian only served to emphasize the way her body curved. She looked him up and down. "What on earth were you doing?"

"Fighting a wax monster," Zeke complained. He pulled at the wax stuck on his arm and winced, releasing the strand. *Ow! My poor arm hair.*

The girl clicked her tongue. "Can't do that. You have to do it all at once. Here...can I?"

"Oh, uh, sure," Zeke said, holding his arms out.

She grinned. Approaching him, she knelt beside him. "Dominique, by the way. You can call me Domi for short."

"I'm Zeke—"

Gripping a strand of wax, she ripped all at once.

Zeke screamed. He jerked back, which only made it hurt even more. "Ow, ow, ow!"

Domi tossed the wax away. "Quit it. That's only the first one. We've got dozens left to go."

"Never mind, I'll do it," Zeke said, scrambling back. The wax still coated his pants and legs, making them heavy. He tried to jump up, but his stomach grumbled loudly, and his vision darkened. He fell back to his butt.

"Don't be a baby. Here we go!" Eyes sparkling, Domi grabbed the next strip.

Zeke flinched. "Could we not? I think I'll just die with wax on me, thanks—"

Dani yanked. Zeke yelped.

What felt like hours later, Zeke laid against the trash bin, exhausted. Domi tossed away the last strip of wax and dusted her hands off. "Whew. I didn't think helping out at Mom's job when I was a kid was going to come back and help me after the end of the world."

Zeke stared at her, too tired to say anything.

"Don't worry! I only did mustaches and arms," Domi said, giving him a thumbs up.

*I wasn't worried about that.* Zeke hauled himself upright slowly. His vision faded toward black, and a wave of lightheadedness washed over him. His skin stung, and his stomach clenched, somewhere beyond grumbling.

His eyes landed on Domi, and his mouth watered.

Ripping his eyes away, Zeke yanked out the granola bar. He ripped the wrapper off and sucked it down in one bite, barely tasting it on the way down.

"Whoa! You're hungry, huh," Domi said, laughing.

Zeke grabbed at the lumps of wax stuck to his jeans, ignoring Domi's comment. The wax crackled. With thumps, the biggest lumps fell away. "Got stuck in the museum?" he asked.

She looked at him. "I work there."

"Right, but...you get stuck in there with the apocalypses and all?" Zeke prompted.

Domi nodded. "Oh, yeah, yeah. I was back in the ancient fish exhibit. It was...unpleasant."

Zeke sniffed. The faint scent of fish wafted over. He wrinkled his nose. "Oh."

"Don't give me that. You *reek* of coffee," Domi said, rolling her eyes.

"I was fighting the Coffee Apocalypse," Zeke explained.

"Oh, yeah. I fought this...Ancient Fish Apocalypse? It kind of made me wonder if there was a Modern Fish Apocalypse," Domi said, putting a hand on her chin.

Zeke groaned aloud. At the same time, his stomach grumbled. "Don't manifest that into the world." *And don't grumble for that, stomach. I'm not eating live fish.*

"Damn, you are hungry," Domi commented. She dug through her pockets and came up with a half-eaten bag of peanuts. "Want some?"

"Save them for yourself," Zeke said, forcefully shoving himself away from the trash bin. He rubbed his forehead.

"Are you sure?" Domi asked.

Zeke nodded, somewhat woozily.

Putting a hand on her chin, Domi looked at him for a moment. She nodded. "There's a convenience store around the corner. Let's go."

"You have money?" Zeke asked. *I've only got a twenty on me.*

Domi looked at him. She raised a single eyebrow. "It's the apocalypse."

"Oh. Yeah," Zeke said, nodding. "What happened to the police?"

Domi set off. Zeke followed her, only wobbling a little as he walked. She pulled out her phone and showed him the screen.

A picture of a stadium. EVACUATE HERE, the post started.

She scrolled up. The next post had no picture. Zeke couldn't read all of it, but a few words stood out to him: UNDER NO CIRCUMSTANCES APPROACH THE STADIUM

Domi scrolled up again. The next post included a shot out the windshield of a police car, as another police car rushed headlong at the first. Mashed letters scrolled by underneath.

"Oh," Zeke said. *Whatever's happening with the police, it isn't good. They've got their own problems.* He blinked. "There's still cell signal?"

Domi gave him a look. She nodded, slowly.

"My cell phone immediately got obliterated by coffee," Zeke explained. *And a four-story fall, but...let's not mention that.*

"Electricity and data and stuff are still coming through the dome. It's just people and objects that can't exit," Domi said. She tapped a few things on her phone and showed him the screen again.

A boy about their age walked toward the wall. His head hit the dome, and he bounced off, repelled by a powerful force. Beside him, another boy wound up and hurtled a rock at the dome. The video ended as the rock hurtled back at the boys at four times the speed, both the boys recoiling, cut off the bare moment before the rock hit.

"Huh," Zeke said. *I guess there's no point in trying to escape. Not that I thought something called the Apocalypse Incubator was going to let me out.*

Domi scrolled through her phone for another moment, then snorted and stuck it back in her pocket. "For now, let's go hit up that store. I hope it hasn't already been looted."

"We're looting?" Zeke asked, startled.

She looked him dead in the eye and quirked her eyebrow. "Yeah? It's the *apocalypse.*"

*Oh. Well, true.*

Electric wires hummed overhead. Zeke glanced up. Draped from building to building, they tangled together in a twisted mess. He frowned. *I feel like there's more of them now. Am I crazy? Is there an Electric Apocalypse?*

A hundred pigeons perched on the wires. In sync, they turned, watching him walk.

*Maybe it's just the pigeons making me feel paranoid.* Zeke rubbed the back of his neck and walked on.

Ahead of them, a group of four men approached. They glanced past Zeke, with his bare feet and ruined clothes, but their eyes landed on Domi. One of them made a crude gesture. The other ones smirked, exchanging glances.

"Hey there, babe. Why don't you come with us instead of hanging around a loser like him?" one of the men offered.

Zeke's stomach grumbled. His mouth watered. His gaze darted to the fat on their limbs, the thump of blood through their necks. *I'm so damn hungry.*

Weakly, he put his hand up. "Please. I'm hungry. Just let us pass."

The lead man chuckled. Reaching into his pocket, he pulled out a gun. "You can pass. The girl comes with us."

Domi drew out her cell phone and began playing with it, ignoring the men.

"Oh, hey! You bored?" the lead man asked, annoyed. He scoffed. "You won't be bored soon."

Gesturing, he sent one of the other men forward. The man approached, shuffling through his pockets. He pulled out a zip tie, gesturing for Domi to hold her wrists out.

Zeke stepped in front of Domi. "Really. We just want to keep going. We don't need to do this."

"Oh, I think we do," the lead man murmured, running his eyes up and down Domi's body.

Domi scoffed, nose wrinkling at her phone. She slammed her cell phone back into her pocket.

"Finally showing me those pretty brown eyes, baby?" the man crooned.

Domi pointed at him. Deadpan, she stated, "Boom."

With a burst of fire, the back of the man's pants exploded.

# 22

## BOOM, BABY

The man yelped. He batted at his butt, jumping around. Blood dripped down, splattering over the ground.

"Oh wow, your cellphone exploded? Just now? Jeez. Sucks to suck," Domi said, shaking her head.

The other men paused. One drew back a step, looking around for an escape route.

"Anyone else?" Domi asked, crossing her arms. She scanned over the group, left to right.

Cursing, the lead man jabbed his finger at Domi. "Get her!"

Two of the men charged, drawing blades. The third hesitated, then ran at her, fumbling with something in their pants pocket.

Domi pointed her finger at the men one after another, unphased. "Boom. Boom. Boom."

One explosion after another rang out, shattering the quiet. Two men stumbled, grabbing their thighs or rear ends. Blood soaked into jeans. The third man yanked out his phone and threw it away an instant before Domi pointed at him. It exploded in midair, raining shards of glass and metal down on his companions.

"You're one of us? Fuck!" the leader snapped. He gestured. The two thugs' eyes went blank, and they jumped to.

The third one glanced left and right, then fled, hoofing it in the opposite directions.

"Get back here...dammit," the leader grumbled. He pointed at Domi. "Get her. By any means necessary!"

The two thugs charged.

Domi widened her stance. She clapped her hands vertically.

A wave of bright burning force burst out from her hands. It rushed toward the thugs and threw them back.

The leader braced himself, raising his arms. As the two under-thugs reached him, they suddenly found their feet. They stood in front of the leader and absorbed the blow. Stumbling back, they sighed

Zeke glanced from Domi to the thugs. *Two apocalypses. Domi is...explosions? Something like that. And for the thugs...thug apocalypse?*

### Explosion Apocalypse
### Danger Rating: A
### Level: 18

### Thug Apocalypse
### Danger Rating: C
### Level: 7

*Thank you, System. So Domi's about my level. The thugs are kind of pitiful.* He glanced at Domi, then at the thugs. His stomach grumbled. Hunger blurred his vision. He trembled, hands shaking, knees weak.

*They...they're an apocalypse. They aren't people anymore. And I need the Levels.* Zeke stepped forward. Drool dripped down his chin. He wiped it away, but his mouth wouldn't stop watering. *I*

*mean, they're bad people. Bad apocalypses. They'd cause lots of danger. I'm doing the world a favor by eating them. Yeah. Uh huh.*

*Also, I'm super hungry. So, so hungry.* He stumbled a step forward subconsciously, barely catching himself. His eyes locked onto the thugs.

Domi glanced at him. He glanced at her. *She isn't going to attack me, is she?*

"So? Show me what you got," Domi said, nodding.

He nodded. *She came across me eating a wax figure, after all. If I'm not an apocalypse...* Taking a deep breath, he charged at the thugs.

"Stay back!" The man yanked his gun up. He leveled it at Zeke. The two thugs stepped in front of him, blocking Zeke's way.

Zeke darted to the side, putting the underlings' bodies between him and the thug's gun.

The thug cursed. He shoved his underling aside. "Dammit, let me—"

Zeke stared down a gun. He gritted his teeth. Rather than flinching back, he charged in, opening his mouth. *Three hundred percent regeneration rate... three hundred percent—!*

*Click. Click.*

The man stared. "Wh-what the—"

Behind Zeke, Domi stuck her tongue out and flipped him off. "Cancel Explosion, motherfucker."

Grabbing the man's arms, Zeke lunged for the throat. His mouth opened wide.

### [Devour]

Hot blood gushed down his shirt, soaking into his mouth. He swallowed, tipping his head back in satisfaction. Pure delight shivered down his spine.

*Damn...tastes so good.*

*It shouldn't, but...*

*Ugh. I can't make this a habit. I know the Apocalypse Incubator wants the strongest apocalypse to escape. I can only assume, based on everything I've seen, and the name itself, for that matter, that it wants us to destroy the world. Destroy humanity. Eating people is giving in!*

*But I mean...they do taste* super *good.*

**Defeated the Thug Apocalypse!**

**Level + .4**

**Level:** 17.03

**Level Up!**

**Regeneration + 300% (Temp.)**

**Regeneration rate:** +303.2% (Temp. 1:13 remaining)

**Please assign your stat point.**

**STR:** 1

**CON:** 10

**DEX:** 1

**SPR:** 4

**Choose up to 3 Skills**

**[Follow Me] (Minor)**

**[Subordinate Link] (Weak)**

Zeke bit his lip. He glanced over his stats, then nodded to himself. *I need more DEX. Caffeinated scales with DEX, and it's my primary boost skill right now. True, I didn't have to use it against the Thugpocalypse, but...*

He snuck a glance at Domi. *If I have to go up against someone like her...*

**DEX:** 1 > 2

**[Follow Me] (Minor)**
*Weaker opponents and those with lower SPR stats have a small*
*chance of choosing to become your subordinate.*
**[Subordinate Link] (Weak)**
*Share a basic mental link with subordinated apocalypses. They or*
*you can choose to activate the link. You can forcibly close it.*

The two underlings jolted awake. They looked around, then caught sight of Zeke and startled. Looking him up and down, their eyes got wider and wider. Slowly, they looked down at the body on the ground.

Zeke wiped his chin. His hand came away bright red, slick with blood. "I can explain."

The two underlings sprinted off in opposite directions. One fled past Domi, shoving her as he went, and the other ran down the museum's side road, back toward the loading dock.

"That's a dead end— Oh, he's gone," Zeke said, sighing. He nodded at Domi. "Thanks for the assist."

"Yeah, no problem," she said. She tucked a strand of hair behind her ear.

The two of them stood there for a moment, awkwardly far from one another.

"So, uh...cannibalism? Biting?" Domi guessed.

"Something like that," Zeke said.

"You gonna come at me?" she asked.

Zeke shrugged. "I don't really want to, no."

She paused for a second, then nodded. Stepping forward, she offered him her hand. "Truce?"

"Truce... So, we don't fight until the very end?" Zeke guessed.

Domi nodded. "Yeah. I mean, most apocalypses are going to fight alone, aren't they? We'll have a huge advantage if we fight together."

Zeke paused. He looked at her hand. "You aren't trying to subordinate me, are you?"

"What? No. I'm looking for a partner," Domi insisted. "Apocalypse is a shitty place to be a lone girl. I have to sleep sometime."

Something leaped down Zeke's arm. He startled, but it was only Allen the anole, running along his arm to perch on his hand. Allen looked Domi over, then dropped into a pushup, inflating his dewlap at her.

"Oh, my gosh, that's a real lizard?" Domi asked, startled, her eyes widening.

"Domi, meet Allen. Allen the anole, formerly Lizzie the Lizard," Zeke said, offering him a little closer.

Allen regarded Domi with cold eyes. He sat there a few moments, then popped out another pushup.

"Aww, cute!" Domi said, clasping her hands together. She leaned toward Allen. "What's he doing those pushups for?"

Zeke cleared his throat. "It's, um. Part of the mating ritual."

Domi burst out laughing. "Aiming a bit high, huh? He's a climber!"

Sighing, Zeke shook his head at Allen. "I think she's out of your league."

As he focused on the lizard, a menu popped up before his eyes.

### Allen the Anole Apocalypse
**Level:** 5.22 (receives some shared Levels while subordinated)

**STR:** 5

**CON:** 2

**DEX:** 3

**SPR:** 0

### Skills

**Limb Regeneration (Minor) +2**
**Strong Jaw (Lesser) +3**
**Fighting Spirit (Minor) +1**
**Cold-Blooded (Condition)**

*Huh. So, he levels up, too? That's nice. Not sure what it's good for, but—*

Zeke narrowed his eyes. He looked at Allen's stats, then his own stats, then back at Allen's. His brows furrowed. *Does the lizard seriously have more STR than me? Allen's stronger than I am?*

Allen looked at him. He tipped his head. With his usual stoicism, he extended his dewlap as if to say, *come at me, bro.*

"What is it?" Domi asked.

Sighing, Zeke clasped a hand to his brow and ran it down his face. "I just got beat out by a lizard."

"Huh?" Domi asked.

"Never mind," Zeke said, shaking his head. "Oh, and... truce."

# 23
## TO DECLARE TRUCE

I t's not as if I completely trust Domi, Zeke thought, following her toward the convenience store. *But she has a point. It's a huge advantage to partner up. If she proves to be someone I can trust, this might be the start of something great.*

*If not...well, I won't let my guard down just yet.*

Overhead, something huge shifted. Both of them froze. On Zeke's hand, Allen turned, his little heart beating fast against his small abdomen.

With a horrible rippling, metal-screaming crash, a billboard tipped forward off the top of a building. One last support held it dangling overhead for a moment, and then it plunged. The billboard bounced oddly off the ground and lay still.

"Was that the Billboard Apocalypse?" Domi joked.

**Billboard Apocalypse**
**Danger Rating:** F-
**Level:** 0
**Deceased**

Zeke snorted. "I guess some apocalypses are just nonstarters." *Unless it crushed some people on the way down, what was it going to do? And it looks like it had to spend all its effort breaking free of its supports. Rather unfortunate in terms of becoming an apocalypse.*

*I guess they can't all be winners.*

"Yeah, guess so," Domi muttered. "Danger Rating F-. Damn."

He glanced at her. *She can see those notifications, too?*

*Okay, no. It only makes sense. She's an apocalypse, too. Still, it raises a question.*

"How does the System look to you?" Zeke asked. Lifting his hand, he set Allen atop his head.

Allen scurried around in his hair a bit, getting comfortable, then settled down.

"What do you mean?" Domi asked.

Zeke nodded. "Like—"

She pulled off her blazer, folding it over her arm, and loosened the buttons of her shirt, revealing soft skin sparkling with perspiration. "Whew, it's hot out here."

Zeke stared, mesmerized, then forcefully shook his head. *Focus, Zeke. Don't forget Mia!* "I mean, like...the menus and stuff. Stats and Skills," he said. *I only know what the System shows me. As far as I know, it could look completely different to Domi.*

"Oh, yeah. Yeah, Stats, Skills. Like some kind of video game or something. It's kind of annoying the way it obfuscates what assists what until you put a point into it or phrase your question the right way. Like the System is one of those annoying teachers who won't tell you the right answer until you guess wrong a few times," Domi said, shrugging.

*Pretty much exactly what I've been dealing with.* Zeke shook his head. "It is annoying. Really wish it would just...say things."

"What was the Coffee Apocalypse like?" Domi asked.

Zeke shrugged. "Uh, weird. Really weird. There was a sea of

coffee, and a coffee bean beach...filter people, cup golems, stuff like that. If you drank the coffee, it brainwashed you... Uh. It was weird. What about the Ancient Fish Apocalypse?"

"Mostly it was just fish bones. Lots and lots of fish bones... and salt. This small exhibit...I was taking a tour group past one of the back exhibits, way in the back of the museum when, suddenly, it started shaking. James went to stabilize it, and the bones...touched him, and he withered into this dried-up pile of ancient bones. Everyone ran, but the fish bones jumped up off the display, and..."

She shook her head. Her throat worked, and her eyes burned red. "Sara...and half the tour group...I thought I was going to die, too, but then I heard a voice in my head, and..." Domi fell silent. Her lips pressed together.

"I'm sorry," Zeke said gently. *For me, aside from Mia, the Coffee Apocalypse was full of strangers. But Domi worked in the museum. She knew the other employees. Whether they were friends or enemies...she lost someone she knew.*

"Ah, well, spilled milk and all," Domi said, waving her hand. Tears glistened in her eyes, but she wiped them away quickly. With some effort, she straightened up and put on a smile. "Store's right up here. It's the end of the world. Let's get some snacks!"

Zeke raised a hand. "Wait."

"Huh? Aren't you starving?" Domi asked.

*Not after I ate that guy's throat. Which, um. I'm not going to think about.* "Yeah, but..." Zeke thumbed at the store beside them.

Domi looked up at the shoe-shaped sign, then down at Zeke's bare feet. "Ah. Yeah. Fair."

Metal grates covered the display window and the door. An alarm blinked in the upper corner, red LED a warning to would-be looters.

"Can you bust open the grates?" Zeke asked. *Domi has explosions. Compared to [Create Coffee] and [Manipulate Steam] or [Manipulate Wind], explosions seem more likely to break the grates.*

Domi frowned. "They look pretty tough. I mean, that's metal, right? Let's check the back."

"You can explode explosive things to create bigger explosions than your usual ones, right?" Zeke asked, tilting his head.

Domi cut her eyes at him. "What?"

"With the Thug Apocalypse, you made their cellphones explode, right? The explosions were bigger than the one you did by clapping, but didn't seem to take as much effort," Zeke explained.

"Ah...yeah," Domi said. She crossed her arms defensively. "So?"

Zeke frowned. *Is she touchy about me guessing her skills?*

*No, it makes sense. If we end up fighting, and I already know all her skills, but she only knows a few of mine, I'd have a massive advantage.*

*Doesn't that mean that I have a massive advantage in general? Even if Domi figures out all my skills, I can find new skills and [Devour] them. If I play my cards right, I'll always have the element of surprise.*

*I should be more careful about revealing when I've figured out Domi's skills in the future. If she knows I know, she'll be able to plan for it. Not that I plan on betraying Domi, but...* He glanced up at the black dome overhead. *Only one can escape.*

Putting his thoughts aside for a moment, Zeke nodded at one of the cars cluttering the road beside them. "What if you exploded a car beside the grate? You know, gas tanks and all?"

Domi looked at the cars. Her eyes glowed with a faint orange light, darting from car to car. She smiled. "Yeah. Yeah, that'll work."

# 24

## BIG BOOM

Zeke tried the SUV's door. It opened, gaping wide. He held his breath. *Come on. Keys in the ignition. Keys in the ignition!*

The ignition stared at him, flat and dead. A button.

Zeke twisted his lips. *Another miss—*

His eyes landed on a plastic-and-metal tab with the car's logo on it, lying on a flat space below the car radio. Zeke grinned. *Hell yeah. Someone forgot their keyless ignition fob!*

Climbing into the seat, he pressed the start button. There was a beat of silence, and then the engine roared to life.

Zeke stood up from the car and waved at Domi. "Got one!"

"What are you waiting for? Drive it over!" Domi called, gesturing from beside the shoe store.

Sitting back in the SUV, Zeke took a deep breath. *Brake on the left. Gas on the right. And...*

*VROOM!* The SUV lurched forward.

Zeke stepped on the brake. The SUV jolted to a halt inches before it hit the car in front of it.

"What, can't drive?" Domi asked, tipping her head.

"I can, I can!" *I just haven't done it much, and I've never driven an SUV like this before. How am I supposed to know how much gas it needs to go?*

Taking a deep breath, Zeke closed his eyes, then opened them. *All right. Here goes.* Gripping the wheel again, he put the car in reverse, navigating back and away from the car in front of him. With a spin, he turned the car. Its wheel hit the curb, and it halted. Zeke pressed the gas, hesitantly at first, and when that didn't work, pushed it hard. The SUV surged over the curb, jumping toward Domi. He stomped on the brake, and it jerked dead.

"Whoa there," Domi said, one hand held out toward him. She lowered it, slowly. "All right. Easy does it. Get her up onto the curb and closer to the store."

"Yep. Getting there," Zeke replied.

The SUV lurched, climbing up onto the curb one wheel at a time. He drove it across the sidewalk and drew it up next to the shoe store. *How close? It can't hurt to get as close as I can, right?* He turned the wheel at the last second. The SUV scraped against the grates, almost rubbing up against them.

He glanced over his shoulder. *There's enough run-up room on the sidewalk.* "We could just use the car as a battering ram."

"Do you want to be inside when it hits the wall?" Domi asked.

Zeke paused. He nodded, pressing his lips together. "You have a point." *There's going to be a ton of kinetic forces at play. Even if the car's safety devices go off...I don't want to be inside.*

*Besides, what if there's an Airbag Apocalypse or something, and they suddenly come to life and start suffocating me? No thanks!*

"Could always ghost-ride the whip," he muttered.

"Or explode it," Domi said shortly, done with the discussion.

Zeke cut a look at her. *She really wants to explode it. Is this her Concept manifesting? Like how I get hungry all the time.*

"Come on, hurry up," she said, waving for him to leave the car.

Clicking the ignition off, Zeke hopped out of the car and slammed the door behind him. He hurried over to Domi's side. "All right. How far away should we get? It's gonna be a big boom, right?"

Domi stood on her tiptoes, taking in the SUV's size. Again, her eyes glowed orange. She hesitated a moment, then nodded, the light in her eyes fading. "A little more, yeah."

*Looks like she has some kind of explosion-gauging skill. I should expect precision attacks if we fight, instead of the slapshot AOE-type explosions she used against the thugs.* Zeke quietly tucked his observation away and nodded, following Domi as she backed away.

The two of them stepped around the corner, slipping into a narrow alleyway.

"Whoa, hey! This's mine. Get out!" a homeless man snarled, throwing away a pile of cardboard boxes and bolting upright.

Zeke flinched back. "Whoa! Sorry, sorry." He turned, heading out of the alley.

"It's exploding out there!" Domi returned, holding her ground.

Zeke looked between Domi and the homeless man, then stopped still within the alley. *If Domi doesn't want to step out of the alley during the explosion...I don't think I will, either.*

The homeless man frowned. "Exploding? The hell is the weather..."

Domi's eyes glowed orange. She snapped her fingers.

*BOOM!*

A wave of force burst through the air. It slammed into Zeke's chest and threw him back. His shoulders struck the wall. Instantly, his ears rang. He shook his head, slightly stunned even though he'd expected it. *Oof. Better remember not to piss off Domi when there's a car in sight.*

Smoke coiled upward.

"Jesus!" the homeless man shouted, scrambling toward the back of the alley. "You'll bring him back! The dinosaur."

Domi glanced at the man, then nodded to Zeke. "Come on. Let's get those shoes of yours and move on. We don't want to stick around too long after that kind of noise."

Zeke shot her a thumbs up. He ran out from the alley and sprinted toward the shoe store.

The homeless man shook his head and drew his cardboard covers back up over himself. "Fucking kids these days."

Raising his hand, Zeke waved at the air, coughing. Black smoke billowed from the crumpled carcass of the car. Bits of plastic, metal, and splatters of mysterious liquids covered the sidewalk. The grate buckled inward, blown entirely away from the wall on one side. He climbed toward the bent metal, carefully avoiding the sharper bits of debris with his bare feet.

*Bang!*

"Domi?" Zeke called, turning over his shoulder.

"I'm fine, I'm fine," she said, coming out of the alley. She hurried over to his side. With a sigh, she tossed her hair over her shoulder. "Come on, hurry up. We don't want to spend too long here."

"Yeah, yeah. I saw that dinosaur. I don't want to wait for it to come back," Zeke muttered.

Domi frowned. "Wait, that's for real? I know the museum had a T-rex, but—"

"Mhm," Zeke confirmed, nodding.

She licked her lips. Nervously, she peered over her shoulder. "Hurry up with those shoes, okay?"

"Yeah, yeah." Zeke wiggled through the gap in the grate. He

stumbled into the shoe shop and blinked, momentarily blinded by the darkness. "Man, it's pitch in here—"

Cold steel pressed against his forehead. A hammer clicked.

Zeke froze. Ever so slowly, he put his hands up.

"Zeke? I can't fit through," Domi said.

"You might not want to!" Zeke called, trying desperately to restrain the panic in his voice.

"Huh?" Domi asked, one leg already through. She squinted into the darkness.

"Tell the girl to come inside and put her hands up," a gravelly voice demanded.

"Domi...please, just move slowly," Zeke begged her.

Carefully placing her hands on the flat parts of the mangled metal, Domi hauled herself up and stepped through. "Why—"

A second gun pressed against her forehead.

She put her hands up. "Fuck."

# 25
## TWO IN CLASS

Gasping, Ryan jolted upright. He scrambled to stand, shoving away from the shoulder he leaned on. "Where-where—"

"Ryan, it's okay, it's okay. We're safe," Mia said gently, letting go of him. She gestured around them. "We're in the elementary school. Mr. Shane brought us here. All the rest of the kids are waiting in the gymnasium for their parents. He said I should take you to the nurse's office, but—"

"I'm fine," Ryan insisted, shoving her away.

Mia reached after him. "You are not—!"

Ryan staggered. He sidestepped sideways, leaning the whole way, until he fell against the wall. The world swirled around him, vertigo twisting the floor beneath his feet. Blinking rapidly, he shook his head. *Settle. Stabilize already.*

"See, what did I tell you? We're going to the nurse's office," Mia insisted.

"I'm fine." He pushed off the wall again.

"Seriously, Ryan. Are you still after Zeke?" Mia asked. She crossed her arms and stared after him, then hurried up, catching up to his somewhat sideways stagger in a few steps.

"Now is the most critical time. If I don't stop him now, it gets much, much harder," Ryan mumbled half to himself.

"What does that even mean? Why do you keep going on about this? You're the one attacking him. He hasn't done anything to you," Mia said, frowning.

"He will. Soon," Ryan muttered darkly. He turned around and pointed at Mia. "You should be on my side, you know. He's your enemy, too."

Mia sighed. She rolled her eyes. "All right, fine. Whatever. If you're so set on getting Zeke, shouldn't you at least be in top shape for it? Let's go to the nurse's office."

"There's nothing there that could help me," Ryan said, voice low.

"Yeah, yeah. Come on, Ryan. What are these B-movie lines, anyway—"

Ryan stopped abruptly.

Mia pulled up short, almost running into him. "What?"

Ryan lifted a hand and pointed.

At the end of the hall, a cute display glittered under the sterile LED bulbs. A sky in blue paper with cotton ball clouds with a rainbow of glitter stretching between the clouds. "We're...here? In Bethel Hannah Elementary School?"

"Yeah? Wait...how did you know the school's name?" Mia asked. She squinted at him. "Were you faking being unconscious? Dude! You're heavy!"

Ryan shook his head. He grabbed Mia's arm and tried to run, only to fall against the wall again. Shoulder dragging against the cold cinderblock, he marched on anyway.

"What? Where are you going?" Mia asked, letting him drag her.

"Out. We have to get out of here," Ryan snapped.

"Why?" Mia said, frowning.

Ryan shook his head. "This place is the epicenter. Everything that's about to happen... Shit! Am I too late? Mia, did he meet her?"

"Meet who?"

"Domi. Did Zeke meet Domi?" Ryan demanded.

Mia put her hands up. "I don't know. We split up after we left the museum. Zeke had to hold off this wax thing... He said we'd meet up here. I was going to double back to check after I had you settled, but—"

"Fuck," Ryan mumbled. He let go of Mia and stumbled on.

"Ryan, seriously. What's going on?" *Ryan's acting weird, Zeke asked me to ask him complete nonsense... 'how many times?' I can't just inject that into random conversation. What does it even mean, anyway? Ugh. Nothing makes sense right now.*

"I told you. You didn't believe me," Ryan replied shortly.

Mia crossed her arms. She followed him, walking to match his shoulder-drag pace. "All right, all right. Let's get you to the nurse's office. After you have a good nap and some time to settle your thoughts, then maybe I'll listen."

Ryan grumbled wordlessly. He rolled his eyes at nothing and wobbled on.

"I mean, today's been pretty crazy. I'd believe about anything you said. But Ryan...Zeke saved us. After you almost killed him! I just...I don't get why you hate him so much right now," Mia said.

"After I almost— Did you ever think about that?" Ryan said.

"Think about what?"

"Why he isn't dead right now," Ryan said ominously. He looked at her. "You lived through the Coffee Apocalypse. You know the danger these things pose. Zeke is the same. He's one of them."

Mia shook her head. "And I keep telling you, he's *helping*. Even if he's one of them—which he isn't—then—"

Ryan halted a second time. This time, Mia bumped into him. She staggered back. "Seriously?"

Silently, he pointed ahead of them, raising a finger to his lips.

A security guard, back turned to them, raised a radio to his mouth. He muttered something, though the static and buzz of the radio swallowed it up. With a *click*, he holstered his radio on his vest once more, his massive stomach bulging below the vest.

"What? The security guard?" Mia asked, frowning.

The security guard turned, slowly.

Two long streaks for eyes, white at the top, black round pupils at the bottom. A blunt, short nose. A big wide smile.

"Why is he wearing a cartoon mask?" Mia asked.

Ryan shook his head, backing away. "He isn't." He ran, sprinting in the opposite direction as fast as his wobbly legs would allow.

Mia blinked at the man, confused. *If he isn't wearing a cartoon mask, then...*

The security guard raised his gun. Still beaming that vacant smile, he aimed at the two of them.

Eyes wide, Mia staggered back. She spun and ran after Ryan.

Bullets sparked over the floor.

Over the speakers, a childish voice blared. "Kill them! Kill the intruders!"

In a few steps, Mia caught Ryan. She grabbed him and yanked him to the side, ducking away from the gunfire into a side hallway. Classrooms opened to either side of the hall, all of them dark and empty. Picking at random, she sprinted into one of them and slammed the door, mashing the lock shut. Still dragging Ryan, she hurried into a corner and hunkered down.

"What the hell?" she muttered, mostly to herself.

Ryan shook his head. He pushed up, staggering toward the door. "He won't stop until he finds us. He's not human anymore. He's just an automaton, programmed to kill anyone he doesn't recognize."

"Anyone he doesn't recognize... So, the kids are safe?" Mia asked. She grabbed Ryan and dragged him back to the corner.

"Safe? Ha," Ryan muttered. He pushed away from her again. "He's going to bust in here. Our only hope is to take him down before he gets us."

Mia took a deep breath, then nodded. She looked around. "Something heavy..."

Ryan drew a dagger from nowhere. He whirled it around his hand and caught it, blade glittering in the light reflected through the door's narrow window.

Mia stared. "Where'd that come from?"

"Don't worry about it," Ryan said. He staggered to the door and pressed his back against the wall beside it, waiting.

"I'm worried," Mia muttered to herself. Her eyes lingered on the dagger, and she shook her head. *It's to save our lives. I can't worry about hurting someone who's trying to kill us.*

Glancing around, Mia bit her lip. *Heavy, heavy...* Her eyes fell on an oversized stapler on the teacher's desk, and she snatched it up. *Better than nothing.*

*Bang!*

*Bang!*

*Bang!*

One at a time, classroom doors flew open. Creeping closer to them, left, then right, left, then right. Closer and closer.

The door opposite them banged open. Mia tensed, tightening her grip on the stapler. *Here we go.*

A shadow fell over their door's window. The handle clacked. *BANG!*

# 26

## SHOES IN THE DARK

Zeke cut his eyes, looking at Domi. Domi cut her eyes back at him. Subtly, she nodded. One of her hands formed into a gun, then an open palm.

*Good. She has the explosion suppressed.* Zeke took a deep breath, then looked up at his captor.

A man in a blue polo shirt, the store's shoe logo embroidered on the breast, looked down at him. Beside him, a kid barely older than Zeke trembled as he pressed a gun to Domi's forehead. Nervously, the boy glanced at the man in the polo. "They don't look dangerous. I don't— I don't think this is necessary."

"They blew open the grate," the man returned, narrowing his eyes at Zeke and Domi.

Domi looked at Zeke. She tilted her hand, turning it into a slash. A blade. She raised her eyebrows. *Attack?*

Zeke shook his head subtly. *Not yet.* Trembling, he looked up at the man. "Sir, I'm so sorry. We heard the blast and came running as fast as we could. Domi—that is, my friend over there—"

Domi gave a little wave.

"—didn't want to, but I said, I said, what if there's people inside? I thought you were in danger, not—"

The man narrowed his eyes at Zeke.

Zeke sniffled a little, willing tears to well up in his eyes. *Come on. It's a reasonable thing to do. More reasonable than the truth, anyway. After all, who'd think Domi could make things explode at will?*

A strange sensation jolted in the back of his mind. He suddenly felt the urge to drop to the ground and pop out a pushup. Zeke blinked, startled. *Why the hell do I want to do pushups? I never want to do pushups. Not even during drylands do I—*

A small message box popped up in the corner of his vision.

### [Subordinate Link]

*Oh...wait, this is Allen?* Zeke composed himself, then sent a wave of calm back to Allen. *I don't want Allen to attack this guy and spook him into shooting us all!*

Allen shifted a little on his head. He did a very dramatic pushup and extended his dewlap, then settled back down.

Zeke sighed. *Whew. Luckily, an anole's idea of intimidating is pretty far from a human's.*

"Rob, they... I mean, they're just ordinary people. How could they even explode the grate? It's not like they have explosives or something." the nervous boy said, starting to lower his gun.

"They don't anymore. Not after they blew the grate," Rob rumbled.

"Sir, please. I work at the local museum. He lost his shoes trying to save me after—" Domi sniffed dramatically. Pretending to choke back sobs, she casually rolled one of her shoulders back to draw attention to her cleavage peeking through the shirt. She fluttered her lashes, ostensibly to shake the tears off but gazing into Rob's eyes the whole time.

Rob's eyes darted to her chest as if drawn by magnets. Still, he held strong. "Uh huh."

"Rob, she's wearing the museum's uniform. I've seen her on her way to work before. They're really just ordinary people," the nervous boy insisted. He lowered his gun and stepped back. "I'm not doing this. This is insane."

Rob hesitated, his gun still pressed into Zeke's forehead.

"Sir, please. I don't know what's happening. We just want to help," Zeke said.

Rob stepped back and holstered his gun. Shaking his head, he turned. "Fine. Can't be too safe, you know."

Domi rolled her eyes and stuck her tongue out at his back.

The nervous boy approached Zeke, and Zeke got a look at his nametag. **TOM,** it read in big bold block letters. "Hi. Sorry about that. And, uh, pity about your shoes. Uhm, if you'd like, go ahead and pick a pair out."

"Really? Wow. Thanks so much," Zeke said, feeling a twinge of guilt. *We were planning to loot your shop, and now you're offering me free shoes? Ugh. He's a nice guy. I feel bad for using him like this.*

*I do need shoes, though, so...* He shoved his guilt down and turned to the racks, picking through the sneakers.

"Comes out of your salary!" Rob shouted from the back.

"It's the apocalypse, Rob!" Tom called in return, his voice a little shrill. He shook his head. "Honestly..."

"Why are you still here, in the shop? Shouldn't you be home?" Domi asked, settling on a bench to wait while Zeke picked out his shoes.

"Oh, me? Well...Rob said he wouldn't pay me if I went home. That, and...once I saw that dinosaur skeleton walking by, I..." Tom licked his lips, then shrugged. "Well, either I was going insane, or the world was and, either way, sheltering in the store with the metal grates sounded like a better deal than trying to make it home."

He turned, looking at the sunlight spilling through the human-sized gap between the grates and the wall and the smoking husk of the SUV outside. Tom chuckled a little under his breath. "I guess they weren't that strong after all."

Domi laughed lightly. "Guess not."

"Says the one who blew them open," Zeke muttered under his breath.

"Huh?" Tom asked, glancing between them.

Domi rolled her eyes. "Nothing. A little inside joke between us."

Tom nodded. "Oh, okay."

Coming around the corner, Zeke held up a pair of sleek, dark-colored name brand shoes and a pair of black socks.

"Going with those?" Tom asked.

Zeke nodded. "I figured dark was best." He knelt to put them on, revealing a brand-new bulging string bag on his back.

Domi put a hand over her mouth, badly hiding a smile.

Tom frowned. He looked at the bag, then down the aisle. "Hey now..."

"Huh?" Zeke asked innocently. *It's the end of the world, damn it! What if I lose my shoes again? I'm not being a thief, I'm preparing for the future!*

*And also being a thief a little, but...*

Sighing, Tom shook his head. "What the fuck ever, man. I'm so done with this shop. Just don't let Rob see it."

Zeke beamed. He gave Tom the thumbs up, then tied up his sneakers and stood.

"You know, I could use a new pair..." Domi muttered thoughtfully to herself.

The lights flickered overhead. All three of them froze and looked up. "What's that?" Domi asked.

Rob came out of the back room, his feet stomping through the store. He marched directly to Zeke and put a gun up against his head again.

"Whoa, whoa! I'm sorry, I'll give them back!" Zeke said, pulling his string bag off his back.

Domi grabbed his arm. "Zeke, he's—!"

A cartoon face smiled down at Zeke and Domi.

"What the fuck!" Tom shouted, startling back.

Rob pulled the trigger.

# 27
## A HERO

BANG!

The door flew open. Smiling down at them with his cartoon face, one hand on the handle, the security guard raised his gun.

Mia swung the stapler at his head. Instinctively, he leaned back. The barrel of the gun pointed up, aiming toward the sky.

Ryan darted in. He grabbed the man by the shoulder and stuck the knife up under the man's ribcage and bulletproof vest. Twisting viciously, he pulled it free. Blood rushed down, soaking the man's jacket in an instant.

The man dragged the gun down and pointed it at Ryan's head. Gunfire rattled, echoing off the cinderblock walls.

Mia screamed. "Ryan!"

The bullets flew through empty space and slammed into the back of the classroom. Ryan appeared behind the man. Grabbing him by his hair, he yanked his cartoon face backward and slit his throat.

The man swung the gun up, aiming behind him. Even as he did, his arms went slack. The gun clattered to the floor, bouncing away. He trembled, then slumped. Falling to his knees, he held there for a second, but only a second before he slammed onto his face.

Hyperventilating, Mia looked from him to Ryan, then back again. "You...you..."

"You saw me push Zeke off the balcony. Why are you surprised now?" Ryan stated. He bent and picked up the gun, then nodded at the man's vest. "You should grab that. It's heavy, but it's better than nothing. Oh, and he has a Taser."

"But...Zeke survived, and—" Mia fell silent. *And it didn't seem real. I didn't want to believe it. Ryan, my friend, the boy I've known since childhood...a killer.*

Against her wishes, her eyes travelled back to the man's body. She shuddered. Her stomach lurched, and vomit welled up in her throat. With effort, she swallowed it down. *I can't deny it any longer.*

"Fine. I'll get them off him. Will you take them?" Ryan asked, kneeling. He grabbed at the man's body, working his gear off him. He scowled, dragging the gear hard.

Mia backed away. She shook her head. "This is insane. This is all—"

"You've been through an apocalypse already. Accept it. This is how the world is now," Ryan said tersely.

Mia shook her head. "It shouldn't be."

"But it is." He slapped the Taser into her hand, then flipped the man over, yanking the vest off his back. Blood pooled on the tile floor.

*There's nothing I can do to stop this. Nothing I can do to make things better. All I can do now, is survive.* Setting her jaw, Mia grabbed the bulletproof vest and slung it on, then shoved the Taser into her belt. Pausing a moment, she bent over and stole the man's handcuffs.

"Good call," Ryan said. He gestured, ready to move on.

"Are you sure you want me to have the vest?" Mia asked,

following him. The vest beat against her body, awkwardly too large and much heavier than she expected. It weighed at her shoulders, dragging her toward the floor. She straightened her spine and forced herself to stand against it. *It's keeping me safe. It might weigh a thousand pounds, but that's good. That's what's going between me and the danger.*

Ryan glanced back. "Yeah. If I can't kill Zeke..." His gaze lingered on Mia.

"What do you mean, can't kill Zeke?" Mia asked. "Why are you so obsessed with killing him?"

"*I'm* obsessed?" he asked, taken aback.

"Are you not?" Mia asked, frowning at him. *Ryan's always been a bit oblivious about himself, but...*

Ryan fell silent. After a moment, he snorted. He shook his head. "We're already on a dead timeline. I'm just running this one out to see what I can see."

"A dead timeline? Ryan, what the hell are you talking about?" Mia asked.

He shrugged. To himself, he muttered, "What the hell. It doesn't matter."

"Yeah? Go on," Mia said, crossing her arms. They fit awkwardly over her too-large vest. Something wet pressed into her stomach. She licked her lips. *I don't feel anything. I don't feel his blood.*

"I've seen this all before. I'm a looper. A time looper. A...a regresser. This is my..." Ryan counted on his fingers. He curled one back down, frowned, straightened another few fingers, then sighed and closed his hands. "Time is weirder than you'd think. It's something like my tenth time. Or hundredth. I'm not... I'm not really sure, anymore."

"Tenth? *Hundredth?* How can you not know?" Mia asked, eyes wide. *Time loops? Regressing? Jeez.*

"Time is *complicated,*" Ryan stressed. He ran his hair back, staring into the distance, his eyes dull. "I've seen this all. Over and over, so many different scenarios, so many different angles. Most of the time, Zeke wins."

"Zeke... What?" Mia asked. "What does he win?"

"The..." He gestured upward, at the black sky, currently hidden behind a drop ceiling and fluorescent lights.

Mia squinted at Ryan. "This whole...whatever's going on... that's something you can win?"

"Yeah. It's— Look, don't make me regret telling you," Ryan said. He took a deep breath. "The point is, Zeke wins it. The black dome goes away. And..."

"And...what's wrong with that?" Mia asked.

Ryan shook his head. "Zeke is an apocalypse. The same as every other monster in here. When he gets out, he's going to destroy the world."

*Going to?* Mia squinted at him. "Are you sure?"

"He's an *apocalypse,* Mia. Duh."

"He's saved me," Mia pointed out.

"Why am I bothering? You die, Mia. You die. Every— *almost* every time. And when you do, Zeke goes insane, and... and we *don't* want that," Ryan emphasized. He shook his head and ran a hand down his face. His eyes gazed at something distant, far beyond Mia. To himself, he murmured, "We don't want that."

"Well, that's bad. Guess I'll do my best to stay alive," Mia said. Internally, she laughed and screamed at the same time. *What the hell am I supposed to do with this information? I die? Multiple apocalypses are going on? Fighting one another for supremacy? Zeke's...like, the final boss or something? Or was, or will be...or would have been if Ryan didn't go back in time, which by the way, haha, Ryan can go back in time... What the hell? What the hell? Can someone tell me what's going on? Please? Someone who isn't Ryan?*

She looked at him. "So, you're riding out the dead loop, or whatever? That's all this is to you? A...test run or something?"

"That, too, and..." Ryan glanced over his shoulder, almost reflexively.

"What?" Mia asked.

He shook his head. "I can't keep doing this forever. I... Just trust me on that. I can't."

"You're asking me to trust you on a whole lot," Mia said, cocking a brow skeptically. *What do you mean, can't do this forever? You can just reset the world if you really have time loop powers. Turn back time if this is a dead timeline.*

*Unless...there's something he can't turn back.*

Taking a deep breath, Mia gathered her thoughts and shoved them all into a box for later. She shook her head, forcing herself to focus only on what Ryan told her. *Time loopers, final bosses...* "Next, you'll tell me this is all a video game."

Ryan paused. "Wait, you know about the System?"

"Oh, you're kidding me," Mia muttered under her breath.

They drew up to a corner. Mia peered around it. A few adults milled around, most of them dressed in office clothes. Their backs to the two of them, they circled slowly toward a glass door halfway down the hallway.

She held her breath. Beside her, Ryan held still as well.

One of the adults turned. A cartoonish face stared blank-eyed down the hallway. Smiling blandly, the adult turned back around.

Ryan pressed his lips together. "They're too far gone. We have to kill them."

Mia held out her hand. "Wait. During the Coffee Apocalypse—"

Ryan shook his head. "I know what you're going to say. You were brainwashed, right? And you got over it. That's as far as you can go. Any further, and there's no coming back. As soon as the apocalypse physically alters someone, like the Cartoon Apocalypse is doing to these people, it's over. They're... Essentially, they're dead."

*Cartoon Apocalypse? What the hell—*

*Focus. Not now. I can have a mental breakdown later.* Mia pressed her lips together. "There has to be something."

Static burst in front of her vision. She blinked, and the static vanished. Mia frowned. *What was that? Am I* actually *having a mental breakdown? In the middle of the apocalypse...apocalypses?*

Ryan nudged her. "Don't drift off. It's time."

"Time?"

Ryan raised his gun. "We can't let them take that office. It'll be hell to flush them out when they can see everything we do through the glass walls and prepare for our every move. You get the leftmost one. I'll take the ones on the right."

Mia gripped her Taser tight. She nodded. "Understood."

Nodding back at her, Ryan snapped around the corner.

The cartoon-faced adults spun to face them. They sprinted toward Mia and Ryan, still grinning the same as ever.

Mia yelped. A round, stubby-limbed man charged her, his teeth bared, his squared off, overlarge eyes maniacal. Clutching a pen in one hand and a box cutter in the other, he closed the distance with surprising speed. Ten feet. Five.

*I have to. Whatever it takes to survive.*

She raised her Taser and fired.

# 28

## CLICK

*lick.*

The hammer thumped down, but nothing happened. Rob tilted his head, then pulled the gun back and looked at it, cartoon eyes wide with confusion.

Unhesitating, Zeke lunged for his arm.

**[Devour]**

Bone snapped. Blood flew.

Tom screamed. He jumped over the counter and hunkered behind it.

Rob's hand flopped to the ground, still holding the gun. He looked at it, then looked at Zeke. His mouth twisted into an exaggerated O.

Zeke swallowed, scowling at the man. "Yeah?"

**You have inflicted a [Serious] wound.**
**If you inflict a [Mortal] or [Life-Altering] wound with**
**[Devour], you have a chance of absorbing a skill. Go for it!**

*Thank you, System. Not exactly being subtle about encouraging cannibalism, huh.*

*But...that being said...what am I supposed to do? I'm stuck at the start of the end of the world, and I'm hungry all the time. I—*

Zeke took a deep breath and closed his eyes. *Calm down. This is the apocalypse thinking. Human Zeke doesn't want to eat people. Human Zeke isn't exactly opposed, but...you know. It's a situational thing. A sometimes food.*

Drawing back his arm, Rob slapped at Zeke. Zeke swayed back, dodging the slap. Rob's meaty palm whooshed by inches from his nose.

Zeke ground his toe into the floor.

### [Crystal Burst]

Crystals burst up, piercing through Rob's foot. Rob stumbled back. Blood poured from his shoe, leaving bloody footprints where he stepped. He crashed into a display of high heels and went down in an avalanche of boxes and shoes. A pair of tasteful, nude, three-inch heels perched at an angle atop the pile, somehow still upright.

"What's going on?" Tom asked, eyes wild.

Domi held out her hand. "Give me the gun. I'll handle it."

Tom hesitated. He pointed at Zeke. "You came in with him."

"So?" Domi asked.

"He *ate* Rob!" Tom shrieked.

"I ate Rob's arm," Zeke corrected him. He regarded the pile of shoes warily. *He isn't dead. I didn't get any levels.*

Shoes flew. Boxes tumbled. Rob burst upward, flying at Zeke, arms already open in a bear hug.

Zeke jolted back, but Rob still caught him. He latched on tight, squeezing tighter and tighter. Turning to Tom, he barked a garbled order, not quite English or any language, but almost.

Arms gripped Zeke tight. Sweaty body closed in all around him. He looked up at Rob's throat and sighed. *His throat is right there...* Almost reluctantly, he opened his mouth.

**[Devour]**

Rob jerked back, but not fast enough. Zeke's jaws snapped shut on the man's throat. Blood spurted, showering down on his head and soaking him in hot liquid. Rob released him, grabbing his throat instead.

Zeke backed away, watching as the man died.

**Member of the Cartoon Apocalypse**
**Level + .2**
**Level:** 16.83
**Please pick a skill**
**[None]**

Zeke poked at the None skill experimentally, but nothing happened. He frowned. *He looked like that, but he had no skills? The brainwashed members of the Coffee Apocalypse could [Create Coffee], and they weren't physically altered. What's the difference?*

*Actually...can Mia still [Create Coffee]? It's not the most useful skill, but it's still a skill.* He frowned, putting a hand on his chin.

Behind him, Domi held her hand out. "The gun?"

Tom's hands trembled so hard the gun clacked in his grip. His eyes darted from her to Zeke, who stood there, soaked in blood, a hand on his chin as he stared at Rob's corpse. He shook his head. "No. No way."

Domi sighed. "Fine." She snapped her fingers.

"Domi, wait—" Zeke protested.

*BANG!*

The gun exploded. Shards of metal shot through the shop

and pierced through Tom's hands and arms, leaving them mangled.

Tom stared at his ruined hands. A mishmash of blood, bone, and gore, Zeke couldn't tell where what went. He grimaced. *Oof. I can't imagine how much that hurts. He pointed his gun at Domi but, even so, that's excessive. I can't tell her off. It's not like she doesn't have the right to protect herself. I just wish she didn't maim him so badly.*

"I told you," Domi said flatly.

Tom screamed wordlessly. As he screamed, his face contorted, growing more and more cartoonish, his cheeks round, his mouth huge, his eyes small.

Before he could finish the transformation, Domi clapped. A wave of force burst from her hands and slammed him into the wall. Startled, Zeke stumbled back, the wave carrying him away.

Tom slumped. Blood ran from his ears and nose.

"Whew," Zeke muttered. He glanced at Domi. "What was that about?"

"I don't know. They seem to be part of some apocalypse, though. The Cartoon Apocalypse?" Domi asked, quirking a brow.

"What does that even mean?" Zeke wondered.

"Nothing good, I'm sure." Domi yawned and stretched. She glanced into the distance, then shook her head. "Let's hurry and hit up that convenience store before someone else busts it."

"What, and not chase the Cartoon Apocalypse?" Zeke asked.

"Why should we? It sounds dumb. It'll probably burn itself out in a bit, or some other apocalypse will handle it. We need levels, sure, but...you need food more. Can't eat levels," Domi said, shrugging.

"Can't level up without fuel," Zeke agreed. He took a deep breath, then nodded. "All right. We'll loot the store. But if there's more of this Cartoon Apocalypse after that, we go beat it."

"All right, deal," Domi said, nodding. She climbed back up toward the gap and pushed her way through.

Zeke glanced at the two bodies and paused. He bowed his head and closed his eyes for a moment. *It's not like I'm religious, but...whatever you believed in...I hope you're there.*

*I'm sorry. I wouldn't have killed you if I had a choice.*

Turning, he followed Domi through the gap and back into the sunlight.

Outside, the street remained much the same, though now a smoking SUV sat half-on, half-off the sidewalk. Domi led the way around it and onward, down the road toward the corner store at the end of the block. Bright red plastic lettering spelled out BUR PHARMACY, followed by a large plus sign. Thin metal grates with big gaps between the chains protected the glass storefront. A small alarm light blinked by the door.

Looking it over, Zeke felt...nothing. No guilt. No fear. Just a vague pressure to stock up, to find his supplies and secrete them away. *If there's ordinary people inside, they'll probably be corrupted by an apocalypse soon. Before long, the only ones left looking normal will be apocalypses, and those lucky enough to be brainwashed, but not physically changed, like the subordinates of the Coffee Apocalypse.*

He frowned, putting a hand on his chin. *I wonder...rather than sending people I find to tenuous safety...would it be better to subordinate them, like I did with Allen? That way, I could keep them relatively safe, or at least, safe compared to being the fodder for any apocalypse to devour and alter at its will.*

*Mia... Damn. I shouldn't have sent her off. Once we loot here, I'll go find her and offer her the chance to become my subordinate. If nothing else, I want to keep her safe.*

*And Ryan...well, he hasn't hurt Mia yet, and she didn't seem afraid of him. He really is just after me, huh?*

Zeke twisted his lips, a hint of irony in his heart. *I am an apocalypse, after all.*

"So...?" Domi prompted, looking at him.

"A pharmacy?" Zeke asked, jolted back to the moment. He nodded appreciatively. *Not bad, not bad. It'll have some food but also medicine and bandages. The kind of stuff you need in an apocalypse. Might even have some clothes, depending on how touristy it is. I might be able to pick up another backpack.*

"It's nothing special, but if we're lucky, we ought to be able to grab some food and essentials," she said, glancing over her shoulder at Zeke.

"Sounds good to me," Zeke agreed, nodding.

"So...wanna go find another car?" Domi asked, looking at the grate.

Zeke paused. He shook his head. "I have a better idea." Gesturing for her to follow, he headed to the back of the shop.

Domi followed him. Around the side of the store, into the narrow road that led to its back door. A nondescript white metal door greeted them, complete with a guard around its lock and dark stains around the handle where many hands had touched.

Zeke nodded at the lock. "Instead of exploding a whole car, why don't you explode the inside of the lock, instead? It should be easier, and it won't create as much noise, either."

Pushing him aside, Domi leaned up against the door, peering into the lock. She tilted her head back and forth, testing different angles to let light into the narrow hole. Drawing her head back, she pointed at the hole, then snapped her fingers.

*Bam!*

Smoke issued from the keyhole. Tentatively, Domi tried the handle, then beamed. Opening the door, she turned to Zeke and gestured. "After you!"

Zeke saluted. "Thank you, Door Opening Officer!"

"You're very welcome, underling!" Domi returned.

As he walked through, Zeke quietly noted, *It seems like she can only explode things she can see. Interesting. I'll keep that for later.*

On the far side of the door, Zeke came out into a narrow white hallway. A large room to the right held the store's inventory in large pallets wrapped in plastic, and a small break room with chairs and a folding table stood to the left, complete with lockers to change clothes and store valuables. He scanned the break room, but it stood mostly empty. Relieved, Zeke let out a breath. *Seems like everyone at this store went home. Good.*

Something crunched underfoot. He lifted his foot, brows furrowed.

Pills. Pills stretched off down the center of the hallway, dusty dry tablets and rounded capsules, dribbled in ones and twos as far as the eye could see.

Zeke swallowed. *Right. Just because every*one *went home, it doesn't mean every*thing *did.* "Domi, be on your guard."

"Got it," Domi said. She pulled up close behind him, hands curled into balls.

A dry *click...click...click...* sounded from ahead, echoing through a half-open door. Light spilled out, illuminating the semi-dark hallway.

*Creeeeeeak.* Unoiled springs groaned with the long-suffering complaints of an old rolly chair. Wheels squeaked over tile.

Zeke held out his hands, readying Wind Manipulation and Steam Manipulation. Behind him, sparks popped as Domi raised her hands, preparing to clap.

A shadow loomed in the spilled light. The door swung wider.

"Come out!" Zeke shouted.

In a blur of motion, something small launched itself at Zeke.

# 29
## PILL HOUSE

Zeke threw his hand out. A blast of wind surged at the small, shiny thing. It fell back, twisting in midair. A syringe clattered to the ground, needle dripping some mysterious greenish fluid.

*Holy shit!*

A rolling chair burst around the corner. Atop it sat a tiny pill, small and dusty, imperiously looking down on them from its throne. The pill shifted a little. A dozen syringes floated out of the pharmacy and flew at them.

Zeke batted at it, backing away. Wind rushed at the syringes in a wide blast. One or two fell back, but the rest hurtled onward, barely rattled. Zeke gritted his teeth. *Dammit. When I can't concentrate the wind, it isn't as strong!*

Domi shoved him back and stepped forward, clapping in the same instant. A wave of force burst from the clap and caught the syringes in midair, shattering them. Bits of glass and fluid splattered over her and Zeke.

Shaking his head to throw the liquid and splinters off, Zeke dropped to the ground and pointed at the rolling chair's wheels.

**[Wind Manipulation]**

The wheels rotated wildly, spinning about on their axis, and the chair flew backward. It slammed into the open door. The pill jumped off it for a second, momentarily dislodged.

Domi charged forward. She snatched the pill off the chair and threw it at Zeke. "Catch!"

Zeke caught it out of the air. Without hesitation, he threw it into his mouth.

**[Devour]**
**Pill Apocalypse [Decoy]**
**Levels:** None
**Warning:** You have gained the Condition [Drugged]
**Time remaining:** 1:32

"Motherfucker," Zeke muttered, and then the world went sideways. Startled, he tried to counterbalance, only for the wall to rush up to meet him. Shoulder propped on the wall, he barely held himself up.

"Zeke? What's wrong?" Domi asked, startled.

Zeke gestured vaguely. "That one was a fake. Find the real one!"

Domi said something, but it wasn't in English. Her face distorted, turning into a monstrous sludge of human-colored putty that melted into red blood and then bone. Zeke stumbled, forcing himself to stay upright. *This isn't real. It's the drugs. Come on. Stay with it.*

Reality popped back, but only for a moment. Domi was gone, but the whole world was full of halos, bright, glistening, star-shaped halos. Zeke pressed onward, heading toward the pharmacy. *There has to be something. Something that can counteract this.*

He fell through a door and thumped to the ground. The earth shifted beneath his fingers, made of pills.

His hands found solid ground. He shook his head. *It isn't made of pills. There's a light coating of pills. Heehee, a light coating... like that good-tasting stuff they put on bitter pills...so you can swallow them.*

He swallowed. His stomach grumbled. He reached out, grabbing a handful of pills. *Damn, I'm hungry. I wonder if these pills will...*

A foot stomped his wrist to the floor. Petulantly, Zeke pulled against it.

"—out of it!" Domi grumbled, frustrated.

"Should've taken Drug Resistance," Zeke told her. *That mugger. The one way back. He had Drug Resistance. Would be nice right now.*

"What?" Domi asked.

Zeke closed his eyes. He waved a hand. *Too late now.*

Cool fingers pressed a pill against his lips. "Here, try this."

Eyes still shut, Zeke opened his mouth.

### [Devour]
### Pill Apocalypse [Decoy]
**Warning:** You have gained the Condition [Drugged]
#### Time remaining: 1:45

Zeke shook his head.

"Damn," Domi muttered.

Time passed, or maybe it didn't. Zeke wasn't sure. The world swirled, colors danced, and he mostly laid on the floor. Occasionally, Domi ran over and made him eat something, but it was never the right something. He twisted his lips, frustrated. *I'm not a garbage can. Come on.*

Something rattled down on him. He blinked awake to find Domi standing over him. Pills fell over him, rattling off like gunfire. Scowling, Domi waved her hand, sending explosion after explosion to meet the pills. She ran forward, leaving him behind.

All alone, Zeke rolled around on the floor. *Hungry... I'm hungry...*

Domi rushed back. She held something tightly between her fingers. "Your Concept is something about eating, right? Here!"

Zeke opened his mouth. Something fell into it, and he swallowed. A moment later, he frowned. *There's something...something I'm supposed to...*

*Oh, that's right.*

### [Devour]
### Pill Apocalypse
### Level + .52
### Level: 16.83 > 17.35
### You [Devoured] the source of your Condition. You are no longer inflicted with [Drugged].
### Please assign your stat point.

"Was that the real one?" Domi asked.

Zeke nodded. He gave her the thumbs up. Slowly, the world began to settle once more, colors snapping back to usual, the floor no longer lurching under him.

"Whew. I was starting to get worried about feeding you so many pills," Domi sighed.

Zeke frowned at her, sitting up. He brushed pills and pill dust out of his hair. It rained down, drifting to the floor in a white plume. Confused, Zeke frowned at the pile of dust. *How long was I rolling around on the floor?* "I only remember two...no, three. Four...? How many did you feed me?"

Domi licked her lips. She shrugged. "Oh, you know. The important part is that you're fine now."

"That doesn't make me feel good about the number of pills you fed me," Zeke said, squinting.

"Hey, no point crying over spilled milk. Let's get to looting!" Domi said. She stepped past him and pushed into the main store.

Still squinting, Zeke heaved himself to his feet. Pills crunched beneath his feet, and he looked down.

A white lab coat and frumpy outfit laid slumped on the floor. Pills spilled out of it, hundreds or thousands of them in every shape and color. Beside them, a pair of jeans, a BUR polo, and an apron splayed out, short sleeve raised protectively.

Zeke gritted his teeth. He looked away. *I guess...everyone didn't make it out.*

At the door, he paused. Bowing his head, he closed his eyes. "I hope you can rest."

Turning away, he took a deep breath. *I can't let all this death get to me. At the end of the day, my life's on the line just as much as anyone else's. If I stop moving from the weight of it all, I die. Once I get out of here, then it's time to mourn.*

So resolved, he pulled up his menus.

**STR:** 1
**CON:** 10
**DEX:** 2
**SPR:** 4 > 5

*It's nice to have good, round, divisible by five numbers,* Zeke decided. *Now, for the skills...*

## Skills

### Create Pill (Weak)
*Create small pills with ordinary effects. Weak painkillers and antibiotics.*

### Manipulate Medical Gear (Weak)
*Manipulate medical gear with your SPR.*

### Inflict Drugged (Weak) (Condition)
*Items you create have a small chance of inflicting the Drugged condition.*

### Mobile (Minor)
*Even if you have no method to move, you can move your body slowly and with weak force. If you are able to move, you can move slightly faster and with more dexterity.*

### Decoy (Weak)
*Create Tiny or smaller decoys of yourself.*

### Bewitching Aroma (Minor)
*Your aroma is slightly disarming and generally positive to some people you encounter.*

Zeke looked over his skills. *There isn't much synergy here, so I might as well go for survival options. Create Pill is much better than Produce since I'm less likely to be able to find pills than food. Manipulate Medical Gear...too situational. Inflict Drugged and Mobile both sound good for survival...if I end up in a situation where my body's broken again, I should be able to move around a little bit with Mobile. Plus, it combos nicely with Caffeinated.*

*As for Decoy and Bewitching Aroma...I wish I could take these skills, but Decoy only creates Tiny decoys, which is useless for someone like me, and Bewitching Aroma...it's nice, but it's kind of pointless.*

[Create Pill] (Weak)
[Inflict Drugged] (Weak)
[Mobile] (Minor)

*All right, so after that, my skills are...*

**Skills**
**Wind Manipulation (Weak) +1**
**Pick Up (Weak)**
**Filter (Weak)**
**Absorb (Weak)**
**Subordinate Link (Weak)**
**Create Pill (Weak)**
**Inflict Drugged (Weak)**
**Crystal Burst (Poor)**
**Engulf (Poor)**
**Manipulate Steam (Medium)**
**Create Coffee (Strong)**

**Passive**
**Resilience (Minor) +6**
**Fighting Spirit (Minor)**
**Teamwork (Minor)**
**Disguise (Minor)**
**Watertight (Minor)**
**Limb Regeneration (Minor) +1**
**Follow Me (Minor)**
**Mobile (Minor)**
**Growth (Lesser) +2**

**Heat Resistance (Lesser) +9**

**Condition**
**Caffeinated (Average) (Condition)**
**Hardness (Lesser) (Condition)**

Zeke took a deep breath. *That's a lot of skills. I wonder if there's some way to combine or truncate them? Since I'm going to get so many skills in the future.*

**Would you like to combine similar skills? Y/N**

Zeke's eyes lit up. He pressed Y.

**Skills**

**Manipulate Aerosols (Medium) +1 (Wind Manipulation + Manipulate Steam)**
*Manipulate Wind or Steam with medium skill, volume, and control. Create a small amount of Wind or Steam.*

**Pick Up (Weak)**
**Osmosis (Weak) +1 (Filter + Absorb)**
*By using osmosis or reverse osmosis, you can either absorb or filter out liquids.*

**Subordinate Link (Weak)**
**Create Drug (Weak) +1 (Create Pill + Inflict Drugged)**
*You can create pills that inflict the [Drugged] status, as well as creating medicinal pills.*

**Crystal Burst (Poor)**
**Engulf (Poor)**
**Create Coffee (Strong)**
**Passive**
**Resilient Regeneration (Minor) +8 (Resilience + Limb Regeneration)**
*You feel less pain and regenerate faster. Limbs can be regenerated using this skill.*

**Team Spirit (Minor) +1 (Fighting Spirit + Teamwork)**
*Gain a small boost when you face a stronger opponent or fight in a team. Boost x2 if both conditions met.*

**Disguise (Minor)**
**Watertight (Minor)**
**Follow Me (Minor)**
Caffeine Rush (Average) (Mobile + Caffeinated) *You move faster and with more dexterity for as long as this skill is active but become exhausted afterward. If your body cannot provide a method of motion, you can still move with some speed and dexterity.*

**Growth (Lesser) +2**
**Heat Resistance (Lesser) +9**
**Condition**
**Hardness (Lesser) (Condition)**

Zeke looked over the skills. *Huh. Teamwork and Fighting Spirit? I would have thought Teamwork and Follow Me, the skill where I have a chance to pick up subordinates, would make more sense. But then, I guess Teamwork and Fighting Spirit both give me a small boost to my stats in certain conditions, so it makes sense.*

*Overall, it seems like I can combine skills to lose a little bit of the skill's specialization in return for getting both skills at the level of the higher-level skill. That's... I'll take it! It's worth it to lose some specialization in return for doing two things well.*

*Still, it'd be nice if I could choose myself which ones went together...*

**You can also fuse skills to create new skills, so long as the two skills are similar enough. Fusing skills is a manual process, and it's possible to destroy or permanently lose skills that aren't similar enough.**

*Ah, I see. So, in return for control, there's a failure chance,* Zeke thought, nodding.

"What are you doing back there? There's a whole store to loot!" Domi called from ahead of him.

"Coming, coming!" Zeke called. Quickly, he closed out of his menus. *Domi's right. We need to get moving.*

# 30
## SCHOOL HOUSE

The Taser buzzed in Mia's hand. A pair of wires leaped from its nose and stuck into the charging man's chest. His cartoon face had a single moment to show pure surprise before the voltage struck. He jerked up onto a foot and both arms and jiggled in place for a few seconds, his bones showing through his flesh. With a *thump*, he hit the floor and thrashed around, contorting wildly.

She backed away. "I'm sorry. I'm so sorry..."

Ryan charged into the crowd, slashing left and right with his dagger. The people he struck clutched their throats dramatically, spun a full circle, and collapsed to the floor, sprawled out dead in the most dramatic death poses imaginable.

One of the men snuck up behind Ryan. Lifting a finger to his lips, he snickered and showed off a pocketknife.

"Ryan, behind you!" Mia shouted.

Ryan whirled. The daggers flashed.

The man stared at his arms. They ended midway down the forearms, cut off where Ryan had slashed. Blood spurted comically from the gory remains, bone and muscles visible along with his severed flesh. He stared at them, eyes widened in exaggerated horror, then collapsed.

"What's happening? Why are they like this?" Mia asked, looking from one to another to another.

"It's the Cartoon Apocalypse," Ryan said tersely. He backed toward Mia, eyes on the bodies. They lay there, bleeding out.

"Ryan?" Mia asked.

Holding out his hand for Mia to stay back, Ryan walked over to one of the bodies. He looked down at it for a second, then drew back his leg and kicked it in the gut.

Startled, Mia screamed. "Ryan! Why?"

The man's body rolled over, front soaked in blood, his face still a horrific rictus of a smile. Its cartoonish eyes stared deep into the middle distance, and his hands laid flat, palms splayed.

Ryan let out a deep sigh. "Thank goodness. It hasn't progressed too far yet. If I don't stop this one right away...these *things* eventually become near-immortal. It's hellish."

"Things? These are *people,* Ryan," Mia protested.

Ryan snorted. "Not anymore, they aren't. Now, they're just mindless drones. No more than an extension of the apocalypse they're subordinated to."

"Is there really nothing we can do? They're people. They *were* people, and they're still alive. There must be something," Mia insisted.

Ryan spread his hands. "Ten loops, Mia. Ten. Or so. I haven't found anything. Once someone's physically altered, that's it. They're too far gone. Which is why you have to stay close to me."

"Huh? Why?" Mia asked. She furrowed her brows. *Come to think of it, everyone we've encountered in the school since that security guard has been a cartoon person. Everyone...but Ryan and myself.* She squinted at Ryan. "Wait, is that why I haven't become a cartoon person yet? Hold on, and you...why haven't you become one, either?"

Ryan opened his mouth, then shut it. He shook his head. "It's complicated. Look, just stick near me. I'll keep you safe."

"Seriously, Ryan, why this piecemeal nonsense? Why tell me little bits and pieces? Just *tell* me," Mia said.

Shaking his head, Ryan set off. He turned back as he walked to shake his finger at Mia. "You won't believe me. I've already lived it. You won't. You never do."

"I believed you that you're a...a time looper, or whatever," Mia said. *Not really, but he does seem to know some things he shouldn't, and...it's better to appease him for now. Besides, the whole world's going to hell. Who knows? Maybe he is a time looper. I mean, hell, I've been stuck in the Coffee Apocalypse, and now the Cartoon Apocalypse. Anything is possible.* "Come on, Ryan. You haven't even tried."

Ryan ignored her. He drew up to the next corner and peered around it, then gestured for her to cross to him. She hurried to his side. Clustered close together, the two of them walked down the school hallway. A thrill ran down Mia's spine, to her surprise, along with an old memory. She chuckled under her breath.

"What?" Ryan asked.

"Nothing, it's just...do you remember when we were little, and we hid in school until after hours? Had to be about ten, fourth grade or something. You, me, and Zeke. The three of us slipped into the closet instead of going to the bus, then came out once everyone left. Wandering the hallways like this...it reminded me of that."

Ryan shook his head, but a small grin touched his face. "Yeah, yeah. I remember us getting chewed out afterwards by our parents. That part wasn't fun at all."

Mia nodded. "Yep. Guess we don't have to worry about that this time, huh?"

"Nope," Ryan agreed.

"Since it's the end of the world, and all," Mia added, half to herself. She took a deep breath. *Focus, Mia. Now isn't the time to get doom and gloom. That can happen after I figure out what I'm doing for food, and water, and where I'm sleeping tonight.*

Around the next corner, a man led a gaggle of small children. Facing away from Mia and Ryan, he ushered the children down the hallway. Mia perked up, recognizing the man's shirt from behind. She raised her hand.

Ryan shook his head. Mia looked at him, confused. He held a finger to his lips.

"Why? It's Mr. Shane..." Mia drifted off. She bit her lip. Her eyes darted to the man again. *No. It couldn't be.*

The man turned slowly. Mr. Shane grinned maniacally at her, his eyes over-large, his mouth distorted into a quirky smile.

Mia gasped, clasping her hands over her mouth in the same moment.

All around Mr. Shane, the children turned as one. Cartoonish faces stared up at her, all grinning.

Mia's heart plunged. She shook her head. Tears welled up in her eyes. "No. No, no, no. It can't be. I won't...no."

"Fuck," Ryan muttered.

In one mass, the children charged Mia and Ryan, Mr. Shane at their rear, a general looming over his miniature troops.

# 31
## LOOTER SHOOTER

Z eke grabbed a handful of candy bags and shoved them into his bag, stuffing them down into the bottom. *Thank goodness I found a new bag here. Would've hated to leave my extra shoes behind. After I lost my shoes the first time...I'm never going to be shoeless again!*

Across the way, Domi shook her head, rolling her eyes at him. "What, have the munchies after that trip of yours?"

"Actually, candy is incredibly calorie dense. In a survival scenario, it's a good way to get burst energy and to keep your energy up without carrying around a ton of unnecessary weight. It's not the only thing you should eat, but you could certainly pick worse foods," Zeke argued. Continuing down the line, he stuffed packets of beef jerky and nuts into his bag, jamming them into the bottom. "Cookies would be even better. And butter, butter is great, too."

"What the fuck kind of bullshit excuse to eat junk food," Domi muttered to herself.

"It's a hundred percent true. When people go trekking through the arctic, they eat straight sticks of butter. It's the only way they can pack enough calories to survive in that environ-ment," Zeke explained.

"But we aren't in the arctic," Domi pointed out.

"Still, calorie density is important in any survival scenario, especially if we have to carry our food ourselves...and we do. Though we should grab any fresh fruits and vegetables we can find while we can find them. They'll be a luxury soon," Zeke said, half-talking to himself. He stood on his tiptoes. "Oh, and vitamins. They're easy to carry, and the chances we can successfully find all the nutrients we need once the world really breaks down are pretty low."

"Now, that's reasonable," Domi agreed.

Zeke looked up, holding a handful of crinkly bags. "Oh, and potato chips! Potatoes have a lot of nutrients, and potato chips can keep for a long time. The salt's a bit of a problem if the taps stop running, and, you know, putting anything heavy on them will destroy them, but..."

"You're insane," Domi said, packing granola bars into a bag she'd found somewhere in the pharmacy.

"Granola bars are a good choice, too," Zeke said, shrugging. *Anything with a lot of calories packed into a small space, and granola bars qualify.*

Domi grunted, ignoring him.

Zeke shook his head and went back to packing his bags. Heading over to the pharmacy section, he grabbed a few bottles of vitamin along with some antibiotic cream and other first aid gear, pushing it all down into his bag. At the end, his bag burst at the seams, stuffed completely full. He gave it a pat, satisfied, then snagged a set of bananas from a display near the checkout. "You ready?"

Domi stood, hauling the bag onto her back. "As I'll ever be."

Zeke nodded. "We should find a place to hunker down. It's getting dark."

Domi looked up at the black sky, then gave Zeke a sarcastic look.

"It is, though," Zeke said, gesturing at the twilight all around them. Although the sky remained as bleak as ever, the light that passed through it changed. Now, only muted twilight escaped the black sky. All the buildings cast long, dark shadows over the street.

"All right, yeah. Wanna head back to my place?" Domi suggested.

Internally, Zeke panicked. *Head back to her place? To a girl's place? For the first time ever, I'm heading back to...*

*No. It isn't like that. This is a survival scenario. Now isn't the time to be an idiot. Down, hormones.* He nodded, playing it cool. "Let's go."

"Unless you have a place?" Domi asked.

Zeke shook his head. "We drove into the city to sightsee. Or rather, Ryan did. I don't have the keys to his car, even if I wanted to sleep there." *I could go find Ryan and Mia, but...Ryan attacks me on sight. He doesn't seem to attack Mia, so I can at least trust him to keep an eye on her, but I don't think it's a good idea to go and provoke him.*

*Ryan...what the hell? I still don't get it. It's like he had a mental breakdown right as the apocalypse started. What was brewing in his head all this time that I immediately became his prime target?*

*Though, he almost seemed to be blaming me for things I hadn't done yet. And what Mia said...he said he came from the future? Hmm...*

*Is he an apocalypse, too? The Future Apocalypse? The next time I see him, I should try to guess his concept. After all, if I get close enough, the System will help me out.*

*For now, though, there's no point in dwelling on it. Focus on the present. On finding shelter and securing food.* He nodded at Domi. "Thanks for letting me crash in your place."

"Sure, no problem. Actually, it's pretty close. We could take a couple trips here and back, load it up with supplies," Domi said.

"That's not a bad idea," Zeke agreed, nodding.

Domi heaved her bag over her shoulder and headed out the back exit of the pharmacy. Zeke followed her, glancing left and right at the door.

A few pigeons sat on the ground across from the pharmacy. At the sight of him, they cooed and took to the wing.

Zeke watched them go. *Somehow... I get the feeling I'm being watched. Is this because I ate one pigeon way back? Surely they can't hold a grudge...can they?*

"Hey. This way," Domi called.

Jolted out of his thoughts, Zeke chased after her, half-jogging down the alleyway.

*Bam!*

A bullet sparked against the asphalt by Zeke's foot. He jumped back, dodging to the side. "Domi!"

"I know!" Domi threw herself behind a set of metal trash bins.

Zeke glanced over his shoulder, hurtling after Domi. Throat torn out, his face fixed into a blank, bloodstained smile, Rob lurched after them. A few seconds later, Tom followed him, his maimed hands outstretched, smiling just as broad.

"What the fuck?" Domi muttered under her breath.

"Are they zombies?" Zeke wondered aloud.

"Shit, zombies? That's the last thing we need," Domi grumbled.

Zeke shook his head. "They're part of the Cartoon Apocalypse. You know how old-school cartoons can take infinite damage without dying?"

"You think that's what this is? But...they're all torn up. In the cartoons, they always visibly take no damage," Domi said, squinting at the two of them.

"Yeah, but...maybe it's not *that* advanced yet. Maybe they're still getting there, and they just hit upon the skill to allow them to keep moving no matter how hurt they are along the way," Zeke suggested. *Like that Mobile skill I got from the Pill Apocalypse. The advanced form of that.*

Domi pressed her lips together. "Well, shit."

"And they have a gun," Zeke muttered.

Domi pointed at the two of them. In a fiery blast, the gun exploded in Rob's hands.

"Okay, never mind," Zeke said, nodding to himself.

"We have to completely destroy their bodies," Domi said, stepping out from behind the bins.

"Yep," Zeke said. Despite himself, his mouth watered. *I hate it, but Devour is a good way to completely destroy something.*

Domi cracked her knuckles. "I take Tom, you take Rob?"

"But there's so much more of Rob to eat," Zeke complained.

Domi stared at him.

"What?" Zeke asked.

"Nothing, I'm just wondering how the hell I ended up stuck in an apocalypse with the world's weirdest cannibal," Domi said.

"Hey. I'm not a cannibal," Zeke protested.

Domi cocked an eyebrow.

Zeke cleared his throat. "I'm not *only* a cannibal. I eat lots of weird things."

"A cannibal with a nasty case of pica," Domi corrected herself.

Zeke put his hands up. "I guess?" *It's not my fault my Concept is weird! I didn't pick it! My stomach just happened to grumble at the wrong moment!*

Rob and Tom charged, dripping blood as they ran. Domi stepped forward. "Here they come!"

# 32
## EATING MEN IN BACK ALLEYS

Zeke ran sideways, away from Domi. As he did, he sent a blast of steam at Rob. In his mind, he shaped the steam into a tight ray, blasting it at the man's head. *Pressurized steam—like that! But my skill isn't high enough, it won't—*

A tight cone of steam shot at Rob's head, nearly as he'd envisioned it. Zeke stared at his hand. *Dang. Manipulate Aerosols is much more powerful than either Wind Manipulation or Manipulate Steam was. I wonder if it's because I can manipulate both the wind and the steam with one skill?*

*Combo skills are the best! Time to merge all the skills!*

*Though...I don't want to lose skills, so I have to be careful. I don't know how high that failure chance is yet.*

Rob turned, jolting after Zeke. Zeke turned and fled, leading him away across the alley and away from Domi. "Yeah, yeah! Come this way! I don't want to get exploded!"

"Hey, come on. It's not that bad," Domi muttered.

Rob lurched sideways at Zeke. Zeke ducked, pointing his head at the man. "Allen, go!"

Allen leaped off his head and slammed into Rob's head. His head snapped back cartoonishly, yoyoing behind him as his neck extended. Blood splattered everywhere.

Zeke grimaced. *Gross.*

He darted in. Before Rob's neck could return to normal, he grabbed the man's head and aimed his mouth at the extended neck.

### [Devour]

His jaws severed the last strand of flesh between Rob's neck and his head. Without a head, his body staggered a few steps, then flopped limply to the floor.

Behind him, something *boom*ed. Spaghetti sauce splattered all over the walls. *Or anyway, that's what I'm going to pretend that is,* Zeke thought, breathing through his mouth. He offered Allen his hand.

Allen darted over to him. The anole jumped. His front claws caught Zeke's fingertips, and he scrambled up Zeke's hand, then scurried up his arm, hauled his way up over Zeke's ear, and settled onto his head.

"You're leaving him like that?" Domi asked, giving Rob's corpse an uncertain look.

Zeke glanced toward her, at the red lump of piled clothes. "I'm using cartoon logic. Cartoons don't get back up once their head has been fully removed."

"Your funeral," Domi said, shrugging. She turned and walked away.

Giving Rob's body one last look, Zeke hefted his bag and hurried after Domi.

"My apartment is right up here, just past the elementary school," Domi said, pointing.

Generic apartments loomed ahead, with the white stucco walls and one-size-fits-all black balconies of apartments constructed in the 1980s. A little around the corner, modern apartments with strangely painted color panels and odd textures screamed out for attention. Across the way, the elementary school lurked in a two-story building even older than the apartments, complete with peeling paint and old wood-framed glass windows without bug nets.

Zeke gazed at the elementary school. He bit his lip. *Mia... should I leave her with Ryan? Maybe I should just go in there. Take her out of there, get her away from him. He hasn't hurt her yet, but it doesn't mean he won't.*

*Still, she's been taking care of him. She doesn't want to abandon him. Even if I came and offered to take her to safety, would she come? Especially if Ryan isn't attacking her...there's no way, right?*

He shook his head. *I'm not going to abandon her, though. I'll check in tomorrow. Maybe, if I find a phone somewhere, I can call her and let her know I'm okay, see if she's doing fine.*

"Hey. You coming?" Domi asked, glancing over her shoulder from the apartment door.

"Coming, coming," Zeke said, hurrying over to her.

The door beeped. Domi yanked it open, pulling with her whole bodyweight.

A chair swung at Domi. Zeke's eyes widened. He darted over. The world blurred, his body moving faster than humanly possible.

### [Caffeine Rush]

He caught the chair leg mid-swing. The momentum of the swing nearly bowled him over. He staggered to the side, into Domi, who shrieked.

Big cartoon eyes beamed at them. The woman winked, drawing the chair back to swing again.

Zeke tightened his grip on the chair leg. The woman yanked. He held on, refusing to let her take it out of his grip.

Domi lifted her hand and snapped, pointing her fingers at the woman.

A narrow burst of explosive power flew at the woman's head. Her head snapped back. Stunned, she released the chair.

Grabbing Domi and the chair, Zeke jumped back from the door. It swung shut.

Both of them stared at the apartment, Zeke panting, Domi wide-eyed.

Domi licked her lips. "Well."

"Well," Zeke returned.

"We can fight our way through an unknown number of cartoon zombies, or go crash in the pharmacy," she suggested.

Zeke nodded, then froze. He whipped around, staring at the elementary school.

"What?" Domi asked.

"Mia's in there. *Mia*," Zeke emphasized.

"Who...?" Domi asked.

"You met her, she's...she's my friend. She went to the elementary school for safety. But the cartoon apocalypse is in your apartment. Doesn't that mean..." He stared at the elementary school.

Through the front office's broad windows, a man paced back and forth, his face mashed up against the glass. Even from here, his big cartoon eyes and vapid expression blared through the window.

Domi bit her lip. She glanced at Zeke. "She's in there?"

Zeke nodded.

"Isn't she probably... I mean...every normal person we've met so far is..." Domi shook her head.

Zeke took a deep breath. "If she's...one of them, then...I want to be the one to do it."

"Those things are a pain in the ass to kill. You can't be serious. We should just get the hell away from here," Domi said.

"Only one can leave," Zeke said.

"What?"

"Only one can leave. When you chose your Concept, didn't you see that message, too? If we let this apocalypse go, it'll just get stronger and stronger. We have to face it now, before it gets too big," Zeke argued.

Domi scowled. She glanced at the apartment, then looked at the school. Apartment, school, apartment, school—

Zeke headed toward the elementary school, slinging his bags off his shoulder. He set his loot down in a bush, then walked around to face the door. He rolled out his shoulders and cracked his neck. *Here we go.*

"Fine! Fine. I'm coming," Domi decided. She tossed her bags in the bush opposite Zeke's and stepped up beside him.

"You sure?" Zeke said.

"Look, you make a good point," she said. She stared at the door. "If we don't kill it now, we'll have to kill it later."

Something thumped against the far side. The door jumped in its frame.

Domi raised her hands, held just far apart for a clap. Zeke quickly checked his status.

**Level:** 17.35

**STR:** 1

**CON:** 10

**DEX:** 2

**SPR:** 5

**Regen:** + 3.6

**Condition:** [Caffeine High]

*Regen went up? Oh, from skill fusion, I bet. Nice! And Caffeine High is still active.*

*No time like the present!*

He pressed his hands on the front door and pushed.

# 33
## SCHOOL'S OUT

The children rushed at Ryan and Mia from the end of the hall, screaming and yelping. One leaped up and bounced off the walls and ceiling, transformed momentarily into a bouncy ball, but none of them moved any faster than the mob. At a surprisingly slow pace, the mob of children hurtled at top speed toward Ryan and Mia, simultaneously fast and slow, all moving as one churning mass.

Ryan raised his daggers. "Fucking Cartoon Apocalypse. Playing mind games already? It's progressing faster than usual. Something's up."

Mia grabbed his arm, forcing it down. "You can't! They're just kids!"

"They're no better than zombies, Mia. There's nothing human left inside them!" Ryan snapped. He twisted free of Mia's grip.

Mia's lip trembled. She looked at the children, at their twisted, cartoonish expressions. *What if? What if it is possible for them to turn back? Ryan says it isn't. But...Ryan also says he's from the future, so...* She set her jaw and glared at Ryan. "We can restrain them. Juke them into a classroom and lock them there. We don't need to hurt them."

"Good luck with that," Ryan muttered under his breath.

"They're just kids. They aren't that hard to push around," Mia returned. She spread her arms and stood in front of them, blocking Ryan's way. "I won't let you hurt them."

"Mia, for fuck's sake!" Ryan turned, only half-hiding his enormous eye roll. "They're already dead. They aren't kids, or anything, they're just part of an apocalypse! They're monsters who look like kids!"

Mia stared him in the eye. "No."

Ryan threw his hands in the air. "We'll give it a try. But when they start beating you to death, don't blame me."

Beaming, Mia nodded. She pointed to a classroom behind them and a little to the left. "I'll bait them toward the door. You make sure to herd them after me."

"And the teacher?" Ryan asked.

"Him, too. Mr. Shane doesn't deserve to die," Mia said firmly.

"When this all goes horribly sideways, remember it was your idea," Ryan grumbled. He stepped back.

"When it all goes well, remember it was my idea," Mia returned. She turned around to face the children once more. "Besides, if it goes sideways, we can always revert to... to fighting them. We might as well try to keep them alive first."

"Whatever. You've already won," Ryan muttered. He reached to his hip, and the daggers vanished. Bare-handed, he faced the children.

The mass rushed them, their legs blurred together into one cloud-like mess. Behind them, Mr. Shane pointed and shouted something garbled, something that almost sounded like a language without having quite the right cadence.

Mia backed toward the room. *If they're the Cartoon Apoca-*

*lypse, then...what would I do in a cartoon, if I was trying to bait someone?* She thought for a moment, then waved her hands over her head. "Hey! Over here! Uh, uhm, free cookies in this room!"

"That's it? That's your gambit?" Ryan asked skeptically.

"It's a Cartoon Apocalypse. We have to think like a cartoon!" Mia insisted.

The Cartoon Apocalypse froze in place. The children looked at one another, their strange faces lighting up with excitement. They dashed toward the room.

Behind them, Mr. Shane continued on the original path, only to find himself alone. He looked around comically, then ran after the others, his other half leaning back behind his hips as if his legs were dragging him forward.

Mia winced. *He's going to feel that when this apocalypse is over.*

The children ran past her, rushing into the dark room without pause. Mia gestured them in. "Come on, come on in! Delicious cookies inside!"

Ryan pressed his lips together. "You aren't serious. This can't work."

"It's working, though," Mia said, shrugging.

Mr. Shane paused at the door. He crossed his arms and tapped his toe skeptically, making a big show of looking into the room.

Before he finished, Ryan ran up behind him and kicked him in the rear. Mr. Shane stumbled forward.

Mia reached around the door, clicked the lock, and slammed the door shut. She looked around, then pointed. Across from the front door, a fancy wooden table held pamphlets about the school. "That table, the big heavy wooden one. Ryan, hurry. Let's barricade them in!"

"The doors open inward," Ryan pointed out.

"But still...it'll buy us time. Like what Zeke did with the

Coffee Apocalypse, there must be something. A central point. Something we can destroy that ends this!" Mia insisted.

"There is, but..." Ryan pursed his lips. "You won't like it."

The door jerked in her grasp. Mia grabbed onto the handle with both hands and dug her heels in, leaning away from the door. "Ryan!"

"All right, all right, I'm coming! It's heavy!" He got behind the table and pushed. Slowly, it slid toward Mia.

The door jumped open again. Mr. Shane stared at her, pressing his distorted cartoon face into the gap. Lifting one hand off the door, Mia punched him in the nose and yanked the door shut again. "Ryan, hurry!"

"Almost..." Ryan slid the table in front of her, blocking off the immediate path.

"All right, now..." Mia glanced around. "If we can find some rope, or an electrical cord..."

Ryan vanished.

"Eh...?" Mia looked around. "Ryan...?"

"I found this in the gym." Ryan stepped out from the opposite side of her, holding up a long, thick blue rope. He wound it around the door's handle, then twisted it around the table, knotting it tight.

Mia released the handle. The door thumped open, but then the rope went taut, and it froze, barely more than a quarter-inch open. The table creaked but held strong.

Breathing out, Mia pushed her hair back. "Now, we need to find the center of this apocalypse. The...uh, the..."

"The core," Ryan said.

Overhead, the PA system crackled. A whiny, childish voice cried out, "They're still here! Kill them!"

Both of them looked up. Mia looked at Ryan, and Ryan looked at Mia.

"It couldn't be that easy," Mia said.

Ryan shrugged. "You heard that voice. The apocalypse's core is a kid. Kids aren't exactly known for their advanced stratagems."

*A child. Again.* Mia took a deep breath, then shook her head. *If it saves everyone else, then…*

*Then…aren't I no better than Ryan, kicking Zeke off a balcony because it* might *help?*

Ryan glanced at the door. "Come on. Let's get moving before this apocalypse mutates again, and they figure out they can get out of there."

"They can get out?" Mia asked.

Ryan nodded, leading the way down the hallway. "After a certain point, they can turn paper-thin and escape from almost anything. This apocalypse is one of the most annoying ones to handle if it doesn't get stopped quickly."

*Right…yeah. That is a classic cartoon technique!* Mia started off down the hallway.

Heavy footsteps echoed behind them, matched by heavy breathing. A sharp whistle blew. Both Ryan and Mia looked over their shoulders.

The gym teacher charged at them, bulging with muscle, eyes vivid red, his teeth bared. Cartoonish clouds of dust burst up behind them. At the sight of them, he growled and sped up.

Mia yelped. She ran, but even with her top striker speed, the gym teacher still gained on her. Meaty hands extended over her head, casting a cartoonish shadow over her body. Pivoting with all her might, she ran out from under them.

The hand slammed down, fracturing the tile floor and the concrete slab beneath. A shiver ran down Mia's spine. *If that touched me, I'd die!*

Suddenly beside her, Ryan grabbed Mia. "Hold your breath."

"Wha—"

# 34
## A LITTLE TOO LATE

The doors flew open. A wall of muscle and force slammed into Zeke, throwing him back. Beside him, Domi yelped, bowled backward alongside him. The two of them rolled down the school's stairs and sprawled over the sidewalk.

A stereotypical gym teacher loomed in the door, so large he filled the doorframe entirely. His white T-shirt barely fit over huge muscles. Red shorts barely contained enormous thighs. A buzz-cut head with a massive forehead glistened in the sun. He raised a whistle to his mouth.

Zeke recovered first. Still lying on the ground, he pointed a finger at the gym teacher's head. *Go for the eyes! No matter how muscular you are, your eyes are weak and squishy!*

**[Manipulate Aerosols]**

A blast of pressurized steam shot into the gym teacher's eyes. Dropping the whistle, he covered his eyes, inadvertently blinding himself.

Domi rolled upright. Blood ran down her forehead, and her

eyes struggled to focus, but she managed to clap anyway. Fiery force leaped from her palms and smashed into the gym teacher. He fell backward, thumping onto the school's tiled floor.

Zeke jumped up from the ground. He sprinted toward the downed gym teacher. The gym teacher half-sat up on the floor, but Zeke leaped onto him, slamming his whole weight onto the man's shoulders and pinning him back onto the ground. He pressed his palm into the man's eyes.

### [Crystal Burst]

Crystals thrust through the tile floor and pierced through the back of the man's head. Squishing and squelching, the man's eyes distorted, then bulged out. Pinkish crystals pierced through them, streaked with gray and white fluids.

Zeke swallowed, resisting the urge to puke. *Gross.*

*I meant to have the crystals burst from my hand, though. I wonder if that skill can only make crystals grow from the ground?*

Despite the crystals shining in his eye sockets, the gym teacher struggled against Zeke's hold. He started to sit up.

Annoyed, Zeke grabbed the man's chin and darted his jaws in. *I didn't want to eat you, but you leave me with no choice!*

### [Devour]

He scraped the man's throat but didn't break through his spine. Holding on, Zeke leaned in, blood soaking his lips and cheeks, and used his skill again.

### [Devour]

This time, his teeth scraped up against the man's spine. *Damn. How thick is this guy's neck?* Pressing even deeper into the muscular recess he'd carved out, he activated the skill once more.

## [Devour]!

This time, his jaws snapped the man's spine. The gym teacher's head lolled off his shoulders, leaving a smear of crimson as it rolled over the tile floor. Even as he died, he stuck his tongue out comically, like an old-fashioned cartoon.

**You've learned [Strong Jaw] (Minor) thanks to your resolve in chewing tough materials! Jaw strength +1!**

Zeke pulled his head back. Blood stained his cheeks to his jaw and dribbled down his chin. Bloodstains crested his nose and smeared almost all the way to his eyes. He lifted his shirt and wiped his face. *Ugh. Gross.*

*At least I learned I can earn skills by doing. I wonder how else I can gain skills? Doing, devouring... Hmm. System?*

**You can also purchase skills.**
**Purchase List:** [EMPTY]
**WARNING:** Due to your unique ability to absorb skills, your Purchase List has been emptied for balance.

*Oh, come on,* Zeke thought. He shook his head at the System and scowled.

Domi eyed him. "Why the long face? You uh, you still hungry? Plenty of gym teacher left."

"Oh, shut it," Zeke muttered, half-laughing at the absurdity of it all. *All right, all right. Come on, System. I downed him. Where are my rewards?*

### Member of the Cartoon Apocalypse
### Level + .5
### Level: 17.85

### Please pick a skill
### Skills

### Whistle Blast (Weak)
*Create a loud sound to distract your enemies. Small chance of inflicting Stun (Condition)*

### Steroids (Condition)
*Your muscles get big, but your brain gets small. +5 STR -10 SPR*

### Can't
### Can't

### Bowl Over (Minor)
*When you crash into an opponent, inflict greater damage and knockback than usual.*

Zeke pressed his lips together. *Given my 1 STR 5 SPR build, I don't think I should go for Steroids. Whistle Blast... hmm. Inflicting Stun sounds powerful. Bowl Over sounds useful, but on the other hand, it requires me to crash into my enemies. I haven't really been able to crash into any apocalypses I've met. The crystal ball was so much bigger I'd be the loser there, the wax body would just engulf me, the espresso machine wouldn't care at all... Yeah, I think Whistle Blast is the winner, here. Plus, it inflicts a Condition. I don't have any skills that inflict Conditions on other people yet.*

### Skills
### Manipulate Aerosols (Medium) +1

**Pick Up (Weak)**
**Osmosis (Weak) +1**
**Subordinate Link (Weak)**
**Create Drug (Weak) +1**
**Crystal Burst (Poor)**
**Engulf (Poor)**
**Create Coffee (Strong)**
**Whistle Blast (Weak)**
**Passive**
**Resilient Regeneration (Minor) +8**
**Team Spirit (Minor) +1**
**Disguise (Minor)**
**Watertight (Minor)**
**Follow Me (Minor)**
**Caffeine Rush (Average)**
**Growth (Lesser) +2**
**Heat Resistance (Lesser) +9**
**Strong Jaw (Minor)**
**Condition**
**Hardness (Lesser) (Condition)**

"You done over there?" Domi asked. She propped herself up on her arm and rubbed her forehead. After a moment, she sighed and climbed to her feet. "Time to press on."

"You sure? You seem kind of..." Zeke gestured at his head.

"I can keep moving. If we stop here, the Cartoon Apocalypse just keeps getting worse, right? You're the one who said that," Domi said.

"Still, you don't want to push yourself if you have a concussion," Zeke returned.

Domi raised her brows. Even with one pupil larger than the other, she still managed to give him a sarcastic look. "Why not? If we kill the apocalypse, that 300% regeneration kicks in. Compared to that, what's a little concussion?"

Zeke opened his mouth, then shut it. *That's fair. I was a mess a few hours ago, and I'm walking around now.*

*Plus, Mia's in there. I don't want to leave without her.*

He offered Domi a hand up. She hauled herself to her feet. Ever so slightly, she swayed in place. Throwing her arms out, she caught herself, then grinned at Zeke and gave him a thumbs up. "I'm okay."

"Are you sure?" Zeke muttered, half to himself. *I'm not going to stop her, though. If she's hurt that bad, then not taking down an apocalypse is basically a death sentence.*

A voice crackled over the intercom, echoing through the open door. Childish and high-pitched, it demanded in a bratty tone, "What's taking so long? Kill them already!"

Zeke frowned. "Is a kid the core of this apocalypse?"

"I don't think the incubator cares. I mean, it picked Ancient Fish and Weird Melty Statue, or whatever you were fighting when I met you. That doesn't speak to high standards," Domi said, shrugging.

Zeke pressed his lips together. He stared into the air-conditioned depths. *I don't want to eat a kid.*

Almost immediately, another part of him pointed out, *but children usually taste really good, right? Suckling pig, veal, chicken nuggets...*

He slapped himself on the cheek. "Don't get sucked into your Concept, idiot."

"Huh? Are you going to start drooling all over yourself again? Do I need to grab some potato chips from the bag or something?" Domi asked, half-teasing.

Zeke shook his head. "I'm fine." *And the whole damn school is an elementary school? Fuck. Can't rely on Devour in here or else I'll get a reputation for child-eating. There's not much worse than being known as a child-eater. Baby-eating, I guess.*

*At least you generally don't run into many babies in the apocalypse.*

Taking a deep breath, he stepped over the gym teacher's body and stepped into the school. Cool A/C blasted him. He closed his eyes, relishing the sensation.

And tipped forward, his foot finding no support whatsoever. Zeke's eyes shot open in time to see the tile floor ripple, falling away in a piece of fabric to reveal a perfectly round hole beneath. Darkness stretched below him, as far as the eye could see.

*Fuck. Not again. Four stories is bad enough,* Zeke thought.

On the far side of the hole, a slender, tall child with a cartoonish face and what looked to be rat ears poking out of their hair raised a hand to their cartoonish mouth and snickered at him, teeth bared in a crescent moon of a smile.

# 35
## GETTING OVER IT

"Zeke!" Domi shouted. She lunged for him, only to slew sideways on her way there. She fell against the middle support of the doors.

Zeke plunged into the hole. His stomach lurched, and his leg ached. *I'm not falling, damn it.*

### [Manipulate Aerosols]

Steam burst out of his hands. It slowed his fall a miniscule amount, but not enough to stop him.

*Okay, that's not working.* With the last of his foothold, Zeke jumped. *Instead, let's go for the other side!* He reached for the opposite side of the hole.

The rat-eared child scurried back. With a *whooooooop* sound effect, the hole grew larger. Its edge receded away from Zeke.

*Motherfucking cartoons!*

A few feet below the edge, Zeke finally struck the opposite wall. Hopelessly, he clawed at it. *Something, anything!*

## Your subordinate [Anole Apocalypse] would like to share a skill. Y/N?

"Yes!" Zeke shouted. *Whatever it is, I'll take it!*

## [Lizard Climb] (Poor) (Temp) granted!

His hands suddenly grew sticky. He pressed them against the wall, spreading out his palms so as much of his hands as possible contacted the somehow perfectly smooth dirt surface. His drop slowed, then stopped. Zeke let out a sigh. *Thank goodness.*

A shadow fell over him. Zeke stared up.

Giggling down at him, the rat-child slung the cloth over the hole. As he did, the hole closed around Zeke. Dirt walls pressed in on him. In seconds, he went from dangling in a deep, ten-foot-wide hole to clinging to a narrow well.

"Fuck!" Zeke shouted aloud. His shoes slipped over the well's wall. Grimacing, he kicked them off and stuck his toes against the wall. They stuck. Zeke dug his hands and feet into the wall and scurried up at top speed.

The hole closed in on him. Dirt pressed against his back and rear. He put a hand on the opposite wall in desperation. *Stop!*

To his surprise, the wall stopped.

*Huh?*

*Wait, wait, cartoon logic. I can hold it off from completely closing for a few seconds like this! But...going off those tropes, I'll get squished in the end.*

"Back off!" Domi shouted.

A blast of fire threw the rat-child back. The fluttering fabric went with it. For a moment, the dirt closed in around Zeke, but then the cloth flew away. The hole opened again.

Zeke skittered up to the top of the hole and hauled himself

back up onto the tile floor. Lying on his back, he let out a deep sigh.

"Zeke, watch out!"

Zeke peered up from where he laid and locked eyes with the rat-child.

In the middle of drawing a circle around Zeke with a crayon, the rat-child froze. They put a hand over their crescent-moon smile and giggled again.

Scrambling to his feet, Zeke jumped out of the half-drawn circle. The rat-child chased after him, following him down the hall with the crayon.

"Domi! Come on!" Zeke called back over his shoulder.

Caught behind the gym teacher and the hole, Domi gestured wildly.

"The other door!" Zeke shouted, pointing at the opposite side of the school's aluminum double doors.

Domi stepped back around the gym teacher and opened the front door that didn't open to a gaping pit. She nodded, slowly, a hand on her head. Putting her other hand on the wall as a guide, she chased after Zeke, who was chased by the rat-child.

From out of nowhere, an upbeat, jokey tune started playing.

Zeke rolled his eyes. *Really?*

"You know what? Fuck this apocalypse. There's no way I'm letting the world get destroyed by this piece of shit," Domi muttered.

"It would be the most undignified way to go," Zeke agreed. "Like, there's at least something classic about zombies, even if they're overdone all to hell. There's a certain solemnity about getting your neck chewed off."

"Says the guy chewing necks," Domi interjected.

"Still not dead, still not a zombie. Anyway, the point is... there's nothing dignified about dying to..." he glanced over his shoulder.

The cartoonish rat-child tilted his head back at Zeke, then covered his mouth and snickered. Bending, he went back to dragging his crayon along the floor. Before Zeke's eyes, the boy's hair turned more gray, fine, and fur-like. The fur crawled down the boy's body. A small tail sprouted from his rear.

A television in one of the classrooms buzzed on. A cartoon boy pointed and laughed at them. "Idiots! Foolish fools! Do you think I'm that foolish? I won't be done in so easily!"

Zeke twisted his lips, glancing between the rat-boy and the television. *The apocalypse is progressing. We have to destroy it soon.*

"I mean, there is a certain...inevitability about it? You know, drawing the circle, being near-immortal...you could work yourself into an existential dread, if you tried," Domi said, shrugging.

"Mmm...I dunno. It might be the worst apocalypse," Zeke mused.

Domi raised her finger. "Nope. Clowns."

"Fuck," Zeke muttered. *It might be a bit overdone, but fuck, I really don't want to die to clowns. It's just so damn stupid. Sure, they're scarier than cartoons, but who wants to have 'Murdered by a Clown" on their headstone? At least "Killed by Cartoons" has some kind of story to it. No one's going to be surprised by "Murdered by a Clown," and it's so, so stupid.*

"I hope there isn't a clownpocalypse," Domi commented dryly.

"Concepts can be anything that exists in the world. It's possible...but who would pick clowns as their Concept?" Zeke wondered.

"A clown," Domi said.

Zeke clicked his tongue. *Her logic is flawless, so why do I hate it?*

The rat-child continued to putter along. Their crayon grew shorter and shorter. The line grew longer and longer.

"Hey, are you tired yet? I don't think you're going to close us in that circle of yours," Zeke commented.

The rat-child giggled at him, then kept going.

"I don't think he has the brainpower to realize that," Domi replied.

Zeke pressed his lips together. *This is what apocalypses do to ordinary people. Brainwash them, alter their bodies, turn them into mindless drones. Is this what having a Domain does?*

**Yes. You gain the ability to shape the world around you, including other humans.**

*Forget it, then. I'm not having a Domain. Never.*

**You are not yet able to choose.**

"I'm not changing my mind," he muttered aloud.

"What?" Domi asked, blinking.

Zeke shook his head. He gestured Domi on. "Let's keep going. Mia's in here somewhere, and I'm not leaving without her."

"What about the apocalypse?" Domi asked, a little whiny.

Zeke pointed up. "He spoke over the intercom, right? Let's find the media room."

Grinning, Domi saluted sloppily. "Roger, Captain."

# 36
## PA ROOM

**A few minutes ago**

The world jumped. One second, Ryan and Mia stood in the entrance. The next, they stood around the corner and halfway down the next hallway, next to a pair of doors, one of which announced 'Mrs. Acher's Room' in reds and greens, the other of which screamed 'WELCOME TO THE WATER CYCLE' in shades of blue.

Mia's chest pulled tight, her body completely out of air. She gasped, pushing away from Ryan to stand on her own. "What... what..."

"Just a momentary time skip. Do you believe me now?" Ryan asked.

"You have superpowers?" Mia asked, looking Ryan up and down.

"More like magic," Ryan explained, shaking his head.

In the distance, the gym teacher roared in frustration. Tiles cracked and smashed, and drywall crunched under his fists.

Ryan glanced over his shoulder, then ran a hand over the back of his neck. He shivered.

"What is it now?" Mia asked.

"One of my skills activated," Ryan murmured. He turned again, walking half-backward.

The front door creaked open. The sounds of the gym teacher faded.

"A skill? This really is a video game, huh?" Mia asked.

Shrugging, Ryan turned away, ignoring her.

Refusing to be ignored, Mia leaned into his vision. "So, this skill of yours. What's it sense, danger?"

Ryan twisted his lips. He looked away again, shoving her head out of his way. "Sure."

*Hmm. He's acting pretty weird about it.* "Does it sense Zeke?" Mia tried, raising an eyebrow.

Ryan pressed his lips together and said nothing.

Mia smirked. *Ooh, I've got him.* "It does, doesn't it? What's the skill called, Stalker?"

Ryan flinched.

Mia snorted. "No way."

"Shut up," Ryan grumbled.

She peered over her shoulder, looking back down the hall-way. Not far behind them, a corner cut off her line of sight, nothing but brutal white cinderblock as far as the eye could see, broken only by the occasional teacher-built art project display. *Zeke's here. I need to tell him what Ryan's told me. Maybe he'll make more sense of it than I can, but, either way, he deserves to know.*

Ahead of them, something rumbled. Ryan stepped ahead of Mia, putting his arm out. "Wait."

"What?" Mia asked.

*Bump. Thud!* Wood clattered off cinderblock. A bright red barrel bumped around the corner, a skull and crossbones emblazoned in white on its side.

Black and white burst in front of Mia's eyes. The world

decayed into static. She knelt and put her hands over her head. *Not now!*

Ryan grabbed her again. This time, she held her breath.

They stood at the far end of the hallway. The barrel bounced away behind them. It smacked against the wall and exploded in a big, fiery ball that instantly imploded in on itself with a fizzle. A pathetic curl of smoke wafted upward.

Mia chuckled. "Okay, that was kind of funny."

"Funny? No way," Ryan grumbled. He took off running.

Mia chased after him. "What is it now?"

"AV room's just up ahead," Ryan said.

"AV... Oh, Audiovisual?" Mia guessed.

The intercom crackled again. In all the classrooms, screens cut on. A cartoon boy, maybe seven, laughed on the screen, pointing at them. Tears crawled out from the corners of his eyes. "Idiots! Foolish fools! Do you think I'm that foolish? I won't be done in so easily!"

Mia glanced over. "Is he...taunting you?"

"He'd better not be," Ryan muttered.

"Shouldn't you know? If you've done a hundred loops or whatever," Mia returned.

Ryan scowled. "Do you have any idea how complex time is? You make one little change, and suddenly everything's fucked. I didn't even fight the Cartoon Apocalypse in most of my runs."

"Didn't you say this was the epicenter, though? Of...something?" Mia asked.

Nodding, Ryan waved his hand. "Oh, sure. I mean, I watched Zeke destroy this school from across the dome more times than I can count. Figured I'd chalk it up as a loss rather than risk my life so early in the run. It's a bad place to be. I made a point of not being here, most runs."

Mia frowned. "If time is as complicated as you say, and a

little change can wreck everything, then why did Zeke always destroy this place so early? Shouldn't that have changed, too?"

"If it wasn't Zeke, it was someone else. Concepts like "cartoons" are far too dangerous. Almost unlimited power that defies physics? The ability to warp reality to one's liking? It would be one of the strongest apocalypses, except it's run by a kid. If not for splashing itself around and drawing attention too early, it could've become incredibly powerful. Top three, at least.

"But being so powerful, and stupidly telegraphing that power, comes with a downside. If Zeke didn't find this place and decide to destroy it, one of the other top contenders did. 'Too dangerous to survive' is a good way to sum it up."

Mia put a hand on her chin. "Did it ever survive? Win, I mean."

Ryan opened his mouth, then shrugged. "I didn't survive long in the timeline...timelines where it didn't get destroyed early." He laughed. "If it makes a go of it now, I almost wouldn't mind. I really fucked this one up by failing to kill Zeke out the gate."

"Seriously, Ryan..." Mia said, crossing her arms. *Zeke isn't dangerous. Even if he was before, it's different now.*

Drawing to a halt, Ryan tapped a plastic panel on the wall. White letters spelled out AUDIOVISUAL ROOM. "Here we are."

Mia took a deep breath. Adjusting the bulletproof vest, she grabbed her Taser and nodded at Ryan.

"Stand back," Ryan advised.

She glanced at him, then nodded and backed away.

Ryan turned the handle. The lock clicked open, and he kicked the door, simultaneously jumping back.

Metal clanked on metal. Mia looked up to find a pail of water hovering in the gap between the door and the frame. It trembled there for a second, defying gravity for no visible reason, then upended itself and plunged, splashing water all over the opening door.

Inside the room, the human version of the cartoon boy they'd seen on the television earlier yelped and jumped up from the audiovisual room's crummy old microphone. Panicked, he jumped onto the table and curled up defensively. "Get back! Don't hurt me!"

"We aren't going to hurt you," Mia said gently. Putting the Taser down, she stepped into the room.

"Mia! Floor!" Ryan shouted.

Mia looked down. A huge mousetrap laid under her foot, somehow the exact color and texture of the tiles. Her foot dropped toward the trigger in slow motion. Her stomach clenched, and her whole body tensed as she struggled not to step down.

Static. The world smeared away.

*Not now!*

In the midst of the static, only the boy remained fully visible. His body glowed a little at the edges, like an animation cel in a hand-drawn animated movie. Before her eyes, his panic melted into a smirk. "Gotcha."

Weight slammed into Mia's shoulder. She thumped against the doorframe, and she stepped beside the mousetrap, outside of its trigger.

The static vanished. Mia took a deep breath and grabbed for the Taser.

Ryan jumped away from Mia. He vanished.

Across the room, the boy scrambled over the desk, half-running, half-crawling for the flickering old monitor in the corner.

Ryan reappeared beside the boy, dagger in hand. He slashed at the boy's back.

"Ryan!" Mia shouted. *Even if he attacked me, even if he's a brat, killing him is—*

The boy's back *schwoop*ed away from Ryan's dagger, distorting with that distinctive sound effect. It snapped back with a rubber-band *bwoing!* and a back-and-forth tremble like a plucked guitar string.

Kicking off the desk, the boy dove toward the screen in full hop-dive cartoon form. The screen bent inward like a trampoline, then snapped back out, and as it snapped back, the boy passed through it. From within the screen, he pointed at them and laughed.

"Mother*fucker*," Ryan snarled. He punched the screen. Cracks burst across its surface.

Inside, his body distorted slightly by the cracks, the boy put on a mock-shocked face, then fell onto his back, rolling around on the ground and laughing even harder.

Ryan yanked the TV's cord, then turned to Mia. "We need to smash all the screens. He can hide in any of them. If there's only one screen left, he has no option but to—"

"Bad news," a familiar voice said.

Mia instantly put her arms out, blocking the route to the door.

Ryan whirled. "Zeke!"

Supporting an early-twenties woman on one shoulder, Zeke nodded grimly at the two of them. He pointed behind him. "The Cartoon Apocalypse has already spread to the apartment across the way."

"Fuck!" Ryan snapped.

Mia's eyes widened. *Apartments? Each apartment will have at least one television, if not two or three. Apartments lock, and there's probably lots of residents hunkering down inside, gun pointed at the door...if not more of these 'apocalypses.' And that's even assuming we make it past all the cartoon monstrosities in the school to smash all the school's screens.*

Zeke nodded at Mia. He gave her a small, reassuring smile. "I have a plan. But...I'll need your help. Everyone's help."

The woman pulled herself upright. She wobbled in place, struggling to make eye contact with Mia and Ryan. With a wave, she smiled. "Hey, I'm Domi. Uh...truce?"

# 37
## DRAWING FIRE

"He found Domi...damn," Ryan muttered.

"Have we met?" Domi asked, squinting.

Zeke's eyes widened. *How does Ryan know Domi? Unless my suspicions are correct, and he's from the future.*

*Unless he wandered off at some point and saw her somewhere in the museum. She is a museum guide.*

*Though, if that's the case, why's he angry at her already?*

Mia glared at Ryan. "Truce. I'll take a truce."

Ryan narrowed his eyes. "What's your plan?"

Zeke took a deep breath. *I'd rather not have to deal with Ryan and everything else, but this plan really depends on everyone working together.* Eyeing Ryan warily, he nodded behind him. "Kill the screen."

Ryan turned.

The cartoon boy leaned toward the screen, one hand to a comically large ear.

"Yeah, yeah. Good call." Ryan pulled the plug.

Eyes flying wide, the boy leaped for the screen, only to wink out as the screen went dark.

Zeke nodded at the dark screen. "This apocalypse is a pain in the ass but, ultimately, a child is in control. He's emotional. Easy to anger. Even faster to taunt us the second we appear weak."

"Zeke, watch out," Domi said, nudging him.

Zeke glanced over. A cartoon-faced boy covered in gray fur with little rat ears crouched past, dragging the remains of a crayon with him. He looped around Zeke and Domi, then headed back the other way.

Ryan squinted. He pointed. "How long has he been following you?"

"Since...the entrance?" Zeke said, shrugging. Leading Domi with him, he sidestepped over the crayon line.

The rat-boy made an over-the-top *oh no* sound. He ran back over to them, then gently led Zeke and Domi back inside the line.

Zeke sighed.

Domi waved her hand. "Wait until he's out of eyesight, then we can step out. Cartoons, remember? It's classic to carefully keep a victim inside a ridiculous trap as long as they can see us, anyway."

"Yeah, yeah," Zeke said.

Ryan clicked his tongue. "You know that's all going to turn into a hole when he closes the circle, right? You've cut off half the school."

"That's fine. We only need half. My point is—"

"He likes to taunt us?" Ryan asked.

Zeke nodded, then leaned his head left and right, not quite shaking his head. "Well...sort of. Again, he's a child. Emotionally simple. All we need to do is..." He leaned in.

The four drew close to the gym's metal double doors. They peered through the narrow windows.

On the far side, cartoons cavorted. Cat-people chased bird-people. Mouse-people scurried through holes in the walls. Cartoon children listened to a cartoon teacher in the corner. Very simply drawn, almost stick figure people giggled beside them, cutting their round eyes left and right. A stereotypical female gym teacher, much slenderer and shapelier than the male gym teacher they'd faced earlier, blew her whistle.

A dozen cartoonish children froze in the middle of playing a strange game of basketball, vibrating in place like a stun anima-tion. The basketball froze, too, mid-throw, and Zeke made out a grimacing face on its surface. Black stick arms hugged its round body to make the basketball's stripes, and orange legs and a torso curled up to form the meant of the ball.

*It's a kid, too? Is everything in here alive?*

Even as he thought it, the circular center marking of the gym yawned, blinking two eyes where the basketball markings looped over one another. The basketball backboards laughed, their nets shaking from their hoop mouths like strange beards. Overhead, the huge gym lights swayed where they hung, flick-ering in time as they chattered with one another.

Zeke took a deep breath. He nodded at Mia. "You were right. This is the stronghold."

"It's where Mr. Shane brought the kids to wait for their parents. Everyone from the school was here, it seemed. If the center was anywhere in the school...I figured it would be the place where everyone gathered," Mia said quietly.

Ryan nodded silently.

Zeke glanced at the other boy. *I trusted Mia's judgement, but when Ryan didn't counter her...he might be trying to hide it, but if he can see the future, then he wouldn't disagree if she guessed right. Him staying silent was the clincher for Mia's idea.*

Mia glanced at Ryan, then Zeke. She opened her mouth.

"I already told you. No," Ryan said, cutting her off before she could speak.

"What's the harm? We're working together," Mia reasoned.

"We're working together for now. Because the Cartoon Apocalypse is too big of a threat to go unchecked. But Zeke is also..." Ryan let his words fade, narrowing his eyes at Zeke.

Mia made eye contact with Zeke and rolled her eyes.

Zeke rolled his back. *Man, fuck you, too, Ryan.*

"Are you sure we can trust them?" Domi asked.

"I'm sure we can trust Mia," Zeke replied.

Ryan crossed his arms. "I want to take down the Cartoon Apocalypse as much as you do. I have no reason to sabotage you."

"I'll tase him if he tries!" Mia said, hefting the heavy-duty black plastic weapon.

Zeke smiled, reassured. "See? She'll tase him."

Domi snorted. "I trust her, anyway."

Ryan pursed his lips but didn't say anything.

Putting Ryan aside for a moment, Zeke nodded at Domi. "Ready?"

"As I'll ever be," Domi replied.

Zeke offered Domi his arm. She leaned against it. Pulling at her bun, she tousled it until it appeared completely disheveled. Flyaways burst off in every direction, while the bun itself sagged halfway down her neck.

*Eh, wait. Should I do this in front of Mia? What if she gets the wrong idea about me helping Domi?* Zeke shot a look at Mia.

Mia smiled and made an encouraging gesture.

*Right, right. Survival scenario. Down, hormones!* Zeke shoved the door open and strode into the gym.

Sneakers echoed loudly against the wood floor. One or two of the nearer cartoon people turned. Their eyes widened, and they leaned toward one another, whispering. The whispers spread, and so, too, did the stares, until the entire gym stared at Zeke and Domi.

Zeke stumbled on, walking with a heavy limp. Domi fell against him, barely able to prop herself up.

As they walked, the cartoons closed in around them, tightening up their circle and blocking their escape route. Zeke's heart hammered in his chest, and his breath came short. He took a deep breath, forcing himself to stay calm. *I have all kinds of Skills. If nothing else, we should be able to break away.*

Out of the corner of his eye, Zeke watched Ryan and Mia vanish from the windows of the doors behind them. His eyes flickered to the next set of gym doors. A few moments later, the two of them appeared in the windows.

A television mounted on the wall played school announcements in a loop. Spitting a hair from her mouth, Domi looked up at the screen. "You've done it. You win."

The announcements flickered. The screen went black, then flashed white. The cartoon boy reappeared. He stared at them, leaning into the screen so his face filled the television.

"We'll become your subordinates. We give up," Zeke said.

The boy's eyes widened. He leaned even closer, until his eye was all they could see.

Domi stumbled. She fell to her knees.

Zeke stopped. He helped her up. The both of them stared at the screen. Exhaustion dripped from their faces, from their drooping shoulders, from their tired backs.

"Please," Zeke begged. "Help us."

The screen trembled. Its surface began to bulge out.

Zeke held his breath. He exchanged a quick glance with Domi. She nodded back, steely determination suddenly shining in her previously defeated gaze. They both turned back to the screen, holding their breath as one.

*Come on out!*

# 38

## KNOCK-DOWN DRAG-OUT

The screen bulged out and out and out, then snapped back. The cartoon boy leaped down from the screen and landed in a three-point landing. Stylized dust clouds swirled up where he landed, though he'd landed on perfectly clean wood floor.

He stood, straightening his shirt and dusting it off, then nodded and gestured them closer.

Unlike most of the other cartoons, the boy's features were barely distorted. His face appeared cartoonish, but his arms and legs were the right length, and he wore ordinary clothes. If not for the faint glow to his body like an animation cel on a painted background, he could have passed for an ordinary human, at least as far as body dimensions. His entire body appeared drawn, his face cartoonish. Cel shading gripped his body, leaving him looking two-dimensional regardless of the angle.

Zeke and Domi staggered over, slowly. Again, Domi tripped.

The boy giggled.

Across the room, all the other cartoons giggled, guffawed, laughed, and chuckled. The basketball boy bounced in place, extending his horrifyingly twisted orange legs to jump on his own power.

Zeke leaned down, helping Domi up. She grabbed his arm and pulled him down. In the mist of the ruckus, she whispered, "Isn't that friend of yours supposed to come out?"

Glancing over his shoulder, Zeke shrugged. Leaning in, he whispered back, "I'll be honest, I never counted on him in the first place. That's why I suggested we take point. Even if we're on our own, we've got a much better chance now that the kid's out here in the real world than we did when he was in the television screens."

Domi snorted. "Fair enough."

*We can't leave this apocalypse alone. It's kind of dumb now, but if it smarts up, we're fucked. Neither me nor Domi can compare to this thing. I mean, Ryan stabbed it, and it shrugged it off without taking any damage. It can teleport between television screens—and how the hell are we supposed to kill it if it goes in there, change anyone into a reality-breaking cartoon person, and spread far further than the Coffee Apocalypse ever could. It's dangerous.*

*Putting all that aside, I honestly don't mind if Ryan decides to betray me here. After all, if he leaves, Mia stays safe. I don't want to put Mia in danger. Unlike Domi, she's just an ordinary person. She has no Skills to help her, no Concept to give her strength. Still, probably shouldn't mention that to Domi.*

They drew closer to the boy.

He looked down on them imperiously, tipping his head back so he could look down from his short stature. "You're willing to be my subordinates?"

Zeke exchanged a glance with Domi. She nodded.

He released her and stepped forward, raising his hands toward his face. "Please. We're just—"

Putting his fingers in his mouth, Zeke whistled.

### [Whistle Blast]
*Rolling Stun chance...*

All around them, cartoons froze in place, or jiggled where they stood, in the same stun animation Zeke had seen from outside the gym. The larger, more cartoonified ones lunged at him, unaffected.

The boy's face twisted into rage. "Liar! Kill him!"

Ryan appeared behind him, dagger raised. Without a word, he plunged it toward the kid's chest.

His dagger struck. The boy's body distorted under it, turning soft and malleable, and gave beneath the dagger.

Shocked but uninjured, the boy stared at Ryan, brows slowly furrowing. "Where did you come from?"

Cartoons closed in all around them. The basketball hurtled at Zeke's head. He dodged, only for it to stop in midair, then swing around and take another pass. Zeke snapped his hands up and caught it.

The ball struggled, its slender black-string arms and meaty orange legs kicking at him. "Let go! Let go!"

Ignoring it, Zeke darted his head in.

### [Devour]

Rubber. A blast of air. The orange ball-person deflated in his grip. It flailed wildly, then went limp.

### Defeated Member of the Cartoon Apocalypse
### Level + .2
**Level:** 17.85 > 18.05

### Please assign your stat point
### Please pick a skill

### Skills
### Bounce (Lesser)
*Your body is flexible and bouncy. Jump higher. Small percentage chance to deflect weak blows.*

### Rebound (Weak)
*Weakly change directions in midair and alter your course of flight. Does not grant flight.*

### Inflate (Minor)
*Increase the size of your body by filling it with air.*

From across the gym, the female gym teacher roared. Bright red energy burst off her body, and her muscles swelled. She charged at Zeke and Domi.

Zeke threw the basketball's remains at the gym teacher. They flopped uselessly to the floor. "Give me, uh, Bounce!" *Rebound sounds amazing, but I don't have the power of flight. Bounce, on the other hand, gives me a jump bonus and the ability to deflect blows! They're both fantastic, but for now, I think I'll focus on the lifesaver that I can use today rather than a great skill I might be able to use tomorrow.*

He stared down the gym teacher. *It's useless compared to her, but...I need more jaw strength. And that's obviously—* "Put my point in STR!"

**Level:** 18.05
**STR:** 1 > 2
**CON:** 10
**DEX:** 2
**SPR:** 4
**Regeneration rate:** +3.6%

**Skills**
Manipulate Aerosols (Medium) +1
Pick Up (Weak)
Osmosis (Weak) +1
Subordinate Link (Weak)
Create Drug (Weak) +1
Crystal Burst (Poor)
Engulf (Poor)
Create Coffee (Strong)
Whistle Blast (Weak)

**Passive**
Resilient Regeneration (Minor) +8
Team Spirit (Minor) +1
Disguise (Minor)
Watertight (Minor)
Follow Me (Minor)
Caffeine Rush (Average)
Growth (Lesser) +2
Heat Resistance (Lesser) +9
Strong Jaw (Minor)
+ Bounce (Lesser)
Condition
Hardness (Lesser) (Condition)

The gym teacher closed in on him. Zeke braced for impact.

**[Bounce]**

She shoulder-checked him into the air. Zeke flew back. He struck the ground and bounced. His shoulder flexed weirdly where he struck the ground, like a ball. For a moment, he had the uncomfortable sensation of his bones bending without breaking, and then he popped back up, flying at the gym teacher.

Her eyes widened. She gasped.

Zeke grinned. He drew back his fist, unleashing a blow just as he reached the gym teacher.

**Condition:** [Harden]

*Your skin grows harder, providing defense but, in return, your flexibility and dexterity lower.*

His fist grew heavier, stiffer. His skin crackled.

*Bam!*

The gym teacher's head popped back, flying back on a neck as flexible as stretched bubblegum. It snapped back into place a moment later, but the gym teacher reeled. She stumbled back a step, then spun around and toppled over.

A fiery blast caught his attention. The cartoon boy reached toward Domi, snarling, his hands clawed, fingertips suddenly sharp and ferocious. Explosions lit his face. His body distorted around them, shedding the damage. He closed in on her second by second.

Behind him, Ryan drew his dagger, then paused. He backed toward the television, letting the boy strike at Domi.

*Oh, that motherfucker! Who's the biggest threat to humanity, huh? Me, who's trying to end this damn apocalypse, or you, the asshole who's too busy stabbing me in the back to help the world?* Zeke jumped at Domi, reaching for the cartoon boy. "Domi!"

Claws struck. Domi screamed.

# 39
## SMASH MASH

Domi screamed, tensing for impact. Zeke grabbed her by the collar and yanked her back, putting himself where she'd stood. The cartoon boy's claws scraped down his hardened skin. Long scratches dug into his forearm, but not deep gouges.

Zeke laughed. *I should've been using [Harden] way more often!* He grabbed the cartoon boy's shoulder.

The shoulder retreated from his grab, but he just kept reaching. At last, his hand landed on the cartoon boy. He squeezed tight, gripping him with all his power.

"Let me go!" the boy demanded.

Zeke darted his face in. He opened his mouth. *I'll bite him, then I'll toss his core at Domi so she can heal—*

"Watch out!" Mia shouted.

Zeke froze mid-bite. He snapped his eyes across the room, catching a glimpse of Mia as she sprinted across the floor. *Watch out for what?*

Taking advantage of his distraction, the cartoon boy wriggled. His body grew soft under Zeke's grip and trembled hard, wiggling like a twanged rubber band. Zeke's grip loosened.

Ryan's eyes widened. He lunged, grabbing for the boy.

Zeke turned back around. He grabbed at the boy with his other hand, too, just as the boy leaped free. He jumped for the television.

"Fuck no," Ryan snarled. He vanished, reappearing in front of the screen seconds later. The boy struck Ryan and recoiled, bouncing back to the ground. He rolled on the floor, gripping his forehead. Ryan jumped after him, but the second his dagger dropped, the boy jumped up. The two dueled. An enormous hammer appeared from the boy's regular-sized pockets. Winding up, he swung it at Ryan's head with a grin.

Ryan's arms moved with preternatural speed. The hammer *clang*ed off his dagger. He laughed at the boy. "You'll have to try harder!"

The boy let out an uncharacteristically uncartoonish grunt of frustration and flung himself at Ryan. Still moving with unusual speed, Ryan fought back, expertly turning the boy's hammer with little twists and flicks of his dagger.

*When did Ryan learn martial arts? No, now isn't the time for that!* Across the gym, cartoon characters reached out for Mia, four-fingered and gloved hands grasping for her.

Zeke turned, lifting his fingers to his mouth. He whistled.

### [Whistle Blast]

A whistle echoed through the boxy gym. Again, about a quarter of the cartoon characters froze, caught up in the stun animations. Mia ducked and dodged, running for Zeke, Domi, and Ryan. Domi jumped toward her. Explosions burst around Mia, propelling her forward and keeping the cartoons back.

"Why now?" Domi asked, exasperated.

Mia took a deep breath. "Giant cat."

"What?" Domi said, confused.

Mia widened her eyes. She gestured wildly behind her. "Giant. Cat."

Behind her, the gym wall exploded inward. Dust sprayed through the air. Chunks of cinderblock thumped down, tearing holes in the gym floor. The gym floor screamed, the boards resonating with pain.

An enormous orange tabby yowled, baring its teeth at the hole. Perched atop its back, a man in a black hoodie glared down at them. Two adorable white cat ears peeped through holes in his hoodie.

*What the fuck?*

The man threw his hand out. On his command, the huge tabby leaped, jumping at Ryan and the cartoon boy.

*Oh shit! They're here to killsteal!* Zeke sprinted for the cartoon boy.

Domi stared as well. She jumped up, only to fall back again, gripping her forehead, dilated eyes squinting. From the ground, she fired an explosion at the tabby.

Spooked, the tabby arched its back and skittered back, eyes wide. It hissed ferociously.

The man on its back kicked it. "Go! Attack!"

"Zeke, go for it!" Domi shouted.

The cartoon boy turned at the last second. His eyes widened.

Zeke dropped down on the boy, aiming for his neck.

The boy's body wavered.

Ryan scowled. "He's about to run!"

Allen sat up on Zeke's head. He did a single, momentous pushup.

### [Intimidating Pose]
*Psychologically intimidate your foes. Anyone who sees your pose has a chance of freezing in fear, especially if their SPR is lower than*

*yours.*
*Requesting to use Leader Apocalypse's SPR? 3x/day*

*That's right. Allen's SPR is 0!* "Granted!" Zeke shouted.

The cartoon boy froze, arms out and eyes wide in a stereotypical expression of fear.

Zeke's mouth opened.

The cat darted forward, only for Domi to unleash another blast of noise and light. It leaped back again, all its hair on end, hackles raised.

"I command you! Attack them!" the man shouted.

*Too late!*

## [Devour]

Zeke's jaws slammed shut. The boy's neck distorted around him, snaking for his teeth. He ground down, yanking his head back as he tore.

Blood spurted. The boy toppled over.

All over the gym, cartoons suddenly bled. Their bodies remained distorted, but suddenly, they were ordinary, living humans distorted past the breaking point. Bones cracked. Organs flopped on the floor. One after another, the cartoons dropped dead where they stood.

Mia gasped. "Mr. Shane... the kids...!"

Zeke turned. His stomach dropped. "No..." *That girl. The one who gave me Allen. All her classmates. Mr. Shane.*

*I failed to save them.*

He lifted a hand to Allen, still sitting proudly atop his head. In true lizard fashion, Allen skittered over and did a pushup at his hand, completely lost to the tragedy at hand.

*Is it* possible *to save ordinary humans, in this apocalypse? Are they nothing but apocalypse fodder, fated for destruction? Even if I wanted to save Mr. Shane and the kids...how would I have?* He looked at the horribly distorted bodies lying all around them, torn into bits, gushing blood and leaking organs from impossibly-shaped bodies. *Once the Cartoon Apocalypse distorted them, there was no hope. The Cartoon Apocalypse was the only thing keeping them alive with their bodies twisted to that extent.*

*If that's the case, then...Mia...* Zeke glanced at her. He bit his lip. *How long can she survive? How long can we keep her alive?*

*There has to be something. Another way.*

*But what?*

Ryan shook his head. "There wasn't any hope from the start. I told you. Once their bodies get distorted, there's nothing we can do."

Mia rounded on him. "Turn back time. You said you can. Do it. Make a loop."

"I said, don't *talk* about that," Ryan snarled.

"Well, that explains a lot," Zeke mused. *Confirms my speculations.*

"Do it!" Mia snapped, stomping her foot.

"I can't! Shut up! Stop talking!" Ryan said, frustrated.

"You can't? What do you *mean* you can't? Aren't you the complete master of time, or whatever?" Mia demanded.

"I-I...shut up!" Ryan shouted in her face, cutting his eyes at Zeke.

Mia grabbed his shirt. "No. Tell me why you can't, or I'll tell Zeke everything."

"I can't. I can't. I really can't. The world is forfeit if I tell you," Ryan said.

"Is it really?" Mia asked, unimpressed.

"Yes. In every loop where I—"

"All ten of them. Or was that a hundred? Can't even remember how many times you looped. Are you the worst time looper or what?" Mia asked, rolling her eyes.

Ryan's face flushed red, though from anger or embarrassment, Zeke couldn't tell. "Mia, please. I'm begging you. I can't. I really can't. If I could control time that well, do you think Zeke would still be alive?"

Domi tugged at Zeke's arm. "The core..."

"Oh, right." Zeke glanced down into the boy's twisted body, not quite human anymore, but a cartoon rendering of human anatomy through and through. He plunged his arm into the torn torso and into a shapeless sack of blood and bones.

Something warm and round met his fingertips. Zeke grabbed it and pulled out a small, multicolored orb, as cel-shaded and animated as the boy had been. Domi reached for it.

Zeke's eyes locked onto the orb. His stomach grumbled, and his mouth watered. Mind empty of thoughts, he lifted it to his lips instinctively. His mouth opened.

"Hey, Zeke—"

**[Devour]**
**Defeated the Cartoon Apocalypse**
**Level + 5.03**
**Level:** 18.05 > 23.08
**Regeneration + 300%**
**Regeneration rate:** 303.6% (Temp. 2:43)

**Please assign your stat points.**
**Choose up to 3 Skills**
**Skills**
**Distort Self (Lesser)**
**Digital Broadcast (Weak)**
**Can't**
**Electric Leap (Poor)**
**Pocket Weapon (Poor)**
**Taunt (Weak)**

**Can't**

**Can't**

Zeke swallowed. He closed his eyes. *Ahh...delicious.*

Domi stared at him, betrayed. "Why?"

Zeke blinked. "Oh, shit! Domi, I'm sorry!" *What happened there? I blanked out. Just...something else took over. Pure instinct.*

*Or...* He glanced at his hand, clenching it into a fist. *Is it...this System? It's nurturing us to be apocalypses. Is it also compelling us to live by our Concepts?*

*Domi and the explosions...Ryan and...I don't know, Time? Is he the Time Apocalypse?*

*No? The System didn't activate on that. Huh. I could've sworn...*

Domi slammed her hand on the gym floor, startling Zeke out of his thoughts. "Sorry isn't enough!"

Behind them, the cat yowled. It reared up, baring vicious claws, and batted the downed cartoon bodies out of its way.

Domi pointed at the cat. Overhead, one of the gym lights abruptly exploded in a shower of shattered glass.

The cat retreated once more, pupils dilating and back arched up. It bared its teeth and hissed ferociously at them, preparing to attack.

Raising her hand again, Domi panted, sweat drenching her hair and running down her face. "Dammit, Zeke. I can't keep doing this forever, and I can't run with my head messed up! We're screwed!"

Zeke took a deep breath. *Shit. I fucked up. I really fucked up.*

**You can share Regeneration and much else with Subordinates, especially if they share [Subordinate Link] and [Teamwork].**

Zeke glanced at the message. He turned to Domi. "Domi. I

know before, I said I didn't... Look, it doesn't matter. I can share my Regeneration with you, if..."

"If?" she asked, cocking a brow.

"If, er...if you become my subordinate," Zeke muttered self-consciously. *Jeez. Asking someone I met today to become my subordinate? I'm not sure I'd be okay with asking Mia or Ryan, pre-trying-to-kill-me, to be my subordinate, let alone a near-stranger, but...*

Domi pointed at his head, arcing her brow. "Like that lizard?"

Allen looked down at her from his lofty perch. He extended his dewlap with all due ceremony.

"He's an anole. Which is a type of lizard, yes, but—"

The cat darted forward.

"Domi. Please. We don't have time!" Zeke said, holding out his hand to her.

She gritted her teeth. "Dammit. I— Fuck! Fine! Give me your damn regeneration rate!"

**Domi has chosen to become your subordinate.**
**New Subordinate:** Explosion Apocalypse
**Share Regeneration Rate?**

*Bathump. Bathump.* The cat galloped at Zeke and Domi, teeth still bared.

"Yes, yes, hurry up!" Zeke shouted at the System, charging to meet the cat.

**Regeneration rate:** 303.6% > 3.6%
**Domi's regeneration rate:** 1.5% > 151.5%

*Huh? Does she get half of whatever I share? That's kind of cheap.*

**In return, you can share your regeneration with any of your subordinates.**

*I guess, yeah. Like if someone was completely incapacitated...*
The cat closed in. It raised a paw, claws bared. Zeke tensed, lifting his arms and planting his feet. *Here we go again—*

# 40
## CAT MAN

The giant cat swiped at Zeke. Zeke raised his arms to block.

**[Hardness]**

Claws bit into his skin and lifted him into the air. He flew for a few brief moments, then smashed into the gym's wall mats. All the air left Zeke's lungs despite [Hardness], and he dropped to the floor.

**[Caffeinated] wore off! You are now [Exhausted]!**

Zeke pushed himself up. His arms and legs trembled, and his stomach screamed, rumbling louder than he'd ever heard it. He managed to get to all fours before his limbs slipped out from under him, and he dropped back to the ground.

*Holy shit. That's more than just [Exhausted]!*

**You've used a great deal of SP-based powers. SP saps your mental and physical stamina.**

*Right, I remember the System saying something about that before...* Zeke's stomach pulled to his spine. He shook bodily as it grumbled.

### Please fulfill your Concept.

Zeke's eyes cut to the horribly twisted bodies all around him, the puddles of blood and mangled limbs covering the floor. His stomach rumbled again. Drool spilled down his chin. He reached out. His hand landed on a piece of flesh. It bounced under his fingertips, slippery and warm. An organ.

Forcibly, Zeke swallowed his drool down. His hand tensed, but he refused to draw it toward him. *I don't want to be the child-eater I don't want to be the child-eater—*

The cat's shadow fell over him. He looked up to find a massive set of pink paw pads dropping toward him.

Zeke sighed. *What an adorable way to die...*

*Hold on. Skills! I need to pick skills! System, show me that list!*

### Choose up to 3 Skills

### Skills
### Distort Self (Weak)
*Weakly change your body shape at will. Body reverts after change, but changes cannot be drastic. 2-3cm of distortion are allowed.*

### Digital Broadcast (Weak)
*Send a message over any television or other digital receiver. Messages can be up to 5s long.*
Can't

### Electric Leap (Weak)

*Movement speed increases when user moves between two electronic devices.*

### Pocket Weapon
*Pull a RNG weapon out of your pocket. Weapon vanishes in 10s.*

### Taunt
*Taunt your opponent. Scales with SPR, fought by enemy SPR. Small chance of inflicting [Anger].*

### Can't
### Can't

Zeke scanned the list quickly. *Obviously Distort Self. None of the downsides of the other body-modification techniques, plus...I'm about to need some distortion! Electric Leap...I wonder if that's the skill the kid was using to jump into televisions? Obviously it isn't powerful enough for that right now, but based on the skills I've seen so far, the enemies have stronger versions of the skills I see. In any case, that's a must-have!*

## [Distort Self] [Bounce]

Soft pink pads pressed down on him. Everything in his body deformed slightly, squishing from both Distort Self and Bounce. Every bone, every muscle, his skin and organs. Zeke pressed flat against the floor but took no damage.

*Hell yeah! It's the kid's invincibility technique!*

*Still, it feels... Ugh. Yuck. Like I'm made of cartilage. Like I'm wobbly.* Every piece of his body screamed that it was wrong, off-alignment, bending past the breaking point, about to shatter... but barely any pain pulsed through him. He shuddered. *I love this ability, but I also hate it.*

A blast of fire slammed into the cat's head. It snarled and leaped back, lifting its foot off Zeke to round on Domi. Exhausted, Zeke laid there, taking the moment to choose his skills even as his body returned to normal with a strange *bwoing!* sound effect.

*For the rest...*

*Taunt...eh. I can do that as a base human. I don't need that as a skill. Which leaves Digital Broadcast and Pocket Weapon.*

*Digital Broadcast is super useful. My phone is broken, and I don't exactly think I'm going to be able to get a new one set up in the apocalypse...apocalypses. Only downside is that it's one-way. Still, I could use it to blast out a warning. Clear people out of an apocalypse and keep it from absorbing them and growing stronger, for example. Imagine, if I could have used that when the Cartoon Apocalypse was just starting to spread...*

*Pocket Weapon, too...damn, that sounds crazy useful. The RNG is the only thing. I don't know how wide of an RNG it's rolling on. What does the table look like? What if I pull out a squeaky hammer or something? It's based on the Cartoon Apocalypse, too, so I feel like there's gonna be a lot of losers in that list, if the user is anyone but the Cartoon Apocalypse.*

He took a deep breath. Giving Pocket Weapon one last wistful look, he nodded at Digital Broadcast. *That one!*

*And for points...*

**STR:** 2 > 4

**CON:** 10

**DEX:** 2 > 3

**SPR:** 5 > 7

*I still need more CON, but I have other ways to grow regeneration rate other than pure CON. For now, I think I should focus on pumping points into offensive skills. Especially STR. I need stronger jaws since that's still my primary melee attack.*

*You know, of all the things I expected to face in the apocalypse... biting people as my main attack wasn't one of them.*

*Wait, no. It was! If I was a zombie, which I'm not, then, of course, my main attack would be biting people. But I'm not a zombie. I'm still alive, obviously. And I don't eat brains.*

His stomach rumbled again.

### Please satisfy your Concept.

**WARNING:** If you do not satisfy your Concept, you will take permanent stat damage. Resisting your Concept for too long will cause death.

*Fuck you, System. Dammit. I guess...I guess I have to...eat...* Zeke drew his hand toward him. Blood smeared across the gym floor. The organ squelched. *Ugh. So gross.*

A gelatinous gray mass wiggled under his hand. Whirls and whorls zig-zagged back and forth under his hand.

Zeke stared the brain down, his eyes dead. *I'm not eating this.*

**WARNING:** If you do not satisfy your Concept, you will take permanent stat damage! Resisting your Concept for too long will cause death!

# 41
## NO BRAINS

Zeke eyed the brains. The brains eyed him back, the one soft eyeball still attached to them lolling gently on the wood floor.

A huge explosion burst through the room. The brains jiggled. The eyeball rolled on the floor a little, just enough to look as though it was rolling his eyes at him.

Zeke pointed his finger at the brains. "You mind your attitude over there."

*Damn. The hunger's making me loopy. Pull yourself together, Zeke. Focus. I need to eat. Something. Anything. Not brains, but anything else.*

**WARNING:** If you do not satisfy your Concept, you will take permanent stat damage! Resisting your Concept for too long will cause death!

"I'm not doing it. I'm not eating brains," Zeke muttered. He crawled over the gym floor, kicking his way toward a different bloody pile. *There's plenty to eat here. If you aren't picky, anyway. And I'm...no longer picky. Except when it comes to brains.*

*They're already dead...they're already dead...they're already dead!*

A red lump loomed in his vision. He clawed his way toward it as explosions and heavy thumps rocked the gym. His hand landed on a piece of mangled flesh. Drawing it toward his mouth, he leaned toward the flesh, drool dripping on the wood floor. *I don't even care anymore. I'm so hungry.*

He tore into the flesh. In a few gulps, he swallowed it down, His stomach quieted, and the intense sensation of hunger abated. Zeke closed his eyes and licked his lips. *Damn. I hate how well that hits the spot.*

*Oh, right. Uh.*

### [Devour]
### Apocalypse already defeated. No bonuses granted.

Footsteps approached Zeke. He turned, face still bloody, a fleshy lump in his hands.

Ryan glared down at him. He flicked his wrist, and his dagger appeared in his palm. His lip twitched in disgust. "I knew it. No matter what, you have to be destroyed for the sake of the world."

"It's not what it looks like. I have to— The System—" Zeke scrambled, pushing himself up. His limbs shook but took his weight. Every inch of his body trembled from exhaustion. *Damn, [Exhaustion] is no joke—*

Ryan kicked Zeke in the chest.

Zeke fell backward, but his shoulders struck the mats, and he managed to keep his feet. He scowled. *Damn, Ryan, how many times are you going to try to kick me backward? Try something new.*

*Or maybe...you're so stuck in your ways after looping through time that you don't even know you're stuck in your ways.*

"So, what are you? The Time Apocalypse?" Zeke asked.

Ryan slammed his dagger toward Zeke.

Zeke raised his forearm. The dagger pierced his [Hardened] flesh and struck his bones. Zeke gritted his teeth. *Oh, damn. That's gonna hurt.*

### [Resilient Regeneration]

The pain faded, no longer so insistent. Zeke's eyes lit up. *Ha. Take that!*

Almost instantly, his stomach rumbled, a pang of hunger shooting through his gut. He scowled. *Really?*

Yanking his dagger back in a spray of crimson, Ryan pointed at Zeke. "That is exactly why you have to be destroyed. You—"

*All right, that's enough.* Zeke rushed him.

Ryan raised his dagger and slammed it into Zeke's back.

### [Distort Self] [Bounce] [Hardness]

Zeke's back gave way before Ryan's dagger. In the depths of the pit the dagger carved in his back, his skin grew harder. The dagger cut into his flesh, but only barely, and with the extra give, barely at all. It was as if Ryan had stabbed a puncture-resistant balloon, which deformed with him rather than taking damage.

*Be nice to have [Bowl Over] right now... oh well.*

Zeke slammed into Ryan, lifting him. Hugging Ryan with both arms, he raised him up, then threw him at the ground.

Ryan's eyes widened.

Halfway to the ground, Ryan flickered and vanished. Zeke wrinkled his nose. *It's not time, but it's definitely time-adjacent.* He spun, activating another skill.

Ryan plunged at Zeke's back, only to suddenly face Zeke's face. Ryan flinched back.

**[Create Coffee]**

Zeke spat boiling hot coffee in Ryan's face.

Ryan flinched, instinctively raising his arms.

Zeke punched Ryan in the gut. Simultaneously, Allen leaped off Zeke's head and chomped Ryan on the nose.

Ryan staggered away. "Dammit, you got a lizard to replace the shirt?" Scowling, he snatched Allen off his nose and threw the tiny lizard away.

Midair, Allen flipped over. He landed on his feet, then skittered around and sprinted up Zeke's leg.

"The shirt?" Zeke asked, confused.

"The—"

"Zeke!" Mia shouted.

Zeke looked up. A massive orange tabby blocked out the lights, arcing high overhead as it dropped down on him.

**[Caffeine High]**
**Warning:** Stacking [Exhaustion] on [Exhaustion] will leave you [Immobile]!

Zeke's stomach roared, but his body sped up. He ran toward the tabby, ducking under its fluffy belly. The enormous cat slammed down behind him and bit at Ryan, perfectly content to swap one target with another.

Zeke gestured to Mia and Domi from across the room. "Let's go! While they're distracted!"

Domi and Mia grabbed each other's hands instinctively and chased after Zeke. Leading the way, Zeke sprinted for the exit to the gym.

"Get back here!" Ryan snarled.

He was answered by the snarl of the cat, which instantly batted him into the wall. The cat-eared boy atop the cat turned as they went, his eyes faintly glowing under the hoodie, and took a deep sniff. A second later, his face distorted into the overly disgusted expression cats make after sniffing something gross.

*Cats do that to remember scents. Wait...is he...is he tracking us?* Zeke squinted, then shook his head and smashed the door open, holding it as the girls ran through. *No way he can smell us through all this gore. No way.*

Ryan glared at him from where he lay, propping himself up against the gym wall. He pointed at Zeke.

Zeke flipped him the bird and turned, letting the door fall shut behind him. He ran after the girls. "Let's get out of here."

"Don't forget the bags at the door," Domi said. She and Mia let go of one another's hands, half-walking, half-jogging toward the school's grand entrance.

"Right, right," Zeke said, nodding.

With the clang of one last set of aluminum doors, they escaped into the twilight.

# 42
## RESTING

The door to Domi's apartment slammed shut. Zeke stumbled. He put a hand to his head, and another to his stomach.

"What is it?" Mia asked, concerned.

Zeke shook his head. "It's... I'm just hungry."

"You already ate half your bag," Domi pointed out. Pushing past Zeke and Mia, she bustled across her apartment and swept everything off the dining room table, quickly stuffing it into a nearby closet.

"I know, but I'm still—"

**[Caffeinated] wore off! You are now [Exhausted]!**
**Warning:** You were already [Exhausted].
**Stacking [Exhausted] on [Exhausted]...**
**You are now [Immobilized].**

Zeke's body froze mid-step, and he toppled over.

"Zeke!" Mia grabbed him before he fell, pulling his weight onto her shoulder.

"The hell?" Domi asked, looking up from across the room.

Zeke limply waved his hand. Even that took an immense effort, as though his hand weighed a thousand pounds. "It's...a penalty. Exhausted and...exhausted, and...now I'm...immobilized."

"What's that mean?" Mia asked, frowning.

"I think that means he needs to sleep it off," Domi said. She gestured. "Over here. I've got a couch he can crash on."

"Oh...thank you so much," Mia said. With some effort, she readjusted Zeke over her shoulder and staggered over to Domi, following her into the living room.

A cozy space awaited them. Pretty white throw pillows sat at the edges of an upholstered black couch, while a knitted pink throw draped over the couch's back. Across the room, paired bookshelves in black flanked a modest flatscreen television on a neat black stand, with a couple of consoles tucked neatly underneath. A round pink shag rug sat under a small, tasteful coffee table, and a single end table stood pulled close to the couch, a dirty mug and a half-finished book propped atop it.

"Need any help?" Domi asked, as Mia dragged Zeke over to the couch.

"Oh no, no. I've got this," Mia said. She hefted Zeke's hips over the couch, then set him down, his torso laid over the cushions. Bending, she grabbed his knees and slung them onto the couch as well, then carefully folded his arms onto his stomach.

Zeke smiled weakly at her. "Thanks."

Mia smiled back, though there was a hint of nervousness in her eyes. "I'm just glad we're all still alive."

Domi nodded at Mia. "Since you're staying the night, you can share the bed with me or take the floor, your call. Bed's a queen. Floor... I've got some blankets, so it won't be a total shitshow."

"Oh, the floor—" Mia started.

"I still haven't driven out all the cockroaches, though. Not sure if it's possible to rid this godforsaken dumpster-fire apartment of cockroaches. So, uh, if one crawls over you in the night—"

"Bed, I'll share the bed," Mia decided abruptly.

*Cockroaches? Free resilience ups!* Zeke's eyes glittered. He glanced at the floor. *Wonder when [Immobile] wears off.*

**[Immobile] lasts 2.5x as long as [Exhausted] would have. You will be able to move again in 10:43. You will be additionally [Exhausted] for 3:21 afterward, as an additional penalty for becoming [Immobile].**

*Damn, harsh,* Zeke thought.

**They would not be punishments if they were not harsh.**

*Fair enough.* Zeke closed his eyes, drifting off. *If all I can do is lie here, I might as well take a nap.*

Gentle snoring rose from the couch.

Peering over at Zeke, Domi snorted. "Out like a light."

"He's always been like that. Able to sleep anywhere, at any time," Mia said, shaking her head.

"You've known him for a while?" Domi asked.

Mia nodded. "We pretty much grew up together in this little dead-end suburb way outside of town. I think there was a grand total of one big, empty lot with a couple of box stores on it. The whole place was total soulless urban rot."

"Sounds like fun," Domi snorted.

Mia sighed. "It was something, anyway. I'm going across state to college just to get away from it." She moved to the window and pressed her lips together, gazing into the black dome overhead. "Or, I guess, I was. I will be. If I get out of this alive."

Domi moved to Mia's side. She sat on the narrow window ledge, crossing her arms and kicking back. Her gaze swooped up and down Mia, taking her in from top to bottom. "But you're headed to college."

"Yeah. Are you not?" Mia asked, looking at Domi.

"Maybe. It's way too expensive, you know? I'd be taking on massive debt. And I'm not sure it's something I could ever pay off, with my ideal career."

"What would that be? I'm guessing...not museum guide?" Mia joked, nodding at Domi's uniform.

Domi glanced down, then snorted. "Yeah. I should change out of this shit. No, yeah. Not my ideal career." She took a deep breath. "Don't laugh."

Mia crossed her hands in front of her. "Promise I won't."

A deep breath. Domi glanced out the window. "Pyrotechnic engineer."

Mia's eyes widened. "Whoa, seriously?"

"Yeah, yeah, I know. I'm nuts. It's crazy competitive, it's super dangerous... I don't know. I'd be happy doing pyrotechnics for a tiny little festival somewhere. I know I'd make pennies, but..." Domi shrugged, "it's what I want to do."

"No, that's awesome! I think it's great to have a passion, to know what you want to do already. That's amazing," Mia enthused.

"What about you? You want to go to college, right? What's your major?" Domi asked.

Mia sighed. She shook her head. "I don't know. I've never known. I mean, I'm good at soccer, I love it, I-I have a scholarship or two, but...even in the highest league, the girls get pennies on the dollar compared to the men, regardless of performance. And even putting that aside, I don't know that I want to play soccer forever. Even in the best case, that's about ten years of a career, and then? What, become a coach?"

Domi shrugged. "Sounds like a plan to me."

"I just... I don't know. I don't have a passion. I don't have something I want to spend the rest of my life doing. I want to make a good salary and live a good life and enjoy my job, but..." Mia shrugged.

"Doesn't everyone?" Domi said, laughing.

"Yeah...yeah, I guess so," Mia agreed.

Outside, the light dimmed. Long rays of gold traced down the buildings' façades, vanishing into shadow where the buildings overlapped. Mia turned away from the window. "Not that any of this matters. We're all going to die in here and—"

Static burst. Mia frowned, rubbing her temple.

**... st an... ...ate...**

*What is that? What's going on?*

Domi put a gentle hand on Mia's back, interrupting her thoughts. "It's all right. We'll get out of here. All of us. Together."

"Will we? Can we? I'm just an ordinary person. I'm not... whatever you guys are. I don't know how Ryan kept me from becoming one of those cartoon things, but I'm not going to last long, am I?" Mia asked. Tears sparked up in her eyes. She sniffed. "And Ryan wants to kill Zeke, and Zeke, I don't know what's happening, but I just watched him eat a kid—a cartoon kid, but still—and—"

Domi said nothing. She just patted Mia's back.

Mia rubbed her face. With effort, she swallowed her sobs and pushed away from the window. "I-I'm gonna go get ready for bed. I can't think about this any longer."

"All right. Take your time," Domi said.

Mia vanished into the bedroom. Domi stared after her, then broke her gaze, looking at Zeke instead. He snored away on the couch. As she watched, he curled up and licked his lips, snuggling into the couch.

She shook her head. "Look at you, snoozing away while your girl looks for help. What kinda childhood-friend-slash-crush are you?"

# 43
## GOOD MORNING RIDE

V*ROOM, VROOM.*
Engine roaring, wheels rolling, the motorcycle ate up the pavement. Smoke burned from its tailpipe, engine louder than thunder. Sleek chrome reflected the dawn. Black handle grips jutted up, defiant. A low-slung seat stood empty. Half a ton of shining steel, chrome, leather, and gasoline blasted down the roadway.

It was King. Lord of the road. It revved its engine, oil boiling, and reared, raising its front wheel in defiance. Blood sprayed from the rubber, evidence of its conquests. Faintly, it remembered them. Not well, because lesser beings didn't deserve to live on in its glorious memory. A few squishy humans. Something large and meaty. All of them no more than roadkill in the making.

Some beings dared to defy The King. None defied it for long.

*No one can stop me. I must roll. To stop is to die! To die is to stop!*

Beside it, its peers rolled. A cheeky crotch rocket in white and neon greens burst ahead of it for a moment, only to fall back at a warning rumble from The King. It cast a wary eye over its fellows, the train, the thunder that rolled in The King's wake.

Two wheels. A motor. These were the beings made in The King's image, and it allowed them to follow it. Some dared to believe they could become The King. But such a thing was impossible. No one could defy The King.

**Please assign your stat points.**

The King looked over its stats with satisfaction. What to add to? DEX? But it was no crotch rocket, seeking nothing but speed at the detriment of everything else, most notably a sense of *style*. Of *kinglyhood*. It would not lower itself to such things.

CON? But its glorious body was already more durable than anything it had ever encountered. Durability was important, but ten points were sufficient. It was built different. Its steel body could resist far more than the lesser beings could, and with another ten points, its body no longer took dents when reducing the lesser beings to their truest state: roadkill. No, it had sufficient CON.

SPR? SPR was for nerds. It had enough SPR to understand it was King, and that was enough.

Which meant there was only one choice.

STR.

**Level:** 27.49
**STR:** 15
**CON:** 10
**DEX:** 4
**SPR:** 3

The King roared in satisfaction. All around it, the peers roared in his echo. They pleased him, except for that cheeky green and white crotch rocket. That one might become roadkill soon if it didn't fall in line.

It eyed the sleek vehicle with utter disgust. Yes, perhaps it was time to destroy it. Although The King appreciated having a fast striker, and no one could beat out the crotch rocket in speed, it was infuriating how the cheeky thing thought itself superior to The King thanks to that.

After all, The King could not risk a threat to the regime.

*Splat.*

The King froze. The other motorcycles rolled forward for a beat, then, realizing their monarch had halted, they all slammed the brakes, screeching to a halt beside The King.

The crotch rocket jutted ahead of The King, then slowly, reluctantly, rolled back behind it.

The King couldn't be bothered to notice. It trembled, furious. Its headlights flickered. Its engine growled, and wheels squealed.

White streaked its immaculate chrome. Black lumps smeared down The King's perfect body, slowly sliding into place.

Overhead, a pigeon cooed, almost laughing. It sat atop one of the tangled electric wires and fluttered its wings in open defiance. That horrible round eye looked down on The King, *down* on it! And then it did even worse and turned away, choosing to peck at its own pathetic back instead of gaze down upon The King in horror and awe!

*Kill it. I must kill that horrible, blasphemous being! Daring to mar this King's faultless form with its filthy oil!*

**You have no skills that would allow you to fly.**
**Would you like to purchase [Improvised Ramp]?**

Yes, yes, a thousand times yes! Anything to crush that profane beast!

**Warning:** You lack the stat points to purchase [Improvised Ramp]! Please acquire more skill points!

For a moment, The King's fury burned hot, and its engine roared. In the next, it suppressed its fury to a low burn of anger, suppressing its roar to a rumble.

So be it. *So be it.* If it needed skill points, then it would earn them.

Earn them the only way it knew how: By turning lesser beings into their true form.

With a howl, The King took off down the road. Behind him, the pack let out howls of their own, chasing after. All their cries mingled together, becoming one cry, one warning:

*The hunt is on! Flee, or die!*

"Fucking hell! This early in the morning?"

The King roared in delight. *Prey! Go forth!*

The hunters sprinted from its pack, leaping ahead in their joy. Even the cheeky crotch rocket, though it would forgive the peer this time. Anything for those stat points. Anything for that skill!

"Domi, watch out!"

"Watch out for what?"

The lesser being raised its hand, defiant. The King laughed. So many lesser beings had faced it. All of them confident. All of them defiant. And in the end, they were no more than blood on its wheel—

The lesser being closed its fist.

Its heart stopped. The King lurched. It skidded forward, no longer able to control itself. Its proud roar quieted to a rumble, then silence. *What? Why? How? The lesser being dares?*

Ahead of it, the strikers tumbled to the ground, crashing and smashing as they skidded to a halt, paralyzed just like The

King. Behind it, the pack rolled to a halt, tipping over or sliding sideways.

"All right, go grab the core. Quickly. I can't suppress them all for long," Domi ordered, clenching her fist tight. Her hand shook from the effort and, in a moment, the trembling reached her arm, until half her body quaked.

Zeke nodded. "I'd love to, but, er…"

"But?" Domi demanded. She gritted her teeth and raised a second hand to her first, holding on with both hands.

Zeke looked over the enormous pack of motorcycles. He licked his lips. "Which one is the apocalypse?"

Deep in the pile of motorcycles, The King's combustion heart thumped.

# 44
## FINDING THE KING

Frustrated, Domi waved her clasped hands vaguely. "I don't know! Go figure it out! Hurry!"

"Just explode them all!" Zeke said, hurrying toward the motorcycles. *What am I even supposed to do? Motorcycles are pretty hard to destroy, and there's, like, twenty of them!* Casting around, he found a stop sign at the corner. Zeke ran over to the sign and slammed his foot on the ground.

**[Crystal Burst]**

Crystals burst up from the ground beneath the sign, severing the bolts that secured it to the ground. He grabbed it and hefted, half-expecting the weight to topple him. Instead, he held it easily in two hands. A faint strain pulled at his biceps, but not enough that the sign became unwieldy. He swung it around experimentally.

*Damn. I guess this is what four STR does.*

"I can't. There's too many of them. It's hard enough to keep them from exploding, and it's easier to stifle lots of explosions than to make them all bigger," Domi said.

"Huh," Zeke said. *I'd have expected the opposite since explosions are her Concept.*

"Psychologically, it's harder..." Domi muttered.

"What?" Zeke asked.

"Hurry!" Domi demanded, gritting her teeth in frustration.

"I'm hurrying, I'm hurrying," Zeke assured her.

### [Team Spirit] (Minor)

*Team activated. +0.5 to all stats for fighting with a Subordinate.*

He quickly took in the motorcycles. *If I was the Motorcycle Apocalypse, which motorcycle would I be?*

A shiny white-and-green motorcycle, sleek and trim, caught his eye. He ran over and smashed it with the stop sign. White-and-green plastic flew in all directions. Metal bits and bobs burst off its frame. The lightweight frame buckled under the onslaught. Creaking and snapping, it fell apart.

Looking over the motorcycle's remains, Zeke pressed his lips together. He shrugged, then grabbed one of the smaller pieces of metal and shoved it into his mouth.

### [Devour]

He swallowed. Sharp metal edges scraped down his throat with some effort. Zeke rubbed his neck. *Ouch.*

### Defeated Member of the Motorcycle Apocalypse!
### Level + .3
### Level: 23.08 > 23.38

### Please choose a skill.

### Ride (Minor)

*Gain Novice-level skill at riding a motorcycle.*

### Nitrous (Weak)
*When active, gain a boost to speed, especially movement speed. Stresses and damages the body.*

### Roll Together (Minor)
*When you travel with someone else who shares this skill or with [Subordinates], everyone in your group gains a small boost to speed.*

### Headlights
*Produce light from the light on your front fork. Small chance of blinding your foe with your bright light.*

As he jogged to the next motorcycle, Zeke scanned the list, then nodded at Roll Together. *Ride isn't that exciting, and while Nitrous sounds fun, I already have Caffeinated. I could have Nitrous Coffee, I guess, but I'm a bit concerned about stacking 'stress and damage' and 'exhausted.' Ride Together could be incredibly useful for moving people across the city, and I don't have anything like it yet. As for Headlights...I don't have a headlight.*

He lifted his stop sign, then paused. Down the street, in the middle of the fallen motorcycles, a huge, gleaming motorcycle with a laid-back seat and high handlebars lay, looming over the other motorcycles even on its side from its sheer bulk alone.

*That one! It's gotta be that one!* Zeke ran over. "Domi! Explode that one!" he shouted, pointing at the huge motorcycle.

Domi growled. She threw her hands open wide.

All around Zeke, motorcycles roared to life. With a horrible squeal of rubber on asphalt, the motorcycles leaped to their wheels and whipped around to face him. Headlights beamed in Zeke's face, blinding him.

Zeke staggered back, blindly waving the sign. *I take it back. Headlight is the most annoying skill ever!*

### [Crystal Burst]

Crystals shoved through the asphalt in a circle around Zeke, pressing outward in a short wave. Zeke's stomach instantly emptied, pulling back to his spine.

Tires popped all around Zeke, deflating with great blasts of air. The motorcycles fell to the side, clunking to the ground. Their bright headlights beamed off into the distance, no longer all focused on him.

Domi pointed at the giant motorcycle. A small motorcycle leaped between her and the bigger one. It exploded midair in a great burst of fire and shrapnel. Zeke ducked, covering his head as bits of metal and plastic rained down.

*Huh. I guess she does need line of sight. Things to tuck away as 'confirmed.'*

Three medium-sized motorcycles charged at Domi from left, right, and center. Backing away, she clapped once. A wave of force burst from her palms. Thrown back, the motorcycles somersaulted away, clattering over the asphalt.

Zeke leaped over the flat-tired motorcycles around him and sprinted toward the giant one.

The motorcycle reared like a wild stallion to accept his challenge. It growled deep in its engine, front wheel spinning in the air. Flying forth, it rushed to meet Zeke.

### [Distort Self] [Bounce]
**You often use these skills together. Would you like to fuse these skills?**

*Just a minute. I'm busy—er—that's right!*

## [Hardness]

The motorcycle struck Zeke, and he flew into the air. Crashing back down, he bounced once, twice, then rolled, coming to a halt at Domi's feet.

He glanced up at Domi and gave her a thumbs-up.

Ignoring him, Domi yanked out her phone and scrolled. Lips twisted, she focused intently.

*Is now the time?* Zeke wondered.

Engine growling, light blaring, the motorcycle charged Domi.

Shoving the phone back into her rear pocket, Domi pointed at it. "Boom."

The motorcycle trembled. Its engine coughed, stuttered, then exploded. Metal shot over the street, shattering windows all around them. Domi crouched down, covering her face. Zeke reached up, blocking what he could. Metal bits stuck into his skin, only to bounce off and fall away, clattering over the asphalt.

### Defeated the Motorcycle Apocalypse
### Subordinate is sharing levels...

"Wait, wait!" Zeke shouted, scrambling to his feet. Motorcycles drove past him, wobbling at random until they struck one another, a car, or a pole. He vaulted a fallen motorcycle and sped up, sprinting for the massive motorcycle Domi had downed.

An orb hovered in its shattered engine cavity. As he charged, it faded. Oily sheen spooled off its surface and vanished into the air.

As it grew translucent, Zeke grabbed the orb. He didn't hesitate a moment, but directly shoved the orb into his mouth. Even there, it faded, weakening to a soap-bubble-like consistency.

### [Devour]

The bubble popped as he swallowed. Zeke held his breath. *Come on...come on! Give me skills!*

# 45
## SPEED EATER

Zeke swallowed. *Come on! Skills!*

**Defeated Motorcycle Apocalypse**
**Levels + 3.41**
**Level: 26.79**

**Please assign your stat points.**
**Please choose 3...**
**Calculating...**

**>Subordinate defeated apocalypse.**
**>Apocalypse core decaying**
**>Devour Skill used.**
**Incompatible!**

"Hey! Domi defeated it, yeah, but I still Devoured it!" Zeke shouted at the system.

"Man shouts at sky," Domi muttered under her breath. She wandered over and tried one of the intact motorcycles, only to scowl. "Out of gas? Seriously?"

**Devour penalties applied...**
**Devour did not destroy...**
**Calculating...**

"Yeah, come on. I got the penalties. Give me the boosts, too," Zeke argued, nodding.

Mia wandered out from the lobby. She frowned at Zeke, then looked at Domi. "Uh, is he okay?"

"Don't worry. He's just fighting the System," Domi said, moving to another motorcycle. Her scowl deepened. "This one too? Fuck!"

**Determination:** Devourer is allowed ONE (1) skill.

Zeke grimaced, then shrugged. "Better than nothing."

**Motorcycle Apocalypse**
**Skills**
**Create Fuel (Weak)**
**Ride Together (Poor)**
**Neat Trick (Poor)**
**King's Demeanor (Lesser)**
**Polished Chrome (Medium)**
**MOTORCYCLE**

Immediately, Zeke's eyes darted to the final skill in the list. *Hold on. The rest of those sound cool—especially Create Fuel and King's Demeanor—but that last one. MOTORCYCLE. What is that?*

**MOTORCYCLE**
*This skill*

Zeke frowned. *This skill... what?*

## MOTORCYCLE
*This skill a46i-1o<?au}Q~*` eir_32jsk1&8::;'f motorcycle.*

*Holy shit, I want that skill. I don't know what it is, but I want it. I mean...* He scanned up the list. *I already have Ride Together. Create Fuel is awesome, but do I want Weak fuel? I know that means that the skill doesn't create much, but...still. Weak fuel, not for me. Neat Trick is...eh, cool, but whatever, King's Demeanor is probably an awesome conditional passive buff, but I have lots of buffs, and same with Polished Chrome.*

*I completely lack CAPITAL SKILLS. It doesn't even have a strength label! It doesn't have a proper description! I have no idea what it is, but...but, but it's worth the gamble!*

Zeke nodded. "That one. Absolutely that one."

**Skills**
**Manipulate Aerosols (Medium) +1**
**Pick Up (Weak)**
**Osmosis (Weak) +1**
**Subordinate Link (Weak)**
**Create Drug (Weak) +1**
**Crystal Burst (Poor)**
**Engulf (Poor)**
**Create Coffee (Strong)**
**Whistle Blast (Weak)Digital Broadcast (Weak)**
**Electric Leap (Poor)**

**Passive**
**Resilient Regeneration (Minor) +8**
**Team Spirit (Minor) +1**

**Disguise (Minor)**
**Watertight (Minor)**
**Follow Me (Minor)**
**Caffeine Rush (Average)**
**Growth (Lesser) +2**
**Heat Resistance (Lesser) +9**
**Strong Jaw (Minor)**
**Bounce (Lesser)**
**Distort Self (Lesser)**
**Roll Together (Minor)**

**Condition**
**Hardness (Lesser) (Condition)**
**MOTORCYCLE**

*It's even on a separate line from everything else,* Zeke thought to himself, frowning. A second later, he glanced over the list. *Come to think of it, I was going to fuse a few of them... Let's see. I'll try manual this time.*

He poked at the list, calling up Bounce and Distort Self. After he selected Distort Self, the two lifted out of the list and appeared next to one another. A small **FUSE?** button appeared below them.

"Let's do it," Zeke decided.

**WARNING:** Skill fusion can result in skill loss. Do you still want to proceed?

"Proceed," Zeke said.

**Calculating...**

A triumphant riff played.

**Congratulations on your first manual skill fusion!**
**Flexible Body (Average)**
*Gain the ability to flex your body 3-6cm past its usual limits. While in this state, your body will rebound to its usual state. If thrown into an object, you will bounce.*

Scanning his skills again, he selected another two skills.

Follow Me and Roll Together appeared next to each other.

Zeke considered for a moment. *They aren't super similar. Follow Me is a skill to gain more followers. Roll Together gives additional speed bonuses to subordinates who are traveling together. Maybe...?*

*Eh, at the worst case...I'll miss Roll Together, but Follow Me doesn't seem to have done much yet. Unless it's been passively helping me pick up Domi, for example.*

**FUSE?**

"Proceed," Zeke said.

**Calculating...**

A neutral riff played.

*Well, that doesn't sound like failure,* Zeke thought to himself.

**Roll With Me (Minor)**
*While travelling together with followers, have a small chance to pick up additional followers. You and your followers travel at a small speed boost.*

*Hmm... What's the difference?* Zeke scanned between the two new skills. After a moment, his eyes lit up. *Oh! I see. Flexible Body took two (Lesser) skills and upgraded them into an (Average) skill.*

*Roll With Me took two (Minor) skills and returned a (Minor) skill. In other words, if the two skills don't have great fusion compatibility, they won't level up on fusion.*

*Understood! So, there's a small chance of leveling up the skills, in return for a small chance of losing the skills. Fusing skills is a bit of a gamble, but it's worth it.*

### Skills
Manipulate Aerosols (Medium) +1
Pick Up (Weak)
Osmosis (Weak) +1
Subordinate Link (Weak)
Create Drug (Weak) +1
Crystal Burst (Poor)
Engulf (Poor)
Create Coffee (Strong)
Whistle Blast (Weak)Digital Broadcast (Weak)
Electric Leap (Poor)

### Passive
Resilient Regeneration (Minor) +8
Team Spirit (Minor) +1
Disguise (Minor)
Watertight (Minor)
Caffeine Rush (Average)
Growth (Lesser) +2
Heat Resistance (Lesser) +9
Strong Jaw (Minor)
Flexible Body (Average)
Roll With Me (Minor)

### Condition
Hardness (Lesser) (Condition)

## MOTORCYCLE

Zeke let out a held breath. *Whew. Enough of that for now. So—*

*Wait. I need to assign my stat points.*

**Level:** 26.79
**Please assign your stat points.**
**STR:** 4
**CON:** 10
**DEX:** 3
**SPR:** 7
**Regeneration rate:** +3.6%

Zeke glanced at his stats, then quickly assigned points.

**Level:** 26.79
**STR:** 4 > 5
**CON:** 10
**DEX:** 3
**SPR:** 7 > 9
**Regeneration rate:** +3.6%

"You done over there?" Domi asked, putting her hands on her hips.

"Yeah. Any of the cycles have fuel?" Zeke asked, glancing at her.

Domi shook her head. "Not a one."

"The Motorcycle Apocalypse had a Create Fuel skill, so it tracks," Zeke said.

Domi squinted at him. "Why would you know that?"

"I mean— Sorry, I said that backward. It would make sense if the Motorcycle Apocalypse could Create Fuel, so it's not a surprise that none of them had fuel after it died," Zeke said quickly. Even as he said it, he felt heat climb up his neck to his ears. *Right, right! Let's not give up the ghost about me being able to devour enemy skills. I'm sure Domi will figure it out eventually, but I don't need to tell her right off the bat.*

*I still don't fully trust her, after all.*

Mia wandered over. She kicked one of the motorcycles awkwardly. "Did you beat them?"

"Yeah. Another threat to the world, vanquished!" Zeke said, smiling.

Mia's eyes tracked over the shining body of one of the motorcycles. Zeke followed her gaze. Bright red splatters tracked over the wheel well, kicked up from beneath. She pressed her lips together. "We ordinary people...the kids. Me. We're just meant to die, aren't we. We're fodder for you...you apocalypses."

"No, no," Zeke insisted. He cut his eyes to Domi, who pressed her lips together and said nothing. He opened his mouth to continue but shut it again. *What can I say? She isn't wrong. This...this Apocalypse Incubator...it isn't meant to help out the human race. Even if I survive, even if I'm the one to break out, even if I choose not to destroy the world...will that really end it?*

He looked up. *There's something else. Something beyond that dome. Something that created this. This dome, this scenario.*

*If I destroy that...will that end this?*

"Zeke," Domi said quietly.

Zeke glanced over. "What?"

She nodded subtly over her shoulder.

A white cat sat on the top of the apartment building's stairs, licking its paw.

"It's cute...?" Zeke tried.

Domi rolled her eyes. She nodded again, more aggressively.

Zeke looked again.

A cat sat in the alleyway, rolling over to show its pale belly. Two orange tabbies stood shoulder-to-shoulder near an overflowing trash can. A black cat watched quietly from across the road.

Zeke swallowed. He backed toward Domi. "Mia, come here."

"What?" Mia asked, still staring at the motorcycle.

The white cat stood. It shook itself and walked forward, toward the stairs.

"Just stay right there. No, wait. Head to the apartment. *Slowly*," Zeke hissed. *There's only one cat that way. I can take a single cat.*

Mia furrowed her brows. Confused, she nonetheless stepped backward. "Okay...?"

The second she reached the other two, all the cats' heads snapped around. From all sides, pale eyes watched silently, pupils slit.

*Shit. Have they already called the big cat?*

"Slowly. Move slowly," Zeke cautioned at a whisper, eyeing the apartment door.

Domi followed his gaze. She nodded.

One step at a time. Zeke and Domi moved in sync, edging toward the apartment. Zeke cast his gaze around the cats, keeping them in view. *None of them are moving. That's—*

All around them, the cats stood. As one, they strode toward Zeke and Domi.

*Not good, not good!* Exchanging a look, Zeke and Domi broke and sprinted for the apartment. "Mia, run!" Zeke shouted.

# 46
## CATS AND CATS AND CATS

The white cat jumped forward. It hopped onto Mia's shoulder. She startled but held still, suddenly frozen, body caught in a tense half-cringe. Her eyes darted to Zeke and Domi, even as they closed in on her. In a small voice, she cried, "Help."

"Mia, we're coming—" Domi started.

The cat looked at them. Mesmerizing blue eyes locked them in place. Both Domi and Zeke froze where they stood. Zeke's mind blanked. Blue filled his vision utterly, so deep he could drown in it.

For some reason, Ryan flashed through his mind. He scowled. *All right, all right. Just because they both have blue eyes...*

Adjusting itself on Mia's shoulders, the cat flicked its tail. "Do not be alarmed. I come in peace, as the representative of a greater being."

At the movement, the freeze on Zeke and Domi broke. Zeke stumbled forward, suddenly snapped out of his reverie. He glanced at Domi, who gave him the same startled look back, then wiped his own face. *Damn. The cat could've killed us.*

*I guess that's what it's like to be on the other side of Stun.*

*I've been neglecting CON lately. I need to go back to mainlining it. If I get Stunned in a real fight, my regeneration rate will be the only thing between me and certain death.*

Domi glanced at Zeke. Quietly, she muttered, "'Be not afraid, for I bring you great tidings?'"

"Fuck. They're angel cats," Zeke muttered back.

Mia's eyes darted from Zeke to Domi. "What? What's going on?"

"Don't worry, you might be pregnant with cat Jesus," Domi said, shrugging.

"What?" Mia squeaked.

The cat swished its tail again. Nothing in its face changed, but it somehow emanated disapproval.

Zeke cleared his throat. *All joking aside...* "You...aren't here to kill us?" *Unlike last night? What changed?*

This time, the cat swished its tail with approval. "Yes. I come as a representative of the Cat Apocalypse to ask for your assistance in freeing us from a great tyrant."

Glancing over his shoulder at the still-slowly-approaching cats, Zeke gave the cat a look. "It doesn't look like you came in peace."

"They are under the control of the tyrant. The Cat Man Apocalypse," the cat explained calmly as if this was all very ordinary, thank you very much.

"Wait... Huh? There's two Catpocalypses?" Domi asked, frowning.

Zeke snorted. "Cat Man? Are you serious?"

"Very," the cat said, utterly unamused.

Mia glanced from Zeke to Domi, expression slightly strained. "What was that about me being pregnant?"

"A joke. It was just a joke," Zeke said.

"I can't tell anymore," Mia muttered.

All around them, the cats paced closer. Zeke shot them a

nervous glance. Unlike the cat in front of them, their eyes all glowed a faint yellow. Not a single iota of variance between one cat and another, but yellow, yellow, yellow. In sync, they stalked toward Zeke, Mia, and Domi.

*Maybe this cat is telling the truth. These cats...they could be scaring us in cahoots with the white cat, but...* Zeke glanced back at the white cat, which was currently curled in on itself to lick its belly. *It doesn't seem to be controlling them.*

Uncurling, the cat licked its paw, then wiped its head. "Shall we go inside before they call him?" It looked up, bright blue eyes flashing in the sun.

Domi and Zeke exchanged glances. Domi shrugged, and Zeke shrugged back. *Might as well. Again, I'm pretty sure I can take a single cat.*

"Can't Cat Man just crash through the wall again? Like he did back in the elementary school," Mia pointed out.

"We'll have to change locations," Domi said quietly.

Zeke nodded. "I have an idea. Follow me."

He led the way up to the apartment and opened the door—or tried to. The locked door clanged against its frame.

Zeke licked his lips. He glanced over his shoulder. "Uh, Domi..."

"Yeah, yeah." Domi shook her head at him and approached the door, casually swiping her key fob to let him in. "Try again now, glorious leader."

"Yes, yes. A momentary setback," Zeke said, pulling himself to his full height. He swung the door open and stepped inside.

The second Zeke vanished, all the other cats sprinted for the door. Leaping and bouncing over the motorcycles, they dashed forth.

Mia sprinted through the door with a yelp.

Reaching the door, Domi paused. She turned back and pointed at one of the motorcycles nearest the door.

It exploded in a big loud *BANG,* and the cats scurried away, instantly burst from their formation. They sprinted off back into the dark alleys from whence they'd come and vanished.

Inside the apartment, Zeke paused for a moment. He nodded at the cat. "Before we get too far...why come to us for help?"

The cat swished its tail. "You have met the Cat Man and know of his tyranny. He rides our noble brethren as if they were mere horses. He dares to command us cats individually, as if cats did not know how to best kill for themselves. Our leader judged that you would be sympathetic to our plight."

"Oh, so because we've fought him before..." Zeke nodded.

"We lost," Domi pointed out.

"We didn't lose. We ran. But everyone was already tired from the Cartoon Apocalypse," Mia argued.

Zeke pointed at Mia. "I could probably take him at full strength. Probably. I'd at least have a chance."

*Although, I guess what this means is that Ryan didn't clean up the mess but just ran away, too. Dammit. Couldn't help us out even a little bit, huh?*

*Unless the Cat Man killed Ryan...*

Zeke pressed his lips together thoughtfully, then shook his head. *No, I don't think that's the case. Ryan's a time looper. In every example of time loopers I know of, the world resets on death. I'm not sure any of us would still exist if he died, since time would loop.*

"That, and you have shown extraordinary cooperation and kindness. You seemed like the type that we could take advantage of," the cat admitted bluntly. It laid down on Mia's shoulder and stared down at Zeke and Domi, daring them to say something.

Domi snorted. "What, you're telling me no one else is working together?"

"I guess...it kind of makes sense? Since there's the whole

'one may escape' thing. It's such a huge advantage to work together, though," Zeke said.

"I mean, evolutionarily speaking, one of humanity's great advantages versus beasts is being capable of communication and cooperation. You'd think more people would be cooperating," Mia argued.

The cat purred. "Several groups of humans are cooperating. You were the closest of them who had also encountered the Cat Man."

Zeke nodded. "That makes sense."

"Speaking of, what's your name?" Domi asked the cat.

It sat upright, drawing itself to a full tall sit. Shaking its head vigorously, it revealed a small blue collar and a shining round tag. "I am Fluffums, Fluffums the Third, First of His Name. You may call me Fluffy."

"Fluffums the Third...but first...?" Mia muttered to herself, her brows furrowing.

"You were someone's pet before the apocalypse?" Zeke asked, nodding at the collar.

Fluffums looked down on Zeke. "I had servants, yes. Kind of you to notice."

Zeke snorted. He glanced at Domi.

Instead of sharing the joke, Domi gestured outside with her eyes.

Zeke turned.

Cats lined the apartment's front steps. Faces pressed up against the glass entry doors, pressed together tight in a mess, three or four cats deep. Tails flicked, but aside from that, all the cats sat absolutely still.

All their eyes glowed faint yellow.

"Shit. We have to move," Zeke said.

# 47
## RUN, RUN, RUN

"I was wondering when you would notice," Fluffums said, sprawling over Mia's shoulders again, front feet on one side of her neck and back feet on the other, tail dangling down on her left and head lolling on the right. He gave her a content slap with his tail. "I grant you the honor of carrying me, servant."

Mia nodded. She looked at the other two, who nodded back. Together, they sprinted to the back of the apartments.

"Won't there just be more cats outside?" Mia asked.

"I'm hoping they're all gathered up front," Zeke replied.

Fluffums yawned. "The Cat Man's army is vast. He has a great number of foot soldiers."

"Remind me why we're helping you again?" Domi asked, raising her eyebrows at the cat.

"Did I not say?" Fluffums flicked his tail. "If you ally with us here, in our weakened state, we will help you later, at a time of our choosing."

"What an offer," Zeke muttered under his breath. *It's reasonable to hear the cat out. After all, it sounds like he's willing to help us take down the Cat Man and, well, Cat Man is a fellow apocalypse.*

*We'd have to take him down eventually. But, damn, that offer makes me want to toss him outside and let him take on that cat army alone.*

Unperturbed, Fluffums licked his paw. "If you show extraordinary capability, our leader might choose to ally with you."

"Oh, really," Domi said sarcastically.

Zeke glanced at the cat. *He's unnecessarily haughty for his tiny size, isn't he? What good can cats do for us? They're small, they're lightweight, they're harmless enough that humans domesticated them. What's the point?*

They approached the back door. Zeke peeked out the small, wire-lined glass window, then slowly pushed it open. No cats awaited them.

*No, no, wait. There's plenty of apocalypses that I don't really have a good solution for, but cats do. Like, for example...* He glanced up.

A hundred pigeons stared back at him, dark eyes as black as the sky above. They crowded the electric wires, occasionally cooing but never moving. Watching. Waiting.

He licked his lips. *They still haven't forgotten that pigeon I ate, have they?* "Will you help us take down the Pigeon Apocalypse?"

Fluffums purred, deep in his throat. His eyes half-shut, pupils expanding. His tail thumped rhythmically against Mia's chest.

*I'll take that as a yes.*

The soft patter of tiny paws caught Zeke's ear. He whirled.

A black cat appeared around the corner. It meowed at them.

"A Cat Man minion?" Domi asked, raising her hand.

"Her name is Shadow. She is one of us," Fluffums said, leaping off Mia's shoulders. He walked over to the other cat, and they exchanged sniffs. Turning back to the humans, he nodded. "Follow us."

"Wait, we aren't going somewhere to discuss this?" Zeke

asked, gesturing over his shoulder. *I was going to take them to the pharmacy...but I guess we don't need that?*

"What is there to discuss between us? You haven't attempted to kill me, and you showed interest in cooperation. That is enough for me to take you to our leader. If you want to negotiate, do it with our leader. Don't waste my time," Fluffums said, swishing his tail.

Domi nodded, smirking a little bit. "He's got a point, you know."

Zeke gave her a look. "Is it a good idea for us to walk into the Cat Apocalypse's stronghold?"

Fluffums cleared his throat. He gave a meaningful look at Domi. "You wield the fearful power of fireworks. If you mean to make your escape, who could stop you?"

"Most cats are terrified of loud noises," Domi agreed, nodding at Fluffums. "And even the ones that aren't will generally spook if they see all the other cats running."

"Fair enough," Zeke said, nodding. *That's right. Even the Cat Man's giant tabby mount was afraid of Domi's explosions. It seems like the System hasn't modified them to the point that they can withstand their native instincts...yet, anyway. Fluffums is intelligent, but Shadow hasn't spoken yet, so I think it's reasonable to assume that most of the cats in the Cat Apocalypse are ordinary cats who should still be spooked by explosions.*

*And if not...* Zeke swallowed down a sudden mouthful of drool and wiped his mouth. *At the end of the day, they're just cats. And, hey, cut that out, me. I don't need to start getting hungry every time I get into a fight. What kind of fucked up conditioned response is that?*

Giving him a sideways glance, Domi offered him a granola bar.

Zeke lifted his hand to refuse, then sighed. He took it.

"Thanks." *Better to eat now before I'm in desperate need and dire straits. Sure didn't enjoy that earlier, when Ryan and the Cat Man were trying to kill me, and all I could do was lie there.*

Fluffums nodded. "Then, please, follow me."

He turned, strutting off into the alleys behind the building. Shadow followed, as sleek and graceful as Fluffums was pompous and elegant. Mia, Domi, and Zeke followed.

Just as they stepped into the alley, a pigeon darted down from the tangled electric wires overhead. It strutted back toward the front of the apartment, bobbling along at a pigeon's pace. Poking around the corner, it waddled into the sunlight.

From on high, the other pigeons watched it, silently waiting, solemn and serious. *Go, our chosen. Arbiter of our will. We pray for your success.*

Every cat clustered at the door whipped around, suddenly focusing on the pigeon.

The pigeon burst up, flapping into the air on instinct. After a moment, it dropped back down. Ever so slowly, it waddled closer.

*You are one of many. Many of one. All pigeons are every pigeon, and every pigeon is all.*

The closest cat dropped into a crouch. The yellow haze over its eyes faded. Laser-focused on the pigeon, it twitched its tail.

Closer. Closer. The pigeon's round eye reflected death. It cooed fearlessly. Chest thrust out, big round eyes empty, it waddled toward the cats one step at a time.

*Our eyes are myriad. Our forms are countless.*

In a silent burst of violence, the closest cat lunged.

Instantly, the pigeon launched into the air in a great loud flutter of wings. The cat snagged one of its tail feathers, but it escaped, flying up into the air.

Jolted back to life, all the cats lunged after it in a messy knot. The pigeon cooed loudly and flew along, dancing between flying and falling as if horribly injured.

The cats followed. Jumping and snapping, lunging and clawing, they chased the pigeon around the corner of the apartment building and toward the rear. One or two started to wander away from the pack, only for the yellow light to glimmer in their eyes and turn them back to face the pigeon.

*None shall escape our vengeance.*

The pigeon turned down the dark alley. Ahead of it, Zeke looked back. Its convex mirror of an eye reflected his form, *the killer, first devourer of true pigeonkind.*

*Never forget. Never surrender.*

*The devourer must be destroyed!*

Spreading its wings, the pigeon flew back up to the telephone wire, its job done.

Zeke frowned. *Huh? What was that? A pigeon? But it didn't attack?*

A cat turned the corner. One. Two. Three. Six. They lined the alleyway, stalking after the trio.

"Guys. Guys!" Zeke shouted. He pushed Domi and Mia. "Go. We've got to go!"

"What?" Domi asked, craning her neck.

"The cats are here!" Zeke snapped.

The girls glanced back. Behind them, a wave of cats leapt forth, twenty or thirty of them chasing after the group. Under the girls' gaze, about half of them froze in place. The rest kept going, then froze and looked back.

All their eyes glowed yellow. The cats twitched, then broke free of their natural behaviors and gave chase.

Fluffums narrowed his eyes. "The tyrant."

Domi raised her hand. "I'll just—"

"Please, refrain," Fluffums requested, flinching.

Domi grimaced. "If I can't explode things to scare them off, then you'd better run!"

Fluffums and Shadow took off, Domi, Mia, and Zeke at their heels.

Behind them, the cats closed in.

# 48
## CATS ON CATS

Yellow eyes glimmering in the dark alley, the cats gave chase.

**[Roll With Me]**
*Speed is boosted due to running with allied and [Subordinate] apocalypses.*

Mia yelped, startled as she suddenly sped up. "What was that?"

Domi glanced at Zeke, arcing a brow. "A new skill?"

Zeke nodded. "Got it from...from...from leveling up from that battle just now." *Don't tell Domi I can eat skills, don't tell Domi I can eat skills.*

She nodded. "Convenient."

"I know, right?" Zeke said. *Almost like I picked it myself because I have a party of sorts, now! Haha! Couldn't be, right?*

The cats sped up, continuing to chase them. Zeke scowled. *It's a good skill, but not enough to outrun the cats on its own. What else do I have? What can I use?*

*Hold on. Obviously! Cats hate being wet!* He turned around

and opened his mouth, half-running backward. The sensation of vomiting welled up from within him, and a dark brown liquid poured out of his mouth.

## [Create Coffee]

A puddle of coffee spread behind them, splashing in the alley.

"Zeke, come on!" Domi shouted.

Zeke shut his mouth and ran on, sprinting back to the girls. He looked over his shoulder. *Did it work?*

The front wave of cats stopped dead, balking at the puddle. One, moving with too much momentum to stop, gathered itself on the very brink of the puddle and burst over it, pulling off an enormous leap. Another cat jumped up on the trash piled around the edge of the alley, nimbly avoiding the liquid. As it jumped from box to box, one of the boxes toppled over. The cat scrambled away, entire body puffed up and eyes wide, and scurried through the coffee puddle in a panic. Behind it, the shifted box tumbled into the center of the coffee puddle.

A cat on the edge of the puddle jumped to the box, then to the far side. Primly, it shook a single paw, as if it might have gotten a little bit damp. One after another, the other cats followed it.

*Damn. Slowed but didn't stop them.* Zeke turned back around and sprinted on.

They turned a corner and came face-to-face with a barbed-wire-topped chain link fence.

"What— How? We're stuck!" Domi called, scowling.

"Not at all. Watch us."

Nodding at Shadow, Fluffums sprinted ahead, moving with speed that belied his fluffy body. With ease, he scrambled up the fence, jumped to an electric box, then jumped up, caught the edge of a rooftop with his paws, and kicked his way up. Shadow followed him a moment later, bouncing up onto the rooftop beside him. Shadow wandered out of sight, while Fluffums sat primly on the edge of the roof and wrapped his tail around his paws.

"There. Like that," he said, nodding.

"We can't—" Domi rolled her eyes. She lifted her hands. "You two move away. I'm about to spook these kitties."

Backing up to the chain link fence, Zeke cast around him. *Something...anything. One of my skills, maybe?*

## Skills
**Manipulate Aerosols (Medium) +1**
**Pick Up (Weak)**
**Osmosis (Weak) +1**
**Subordinate Link (Weak)**
**Create Drug (Weak) +1**
**Crystal Burst (Poor)**
**Engulf (Poor)**
**Create Coffee (Strong)**
**Whistle Blast (Weak) Digital Broadcast (Weak)**
**Electric Leap (Poor)**

## Passive
**Resilient Regeneration (Minor) +8**
**Team Spirit (Minor) +1**
**Disguise (Minor)**
**Watertight (Minor)**
**Caffeine Rush (Average)**
**Growth (Lesser) +2**
**Heat Resistance (Lesser) +9**
**Strong Jaw (Minor)**
**Flexible Body (Average)**

### Roll With Me (Minor)

### Condition
### Hardness (Lesser) (Condition)
### MOTORCYCLE

Zeke pressed his lips together, looking over the skill list. *Hmm... no, no, no...*

*Wait!* His eyes lit up. *Subordinate Link! Allen is an anole. A lizard! Specifically, a lizard that's great at climbing! I bet he has a climbing skill. Can I borrow it?*

**You can borrow subordinate skills, but you cannot share them with other subordinates or neutral parties.**

*That's no good. If only Allen and I can escape, but Domi and Mia get left behind... I can't abandon them.*

*Whistle Blast? It won't stun all of them, but some of them...but I want to stop all of them. Come on, something else, something else...*

His eyes landed on Create Drug, and he smiled. *Oooh. Yes, I think I've found it.*

"Domi, do you have a skill that can get you and Mia up to the roof?" Zeke asked, clenching his hands together. Focusing on the space between his palms, he activated his skill.

### [Create Drug]

Something lightweight tickled the inside of his palms, just a small amount. He snorted to himself. *Not enough. More!*

### [Create Drug]

"I've got Grenade Jump. It's, uh, it's a bit dangerous, but it works," Domi said, shrugging.

"It won't leave you so injured we'll have to do the apocalypse-defeating trick again?" Zeke asked.

"Nah. Couple scratches. You might want to back up, though," Domi warned.

"Got it." Zeke strode forward, toward the oncoming wave of cats.

"Zeke, you aren't going to take them all alone, are you?" Mia asked, concerned.

"Who do you think I am, Ryan?" Zeke asked, rolling his eyes. He shook his head. "I'll be right behind you. Trust me. I'm not stupid."

**[Create Drug]**

Mia nodded. She looked at Domi.

Domi sized her up. Mia's head reached about the top of Domi's shoulder. Nodding to herself, Domi knelt, scooping up Mia in a princess carry.

"E-eh?" Mia asked.

"All right, hold on," Domi said. Bending her knees deep, she jumped with all her might. An explosion burst beneath her, and she flew upward, propelled toward the roof. Curling Mia to her chest, she struck the roof and rolled.

Staring down the cats, Zeke created a little more space between his hands. His stomach grumbled, and his strength flagged, but he pushed on. *Come on. Just a little more. I need a ton of this for it to work!*

**[Create Drug]**

The cats locked onto Zeke, standing there all alone. They

sprinted, closing in for the final leap. Zooming forth, they bared claws and teeth.

With one final **[Create Drug]**, Zeke threw his hands open, tossing the light green herb at the cats.

The cats' pupils went wide. Almost as one, they shivered in delight. Instantly, they lost all interest in Zeke. Instead, they chased down the deepest patches of the herb and dropped to the ground, rubbing their necks in it. They purred loudly, rolling around on the ground. As more cats arrived, they began to fight, jostling for the best spot in the herb.

Zeke grinned. *Catnip! There's no risk to humans, but it's a great way to distract cats without hurting them. After all, we're allied with the Cat Apocalypse. They probably won't look kindly on us wildly attacking cats.*

He looked up at Allen on his head. "Can you share a climbing skill with me?"

Allen looked down at him. Superiority gleaming in his eyes, he gave a single pushup.

### Subordinate [Anole Apocalypse] has shared the skill [Sticky Feet] (Strong) +5 with you!

Zeke pressed his hands against the nearby wall. They stuck, and he lifted them, pulling himself up. His feet scrambled against the wall. He stared down, confused. *My hands work, but my feet—*

*Oh. Right. Shoes.* Reaching down, Zeke plucked his shoes off his feet with one hand, then quickly tied them around his neck. Pressing now bare hands and feet to the wall, they stuck easily. He ascended the wall one push at a time, steadily climbing to the top.

Domi reached down. She offered him a hand. Zeke grabbed it, pulling himself up the last bit. Panting, he wiped off his hands, deactivating the skill. *Whew. That was exhausting.*

Across the roof, Fluffums thumped his tail. "See? As I said. Easy."

Zeke scowled at him. "Easy for you to say," he muttered.

Fluffums stood and stretched, giving a big yawn. He turned away, flicking his tail. "While they're distracted...shall we?"

Zeke nodded. "Let's go."

# 49
## HEADQUARTERS

Taking a final leap down, Fluffums descended into a destroyed building. The roof gaped to the sky, sunlight pouring down from the black dome to illuminate what had until recently been the inside of a quaint house. From the roof, a massive hole penetrated the house down to its ground floor, as if something huge had punched it from above. Stairs crawled down the gap, cut off halfway only to resume below. Rooms laid open and exposed, two stories cut clear open from above. A cute pink children's bed set laid scattered amid a chic dining room, the upper floor spilling down into the lower. A home office crunched under the weight of a bathtub, while a toilet perched precariously on the newly cut edge of the second floor.

Grabbing the edge of the roof with the assistance of Sticky Feet, Zeke lowered himself to the rafters, then reached up, helping the girls down. From the rafters, he grabbed Mia's hand and slowly dropped her into the room below. Her feet dangled a foot over the ground, and he released her. She landed, then reached up to help Domi down.

Shadow jumped on Zeke's shoulders, pounced to the rafters, jumped to Mia's shoulders, and dropped to the ground.

"Thanks, you were a huge help," Zeke muttered, offering Domi his hand. She took it, grabbing the rafters with the other, and swung herself down. Mia grabbed her around the waist, and she slid down to the floor. When the girls were safe, Zeke grabbed the rafters and dropped himself, landing not far from the edge of the hole in the building. The floor gave under his feet, bending down. Startled, he scurried further into the building, away from the hole.

Sitting on the rubble-dusted kitchen counter on the first floor, Fluffums looked up expectantly, waiting for them to join him. Glancing down, he casually batted a bit of rubble to the floor, then sat once more.

"Why'd we come in through the roof, anyway?" Domi muttered.

Zeke shrugged. "It's the way Fluffums led us."

"And I'm asking, why did we follow the dumb cat?" she muttered back.

"Cuz we didn't know where he was going," Zeke returned.

"That's fair, and yet..." Domi said, shaking her head.

Mia snorted. "This whole situation is ridiculous."

As they climbed down to the first floor, cats appeared. From every corner, from under the couch, in through the shattered windows. Some wore collars, with sleek coats and plump bodies, while some were slender, mangy and weather-worn, no collar to be seen around their bony necks. Dozens and dozens of cats, hundreds of them. They sat at the edges of the broken second floor and paced up and down the stairs.

"Whoa," Zeke murmured. *That's way more cats than the Cat Man had chasing us. Seems like the Cat Apocalypse has more pull among cats than the Cat Man does.*

Domi's eyes burned orange. She raised her hands. "Was this a trap?"

Mia looked at Fluffums. Her eyes narrowed.

"Excuse me for the...slight deception, friends," Fluffums said, sitting up perfectly straight. He took a deep breath. "In truth...I am the Cat Apocalypse."

## Cat Apocalypse
## Danger Rating: A
## Level: 25.44

"I guessed," Zeke said.

"And you didn't tell us?" Domi said.

"Didn't seem important, and I didn't want to spook him," Zeke said aside, saying the second part quieter. He nodded at Fluffums. "He's a talking cat. How much SPR do you think he had to buy to be capable of human speech? Not to mention, it's probably a skill investment, too, with the shape of his mouth not being particularly good for speaking human languages. Plus, Shadow didn't speak, only Fluffums. That was really the clincher. Why would only one cat be able to speak? Unless, of course...that one cat *was* the apocalypse."

Fluffums lowered his head in acknowledgement. "Impeccable deduction."

"We would have trusted us more if you revealed that from the start," Domi grumbled, crossing her arms. Her eyes' glow faded.

"Cats are solitary hunters. Although we live in loose families, we prefer to move alone, unseen and in silence. I don't understand what it takes to gain a human's trust, nor do I care to. I moved according to my superior instincts and succeeded. Perhaps you humans should take notes," Fluffums declared pompously.

Zeke sighed. *Well...he is a cat, after all.*

"However...I enlisted your aid because we are small, and though we are many, we are not like those suicidal pigeons, willing to risk life and limb to kill a large foe. We are solitary hunters not herbivores. A single injury can leave us starving on the street, fated for death. And when we face a man who can create huge cats, easily able to throw us aside..." Fluffums shook his head.

"You can't take on the Cat Man's giant cats alone, so you need our help," Zeke translated. *It does make sense. Herbivores, as he says...and as Resilience says, can take a hit and keep trucking. Biologically, it's what they're designed to do. The longer prey animals can run from their predators, the more they protect all the other prey animals like them in the vicinity. On the other side of that equation, though, a mildly injured predator can no longer run down its prey and dies...hence why predators tend to die more easily to small injuries and have more risk-adverse behavior in the wild.*

*In that sense, the risk each individual cat faces from one of Cat Man's giant cats... Well, Fluffums is literally trying to herd cats. And not even that, but herd cats to do something they're biologically programmed to avoid, that is, take on a larger foe with a high chance of their personal destruction. No wonder he needed to enlist our help.*

Fluffums nodded. "Indeed."

Zeke nodded. He turned to Domi and Mia. "What do you say?"

Domi leaned in close. "So, we have two options here—"

"Ah, excuse me. I'll give you room to think," Fluffums said. He stood and walked to the far end of the kitchen's countertop, then sat down, curling his tail around his feet once more.

"So, two options—" Domi cut off again. She glanced over.

Fluffum's ears pivoted, both locked on the three of them.

Zeke sighed. "Just go ahead." *We can leave things unsaid.*

Domi nodded. "One. We walk. They still have to deal with

the Cat Man, but so do we. We potentially risk coming back to a much more powerful Cat Man or Catpocalypse, but now with a grudge against us."

"Right. Reaching out to us was already a power move," Zeke agreed.

Mia pressed a hand to her forehead. She winced, blinking rapidly. "Ow..."

"You okay, Mia?" he asked, leaning in.

Mia waved her hand. "I'm fine, I'm fine."

Zeke nodded. He stood but kept his eyes on Mia, faintly concerned. *Maybe I should make some painkillers with Create Drug later...?*

"Or...we stand our ground here and take down a weaker Cat Man with the assistance of the Catpocalypse. Forge the foundation of an alliance between us and the cats—"

"With the Pigeon Apocalypse in mind," Zeke agreed.

Domi nodded. "By the way, why are they after you? The pigeons, I mean."

"I, er. May have eaten one of them," Zeke confessed.

Mia and Domi both stared. From the kitchen countertop, Fluffums nodded with approval.

"You cooked it first, right?" Mia asked.

"Would it make you feel better if I said yes?" Zeke replied at a whisper.

"Jeez," Mia muttered.

"He hasn't always had pica?" Domi asked.

Mia shook his head. "This is all a new development to me."

"Guys, it's the Apocalypse, okay? Things are weird," Zeke muttered back.

"I'm still eating food," Domi said, shrugging.

Zeke put his hands up. "We're deciding what to do. So far, I'm mostly hearing... join hands with the Cat Apocalypse."

Domi nodded. "I mean... yeah. We gotta take down the Cat

Man. Those big cats are scary. Plus, he's already tried to swoop in and pick off the scraps once. For as long as he's around, there's always a chance we finish off an Apocalypse, only to find a tiger-size tabby breathing down our necks."

Zeke nodded. "Mia?"

"I..." Mia shook her head, blinking rapidly. She wiped her eyes and nodded at him. "I'm not an apocalypse. I'm along for the ride."

"You— You're not an Apocalypse, but that doesn't mean you don't get a say," Zeke said.

Mia put her hands up. "I agree with you, anyway. I... Jeez. Everything's moving so fast. One second, Ryan's trying to kill you, then there's coffee everywhere, then the school's a cartoon hellscape, and now we're allying with cats?" She let out a laugh, her voice just a little hysterical. "I-I mean, I feel like I'm losing my mind."

"It is pretty nuts," Domi agreed without expression.

"I guess I'm just rolling with the punches," Zeke admitted. "Ryan trying to kill me was rough. I still haven't really wrapped my head around that one."

A soft paw on the back of Zeke's arm. He turned. Fluffums looked up at him, brilliant blue eyes impatient. "So, have you decided?"

Zeke took a deep breath. He looked at the girls, who nodded. Turning to Fluffums, he nodded. "Yes. We'll help you."

Fluffums purred. "Then, let an alliance be forged."

**You have Allied with the Cat Apocalypse. The terms of the alliance are: Until the Cat Man Apocalypse is defeated, the Explosion Apocalypse, Hunger Apocalypse, and Cat Apocalypse will cooperate.**

"Huh. Hunger, huh?" Domi said, glancing at Zeke.

Zeke spread his hands. "I thought it was pretty obvious."

"It was that or the Pica Apocalypse," Domi agreed, nodding.

Mia frowned. She glanced at the air, then squinted. Her brow furrowed.

# 50
## AN UNEXPECTED GUEST

Fluffums flicked his tail. "It has been decided. Come with me. I'll show you his hideout."

"The Cat Man's?" Zeke asked.

"Who else?" Fluffums returned primly.

"We're going now? Like, right now?" Domi asked.

Fluffums tilted his head. "Why wait?"

Zeke nodded. "He's got a point. The longer we wait, the higher the Cat Man levels."

"Fair enough," Domi muttered. She rubbed the back of her neck, then glanced at Zeke. "Is that Ryan jerk going to show up again?"

Zeke shrugged. "*I'm* not the one who can see the future or whatever."

"Time loop, he could time loop. I guess...unless this is something we do every loop, he probably won't come?" Mia said.

"But Fluffums came to us because we encountered the Cat Man, and Ryan knows we encountered the Cat Man," Zeke pointed out. "This could be a common route, or at least a common reaction to encountering the Cat Man. We should be on guard."

Mia nodded. "Right, right. I... Er... Well..."

"What?" Zeke asked, frowning at her.

Mia took a deep breath. Slow at first, then rushing out all at once, she said, "Um, talking about time loops...Ryan said I usually die."

"You die? Holy shit! Mia, why didn't you say anything?" Zeke asked, startled. *Should I not have brought her? Wait, but what if not bringing her kills her? I should keep her close. I can't let Mia die!*

"What did he say about me?" Domi asked cheerfully, breaking into the mood.

Mia looked at her, somewhere between tears and laughter. She let out a choked sob that sounded almost like a laugh. "He was scared of you or something. He didn't want to let you meet Zeke."

"Oh. Why not?" Domi wondered aloud.

Taking a deep breath, Mia visibly swallowed and shook her head. She took a few moments, but ultimately looked up, forcing herself to smile. "I don't know. I don't know anything. Ryan just kept saying he couldn't trust me, I wouldn't understand..."

"Oh, sweetie. Come here," Domi said. She drew Mia to her chest, and Mia went, tears running down her face. Domi patted her back comfortingly, holding onto her. "Have you been keeping it inside this whole time? It's okay."

Mia sobbed. She grabbed onto Domi, her knuckles white, her shoulders shaking. Her voice trembled, tears rolling down her face. "I don't wanna die. And the kids, the kids, I couldn't do anything, I couldn't do anything! Zeke and Ryan, and Ryan, and Ryan, he's...he's...he's—"

"Shh. It's okay. It's okay now. We'll take care of you," Domi whispered soothingly, stroking her back.

Standing there awkwardly, Zeke cast a jealous look at Domi.

*Why couldn't I be the one she ran to? No—I should've reached out for her first. Okay, come on. I can still rectify this.* He put a hand on Mia's back gently, almost too gently. "It's...it's okay."

*It's okay? Is that the best I can do? Am I kidding, me? Come on! Something better!*

Mia took a deep breath. She pushed away from Domi and rubbed her eyes. Another deep breath, chest heaving, and then she nodded. "Okay. Okay. I'm okay."

*Damn. Missed my chance.* Zeke fell back, a pained smile on his face.

"You're sure?" Domi asked, a hand still on Mia's arm.

Behind them, something crashed. All three of them jumped and turned.

Fluffums stared at the floor, where a piece of rubble rattled on the ground, his paw still outstretched. Unashamedly, he slowly retracted his paw, then looked up at them, somehow exuding boredom. "Are you ready?"

Mia nodded. She clenched her fist and grinned, and it only looked half-fake. "Let's go take on the Cat Man."

"At last," Fluffums muttered under his breath. He hopped off the countertop, then froze.

"What is it?" Zeke asked, confused.

Fluffums turned wide eyes to Zeke. "Hide."

"Huh? But—"

All around them, cats fled. Vanishing into nooks and crannies, fleeing over rubble, tails flicking as they vanished under beds and furniture. A moment later, Zeke felt it. The earth trembled.

*Thump. Thump.*

"What *is* that?" Mia hissed.

"Not good, is what it is," Domi replied. She glanced around, searching for a spot.

Zeke glanced up at the hole in the roof. His stomach dropped as a thought came to him, simple as it was terrible: *Something* made that.

He glanced around, then pointed at the kitchen counter, at the big cabinets under the sink. "Domi, Mia, you two should fit in there."

"Sure, but what about you?" Domi asked, shepherding Mia toward the cabinet.

"I-I have skills," Zeke said.

"Good luck," Domi said. She pulled the cabinet's doors open, and she and Mia vanished inside.

*Thump. THUMP. THUMP.*

Zeke ran toward the collapsed part of the house, careful to choose a spot of rubble away from the edge. He laid down on it, scraping the rubble over himself, then activated a skill he'd never called on before.

*Here goes nothing.*

## [Disguise]
*Disguise yourself, especially as a pile of garbage.*

Zeke's vision changed. Suddenly, he saw everything from above, saw himself, lying there, covered in rubble. He moved, and the him below moved, exactly the way he meant to. *Huh. I don't look very hidden. But if I do this...*

Reaching out, he pulled a piece of fallen drywall over his body, hiding his face and the shape of his limbs. From below him, he adjusted the shape of a curtain so it outlined his body less, then swept another dozen nearby bits of rubble and trash over his left arm, finally hiding his right under the drywall with his head.

From the detached perspective, he turned away from

himself and watched the sky. *How can I see things like this? Is it because the skill is active? Disguise...this skill might be more useful as a vision technique than a disguise technique.*

*Well...I'm not complaining. I don't feel too hungry yet, so let's ride this out and see what I can see.*

*THUMP. THUMP. THUMP.*

Dark beige. Deep shadows. Cracks, zagging through the old bone. An empty eye socket loomed in the hole where the roof had been, then a long muzzle, lined with teeth longer than Zeke's hands. The T-rex skeleton stared into the house.

### Dinosaur Apocalypse (Skeleton)
### Danger Rating: SSS
### Level: 39.23

*Fuck! It's still around?* Cursing under his breath, it took Zeke a moment to notice the second half of the message. *Level 39.23? Wait, then it* could *have a Domain...but it doesn't?*

### You do not have to choose a Domain.

Zeke frowned. He glanced at the System. *What else can I choose?*

...

Still not going to say anything, huh.

Slowly, the enormous skull turned left and right. A long, slow inhalation sounded, a deep huff despite the skeleton's lack of lungs or a proper nose. Fierce, cold breath like a wind rolled over Zeke, jostling his curtain and the stray drywall.

*Shit! Not now!*

## [Disguise]

Just as the drywall was about to slide off his body, it suddenly stopped, snagging on a bit of Zeke's bloodstained shirt. The curtain fell back down, forming a shapeless mess over his legs.

The T-rex snorted. It lifted its head out of the hole and turned away, looking over its shoulder. A low grumble sounded from its throat.

Clicks and thumps came in return. Smaller feet pattered away, clattering dry as bone on the asphalt outside.

Zeke's heart jolted. He held his breath. *Shit. It's making more?*

*Wait. How the hell can a skeleton make babies?*

*I guess there's a skill for everything.*

Earth shaking, claws thumping, the T-rex walked away.

Zeke waited until the sound faded, then sat up, pushing the drywall away. Across from him, in the kitchen, Domi peeked out of the cabinet, her jaw dropped. Silently, she mouthed, *was that really the—*

"The T-rex from the museum, yeah," Zeke whispered, nodding.

Domi mouthed something else less polite.

Fluffums appeared from behind some rubble and hopped down to the countertop once more. "So, the Cat Man?"

"You aren't going to mention the giant T-rex skeleton that just—" Domi gestured wildly.

Fluffums blinked at her. He tilted his head. "What T-rex?"

"The—" Domi took a deep breath.

Zeke leaned in. "Cats like to pretend they can't see things they can't beat."

"Yeah, yeah, I know," Domi muttered back.

"There is nothing I can't beat," Fluffums declared primly. He hopped off the countertop and strode toward the back door, the opposite side of the house from the T-rex. "Shall we?"

Crawling out from under the countertop, Mia nodded at Zeke and gave him a thumbs-up.

Zeke nodded. "We shall."

# 51
## SCOPING OUT THE CAT MAN

Fluffums led them through the back alleys and twisted streets toward the seedier part of town. Pawn shops and run-down convenience stores dominated the landscape, advertising GUNS, CBD, and VAPES in big, bold letters. Filth piled up in the streets, overflowing from the public trash cans and spilling out onto the sidewalks. Here, the abandoned cars sported smashed windows, each and every one. If not for iron bars and shutters on the shops' windows, Zeke had the feeling the shops would be the same. Even then, half the shops' doors laid half-open, the shutters pried apart, locks smashed. A fire burned somewhere in the distance, dark smoke billowing into the black sky.

"This is where the Cat Man hangs out?" Domi asked, glancing around, her brows furrowed.

Fluffums nodded. "There are several good trash cans back here."

"Damn. Cat Man is more hardcore than I expected," Domi muttered, twisting her lips.

Zeke nodded. "Yeah, I didn't exactly expect a guy with fluffy white cat ears to hang out in the bad part of town."

Fluffums' own fluffy white cat ears twitched. "His what?"

"Cat ears... Oh. They aren't as nice as yours," Zeke hurriedly assured Fluffums.

"He dares to impinge upon my perfect form?" Fluffums muttered to himself, horrified.

"That's your problem?" Domi asked, shaking her head.

Mia put a hand on her chin. "Cat Man...what kind of guy is he? You've run into him before, right, Fluffums?"

Fluffums lowered his head in acknowledgement. "He was a lesser being who knew his place and would offer gifts and service, as is my right, and the right of every greater being, to demand from you lesser beings. Back then, I considered him a relatively enlightened lesser being. Who knew that he secretly hid a horrible envy for my beautiful self, one that would drive him to abandoning his righteous place and falling from grace?"

"He...was someone who would give you and the other cats treats?" Zeke translated after a moment.

Fluffums nodded. "Indeed. A lesser being who *knew his place.*"

Mia glanced at Domi. "Why do I feel like we're on the wrong side of the French Revolution?"

Domi snorted. "More like the Cat Revolution."

"That wasn't funny," Zeke replied over his shoulder.

"I was gonna say 'Catch Revolution,' but then I realized that catch is a word," Domi said, shrugging.

Mia chuckled.

"Don't laugh at her. She doesn't deserve it for that horrible... Does that even qualify as a pun?" Zeke said, shaking his head at Domi.

Domi clicked her tongue. "Don't be jealous just because you can't sling this level of pun."

"'This level of pun' being negative one thousand?" Zeke asked.

"It wasn't *that* bad," Mia said, glancing at Domi.

Domi glanced back with a grin. "She gets it."

Fluffums halted. His tail curled up. He looked over his shoulder. "We have arrived."

Zeke blinked. He frowned. "That?"

Domi glanced at Fluffums. "You aren't serious."

Squeezed in between a locked-down coffee shop and a grated-up tattoo parlor, a large, flat store awaited them. **PETS LIFE** spelled out in bright green letters over a generic, slightly run-down storefront. No grates covered the windows, and the automatic doors stood ready for the next customer. Bright florescent panels lit the store from within. If not for the shattered windows and locked shutters all around them, Zeke might have mistaken it for an ordinary afternoon.

Mia frowned. "The...pet store?"

Fluffums' ears flattened to his head. "He has captured our brethren within and wiped their minds. We must destroy him, swiftly!"

"Wait, hold on. Ryan probably knows we're headed here. We need to proceed with caution, not bust down the front door," Zeke said, gesturing the group back around the corner.

"What do you suggest, then? Going in the back?" Domi asked.

"I suggest...scouting it out," Zeke said.

Fluffums sat down. He sighed. "If we could enter this place, do you think we would not have already done so? Inferior beings and their small minds."

Ignoring Fluffums, Zeke lifted his hand to his head. Allen the anole hopped on, and he put the lizard on the ground. "Go!"

Allen paused to do one last push-up, making intense eye contact with Zeke, then scurried away. He darted around the corner and slipped between the automatic doors with a flash of green.

Leaning against the wall, Zeke closed his eyes. "Domi, keep an eye out."

"Roger." Domi gave a sloppy salute.

"What're you doing? What's he doing?" Mia asked.

Domi shrugged. "Fucked if I know."

"I'm...I'm gonna borrow Allen's eyes. The lizard's," Zeke explained.

"You can do that?" Mia asked.

Zeke shrugged. "Probably?"

**[Subordinate Link]**
**Who would you like to link with?**
**-Anole Apocalypse**
**-Explosion Apocalypse**
-

Zeke's brows furrowed. *Why is there a third empty slot? Fluffums, maybe? Is the Subordinate menu glitching now that I have allies?*

*Can the System glitch? That's a horrifying thought. Let's just... focus on the now. I can worry about that later.* He selected Allen from the list.

Instantly, he saw the world from a low angle. The edges sloped away, the center magnified almost like a fisheye lens. Zeke tried to turn his head but couldn't move.

**Please level up Subordinate Link if you want to exercise more control over your Subordinates.**

*That's actually kind of terrifying, isn't it? I never thought about it, but Subordinate Link is incredibly dangerous. When I use it with a small lizard like Allen, it isn't that troublesome, but if I used it on Domi? If I leveled it up to the point I could fully control her body?*

*Fuck. I-I don't like this skill. I don't like where it's going. System, are you trying to make me a criminal?*

### You are an Apocalypse.

Zeke sighed aloud. *All right, you got me there. I guess the System doesn't really have an incentive to keep the powers from getting dangerous. If anything, it wants our skills to get as dangerous as possible, just as quickly as powerful.*

*Still, I have to remember this. I shouldn't use Subordinate Link without thinking.*

"Everything okay?" Mia whispered.

Zeke gave a thumbs up and turned his attention back to Allen.

The lizard blinked, then looked around. He stood in the entry of the pet store, beside the checkout counter. The store loomed around him, deeper and taller than it appeared from outside. In the distance, a massive fluffy tower constructed of boxes and platforms propped up by tall poles climbed toward the corrugated metal ceiling, a dangly pompom easily as large as Zeke's head dangling from the ceiling of its highest chamber. A huge cat sat atop the tower, splayed out on its side, napping.

*That's a Domain if I've ever seen one,* Zeke thought, taking in the huge cat tree.

Allen scurried forward. The world flashed past, distorted as the tiny anole darted. Zeke rubbed his forehead, waiting for it to clear.

A pause. The anole stood on the cabinets, staring hungrily into the plastic bin of live crickets.

*Not now. Keep moving!* Zeke ordered him.

Allen ignored him. He tilted his head, getting a better angle on the live crickets.

Zeke groaned. "Honestly..."

"What is it?" Mia asked.

"Well, do you want a live feed of the store's cricket supply? Because I've got the best possible view of that," Zeke complained.

Domi snorted. "What did you expect, sending a lizard in there?"

"Indeed. A lowly being like that one. He's barely worthy to qualify as food," Fluffums opined.

Zeke stiffened. "Eh... Wait, what was that?"

"I was saying, I wouldn't bother eating such a tiny prey as that one," Fluffums said, tossing his fluff.

"Shit! I forgot. Cats are natural born killers," Zeke muttered. He closed his eyes, reaching out to Allen. *Come back! You're in danger!*

Allen ignored him in favor of scurrying closer to the crickets.

*What did I expect from a lizard? Honestly.* Zeke sighed. He stepped away from the wall. "I didn't see Ryan. Let's go rescue my dumb subordinate before he gets himself killed."

"You're in danger," Ryan said, his voice fuzzy and distorted.

Zeke froze. He raised a hand to the others. Closing his eyes again, he focused on Allen's perspective.

The crickets hopped around in the bin. Allen darted to the side, searching for a way in. In the distance, a voice responded to Ryan.

*What's he saying? Dammit! Allen, stop running around! This is the important part!*

"I'm serious. He's going to kill you. Not just that, eat you. If you take my hand—"

"I won't become your subordinate."

Ryan let out a frustrated huff. "I'm not telling you to become my subordinate. Let's fight together. If we work together, we might be able to—"

"Or I could destroy you here, level up, and defeat him with

the levels," the man returned—*probably the Cat Man,* Zeke deduced.

"Sure. Try it," Ryan said. Though Zeke couldn't see him, he could hear the eye roll in Ryan's voice.

A loud *crash* smashed through the store. Allen jumped, turning to run, then froze. A wall of orange and black fur blocked his way. Sharp claws hid beneath padded paws. He looked up slowly.

"Meow," a calico cat said, its pupils widening in hunger.

Zeke pushed away from the wall. "Cat Man and Ryan are fighting. Now's our chance."

"I feel like I'm repeating myself, but...right now?" Domi asked.

"And Allen's in danger," Zeke said. *Though...he is an apocalypse, so he can probably hold his own against a single cat.*

*Probably.*

Fluffums stepped forward. He nodded at the humans. "He's distracted. Let's go."

# 52
## BUM RUSH THE PET STORE

Three people and a cat rushed at a pair of automatic doors, slowed down a moment as the automatic doors took a second to detect them and open, then ran into the store. A few betta fish swam lazily in a display to the left, while the checkout lanes stood emptily to the right. A long, long hallway sloped off ahead of them, stretching seemingly to infinity. Dog toys and chews lay strewn across the hall, torn off the walls and thrown to the ground. Puddles slicked the floor, a few bait fish still struggling in the shallow water.

Distantly, the sounds of battle echoed down the shiny tile floor. Blades clashed. A cat yowled in fury. A giant orange tabby flashed by the end of the aisle, chased by Ryan, only for a boy in a black hoodie with fluffy white ears to drop down from above. With acrobatic ease, Ryan leaped out of sight, and the Cat Man's claws slashed the tile floor instead.

Zeke beelined to the left, charging past the betta fish and aquarium accessories in the aisle. A calico cat sitting atop a bin at the end of the aisle startled, then fled. The top of the cricket bin lay empty, no anole in sight. *Shit. Was I too late?* "Allen!"

Scuttling from within the bin. Allen looked up at him, eyes

void of remorse, mouth full of crickets. He swallowed, licked his lips, and gave Zeke a pompous pushup.

Zeke sighed. *At least he's safe.* Opening the bin, he reached for Allen. The anole scurried away from him, thrashing wildly, but Zeke cornered him in the back of the bin and scooped him up. Several crickets clung to his hand.

Extracting Allen from the crickets with his free hand, Zeke regarded the crickets for a moment, then shrugged. *Can't hurt.*

### [Devour]

He slurped up the five or so crickets that had jumped on him.

"Seriously, dude?" Domi asked, arching a brow.

Zeke shrugged. "Why not?"

"Is that even a question? You just ate crickets! First cockroaches, now crickets. Is this a thing, now? Eating bugs?" Mia asked, exasperated.

Zeke considered, then nodded. "Yeah, I guess it is."

**Feeder Cricket (Food)**
**Worth 0 Levels**
**Special Effect:** Sates [Hunger].

**Please choose a skill.**

**Food (Strong)**
*When you are eaten, you sate the eater's hunger.*

**Strong Legs (Minor)**
*Small boost to jump strength.*

Zeke pressed his lips together. *I don't really want to become better food, so Strong Legs it is.*

Fluffums darted back over, slowing to a strut as he approached the humans. He walked up to them, then turned his head to look at them. "The Cat Man?"

"Right, right." Zeke cast the feeder crickets one last longing look, then turned away. *The crickets will wait for me. It's time to take on the Cat Man Apocalypse.*

"Speaking of, what're you going to do?" Domi asked Fluffums, as they ran along the back wall, away from the center aisle. Shallow water splashed under their feet, actively spilling from a seemingly endless array of aquariums lining the left wall. Not all the aquariums were shattered, but enough were that they rarely ran on dry tile. For all the shattered aquariums, only a few fish laid lifeless on the ground.

*There's a lot of cats to feed, after all,* Zeke noted.

Fluffums swished his tail. "I pledged to assist you with the Pigeon Apocalypse."

"Aren't we *helping* you with the Cat Man?" Domi asked skeptically.

"Helping me by defeating him, yes," Fluffums replied primly.

"Mother *fucker*. Played by a cat," Domi grumbled.

Zeke narrowed his eyes at Fluffums. "You're fighting with us, though, right?"

Fluffums flicked his tail non-committally. "Perhaps."

Zeke took a deep breath, then shook his head. *It's fine. Last time, we were exhausted from defeating the Cartoon Apocalypse. This time, we're taking on the Cat Man fresh. Ryan's there, but even so...we should be fine.*

*At the end of the day, there's just too many pigeons for me and Domi to take on alone. Even if we have to take on the Cat Man without Fluffums' help, we're still benefiting from this partnership.*

After a moment, Fluffums lowered his head slightly. "To tell the truth, it is very dangerous for me to fight the Cat Man. The Cat Man is higher level than me and is able to steal my cats away from me. To take my army here would be to throw it directly into the Cat Man's hands."

*Oh. That makes sense, kind of. Like how the Cartoon Apocalypse infected people, I guess the Cat Man Apocalypse can infect cats.*

*No...it makes sense. The Cartoon Apocalypse primarily affected people, while the Cat Man Apocalypse targets cats. But if that's the case, why can't Fluffums steal the Cat Man Apocalypse's cats away? Shouldn't they have about the same pull? Is it really a matter of levels? Or...*

He glanced up, taking in the enormous cat tower at the back of the store. *Or is it because the Cat Man Apocalypse has a Domain and Fluffums doesn't? After all, the Cartoon Apocalypse's Domain seemed to involuntarily infect everyone who stepped inside, whether the Cartoon Apocalypse was aware of them or not. If Fluffums brings his cats here, even though they're members of the Cat Apocalypse, will it be the same? Or maybe the same but slowed.* Zeke glanced at Mia. *Mia survived the Cartoon Apocalypse, after all.*

"So long as we have the element of surprise, we have this in the bag," Zeke muttered, half to himself.

"What, the cat?" Domi joked.

Mia rolled her eyes. "Okay, that one was bad."

"*That* was worse than the Catch Revolution?" Zeke asked skeptically. "That's a low—"

Beside them, shelves creaked. Startled, Zeke looked up.

Black fur. Sleek, streamlined body. Slicked-back ears, wide pupils, golden eyes. The adorable face of a housecat as large as a panther's head. The black cat yawned, displaying enormous fangs. It looked down at them in a lazy, hungry sort of way.

"Fuck," Zeke muttered.

All but smirking, the cat pounced.

# 53
## BAD LUCK BLACK CAT

The black cat pounced, golden eyes burning.

Grabbing Mia, Zeke jumped to the side. He soared, leaping far enough to cross the next aisle over.

**[Strong Legs]**

*Damn. I couldn't jump that far to save my life before that new skill, but now I can carry Mia around like it's nothing. These skills are no joke.*

The cat hit the floor and pivoted, charging at Zeke's back. It raised a paw, claws bared.

Domi clapped. An explosion slammed out from her hands and threw the cat to the side. Startling, all its fur puffed up and its hackles raised, the cat galloped in place and skittered away, flying off down the aisle.

Zeke set Mia down. "Hide."

Mia nodded. She ran into the next aisle and hid behind boxes of dog treats, hunkering down on the shelf.

The cat slowed. It turned back around, murder in its eyes

once more. Lowering its head, it stalked toward them, one shoulder slinking after the other, eyes faintly glowing.

Zeke charged at it. Surprised, the cat flinched back and fled, vanishing into one of the seemingly endless aisles.

*It might be as big as a panther, but on the inside, it's still a housecat,* Zeke thought, snorting.

"Behind!" Domi shouted.

Zeke whirled. A furless sphinx as big as the black cat bared its teeth at them, hissing ferociously.

Domi threw her hand out.

*BOOM!*

The sphinx flinched back, delicate skin bright red. It fled, high-tailing toward the entryway.

Jumping onto the shelves again, the black cat yowled in fury. Pet food bags rained down into the aisle. In the near distance, paws padded over the shelves and claws skittered on tile. A thousand tiny shapes darted toward them, closing in from all directions.

Domi backed up to Zeke. "Got any brilliant plans?"

"I have *a* plan, anyway." Zeke muttered back. He rubbed his hands together. *It worked once. It might work again!*

### [Create Drug] +1

*Nice. Guess I used it enough to level it up!*

A small pile of catnip formed in his hands. Zeke gritted his teeth. *More!*

### [Create Drug]

More catnip dropped into his palms.

The sound of paws grew louder. A cavalcade of paws,

rumbling over the shelves, slapping against the tile floor. Hidden in the pet food, Mia hunkered down.

Zeke and Domi exchanged a look.

"Mia!" Zeke called.

"What?" Mia asked, peeking out.

"I think we're running for it!"

"You should probably run for it. I was counting, but I ran out of numbers," Fluffums offered from above them.

Zeke glanced up. The cat perched on a rafter, well out of danger. Licking his paw, he ran it over his head, smoothing his already-immaculate white fur. He sighed. *Typical cat.*

"Fuck off," Domi muttered. "Mia, come on, time to go!"

Mia jumped up, knocking over the pet food. She ran.

Giving her a moment to get ahead, Zeke and Domi chased after her.

### [Roll With Me]
*Boost to speed while traveling together.*

### [Team Spirit]
*All stats + .5*

As he ran, Zeke rubbed his hands together, using **[Create Drug]** once more. *I'll toss it at them when they pop out of the aisles. Give us a bit of a head start. Though...not much of one. I really need some time to work up a good handful of catnip.*

*Or... Hmm.* He glanced at his skills again, eyeing one of them. *It's worth a shot!*

A wave of cats crested the aisles. Orange, black, white, brown, tabbies and calicos, patches and tuxedos, tiny Scottish Folds and huge Maine Coons. All with glowing gold eyes. All moving as one. In a yowling wave of flesh, teeth, and claws, they descended on the humans.

As they dropped, Zeke cracked his palms open, just a tiny amount. He pointed it at the nearest cats.

### [Manipulate Aerosols]

Steam infused with catnip sprayed from the tiny gap in his hands. Zeke waved it wildly, painting the catnip-infused steam over the oncoming cats. *Come on...come on!*

The struck cats trembled, then flopped over, suddenly more content to roll around on the ground than attack the humans. A handful of their fellows dropped out as well, now desperately rubbing themselves on their catnip-scented friends rather than chasing Zeke and Domi. Zeke ran as he sprayed, even as the small portion of catnip he'd managed to gather rapidly dwindled.

Beside him, Domi clapped her hands. Bright light, heat, and explosive noise burst from her hands. The cats nearest her flinched from the *boom*s, but the moment they froze, another dozen cats boiled over them to take their place.

Mia grabbed a dog bed off a shelf and swung it at the cats, battering them away with the fluffy material. The cats flew back, bounced to the floor, and jumped at her again, unharmed. Her eyes flashed. She grabbed a second dog bed and dual-wielded, striking the cats away with both hands.

"Fluffums! Which way should we go?" Zeke shouted. He threw the last of the soggy catnip at the cats and glanced around, searching for a bludgeoning weapon. *Damn. Should've picked Pocket Weapon!* Grabbing up a random bag of cat litter, he swung it two-handedly at the cats.

Overhead, Fluffums considered. He glanced left and right, humming under his breath.

"Take your time!" Domi grumbled.

"Behind you, there's fewer cats," Fluffums said at last, as casually as if he was suggesting a walk in the park.

"Thank you," Domi said, rolling her eyes.

Zeke nodded. "Then we'll go—"

"But the Cat Man and his giant cats are that direction. To the right, there's more small cats, but there's a gap in a small distance," Fluffums continued.

"So, right?" Zeke asked.

"The human is there, though," Fluffums said.

"The human? Ryan?" Mia asked, heaving panted breaths as she fell back between Domi and Zeke, giving herself a momentary breather.

"Is that his name? The one who was fighting the Cat Man. Oh, they seem to have reached an accord of sorts," Fluffums offered.

"Is it worth it. Is he really going to help us with the pigeons," Domi complained.

"Too late now," Zeke said.

The black cat jumped down from overhead, diving at Zeke. Zeke slammed the bag of cat litter at the cat's head. It burst open, spraying cat litter across the floor. The black cat's head snapped to the side. Shaking its head, sending cat litter flying, the black cat turned and looked at Zeke, already raising its claw.

Zeke blocked, bracing his legs.

**[Hardness]**

The cat's claws scraped across Zeke. Shallow cuts opened on his forearms. Swatting left and right, the black cat beat Zeke back and forth. The shallow cuts deepened. Slices striped his forearms.

**[Hardness] +1!**

## [Hardness] +2!

Gritting his teeth, Zeke held on. "Domi! Help!"

"I'm busy!" Domi shouted, pointing both hands at the smaller cats. Light and noise pushed them back, but only temporarily.

Mia glanced over her shoulder. A cat clung to one of the dog beds, while the other had tear marks up its back where sharp claws had cut open the fabric. Fluffy white stuffing spilled out like blood. "Zeke! I'm coming!"

*Dammit, I don't want Mia to put herself in danger! She's just an ordinary person, not an apocalypse.* Zeke spun his hands, pointing his palms outward, and caught the cat's paws. Dragging it forward, he opened his mouth wide.

## [Devour]

Hot blood streaked down his face. The giant cat thrashed. Zeke held on, tightening his grip. *You won't escape!*

## [Strong Jaw]

His jaws ground shut. Zeke yanked backward, tearing out the cat's throat. Struggling one last time, the giant cat fell to the ground. With a final flop, it laid still.

Bright red blood streaked his face and dripped down his jaw. Wiping his mouth, Zeke swallowed.

**Member of the Cat Man Apocalypse**
**Level + .41**
**Level:** 26.79 > 27.2
**Please assign your stat point.**

**Please choose a skill.**

**Skills**
**Claws (Large)**
*Grow claws from your fingertips.*

**Giant (Condition)**
*Become large permanently.*

**Catlike Reflexes (Minor)**
*Small boost to reflexes. Will react more strongly to all stimuli.*

Falling back, Zeke took a moment to consider his options. *Catlike Reflexes is nice and should combo well with my other buff skills, but...* He glanced aside at Domi. *If it makes me startle every time I hear an explosion, that's no good! I'll become worthless in a fight alongside Domi...or against her. Still, it isn't a bad skill. If I don't see something better, I should pick it up.*

*Giant sounds nice, but permanently? I don't want to be huge all the time. It'll make it super easy for Ryan to find me. Sure, I'll get a big advantage...but I'll also be a big target. I don't think I'm ready for that yet.*

*Which leaves...*

Zeke eyed Claws. *I do need a melee weapon. Right now, I don't have any weapons at hand. I have to use whatever's lying around. With Claws, I'll always have a weapon, even if someone tries to disarm me.*

*This time, I think Claws is the right pick.*

**[Claws] (Large)**

As soon as he picked the skill, his fingertips burned. Zeke bit his lip, his fingers clenching subconsciously. *Ow, ow, ow, ow, ow—*

**[Resilient Regeneration]**
**[Resilient Regeneration] +9!**
**[Resilient Regeneration] (Minor) +9 > (Lesser)!**

The pain faded to the back of his mind. His fingerbones morphed, growing sharp, and pushed through the tips of his fingers just under his fingernails. Little droplets of blood welled up as they pierced his skin, only for the skin to reshape around the claws, creating divots for the claws to sit in. Muscles in his fingers restructured, forming around his new claws.

A shadow dropped down on him from the rafters. Zeke whirled, baring his claws.

Ryan glared at him, dagger aimed at Zeke's head as he plummeted toward Zeke.

Glancing up from licking his nether regions, Fluffums peered down at Zeke. "Oh, watch out."

# 54
## CAT MAN AND REGRESSOR

Ryan dropped down on him. Zeke jumped backward, simultaneously pressing his toe into the ground.

**[Crystal Burst]**

Crystals broke through the tile floor where he'd been standing. Ryan fell toward the razor-sharp growths, unable to change his trajectory midair. As he fell, Zeke swiped at him from the side, extending his claws for the first time.

A small prick of pain bit through his fingertips as his raw claws touched the air for the first time, but it quickly faded. He aimed at Ryan's throat, ignoring the dagger. *So long as I strike first, I win!*

**Please assign your stat point.**
**STR:** 4 > 5
**CON:** 10
**DEX:** 3
**SPR:** 7

Ryan grimaced. He raised his dagger, blocking Zeke's blow. Steel clashed with claws. The swipe slammed him into the shelves. He flopped toward the crystals in a rain of dog harnesses and leashes.

As he fell, Ryan thrust his hand toward the crystals. His fall slowed. Twisting in midair, he dropped down between the crystals instead of crashing into them.

Zeke didn't hesitate. He pushed his toe into the ground, calling more crystals from the floor beneath Ryan. *I'm done. He's clearly trying to kill me, at any cost. I won't hold back anymore. If he's going to attack me to kill, then I'll fight back.*

Ryan threw himself backward, vanishing under a wave of cats. They swarmed Zeke, darting around the crystals to attack him, but refused to get too close to the crystals.

*They don't want to jump over the crystals or walk through them? Excellent.* Zeke backed up to Domi and Mia, swiping his toe from left to right along the ground as he went. A wall of crystals burst forth from the tip of his shoe, about half a meter deep and a few centimeters tall. The cats backed away, balking at the edge of the crystals.

Domi took a deep breath, stepping back for a moment. She shook her hands out, her palms smoking lightly. "There's too many of them. I'm getting tired."

"Me too," Mia panted, wiping her forehead on her sleeve.

"We can't keep this up for much longer," Domi said.

"No," Zeke agreed. "Where's the Cat Man?"

"Deeper in," Mia replied, pointing.

Zeke looked over his shoulder. Cats blocked them in, packing the long aisle as far as the eye could see. He took a deep breath. "We have to run for it. If we get stalled out here, the cats will exhaust us long before we reach the Cat Man."

"How?" Domi asked.

Zeke called up his skills. The list scrolled by. *Something...surely I have something...*

His eyes fell on one of the skills. He raised his eyebrows and smiled. *Time to find out what this skill does.*

"Watch my back for a second. I've got an idea," he said. He turned, facing the rear.

Domi rolled her eyes. "Sure, sure. Easy—"

Ryan jumped out of the cats, dagger darting for Zeke's back.

Pushing Zeke forward, Domi pointed at Ryan. He flinched to the left, falling back.

Nothing happened. Domi smirked. She pointed her finger slightly to the left, a little further than he'd ducked. An explosion blasted the remaining dog leashes and collars off the wall. Ryan raised his arms, covering his head as the paraphernalia rained down on him.

"—peasy," she finished, grinning.

Maintaining his focus through the shove, Zeke focused. Energy drained out of him, his stomach growing emptier by the moment. *Where are those feeder crickets? I'm starving...*

"Zeke, you're *hungry?*" Mia asked, confused. She batted another few cats away. Some of them sat in the distance, now, choosing to sit, watch, and wait rather than charge Mia.

"Yeah, i-is there any animal food around?" Zeke asked, as his knees began to shake. His arm trembled, all the energy leaving him. *At this rate, I'm going to pass out before the skill finishes!*

"Lots of cat food," Mia said, pointing to a wall of tins in the next aisle down.

"Could you—this is going to sound insane, but—could you open a few of those and dump them into my mouth?" Zeke asked.

"I know it's the apocalypse, but are you that desperate already?"

"Mia, please," Zeke begged her.

Mia slapped another cat down, stepping forward. "I got it, I got it," she said, kicking her way into the aisle. Throwing one of the dog beds at the cats, she grabbed a stack of tins and yanked open the flip top.

Zeke opened his mouth. *Of all the things I've eaten...at least it's food!*

Putrid, strangely seasoned room-temperature fish fell into his mouth. Grimacing, he swallowed.

### [Devour]

His hunger abated a small margin, barely enough to be worthwhile. *Still, it's better than nothing!* He nodded at Mia. "More. Hurry!"

Mia tossed the empty can at a jumping cat. It yanked its head back, offended, then darted after the can, chasing it down to lick the residue. A few other cats darted after it, while some of the chubbier ones sat down obediently despite the yellow glow in their eyes, licking their chops, eyes locked on Mia's hands as she opened another can.

### [Devour]
### [Devour]
### [Devour]

Can after can of cat food vanished into Zeke's gullet. Mia threw the empty cans around, holding off the cats with wild tosses. The stack she'd grabbed vanished, and still Zeke's stomach grumbled. His hunger abated, but slowly, so slowly. *So long as I don't pass out mid-way...so long as I can keep going!*

*Damn, good thing I used this skill in a pet shop, surrounded by food sources. I'd have died if I'd tried it on the streets.*

At last, Zeke's hand began to heat up. The energy drain dropped off. He pushed Mia back protectively, putting his hand out ahead of him. "Go!"

## [MOTORCYCLE]

A blob of metal emerged from his palm. The metal morphed, taking form. A body frame emerged from the shapeless mass, then pipes, an engine, handlebars and finally wheels. With a screech of rubber, a motorcycle appeared before him.

"Holy shit, what the hell?" Domi asked, whipping around to find a fully formed motorcycle.

"Hop on!" Zeke called.

Ryan crawled out from under the fallen dog leashes. "I won't let you!" He ran at Zeke and the motorcycle. Mid-step, he vanished.

"He has some kind of teleportation skill. Watch out!" Mia shouted. Tossing the final can of cat food at the cats, she hopped on behind Zeke.

Domi slid onto the rear of the seat, perched up high behind Zeke and Mia. "Just hit the gas! He can't keep up with a motorcycle!"

Zeke peered at the controls. *Dials, switches, buttons... this is all more than I need. Come on. How do I start this thing?*

"Right there," Mia said, pointing at a button labeled START.

"I knew that," Zeke muttered. He pressed the button. The motorcycle roared to life. Cats skittered away in all directions, fleeing into the aisles.

Ryan popped into view in front of them, his dagger aimed at Zeke's heart as the motorcycle lurched forward.

Zeke's eyes widened.

## [Caffeine Rush] [Hardness] [Flexible Body]

Thrusting his arm in front of his heart, Zeke released the motorcycle's handles. The motorcycle immediately skewed off to the side, hurtling toward the aquariums lining the left wall. Glass flew at them.

The dagger skittered over Zeke's arm and carved across his chest. The motorcycle glanced against Ryan, slamming him into the aquariums. Water sloshed, and one of the aquariums tipped over and crashed to the ground. Small tropical fish flopped over the ground.

Eyes wide, Mia lunged for the handlebars and turned the motorcycle away. The handlebar dragged along the glass, leaving a black smudge behind it. They bounced away from the aquarium, front wheel barely dodging the downed aquarium, and blasted down the aisle, careening toward the shelves.

Zeke grabbed the handlebars back from Mia and wrestled the motorcycle back away from the shelves. It lunged for the aquariums instead.

Mia yelped and held on tight. Something soft pressed up against Zeke's back.

*Fuck! Zeke, focus! Now isn't the time!* Gritting his teeth, Zeke ignored Mia's body pressed up against his and gripped the handlebars with both hands. With all his might, he fought it left and right, finally forcing it to head straight down the aisle.

"Whew! First time on a motorcycle?" Domi asked, running stray strands of hair out of her face.

"Yeah," Zeke muttered, focused on the floor in front of him. Brutal metal shelves reached at him from the right, while the unfeeling glass of the aquarium awaited on his left. He clenched his teeth, barely keeping the beast beneath him from rushing wildly off to either side. *Fuck! This is terrifying!*

"Whoa, whoa, whoa, Zeke!" Domi shouted.

Zeke yanked his eyes off the immediate floor in front of him.

The sphinx cat hissed from a shelf ahead of him, watching with narrowed eyes. "I see it!"

"No, in front!" Domi corrected him.

Zeke looked up.

An orange tabby blocked his way ahead, lips lifted in a dangerous snarl. Atop it, a slender teen in a black hoodie sat, fluffy white cat ears poking out from the hood. The teen smirked. Beneath him, the orange tabby lifted its paw, ready to swipe them off the motorcycle.

"Fuck!" Zeke tightened his grip on the handlebars. He revved the engine, ducking low to the handlebars as the wind swept through his short hair.

"Zeke...Zeke! We're going to hit him!" Mia shouted.

"Brace for impact!" Zeke shouted, aiming for the tabby's front legs.

# 55
## BRACE FOR IMPACT

The motorcycle roared. Its front wheel chewed up the ground between Zeke and the tabby. Mia and Domi grabbed onto him and one another, holding tight as he revved the engine at the giant tabby.

The giant tabby reared up, pouncing down on the motorcycle. Enormous paw pads dropped toward them.

Releasing the motorcycle's handlebars, Zeke reached up and scratched the cat's paw pads. Blood beaded up. The cat leaped away, limping down the aisle, leaving small bloodstains behind.

Zeke sped up again. "Hold on."

"Wait, again?" Mia asked.

"Let me off!" Domi shouted.

Atop the giant tabby, the Cat Man's eyes widened, then narrowed. Kicking his tabby's flanks like a horse, he pointed the cat at the motorcycle. He and the cat charged at one another, running at one another like a medieval joust.

The Cat Man flicked his hand open. Claws burst from his fingertips.

"Domi, ready up Grenade Jump," Zeke said darkly.

"You're kidding," Domi replied.

Zeke glanced at her over his shoulder.

Domi pressed her lips together. "You're serious." Yanking out her phone, she started tapping rapidly.

The cat and the motorcycle closed in on one another. Mia grabbed onto Zeke for dear life. Zeke dropped low over the handlebars. Wind rushed past.

The tabby loomed over him. Opening its mouth, it pounced.

Zeke tensed. "Domi!"

Domi put her phone away. She snapped her fingers.

A blast of force burst out from beneath the motorcycle, lifting it up into the air and over the pouncing cat's head. The Cat Man's eyes widened. He stared up at the motorcycle as it rose over him, a half ton of steel, chrome, and leather flying through the air. For just a moment, Zeke caught a glimpse of a terrified, handsome face framed by perfectly airbrushed white hair, and then the motorcycle eclipsed the man.

*Splat.*

Blood, brains, and bone spewed over the tabby's back, dying the orange-and-white stripes a gaudy crimson. The Cat Man fell backward on his mount, lifeless, little more than a skid mark where his face had been.

They smacked the giant cat's rear on the way down. It yelped and sprinted off, charging toward the doors, dropping the Cat Man's corpse as it escaped. The motorcycle slammed into the tile floor and careened off, barely under control. Slamming the brakes, Zeke drifted to a hockey stop. He glanced up as messages appeared before his eyes.

**Congratulations! You've defeated the Cat Man Apocalypse!**
**Level + 0.51**
**Level: 27.71**
**Regeneration + 300% (Temp.)**

**Regeneration rate:** +303.6 (Temp. 1:01 remaining)

Zeke frowned. His forearms faintly burned as the cuts healed, but he ignored it, focusing on the messages instead. *This is weird. Only half a level for defeating an apocalypse? That's insane. Especially an apocalypse with a Domain like Cat Man. I should get at least a full level from beating a higher-level apocalypse.*

All around them, the ordinary-sized cats milled around, suddenly leaderless. The giant sphinx cat stood up from the aisle and jumped away, no longer hissing viciously at them.

*And that...that's strange, too.*

Peering over his shoulder, he took in the enormous cat tree. His brows furrowed.

Beside him, Domi followed his gaze. The two of them slowly exchanged a look.

"Huh?" Domi said.

"I know," Zeke returned.

Fluffums walked over. He sat down primly and looked up at the three on the motorcycle. "Is he defeated?"

Zeke and Domi exchanged glances.

Taking a deep breath, Mia nodded. "He's dead. He's...he's dead. We killed him."

"Excellent. Shall we claim our prize?" Fluffums asked, tilting his head at them.

"Our prize?" Zeke asked.

Fluffums coughed, then bent over, hacking. He spat up a hairball and sat back down, as primly as though nothing had happened. "Oh, that's right. *My* prize."

All around them, the cats milling about froze. They shivered, trembling from skull to spine. With perfect synchronization, they turned to face the motorcycle.

"This isn't good," Domi muttered.

Fluffums stood and walked behind them. Sitting, he licked

his paw, then smoothed the fur on his head. "Good job, lesser beings. I knew I could rely on you servants one final time. However, as cats are the ultimate life form...it is time for you to choose. Do you commit to becoming my servant? Excuse me, subordinate. Or do you die?"

Zeke licked his lips. "You know, I really feel like I could have seen this coming. I mean, cats, right? They're pretty self-serving."

"Yeah...yeah," Domi agreed, sighing.

"Why attack us now? Aren't we allies?" Mia asked, her voice breaking.

Fluffums shrugged. "Only so long as it benefited me. Now that I have the might of the Cat Man's allies behind me...well, the Pigeon Apocalypse is merely made up of those lesser delicious creatures known as birds. It shouldn't be a problem for me to take on alone, now."

The giant tabby and sphinx crept up behind Fluffums, blocking the route to the door. Shaking itself, the giant tabby kept reaching over its shoulder to lick itself clean, bothered by the blood slick on its back. Leaping from shelf to shelf, crossing the store at speed, another giant cat appeared, sleek tuxedo-patterned body shining under the store's distant lights.

"You have three seconds. Subordinate yourself to me, or die," Fluffums declared.

"Drive. Drive!" Domi shouted, slapping Zeke's shoulder.

"Right, on it!" Zeke shouted. Whipping the motorcycle around, he gunned it. The cycle leaped down the aisle toward the distant cat tree.

"Destroy them," Fluffums ordered.

**The Alliance has been broken.**
**Temporary penalty:** Cat Apocalypse -5 SPR.

The giant cats surged after Zeke and Domi, sprinting down the aisle after them. Paws slapped against tile floor and clattered over steel shelves. Ahead, the back wall of the store loomed.

"Exit sign, look for an exit sign!" Domi shouted. Putting a hand on Mia's shoulder, she turned around and pointed. A box of dog treats exploded, bursting hard biscuit fragments over the lead cat.

"I'm looking!" Mia shouted.

Zeke clenched the handlebars and gritted his teeth, counting down the aisles until they reached the wall. *Five... four...three...!*

# 56

## CAT AND A HARD PLACE

J ust as they were about to reach the wall, the space around them expanded. The last aisle gave way, and they burst out into a huge empty space at the back of the store. The giant cat tree extended into seeming infinity, vanishing into fog overhead. Cat statues lined the wall, all manner of them. Cats standing, sitting, crouching, pouncing, even *maneki neko,* sitting upright with their distant expressions, holding an oval-shaped coin in one paw and beckoning with the other. Cat art plastered the wall, from cat-eared girls in an anime art style to handsome cat portraits in oil paint. Cat beds laid over the floor, and a neat line of bowls sat behind the final aisle. A gentle waterfall sent fresh water spilling down into a shallow cat-height pool, perfect for sipping, while an enormous sand pit served as a litter box, complete with a Zen-garden style rake and several large, smooth stones.

Small cat trees grew in a forest around the enormous one. Cat wheels and cat toys lay strewn around the space, while boxes of treats, neatly sealed, awaited only a human hand to open them. Stockpiled cat food stacked in a corner, while a much smaller lump of human food piled up beside it, some of it stuffed in the cat food refrigerator to keep it safe.

*Huh? Compared to the Cartoon Apocalypse's chaotic domain and Fluffums' dangerous abandoned house, isn't this kind of a paradise for cats?* Zeke frowned. He looked up at the cat tree again and swallowed. *Aside from him trying to kill-steal us, which, I mean...who wouldn't, the Cat Man doesn't seem like a bad person. He isn't infecting people. He isn't out of control.*

*Sure, he's controlling the cats, but if that's a crime, then so is Fluffums, and it seems...if this room is any indication, it seems he isn't controlling them all the time, only when he considers himself under threat. And, well...we're all Apocalypses. We're all trying to win this.*

*Only one can escape, after all.*

*But that does beg the question...did we attack the wrong guy?*

Nestled in a pile of dark clothing, a small, weak kitten blinked up at them. Still blue-eyed, its fur so soft and thin they could see the delicate skin and tiny body beneath, it couldn't have been more than a few days old. Letting out a pitiful meow, it dug at the clothing, desperate to hide away underneath.

"Poor baby," Mia whispered.

As if on cue, the motorcycle's engine growled to a halt beneath them. Powerless, they drifted to a stop not far from the kitten.

"Next time, Zeke, try materializing a motorcycle with a full tank of gas," Domi advised, hopping off it.

"I had no idea what I was doing. I was more worried about not passing out than I was about filling the tank," Zeke muttered. He cranked the engine again. It spluttered but didn't turn over. *Guess it's dead.*

He peered behind them. The giant cats hurtled down the aisles, galloping closer with every passing moment. "Domi, you ready?"

"I'm exhausted. We need to gank Fluffums as fast as possible," Domi returned.

"Agreed," Zeke said, climbing off the motorcycle. *I'm not starving right now, but I'm not full either. Too much longer, and I'll have to start eating cats left and right. Can you imagine? Eating cats all day long...*

Mia ran over to the kitten. "Where's your mommy? Little thing, all alone."

Mewling, the kitten crawled weakly toward Mia. It extended its little claws and wobbled toward her.

She knelt, picking it up, and cradled it to her bosom. "Poor little baby."

The cats swarmed around the corner. Giant cats in the lead, a wall of smaller ones behind them, and Fluffums overhead, watching from the rafters.

"He isn't making it easy, huh," Zeke muttered under his breath.

"Ha," Domi muttered back.

Zeke peered past the cats, looking for a familiar form. *Where's Ryan? Did he take off after Fluffums swapped sides? I guess... well, I guess Fluffums isn't allied with him. Might as well take off before Fluffums decides to attack him, too, and let us get slammed by the Catpocalypse.*

Mia ran back over to Domi and Zeke. She pointed. "The cat trees. We can head there, limit them—"

"No good. They're *cat* trees. They're built for the cats!" Domi returned.

Gritting her teeth, Mia glanced left and right. She held the kitten up to her chest, protecting it from the world. "We have to get Fluffums down from the top, right?"

"Right," Zeke agreed.

"Domi, you can use your phone to send explosions... farther?" Mia asked, squinting.

"Places I can't see, farther, whatever. It takes a shit-ton of battery, though... Wait, hold on. How do you know that?" Domi asked.

Mia pointed. "Explode him down. Zeke can take care of it from there."

Zeke looked up at Fluffums, then at Domi. "Can you do it?"

Domi grabbed her phone out. "I've got enough charge for one more shot."

The cats closed in. Fluffums strutted overhead, a bit back from the front of the wave. Zeke knelt. *Here goes nothing.*

## [Caffeine Rush] [Strong Legs]

Yowling, the first of the cats jumped at Zeke.

He took a deep breath and whistled.

## [Whistle Blast]
*Small chance of inflicting stun.*

About a quarter of the cats froze in place. Zeke sprinted into the cats.

Cats flew at him. Claws bit into his legs and hips. One jumped onto his back. Zeke pointed his hand over his shoulder.

## [Manipulate Aerosols]

The cat fell back, screaming.

The giant sphinx swiped at his head. Zeke ducked. The paw swooped over his head, swiping through his short hair. He slid over the tile floor, kicking his way through the small cats, then jumped back to his feet.

*Come on, Domi!*

Domi shoved her phone in her pocket. She pointed at the rafters. "Boom."

An explosion burst overhead. Fluffums jumped into the sky, scrambling with all four paws in the air, his eyes wide. He dropped back down toward the rafter.

*No, I don't think you will.* Zeke whistled again, narrowing his eyes at Fluffums and focusing on him with all his might. *Him. If it stuns no one else, at least him!*

### [Whistle Blast]

Fluffums froze in midair. His pupils blurred. He plunged past the rafter.

*Yes!* Zeke sprinted for the falling cat. Activating **[Strong Legs]** again, he leaped up to catch the cat, ignoring the pang of hunger in his stomach.

The sleek tuxedo leaped into the air and slammed into him. The two of them dropped toward the floor. Grabbing Zeke in its mouth, the cat used all four of its paws to scratch at his stomach even as they fell. His shirt fell apart in shreds. Blood ran down his stomach, pooling in his waistband.

### [Hardness] [Flexible Body] [Resilient Regeneration]

Even with all his skills, the claws tore him up. His stomach hurt as much as it ached, his pain equal to his hunger. *If not for Resilient Regeneration, I'd probably have to stop fighting from the pain,* Zeke realized dully.

Extending his own claws, Zeke scratched at the cat's legs. The two of them bounced over the floor. He gritted his teeth and clawed harder, only for the cat to wrestle him onto his back, its four long limbs giving it the advantage. *Dammit! Fluffums is going to get away!*

Domi twisted her lips. She hung back, watching silently, her arms crossed.

Midair, Fluffums broke free of the stun. He looked around, then startled and kicked, rolling around to point all four feet down.

Mia looked at the kitten in her arms, then at Zeke and the falling Fluffums, then at Domi. She took a deep breath, then shoved the kitten into her shirt and sprinted off.

"Mia!" Domi ran after her. Explosions flew out ahead of Mia, cutting a path through the cats. She ran through it, sprinting for Fluffums.

Fluffums extended his claws, reaching out to grab for Mia.

Her eyes narrowed, Mia reached out with both hands and snatched Fluffums out of midair around his middle. He instantly reached out all four limbs to scratch her arms. Bright red lines lit up her forearms as blood welled up.

Gritting her teeth against the pain, Mia threw the cat at Zeke. "Zeke!"

Domi hesitated just one moment. Gritting her teeth, she clapped. Bright light burst inches from the tuxedo cat's nose. It released Zeke and darted backward.

Zeke jumped up. Without bothering with arms, he dove at Fluffums, mouth wide.

### [Devour]

Fluffums twisted in midair, but Zeke darted in, seeking out Fluffums' throat with his mouth. His jaws snapped shut on fluff, but he snapped his arms up and stuffed Fluffums toward his mouth. Claws latched onto his face.

"Lowly creature, know your place! You are *not* allowed to touch this higher being! I disallow it! Puny being, bow before me!"

*How about you shut the fuck up.* He shoved the cat in with all his might and took a big bite.

Hot blood spurted in his mouth. Fluffums twisted. The claws dug deep into his face. Struggling to the last, the cat finally went still.

**Congratulations! You've defeated the Cat Apocalypse!**
**Level + 2.34**
**Level:** 27.71 > 30.05

**Please assign your stat points.**

**Please choose up to three skills.**

**Skills**
**Claws (Small)**
**Fangs (Small)**
**Defensive Fluff (Small)**
**Catlike Reflexes (Lesser)**
**Cat Call (Medium)**
**Claw Fighter (Lesser)**
**Perfect Landing (Lesser)**
**Can't**
**Can't**

Zeke twisted his lips, then quickly chose Catlike Reflexes, Claw Fighter, and Perfect Landing. *I have claws now, so that makes Claw Fighter a no-brainer. Perfect Landing sounds like a great all-rounder...always land on my feet like a cat, who doesn't want that? Likewise, Catlike Reflexes is an all-rounder skill that syncs well with Caffeine Rush. Again, not the greatest combo with Domi, but it's such a good baseline skill I can't ignore it. Not the most exciting skills in the world, but I'll take them.*

**Congratulations on reaching level 30!**
**Reward Loading... Please wait.**
**Due to a recent surge in requests, reward may take up to 24**
**hours to load.**

Zeke snorted. *Guess I still have to wait to see what I have available for me. Obviously, I'll have the choice to pick up a Domain, but the System has hinted at other options. I don't want a Domain, so I'll have to see what those other options are.*

*As for my stat points...*

**SPR:** 7 > 10

*SPR is what powers all my nonphysical attacks, and it provides safety against stun and other mental effects. I can't neglect it.*

Once again, the cats surrounding Zeke fell back. They backed away from him, some fleeing into the cat tree forest, while others yowled and vanished into the aisles.

Mia sighed, clutching her wounded arms to her chest. The kitten crawled up to the neck of her shirt and looked around, shaking its little ears. "Whew. Thank goodness."

"What were you thinking?" Domi admonished her lightly with a smile, shaking her head at Mia. "Charging in there?"

"What were you thinking?" Mia returned, rounding on Domi. Unlike Domi's teasing tone, hers was serious. "Standing back while Zeke struggled. Risking defeating the entire Cat Apocalypse... for what?"

"I..." Domi crossed her arms. "I didn't want to waste my energy unless victory was sure."

"So, you—"

"Wait. Domi, we're coming back to this, but first," Zeke said. He paused, spitting bloodstained white fluff from his mouth.

"First?" Domi asked.

Zeke locked eyes with the tiny white kitten, staring it right in its baby-blue eyes. "First, why don't you join us? Cat Man."

# 57
## CAUGHT OUT

"What?" Mia asked, pointing at herself.

"Zeke, have you gone nuts? The Cat Man's dead. You saw that message." Domi asked.

"And you saw the levels. The Domain remains. And isn't it strange how the Cat Apocalypse couldn't control exactly one of the cats?" Zeke asked, still staring at the kitten.

The kitten stared back innocently. It yawned, baring adorable little milk teeth.

"Zeke, it's a kitten. It could barely move, let alone fight," Mia said, cupping her hands around the small creature.

Zeke stepped forward. "Give it to me. It's dangerous."

"No. Not unless you promise you aren't going to eat it." Mia stepped back, still protecting the kitten.

"Oh, I'm going to eat it. I'm going to slurp it right down," Zeke growled. He jumped forward, reaching for the kitten. Mia jumped away, but too slow. His hand closed in on the cat.

Domi ran forward, grabbing Mia protectively. "Zeke, are you insane—"

The kitten shifted. Its body grew larger, white fluff accumulating at the top of its head. It wriggled free of Mia's top and flopped to the ground, growing larger and larger with each passing moment. In a few moments, a white-haired, cat-eared boy about their age, slender as a model, stood before them, naked as the day he was born. He put his hands on his hips and narrowed his eyes at Zeke. "Good guess."

"The Domain didn't vanish, the huge cats didn't die, the levels we gained were too low...and then I thought, don't cats have nine lives?" Zeke asked, crossing his arms.

The Cat Man frowned. "Wait, you knew?"

*Damn, my shot in the dark was right? Awesome?* Zeke scoffed. "It was obvious."

*Hmm. Wonder if I could learn that skill if I eat him? Be nice. Chances are, it'd end up as one of those 'Can't' skills.*

*I don't fully understand what the System classifies as 'Can't' skills. Overpowered skills? Skills that don't make sense for a human being to have? I can't see what they are, so it's hard to guess the System's reasoning.*

He looked the Cat Man in the eye, refusing to look any lower. "So? Are you friend or—"

"Guys, guys. Please. Sorry to interrupt this bro talk, but..." Domi looked the Cat Man in the eye and raised her brows, "could you put on some clothes, dude?"

Covering her face, Mia blushed furiously. "Please!"

The Cat Man glanced down. Startled, he covered himself and scooted off into the pile of dark clothes. He yanked on a pair of black sweatpants and a baggy black T-shirt. He turned around. "There. Better?"

Zeke eyed the huge cat face printed on the front of the T-shirt. *He really does love cats, huh?*

"Better," Mia said, nodding emphatically.

"I dunno. I mean, it wasn't all bad," Domi murmured to herself. She put a hand on her chin thoughtfully, eyeing the Cat Man up and down. "I mean, the...cat ears are adorable."

Cat Man's ears twitched. He smiled to himself.

"Domi!" Mia protested.

"What's your name, first off," Zeke said, nodding at the Cat Man.

"Isaac," the Cat Man said.

Domi snorted.

Isaac looked at her, raising an immaculate brow.

"Nothing, nothing," Domi said, waving her hand.

"We're Zeke, Mia, and Domi. So. Are we going to fight now, or...?" Zeke said, eyeing him up.

Isaac looked them over. "You're the ones who came after me."

"That was Fluffums. And you tried to kill us after we wiped out the Cartoon Apocalypse," Zeke said, giving him a look.

"Wouldn't you?" Isaac said.

"I mean..." Zeke muttered. *He's got a point. I need to kill all the other apocalypses in here if I want to survive. If I saw a weakened apocalypse, I'd swoop in to land the finishing blow without thinking. Levels, skills...no reason not to.*

At the same time, Mia shook her head. "Of course not!"

Isaac looked at Mia. He took her in slowly, his frown deepening the whole time. He looked at Zeke and Domi. "She's... normal?"

"Yeah," Zeke said.

"Mostly," Domi replied.

"How?" Isaac asked.

"What do you mean?" Zeke asked.

Isaac turned to Mia. "Almost every normal person has been killed or infected by now. Ordinary people are worth a lot of levels for something that basically can't fight back. And if you don't want to kill to level up, you can use them as fodder for your Concept instead. Servants, fighters, you name it. Neither of you killed her? No apocalypse has infected her?"

He licked his lips. His eyes traced over Mia again, this time with a predatory hunger. "It's...*she's* almost a delicacy."

Mia flinched back. She reached for her back pocket, hand resting on a dark handle.

As she stepped back, she stepped into the dark pile of clothing. It toppled over. A body spilled out, still wearing the uniform of the pet shop.

Mia shrieked.

"Easy levels," Isaac said, shrugging.

A few of the cats ran over. Fighting one another, they struggled over the rights to eat the body's face, while the quicker ones darted in to chew on its eyes before the bigger cats fought them back.

Zeke stepped protectively in front of Mia. *If anyone's going to eat Mia, it's me. I'm not giving her away to—*

*I— What? Huh? I mean, I'm going to protect Mia. I want to keep her safe, not eat her. Where did that come from?*

"Why don't we get out of your hair? We're all tired, we're all injured. Let's call a truce for today and come back tomorrow at our best," Domi suggested.

Zeke glanced at the dead body, then at Domi. He frowned. *We're leaving him? After that?*

*For today. Just for today,* Domi mouthed back.

"I'll let you go. So long as you leave her," Isaac said, staring at Mia.

"No," Zeke said.

"No?" Isaac asked. The giant cats crept up behind him, slinking along slowly, their powerful paws almost silent on the tile. He backed away, quickly growing abreast with the cats. Smaller cats crowded around him as the army formed once more.

"No," Zeke replied decisively.

Domi stepped up beside him. She raised her hands despite

the scratches running down her limbs. "Fuck off, cat boy. Mia's with us."

"You're the ones throwing away free levels, not me." Isaac chuckled, hopping up on one of his giant cats.

"What did we learn today, class?" Domi asked, pushing up invisible glasses in her best impression of a teacher.

"We didn't ally with the wrong cat-slash-person. The problem is that, fundamentally, everyone's a douchebag," Zeke returned.

"It's a battle royale, what did you expect?" Domi asked. She cracked her knuckles.

The giant cats knelt. Eyes wide, tails swishing, hindquarters high, they prepared to pounce.

"I mean, you're right, but still. Am I wrong to have faith in humanity?" Zeke muttered. He extended his new claws, baring them at the cats.

"Not everyone can be as cool as me," Domi said, flashing a smile.

"Oh, come on," Zeke said, rolling his eyes back at her.

Mia stepped forward, passing both of them.

Zeke startled. "Mia!"

Domi jumped, reaching for her. "What are you doing? He's going to kill you!"

Grinning, Isaac kicked his mount. The cat leapt forward, stretching its claws toward Mia.

# 58
## AWAKENING

Mia's head buzzed. She pressed her hand to it, squinting against the pain. *Ow. Again? Why?*

A blue box appeared in front of her eyes.

**ACCEPT? Y/N**

*Accept what? Huh?*

*Wait, is this that video game system thing they've been talking about? But...what does it want me to accept?*

She looked at the box again.

**ACCEPT? Y/N**

*The kind of power Zeke and Domi have... it could be mine? I wouldn't have to be protected. Ryan wouldn't go on about me not understanding.*

*I wouldn't have to die.*

"Accept," Mia whispered.

Something descended onto her. A weight on her shoulders. She jolted, almost toppled by the weight.

**Welcome, Hero.**
**This world must have a chance. You are that chance.**
**Good luck.**

The weight left her. *No. It has become part of me.* Mia lifted her hand, and cool metal filled her grasp. A sword shone in the fluorescent light.

*I am this world's chance.* The responsibility weighed on her shoulders more than the ability itself had. She strode forward, passing Zeke and Domi.

"Mia—" Zeke cut off, his eyes wide.

"You..." Domi's eyes travelled then length of the sword. She frowned, confused. "You're an apocalypse?"

"No. I'm the Hero," Mia replied.

"You stealing Ryan's lines now?" Zeke muttered, struggling to process the scene before him. *The Hero...Apocalypse? But...the System did say that there were other classes aside from Apocalypses. Survivors, for example. Is Hero another one of those other classes?*

*Ah, shit. Don't tell me Mia's going to start trying to kill me now, too.*

Across from them, Isaac backed away. "She's an apocalypse? Not an ordinary person? Why'd you bluff if she could fight this whole time?"

"You're the idiot for falling for it. Now we've got you right where we want you," Zeke instantly bluffed, stepping up beside Mia. *I'm tired. I'm hungry. I don't want to keep fighting. I need time to recover. If I can get Isaac to back off now, we have the advantage. We know where his Domain is. Unlike us, he can't easily move around. We can come back any time.*

Isaac swept his hand without another word. The cats tensed.

Mia lunged forward. In a single motion, almost too fast for Zeke to see, she dashed past Isaac.

Isaac's head fell away. A startled expression pasted permanently on his face, his head struck the ground and rolled. Blood spurted from his neck as his body crumpled to its knees, then fell over.

Zeke stared. *This is Mia? Mia, who was protecting a kitten seconds ago? Mia, who didn't want to kill a single member of the Cartoon Apocalypse?*

Mia turned. She flicked the blood off her blade, her expression flat. Nodding at Zeke, she sheathed it in a sheath that materialized as she reached for it. "He isn't dead. I've bought us time."

*Oh, right. Nine Lives, or whatever that skill is called. But still. Still! She just beheaded a man!*

Domi nudged Zeke. "You aren't going to try to eat him?"

"Oh, shit!" Zeke snapped to life. He lunged for the falling body. *I don't know if I can eat his Nine Lives self, but it's worth a shot. Free skills are free skills!*

A transparent bubble fell out of the Cat Man's body, on the verge of bursting. Zeke lunged for it and grabbed it up, stuffing it in his mouth even as it vanished.

### [Devour]

He held his breath. *Did I make it in time?*

Nothing. No messages.

Zeke wrinkled his nose. He shook his head.

"Nothing?" Domi asked.

"Nothing," Zeke confirmed.

Mia froze. She looked up at the sky.

"Mia, you all right?" Zeke asked.

"I'm hearing...something," Mia muttered.

"You can hear the System? Usually, it talks to me with messages," Zeke said. *Except when it asked me to pick my*

*Concept. I heard something then. Something... A voice? Not quite, but...*

"No, I think it's..." Mia trailed off.

Zeke waited. Mia frowned, focusing intently on something Zeke couldn't hear. He looked at Domi and shrugged.

Domi shrugged back. "I can't hear anything, either."

*Oh, that reminds me.* Zeke stood on his tiptoes, peering into the pile of black clothes. No kittens curled up there. He walked out into the mess of cats. They fled before him, keeping a respectable three-foot personal space bubble around him. One or two came up to him and rubbed on his legs, asking to be pet. Absentmindedly, Zeke rubbed their backs.

*I don't see any kittens. I wonder if he's...* Zeke turned, looking at the cat tree forest. He bent back, and back, and back, taking in the enormous cat tree.

Zeke licked his lips. *If he's in there, we're fucked if he wakes up and becomes able to command the cats again before we kill him.*

*But on the other hand...cat trees are covered in fabric. Flammable, flammable fabric.*

Domi nodded at Zeke. "Burn it down?"

Zeke nodded back. "Just what I was thinking."

Mia jolted, coming back to life. "Hold on. Give me a few minutes. There were still some animals alive at the front of the building."

"Hurry. Give us a shout when you finish," Domi said.

Mia nodded. With a wave, she ran off.

Zeke glanced at Domi. Domi glanced back. "What?"

"Mia...does she seem different to you?" Zeke asked.

"Huh? Not really," Domi said.

Zeke frowned. "Really?"

Domi spread her hands. "I've known her for maybe a day. I'm not going to pick up on subtle differences."

Zeke pressed his lips together thoughtfully, gazing after

Mia. *As soon as she became the Hero, she became cold and emotion-less. Is that the Hero's Concept controlling her?*

*But she's still devoted to saving people and things...unless that's also the Hero's Concept.*

*Does she have a Concept? Maybe Heroes work differently.*

*Even so, she definitely changed. I'll have to keep an eye on her. I don't want to end up on the pointy end of her sword eventually.*

In the distance, bangs and clangs sounded out. Birds flew out of their cages, fleeing out the open doors. Small hamsters and rats that had survived the cats scurried out into the daylight. A few small puppies loped away, vanishing onto the streets.

"Guys! All done!" Mia shouted.

Domi stepped forward. "Time to get down to business."

# 59
## BUSINESS TIME

Clapping her hands, Domi held them slightly apart. Sparks darted between her palms. She knelt, letting the sparks dart through the fabric. The fabric began to smoke. A small flame flickered in the fabric, then burned bright, charging into the cat tree.

She stepped back, then pulled out her phone. Tapping it quickly, she stuck it in her back pocket and pointed. An explosion rocked the cat trees from deep within. A few toppled over. The remaining cats hidden in the forest burst out, fleeing with their tails high.

*Whew. I don't want to burn any cats to death, excepting a certain Cat Man.*

*But wait, hold on. She's helping the cats, but...* Zeke frowned, turning to Domi. "Speaking of. What was that leaving-me-to-die moment last battle?"

Domi glanced away, distracted. "Huh?"

Cats ran by them. The large ones galloped away, while the little ones high-tailed it, streaming through the aisles in river-like masses. Looking at the large one, Zeke narrowed his eyes. *Guess the Cat Man isn't out of lives yet.*

He put his hands on his hips, looking Domi in the eye. "You heard what I said. Why didn't you help? I noticed you leaving me to die. Mia noticed, too. We know what you were doing."

Distracted, Domi waved her hand and began to jog off. "I was saving my energy. I told you. Come on, let's get out of here before we get killed by smoke inhalation."

"Saving your energy? Or seizing an opportunity to bump me off?" Zeke asked, following her.

"What's the difference?" Domi said, laughing.

"Domi. This isn't funny," Zeke said.

Domi rounded on him. "So? We're in a *battle royale*. Only one can survive. I'm your subordinate. The only way for me to survive is to kill you. I don't want to kill you, but I'm not seeing another way out of this."

"What if subordinates can survive as one unit with the main apocalypse? We don't know how this works. I mean—" Zeke paused. He glanced up. "System, can subordinates survive?"

**So long as they are sufficiently subordinated.**

Domi paused. She licked her lips.

Zeke cut his eyes at her. "So? Did you not ask?"

"Look, man, I'm stressed out. I'm tense. We're out here killing people to survive, fighting, I don't know, cats and pigeons and cartoon kids and shit. I'm not running at a hundred percent, okay?" Domi said, throwing her hands up.

"Right, but you almost let me die because you didn't ask. Maybe next time, ask first, kill later?" Zeke said, narrowing his eyes at her.

Domi took a deep breath. "I get it, but like, seriously. Based on everything we've seen so far, the damn System wants us all to fight to the death. I mean, I imagine you can't subordinate everyone, right?"

...

Domi squinted. "Right?"

Zeke put a hand on his chin. His eyes widened. *Is that the ultimate way to win? Subordinate everyone else?*

*But...that's incredibly difficult. As Domi showed, subordinates can still choose to kill me, or at least let me die. For example, I wouldn't trust Cat Man Isaac with my leftover cheese curls, let alone my life. And the T-rex skeleton, too... I don't think it understands English, and even if it did, I'm pretty sure it isn't interested in cooperation. It's too powerful. It doesn't have a reason to subordinate itself to me.*

*Hmm. Subordination is obviously a powerful skill, on the other hand. If I level it up, I could even control my subordinates' bodies. Control them all at once? Control one at a time? If it's one at a time, betrayal is still a problem. If it's all at once, it ceases to be a problem... but then I've become a true evil overlord, a complete and utter tyrant like no tyrant so far on Earth. Even the most domineering king can't literally control the bodies of their citizens.*

*I-I don't want to do that. So...I think...I'll use subordination. But not exclusively. I'm not going to try to subordinate everyone. If I can trust them, if they aren't going to try to kill me, I'll subordinate them rather than killing. If they're dangerous and given to traitorous actions, like the T-rex or Cat Man Isaac, it's probably better to just kill them outright.*

*Besides, I still need to level up and gain more skills. I don't get as much from subordination as I do from killing. True, I can share subordinates' skills eventually, but I can't use them forever, I can't use them without my subordinate's permission, and I can't use them as skill fusion fodder, either.*

*Subordination is a powerful tool. I should keep it in mind. Still, it would be foolish to make it my default. Subordinates aren't mindless clones. They're beings with thoughts, desires, wants, goals. I need to find someone, or something, I can trust before I subordinate them.* Zeke reached up and patted Allen on the back.

Allen turned his head up and latched his teeth onto Zeke's finger.

Pulling his hand down, Zeke sighed and carefully freed the anole. Carefully, he set Allen on his head again. *...Or, if not trust, at least something that can't harm me.*

"So?" Zeke asked, as he ran alongside Domi, and smoke began to pour into the ceiling overhead. "Are you going to continue to try and kill me? Should we hash this out now? Or do you want to win together?"

Domi twisted her lips and rolled her eyes. "I don't want to kill you. I really don't. I like you, Zeke. If I don't have to, I'm not going to try to kill you."

Zeke eyed her. *On one hand, she definitely left an opening for the Cat Man to kill me. On the other hand, I passed out in her apartment, and she didn't do anything to kill me or Mia.*

*I-I think I can believe her that she was just seizing the moment, rather than deliberately planning to kill me. After all, if she was premeditating murder, she could've killed me easily while I slept. Deciding not to step in and see if I beat a powerful foe... it's not something I like, but it's not ganking me in my sleep, either.*

*For now, I'll trust her. Still, I'll keep my eyes open more than I was before. If anything, this is a good reminder that I can't trust anyone. Not even my subordinates.*

The smoke billowing through the store grew lower. The three of them started to run. As he ran, Zeke snagged a bag of dog food off the shelf. The heavy bag drew him to a temporary halt. Kneeling, he worked the bag up onto his shoulders, then ran on again, chasing after Domi.

"Hungry?" Domi asked, eyeing the bag.

"Guys! Hurry up!" Mia called from the door.

"Perpetually," Zeke returned. He paused, giving a longing gaze toward the feeder crickets. *Too bad about those. I could've eaten so many of those...*

Domi snorted. "Fair enough."

# 60

## ARENA

They burst out into the street. Black smoke streamed off the building, rising into the sky. Zeke bent over, panting. He waved his hand in front of his face. "Whew!"

"That was *brutal,*" Domi muttered.

"Try doing it with fifty pounds of dog food on your back," Zeke muttered.

Mia frowned. "Why'd you grab dog food?"

"Dinner," Zeke said, only half joking.

Mia pulled a face. "We need to find real food."

"Dog food is real food," Zeke said.

"Real food... for *dogs,*" Mia pointed out.

Domi shrugged. "Dog food is food, too."

Zeke nodded at Domi.

Mia crossed her arms at Domi. "Are you going to eat the dog food?"

Taken aback, Domi frowned at Mia. "Are you insane? No. Of course not. That shit's for Zeke."

"Oh, hey," Zeke muttered.

"I saw how you looked at those crickets," Domi said, shaking her head at him.

Mia's head snapped up. She put her hands over her ears and frowned, staring into the sky.

"Mia? You hearing things again?" Zeke asked.

"People. They're hurt," Mia said. She turned slowly, facing into the heart of the city.

Domi followed her gaze, then shook her head. She backed away. "No. No, no, no. We are *not* going over there."

"What? Is it a bad part of town?" Zeke said, frowning. *Worse than here?*

"Nope. Nice part of town, actually."

Confused, Zeke looked at her. "So... what's the problem?"

Domi pulled out her phone and tapped away, then held up her screen, showing him the crashing police cars again. "It's the *stadium.* Remember? With the police, where everyone was evacuating to?"

Zeke drew a slow breath. "In other words...full of people. Which the average apocalypse sees as level-up fodder, and little else."

"Right. Now you're getting it. Any apocalypse over there is going to be insanely strong. Massively over-leveled. We'd be charging into the lion's den. It's just plain stupid," Domi argued.

"But...I can hear them. They're still alive," Mia said, rubbing her ear.

"Still alive like the Cartoon Apocalypse, or still alive like the Coffee Apocalypse?" Zeke asked, skeptical.

"Like—like I was. Like the Coffee Apocalypse. There're people there, but they're in danger." Mia stepped forward, almost dragged toward it. "I can't... we can't leave them to die."

Zeke drew a breath. He met Domi's eyes.

Domi backed away. She shook her head. "No. Whatever you say, no."

"Domi, listen. If they're level up fodder, and we ignore them, then what? We've made our own job harder in the end. We still have to fight all of the other apocalypses, no matter what. If they're keeping people around for some sick reason, that just means they're not as high level as they could be later," Zeke argued.

"I know, but we're tired. We've already taken on two apocalypses today. Do we need to plunge into danger again?" Domi asked, shrugging.

Zeke took a deep breath. "I hate to say it, but...better now than later."

"Yeah?" Domi quirked a brow.

"Right now, we still have food, running water, electricity... who knows when we'll be unable to find food, when the water and electricity stop running. We're tired today. Tomorrow, if the water cuts off, we might be tired *and* thirsty. And if the apocalypses in the stadium aren't human-based, if they're inanimate objects...our humanity immediately becomes a huge detriment. They can wait us out," Zeke said.

Domi pressed a hand to her forehead. "So, if supplies cut out—"

"Even if they don't... the other apocalypses are leveling up. We can't afford to sleep on this, Domi. Especially if they have a bunch of—I hate to say it this way—but... a bunch of levelling resources lying around. We're talking about apocalypses that could gain another ten levels in the blink of an eye, if they really have ordinary people lying around like that."

"They do," Mia said urgently. She glanced toward the stadium and took another few steps toward it.

"Plus, Domi, what do you think the other apocalypses are going to think, if they catch wind of this? Cat Man Isaac over there...do you think he's gonna sit around, twiddle his thumbs, and say 'good for them?' Or is he going to charge on over there and try to catch a few ordinary-people-levels for himself?" Zeke argued. "If we don't act now...even if the apocalypses that caught them are sitting on them, those ordinary people aren't going to stay alive for long."

Domi took a deep breath. She nodded. "Yeah. Yeah. I hate it, but you're right."

He turned to Mia. "What can you do? What does a [Hero] get?"

Mia gestured. Her sword appeared again, along with a glowing set of translucent armor. "I have lots of attacks, I think. Um. These things called skills?"

"So don't tell me exactly what they are but give me an idea. Melee attacks, ranged attacks?" Zeke asked.

Mia's eyes glazed, darting back and forth across a list Zeke couldn't see. After a moment, she nodded. "Melee, I think. Uh, some movement stuff."

"All right. Domi, you're ranged mostly, right?"

Domi nodded. "Mostly, yeah."

"And I'm... well, kind of a mix of everything," Zeke muttered. He nodded to himself.

Feathers fluffed in the air. A bird swooped down at Zeke, its dark eyes glimmering with hatred, claws bared to attack.

## [Catlike Reflexes]

Zeke snatched the bird out of the air. Almost instinctively, he stuck it in his mouth.

## [Devour]
## Member of the Pigeon Apocalypse
## Level +.02

**Level:** 30.07
**Congratulations on reaching level 30!**
**Reward Loading... Please wait.**
**Due to a recent surge in requests, reward may take up to 24
hours to load.**

*Are they going to say that every time I gain levels?* Zeke
wondered.

**Choose Skill**
**Resilience (Minor)**
**Steel Stomach (Minor)**
**Wings (Tiny)**
**Claws (Tiny)**

Zeke started reaching for Resilience, then paused. *You know
what? I'm going to need Steel Stomach if I want to actually process
everything I eat. It hasn't bit me yet, but...I'm just going to keep
eating bad things. It'll keep getting worse unless I do something
about it.*

**Steel Stomach (Minor)**

Turning from the screen, Zeke clapped his hands together.
"Off to the stadium?"

Two disgusted faces met him.

Zeke blinked. "What?"

Domi wrinkled her nose harder. "You just keep doing more
impressive yet disgusting things."

"Did you just casually snatch a pigeon out of the air and eat
it?" Mia asked, flabbergasted.

"Oh. Yeah. I was hungry," Zeke said.

"You were—" Mia took a deep breath. She looked at Domi, disbelief written all over her face.

"I don't know. He's been like this as long as I've known him," Domi said, shrugging.

Mia rubbed her face. "Zeke, what the hell is happening? To you. To us. With...everything."

Zeke shrugged. "It's the apocalypse. What isn't happening?"

Mia waved her hand, putting the armor and sword away. "All right. Let's go."

"Wait," Domi said.

"What now?" Mia asked, antsy.

"It'll be faster if we take a motorcycle," she said, cutting her eyes at Zeke.

"What? Oh, come on. It'll take like, half the bag," Zeke said. He hefted the bag of dog food.

"Do you really want to carry around fifty pounds of dog food, anyway?" Domi asked.

"Come on, Zeke. We need to get there quickly," Mia said, nervous.

Zeke scowled. *They're right, but still.* He tore open the dog food bag and grabbed a handful. "All right, fine. But don't' complain when it runs out of fuel. I still don't know how to give it more."

"About that...I have an idea." Domi flexed her hand, then clenched it.

Grasping a handful of dry food, Zeke licked his lips. "Here goes nothing."

### [MOTORCYCLE]

Half a bag of dog food later, Zeke panted and stepped back. He wiped his mouth. "There. What do you think?"

Domi looked over the cycle. A black tank, a big round headlight, a swooping black leather saddle. She nodded. "Eh, good enough."

"Good enough? What does a man have to do to get a 'thank you' around here?" Zeke clicked his tongue, shaking his head at her.

Slinging a leg over the saddle, Domi grabbed the handlebars. She grinned at the two of them. "Hop on, bitches! Let's go to the stadium!"

Zeke stepped forward, but Mia got there first. She hopped on behind Domi, then turned to Zeke. "Hurry!"

Zeke pursed his lips. "I made the motorcycle. Why am I riding double-bitch?"

"Hop on, double-bitch, before you get left behind," Domi said, grinning.

Zeke sighed. He climbed on, setting the dog food bag in his lap, then looked at his hands. *Uh. What do I hold onto?* He reached for Mia, then paused. *Maybe not? Er...should I ask permission?* "Mia, can I—"

Domi cranked the motor. The cycle reared and burst off, roaring down the road.

Yelping, Zeke grabbed onto Mia's waist as Mia latched onto Domi.

"Haha, yeah! Hell yeah! Here we go!" Domi shouted, speeding up.

"Zeke, I'm scared," Mia cried.

"Domi, you're never allowed to drive again!" Zeke called over the screaming wind.

Domi grinned. "You can't stop me!"

# 61

## CAN'T STOP WON'T STOP

Halfway down the street, before they reached the next block, the engine spluttered and died. The motorcycle slowed down.

Zeke gasped a breath, relieved. He shook his head. "Whew. At least she can't do it for long."

"Domi, don't play on your cellphone! You're driving!" Mia called, shocked.

"Yeah, yeah. Just give me a moment..." Domi tapped something, then shoved her phone back in her pocket.

Below them, the motorcycle's engine rumbled to life.

Grinning, Domi grabbed the handlebars. "Haha! It's go time!"

"Oh, right. Explosions," Zeke muttered, half to himself.

Pointing the nose of the motorcycle at the stadium, Domi blasted off down the road. Zeke held on to Mia, Mia held on to Domi, and Domi gripped the handlebars. Overhead, countless electric wires crisscrossed the sky, while thousands of pigeons watched them from on high.

Zeke narrowed his eyes at the pigeons. *I'm onto you. Come at me, birdbrains!*

The pigeons leaped off the wires, swooping down on the motorcycle. Zeke extended his claws. "Be ready!"

"Be ready for what?" Domi asked.

Gray feathers filled her vision. Cursing, Domi ducked. The motorcycle swerved as she dropped to its handlebars. "Can't... see!"

A shining sword flashed out. Split in two, the pigeon tumbled to the ground on either side of the motorcycle.

"Be ready...for birds," Mia said darkly.

"Pigeons, specifically," Zeke added.

From left and right, pigeons shot at them. Zeke's hands whirled, and Mia's sword blurred. Pigeons fell to the ground left and right, while Zeke stuffed them into his mouth as fast as he could catch them. Tiny scratches accumulated on his arms and face, annoying if not dangerous.

### [Catlike Reflexes] [Claws] [Devour]

Battering away a pigeon with the back of his hand, Zeke grimaced. "Is there no end to these things?"

"Keep going!" Mia said. She panted, breath ragged. Blood clung to her blade. She flicked it free, but it clung, nonetheless. A pigeon dive-bombed her head, only to bounce off a barely visible helm. It flopped to the ground behind them and fluttered upright, already flying after them again.

"Help...help!" Domi grumbled, slapping a pigeon away. It flapped in her face, battering her with wings and claws.

Mia lunged forward. Grabbing the pigeon in her bare hand, she tossed it into the air and cut it down.

"Damn, thanks," Domi said, nodding.

Another pigeon swooped toward her face. Seeing it coming, Zeke pointed his finger at it. A blast of steam smacked the pigeon in the eyes, and it batted its wings wildly, blinded, and flew off course.

Even as he struck the pigeon down, another one flapped into his face, battering his eyes and nose with its wings.

"Back off!" Zeke shouted, annoyed. Reaching up, he shoved the attacker into his mouth.

## [Devour]

Mia swiped to the left. Zeke pointed his finger to the right, blasting steam at the oncoming pigeons with one hand and scooping handfuls of dog food into his mouth with the other. Together, they managed to keep the pigeons off Domi's face.

Abruptly, the pigeons fell back. Mia wiped her brow with her sleeve, and Zeke used what little remained of his shirt to clean his face of pigeon blood. *Whew. That was annoying. But at least I got a few pieces of levels and some skills.*

**Level:** 30.05 > 30.19
**Resilient Regeneration (Lesser) > (Lesser) +7**
**Regeneration rate +3.6% > 6.1 %**

A thought struck him. Zeke licked his lips. Craning his neck, he peered at the pigeons. They drew a sharp line on the road, not crossing another inch closer.

*They didn't stop because they got tired...they stopped because they chose to. Because...*

He turned his eyes forward, toward the stadium. *Because... they were afraid of something.*

"Zeke, is something wrong?" Mia asked.

"No, just... nervous," Zeke said, muttering the last bit under his breath. He rubbed the back of his neck. *What do those bird-brains know, after all?*

The bass thump of distant music rattled Zeke's chest as they approached the stadium. Fewer abandoned cars blocked the road, but the cars parked on the side of the road sported shattered windows and broken windscreens as a rule. Human and humanoid bodies laid scattered across the sidewalks, snarled in tight knots around the entrance gates. Blood stained the sidewalk and pooled in the gutters. Big black flies burst away as they arrived, scared off by the loud engine. A thick, rotten scent hung in the air, heavy enough to choke on.

Mia gagged. Zeke grimaced. Domi frowned, lifting her shirt over her nose.

*This is the stadium. The place where they told everyone to gather at the start of the crisis. The apocalypses, who were also gathered... isn't this nothing more than a smorgasbord to them? All these human lives are nothing but levels to the other apocalypses.*

*Whatever we find here is going to be incredibly powerful. We have to be ready.*

The motorcycle's engine quieted as they slowed, slowly petering to a halt. Domi kicked the stand and parked it, climbing off. She kept her eyes away from the bodies, locking her gaze onto Mia and Zeke. "Ready?"

"I don't think we are," Zeke said quietly.

"Are we ever?" Domi asked.

Zeke grabbed one last handful of dog food, gobbling it down as he hopped off the motorcycle. "Never."

Stepping away, Mia closed her eyes. When she opened them, a decisive light burned in their depths. "They're still alive. For now."

Zeke nodded. He headed for the door, then paused. Looking over his shoulder, he nodded. "Domi...don't take a Domain."

"Huh?" Domi asked, startled.

"You're level thirty now, right? Or close to it. The System, it's going to offer you something called a Domain. Don't take it. It's a trap," Zeke said.

"Domain... Oh, like the Cartoon Apocalypse or Cat Man Apocalypse had? That thing that changes the world around you?" Domi frowned. "Is it a trap? It seemed to work out for them. Like, it was a huge power boost, especially if we're talking the Cartoon Apocalypse."

"Only one can escape," Zeke repeated. He shook his head. "How can we escape if we're locked to one area of the city?"

"But...wouldn't we just have to expand our Domain out of the city? Isn't that the point of the Domain, spreading it across the world?" Domi asked, confused.

Zeke pressed his lips together. He looked her in the eyes. "I don't want to destroy the world, Domi."

"I mean, we're apocalypses, man. I get it, but—" Domi fell silent. She paused. "You think that once we have a Domain, there's no way back. In other words...once we have a Domain, we destroy the world no matter what we want."

"That's what I'm afraid of. Think of the Coffee...Cartoon Apocalypse. That kid had no idea about the people in the shoe store, didn't even know they existed, but they still got turned into cartoons. If we take Domains...that's game over in terms of not destroying the world. We're on the path of no return," Zeke said.

"And you think there's something else?" Domi asked.

Zeke shrugged. "The System's being sketchy about it. I'm not sure, but...I might have evidence."

"Evidence?" Domi asked, brows furrowed.

"The Dinosaur Apocalypse. It didn't seem to have a Domain. If nothing else, it was roaming freely through the city, right? And it didn't infect Mia or any of the cats." Zeke pointed out.

"That's true... unless it's like the Cat Man. Mia didn't start turning into a cat, after all. I think his Domain only infected cats," Domi returned.

Zeke spread his hands. "I don't know. I just know that Domains are bad news... if we want to avoid destroying the world." He gave Domi a look.

Domi put her hands up. "I don't want to die, but I don't want to destroy the world if I can avoid it. Fuck, I like having internet and air conditioning, okay? I want to become a pyrotechnical engineer. Fireworks! Who's going to want fireworks at the end of the world? We lose society, we lose all of that."

Zeke nodded, then grinned. He put a hand on his chin. "I don't know. Fireworks at the end of the world? Sounds nice, actually."

Domi snorted. "If we get there, I'll set them off for you. A whole show's worth. Turn the night sky to day, with booms so loud they roll like thunder."

"It's a deal," Zeke said, snorting. *That'd be a sight to see.*

Mia turned. Her hands shook, subtly, and she kept her eyes on the sky, unwilling to look at the bodies. "I don't want to spend any more time out here."

"Domi?" Zeke asked.

"Huh? No, I don't really wanna stay out here, either," Domi said, shrugging.

The bass thumped from the stadium. Distorted voices boomed forth. Half-visible over the stadium seating, huge screens flashed, though they only showed blobs of bright colors rather than meaningful images. Distantly, screams echoed, though the bass and announcers' voices drowned them out.

Flies buzzed. Somewhere, a body let off gas. A rat jumped up from the bodies and scuttled away, vanishing into the shadows.

"It's already hell out here. How much worse can it be in there?" Zeke asked.

"Don't say that," Domi muttered.

Mia nodded. "Let's go."

Together, they strode through the entrance gate.

# 62

## MAIN EVENT

The noise of the stadium grew clearer as they walked inside. They passed under the stands, and darkness swallowed them up. Distantly, green light glowed at the end of the long tunnel, hinting at the grassy field beyond. Their footsteps echoed through the tunnel, bouncing off the smooth concrete walls. The distorted voices slowly resolved, while the deep thumping became upbeat music with a driving bass line.

"A strong showing from the Reds! Can they recover this? What do you think, Rob?"

"I don't know, John. It's a close game! My money's still on the Blues. Let's see them hustle!"

Around them, the tunnel widened out. Darkness stretched in both directions, seemingly infinite, too dark for Zeke's eyes to pierce.

*Damn. Maybe I should've chosen the Headlight skill from the motorcycle.*

Mia jumped and grabbed Zeke. Zeke startled. He raised his hand, ready to shoot steam at the threat. "What? Where?"

Mia pointed, her finger trembling. A strange figure loomed out of the darkness, one hand raised.

Domi raised her cellphone, turning on the flashlight. It illuminated a cartoonish bird mascot standee. The cardboard figure gave the group a friendly smile, while a speech bubble said, *Robbie the Robin invites you to remember to throw out your trash on the way out!*

"He's gonna get you," Domi chuckled. She walked over and gave it a kick. "Dumbass thing. I never liked it anyway."

The cardboard went flying, bouncing off into a corner of the room. Lit up for a moment in the swing of Domi's cellphone light, dark concessions stands and a retail shop selling jerseys stood to either side, all closed off behind bars. Domi shut off her flashlight, and everything plunged into darkness once more.

Mia breathed out. "Whew. Seeing that in the dark...I thought it was another apocalypse, coming for us."

"That is a good question, though. Why isn't anyone out here? It's a great place to sneak attack," Zeke wondered aloud.

Domi shook her finger at him, silhouetted against the growing light. "Don't you speak that into the world."

"But...seriously. Dead bodies at the door, then...nothing. Not even any bodies. It's like...no one was allowed in here, or something," Zeke muttered.

"That's...a good point," Mia agreed.

"But why?" Domi asked.

Even as she spoke, the announcers' voices boomed out again. "Wow! What a play from number fifteen! Do you think she'll be able to replicate that action ever again?"

The other announcer chuckled. "Not with her legs mangled like that, John."

In the growing light from the field, the three of them exchanged a glance.

"Sports Apocalypse? Announcer Apocalypse? Stadium Apocalypse?" Zeke tried.

**Stadium Apocalypse**
**Danger Rating:** A
**Level:** 30+

"Here we go," Domi muttered. Putting her cellphone in her back pocket, she flexed her hands.

Beside her, Mia drew her sword.

Zeke bared his claws. Quickly, he checked his stat menu.

**Level:** 30.19
**STR:** 5
**CON:** 10
**DEX:** 3
**SPR:** 10
**Regeneration rate:** +6.1%

**Skills**
**Manipulate Aerosols (Medium) +1**
**Pick Up (Weak)**
**Osmosis (Weak) +1**
**Subordinate Link (Weak)**
**Create Drug (Weak) +1**
**Crystal Burst (Poor)**
**Engulf (Poor)**
**Create Coffee (Strong)**
**Whistle Blast (Weak) Digital Broadcast (Weak)**
**Electric Leap (Poor)**

**Passive**
**Resilient Regeneration (Lesser) +7**

**Team Spirit (Minor) +1**
**Disguise (Minor)**
**Watertight (Minor)**
**Caffeine Rush (Average)**
**Growth (Lesser) +2**
**Heat Resistance (Lesser) +9**
**Strong Jaw (Minor)**
**Flexible Body (Average)**
**Roll With Me (Minor)**
**Strong Legs (Minor)**
**Catlike Reflexes (Lesser)**
**Claw Fighter (Lesser)**
**Perfect Landing (Lesser)**
**Steel Stomach (Minor)**

**Condition**
**Hardness (Lesser) (Condition)**
**Claws (Large) (Condition)**
**MOTORCYCLE**

Zeke snorted. *A CON/SPR build? Not exactly a normal build. Most casters don't have much CON. But, hey, whatever it takes to survive. Survival is more important than anything else!*

*My skill choices line up with that, too, don't they? A few ranged attacks, a few melee attacks, but a lot of resiliency and damage-lessening skills.*

*After all, the last one alive escapes. It doesn't matter if I kill everyone else. I just have to survive. I'd just sit quietly in a room somewhere, but I don't think poison mist is going to come out and kill everyone else. I have to level up to win. I have to fight. But, most of all, I have to survive those fights.*

"Ron, we've just got word...new contenders are on their way in!"

"Do you think they'll have what it takes to freshen the game, John?"

"Only time will tell. Are they benchwarmers or playmakers? Let's find out. Here they come!"

Zeke, Domi, and Mia stepped out into the light. Glaring sunlight burned into their eyes. Zeke raised a hand to block the sun, squinting out onto the field. *Here we go. What's going on here?*

They came out on the short side of the field, the long side stretching away from them. Men, women, and children filled the field. Every person wore either a red or a blue jersey. Those in red jerseys stood to the left, while those in blue stood to the right. They faced one another, tensed, hands bared.

Bodies littered the field around them. Some crumpled into strange shapes, others plainly beaten to death. Many were old, young, or infirm, though plenty of the dead were fully grown men and women as well.

Zeke lifted his eyes from the field to the seats around them. Strange, shifting shapes sat in the seats, not quite human, but not quite anything else, either. *They kind of remind me of those background characters in video games, the ones that are only half programmed in to save polygons. They're almost approximations of real people, but half-assed ones.*

Up in the box, two wrinkly old white men in headsets smiled down at them. "Reds and Blues! It's time to shake it up. We're going to transition here to everyone's favorite game... Battle Royale!"

"Uh... wasn't it a battle royale the whole time?" Domi muttered.

"I think... I think he means right here, right now," Mia muttered back.

The people in red and blue jerseys turned to face the three

of them. A few of them raised weapons, chairs torn from the stands or improvised bits of sporting equipment.

Zeke bared his claws. "Are these all normal people?"

Mia closed her eyes. She nodded. "Yeah. Yeah. They're under the Stadium Apocalypse's control, but they're normal people."

"In other words, the real mastermind is somewhere else," Zeke muttered.

Domi pointed at the announcer's booth. "Who the hell would choose 'Stadium' for their concept except for them?"

"Unless it's the Stadium itself that's an apocalypse," Zeke countered.

"It's a place to start," Domi said.

"Mia?" Zeke asked.

Mia shook her head. "I can't sense that precisely. They're too far away. All I can sense is that there are some ordinary humans here, and most of them are..." She gestured at the people on the field.

"All right. Make a run for the announcers?" Zeke suggested.

Domi gave a thumbs-up.

Mia took a deep breath and nodded.

"All right, folks! Murderball is over! But don't get yourself down because that means it's time for another game. Here we go! The Battle Royale you've been waiting for! Either the new kids win, or you do!"

"Ten minutes on the clock, Rob!"

"Thank you, John. And...time starts...now!"

The people in jerseys charged at the three of them, eyes vicious, teeth bared.

The three of them charged in, sprinting for the announcer's booth.

# 63

## TAKE THE HEAD

The three of them ran, feet churning up the turf. The red- and blue-jersey-wearing people charged at them from both sides, eyes wild with anger. Their muscles swelled, and their teeth bared, savagery in every inch of them.

Domi dropped to one knee, holding her hands at mid-calf height, and clapped. A wave of force blasted in front of her. It clotheslined the closest attackers, blasting their feet out from under them. They fell to their faces and immediately shoved themselves up, but before they could, the next wave of people trampled over them. They dropped back into the turf, bowled to the ground.

Running ahead, Zeke threw his hands out in front of him.

**[Manipulate Aerosols]**

A mist cloud formed up around them, momentarily hiding them from view. Without pausing, the attackers continued to rush the three of them.

"What's the point of that? They still know where we are," Domi grumbled.

Zeke raised his fingers to his mouth and blew.

## [Whistle Blast]

All around them, the people froze, stunned in place. Taking advantage of the freeze, Zeke ducked around the stopped bodies and went back to using **[Manipulate Aerosols]** to spread the fog out farther.

"Ohhhh," Domi said, nodding in understanding.

Mia stepped forward. As her foot hit the ground, she shouted, "Wake up!"

Gold light burst from her foot, blasting over the surface of the turf. Some of the people it struck blinked and looked around, plucking at their jersey in confusion.

"Hero skill?" Zeke asked.

Mia nodded. "It says it has a chance of breaking people away from an apocalypse."

"Damn!" Domi said, grinning.

"What's going on down there? It seems like a lot of exciting action is happening, but we can't see a thing!"

"That's right, John. This mysterious mist is completely covering our view! I guess all we can do is wait for it to clear."

"Ron, what do you think? Should the coaches call a time-out?"

John chuckled. "What's a time-out?"

"Right you are, John!" Ron returned, laughing.

"Motherfuckers. I'm gonna kill them whether they're the core or not," Domi grumbled.

"Hey," Mia warned.

"They're the ones cooperating with the System and narrating this shit!" Domi returned.

Mia shook her head. "They could be brainwashed. I was—"

A freight train slammed into Zeke's head. Static buzzed in

his ears, and his vision went black. He stumbled to the side, crying out. *What the—*

"Zeke?" Mia asked, concerned.

The pain faded. His vision returned, and the static faded. He rubbed the side of his head, confused. *Ow. Is this one of the Stadium's skills? It came out of nowher—*

### Targets Identified. Opening Domain.

"No! I don't want it!" Zeke shouted desperately.

Off to the side, Domi gripped her head, too.

"Domi, stay strong!" Zeke called.

### Initializing...

"Stop," Zeke snapped, annoyed. *Why isn't the System listening to me? It's never ignored me before!*

### This is a Free Trial. Please enjoy.

"I don't want a free trial. I don't want a Domain, I—"

All around him, the people who'd been shaken free of the Stadium Apocalypse's grasp stiffened. They turned toward Zeke, reaching out for him.

"Stop it!" he snarled at the System.

### This is only a Free Trial. Please relax and enjoy.

"All right, I've had enough trial, so—"

Hunger thundered into his stomach. Zeke crumpled. All the energy left his body, and he fell to his knees. Startled, he slapped his hand down just in time to catch himself before he fell onto his face.

*What...what the—*

Around his hand, the turf rotted away, blackening, then turning to dust. The earth underneath blanched to sand as nutrients poured out of it. Farther and farther, the emptiness spread. In return, ever so slowly, the hunger faded from Zeke.

### [Absorb] (Level 30 Skill) could be yours.

"Zeke, Domi, what's happening?" Mia asked, panicking.

"Get back!" Zeke shouted.

The ring of decay struck one of the Stunned people. Their shoe fell apart, their foot desiccated to bone, and still the absorption pulse grew. Zeke pulled at his arm, trying to lift it off the ground, but couldn't. As if it weighed a thousand pounds, it refused to budge. Instead, it plunged deeper into the destroyed ground.

"Stop it. Stop it!"

The devouring crept up the man's leg. His flesh withered while Zeke's stomach filled. His bones flaked away, and he fell to his knees, face twisted in a rictus of confusion and horror. Now the same height as the man, Zeke stared into his eyes. He shook his head, not sure what to say. "I'm sorry. I'm sorry!"

With both knees on the ground, the devouring pulse spread all that much faster. The man's body withered away, leaving only the bones. A wind blew, stirring the steam around them and tearing the bones apart. Fine white dust flew off on the breeze. Nothing remained.

"I'm sorry...I'm so sorry," Zeke whispered. *Is this what Ryan meant? Is this what he was afraid of?*

*How do I control power like this? Can I? Can anyone?*

*Is this...is this how we end the world? Even if I don't want to, this hunger...this hunger, the Absorb ability, and the Domain...*

*The Domain. What is my Domain doing?*

Bright orange glow lit the foggy steam. Zeke glanced over. A different attacker's body bloated, glowing bright from an intense internal heat. The attacker trembled. Her eyes rolled back, hands shaking. Pressure drove her skin taut, while light beamed out of her eyes, nose, and mouth.

"What are you two doing? Stop it!" Mia shouted. Her sword beamed in the fog, cutting a swathe of light through the misty air.

"Stop," Domi said weakly. Her own eyes glowed a bright orange, while orange flashed from the inside of her cheeks as she spoke.

The taut, glowing woman staggered away, disappearing into an orange blur in the fog. An earth-shattering explosion burst.

Something wet and hot splattered over Zeke. Zeke flinched. He raised his hand, wiping his forehead. A smear of bright red stretched over his palm.

Against his will, his hand lifted toward his mouth. Zeke stiffened. Grabbing his arm with his other hand, he forced it down, away from him. "System! This isn't what I want. I don't want this, I swear!"

One of the old ladies in a red jersey staggered by Zeke, appearing out of the fog. Her body curved inward, concave. Drool dripped from her lips. Her limbs shook from hunger, but she walked onward with a strength and determination that gave lie to her great age. She laid eyes on one of the children. A long tongue stretched from her gaping mouth and licked her entire face. She staggered toward him, drooling even heavier than before.

**Someone inflicted with your Domain will look like this. Look at how powerful she is!**

"I don't want this. I don't. Stop this, System," Zeke demanded, halfway between pleading and demanding. *It's going rogue. It's not listening to me.*

*Could it do this the whole time? If so, why was it playing along?*

*Was it waiting for a foothold? A grasp on this mortal plane, from which to impose its will? Is this what happens to everyone with a Domain?*

*Or is this just because I'm refusing it? Because I don't want to destroy the world? Because I don't want a Domain?* Zeke gritted his teeth.

"Gramma? Gramma, what are you doing?" the boy asked, backing away nervously.

The old lady lunged at him. She snatched him up, far spryer than she appeared. Grabbing his arms in one hand and legs in another, she opened her mouth wide.

The boy screamed in fear. Tears ran down his face.

"No. No! Stop it! I don't want this!" Zeke shouted.

**This is a Free Trial. Please enjoy.**

Zeke's stomach suddenly felt empty once more. Faintly, he saw a blue message box appear above the grandma's head.

**[Devour]**

"No! Stop it!" Zeke screamed. *Something. There has to be something I can do!*

The grandma's jaws arced toward the child's stomach.

# 64
## WAKE UP

**[Caffeine Rush] [Catlike Reflexes] [Strong Legs]**

Activating all his skills at once, Zeke forced himself upright despite the weakness. He charged for the grandma and tackled her to the ground. The boy fell out of her hands and rolled away, bouncing off into the fog.

"Wake up!" Zeke shouted.

"Huh? Oh!" Mia jumped forward. She stomped again. "Wake up!"

A pulse of gold light sent the fog flying away. Across the field, glowing people suddenly faded back to normal, their skin and bodies deflating, the glow burning away to nothing harmlessly. Hungry men and women released each other. Confusion glimmering in their eyes, they wiped their mouths and backed away while their would-be victims fled in fear.

The System popped up before Zeke's eyes.

**Are you sure you want to terminate the Free Trial?**

"Yes!" Zeke snarled. *How many times do I have to say it before the System listens?*

The System paused as if surprised.

## Even after you see the Domain's power for yourself, you reject the Domain?

"If I can't control it, it isn't useful at all. Power without control isn't power at all," Zeke spat back. *Without control, I'm nothing but an avatar of the System's will. A mindless beast, without a mind of my own. I'd be playing into its hands. And that's the last thing I want to do.*

Panting, Domi wiped her sweaty brow and fell backward, dropping to her butt. She looked at her hands, blinking rapidly. "Whew. What *was* that?"

"Guys? Seriously. I just watched Domi blow up someone for no reason. What happened?" Mia asked. Her eyes darted back and forth between Zeke and Domi, her trembling hands begging for an answer.

"The System tried to force us to take Domains. W-we lost control for a second. We couldn't do anything about it," Zeke said. He looked at his hands, then clenched them into fists. *I need to break free from the System.*

*The System wants us to destroy the world. It's giving us power to destroy the world. It's guiding us to destroy the world. Right from the start, it said so. To think I can use it and avoid destroying the world is hubris.*

*It didn't call us Apocalypses for nothing. If we keep relying on the System, we'll wind up causing the end of the world, whether we want to or not.*

*But...what else can we rely on, if not the System? Without the System, I'm nothing. I have no powers. I'm just an ordinary kid. I couldn't beat the Cat Apocalypse without these powers, let alone this*

*Stadium Apocalypse or any of the seriously dangerous beings out there right now.*

*And, of course, if I give up now, die happily the way Ryan wants me to for 'the good of humanity' or whatever, I lose. We all lose. Some other apocalypse will win, and the world ends anyway.*

*Why is Ryan so obsessed with me? Is that his apocalypse? Or maybe...it's a facet of it.*

*Does he have a Domain? What is his Concept? I know far too little about him. True, he hasn't really been a threat for a while, but I can't ignore him, either. If he's left to his own devices, he'll eventually turn back time...and then all of this will be for nothing.*

He looked at his hand, then at the withered circle on the ground around him. *I can't give up the System, or else I lose my life. But, with the System...I'm a threat to all life on this planet.*

*Catch-22. I can't win.*

"Is it going to happen again?" Mia asked.

"I don't know! I don't know." Zeke's voice fell to a mutter, his words half to himself. *The System didn't warn us about the "Free Trial." What else does it have up its sleeve?*

The field trembled underfoot, startling Zeke out of his thoughts. He looked around, wide-eyed.

"Zeke, look sharp. Something's coming," Domi warned.

"All right, third-string players! Let's clear the field out for the real players," one of the announcers called.

"These boys and girls are the real deal. If you aren't on your toes, prepare to be flattened!" the other returned.

The people in blue and red jerseys turned and fled, leaving only the three of them on the field. The thumping grew louder and louder. The floor shook harder. Zeke spread his legs instinctively, lowering his center of gravity to avoid toppling over.

"We'll talk about it later," Zeke said tersely, backing toward Domi.

Mia joined them, brandishing her sword at the field. "I won't let you become killers. I don't care what Ryan says."

"Bit late for that," Domi muttered under her breath.

Zeke elbowed her.

"*More* killers. I mean, I won't let you kill any more," Mia declared. "Not innocents, anyway."

"Oh, okay. We're good, then," Domi said, nodding.

*In the space of a day, I've gone from being unwilling to kill, to seeing no way to avoid killing if I want to survive. Is this what the System wants from us?*

Zeke bared his claws.

*It doesn't matter. No matter what, I won't give in.*

Bulky figures thundered out of the tunnel at the opposite end of the field, not a one of them less than seven feet tall or three hundred pounds, every ounce of them pure muscle. Zeke gaped, his eyes widening as he counted them. *One, two ... ten ... fifteen...*

"Motherfuck," Domi whispered.

"Here they come! Let's see if defense can hold the line!" one of the announcers called.

Abruptly, Zeke stood. He blinked. *Hold on. What are we doing here? Why are we standing here on the field?*

*No, I have to fight. If We don't beat them, then...*

*Then...what?*

"Zeke! Now is *not* the time to get distracted!" Mia shouted.

"Guys, wait. Why are we here, facing off against these guys? What happened to killing the announcers?" Zeke asked, pointing up at the booth.

"We— Huh?" Domi furrowed her brows. She looked up. "Why?"

Mia startled, eyes widening. She whirled around and clapped her hands. "Wake up!"

Gold light passed over Zeke and Domi. Abruptly, Zeke's

mind cleared, and Domi's eyes lit up. The two of them exchanged a look.

"Damn. We fell into the Stadium Apocalypse's pace," Domi grumbled.

"It's powerful enough to influence other apocalypses?" Zeke asked, surprised.

"Why not?" Mia returned with a shrug. "You're assuming apocalypses can't affect other apocalypses, but do you have any proof?"

*We didn't get affected by the Cartoon Apocalypse, but maybe that only applies to physical alteration not mental influence.* Zeke rubbed his head. *Damn. One more thing to guard against.*

Looking at the monstrous people thundering toward them, more muscle than human, Zeke pressed his lips together and turned toward the press box instead. "What do you guys say we slap around some old white guys instead?"

"I'm for it," Domi said, chuckling darkly as she cracked her knuckles.

Mia nodded just once, short and sweet.

As one, they turned and fled, hurtling toward the announcer's box.

"And it looks like the challengers are exiting the field. I've never seen a play like this before in my life! How about you, Ron?"

"Right you are, John. And I think... it looks like they're coming right for us!"

Zeke jumped the fence from the field to the stands. Cutting a sharp corner, he leaped up the stairs into the seating, then jumped from one seat to the next. Domi and Mia followed him. Their steps *ping*ed up the metal structure, echoing in the hollow space below.

Behind them, the muscular people smashed through the fence without pause. The fence went down, chain link and aluminum supports crumpling under their weight. Wordlessly, they bounded up the stairs after the trio.

Panting, Zeke glanced back. "Damn. They just don't stop."

On Zeke's head, Allen scurried upright. Looking down on the muscular monstrosities, he extended his dewlap, then slowly, precisely, executed a single pushup.

### [Intimidating Pose]
### Subordinate Allen would like to borrow your SPR. Allow?
### Yes/No

"Yes!" Zeke shouted.

The muscleheads' feet fell silent as they froze in awe of Allen's pushup.

Ahead of them, the announcer's booth loomed. Huge windows reflected their faces back at them, while the sun glanced off the glass, obscuring the announcers for the moment.

"Go, go, go!" Zeke shouted.

The sword materialized in Mia's hand. Domi raised her hands, sparks glowing in her palm. The three of them closed in on the booth.

# 65
## ANNOUNCER'S BOOTH

Mia reached the announcer's booth first and slashed out. A line opened in the glass. Cracks branched off it, cutting through to its edges.

"Everyone, get down," Domi declared.

Zeke dropped, hunkering below the level of the seats. Leaping back a row, Mia ducked, hands over her head.

The muscular people closed in on them. Five rows of stairs separated them from Zeke. Four. Three. The seats rattled around him. Bits of trash bounced down the stepped floor. Zeke's bones rattled in his chest.

"Domi!" Zeke snarled.

"Don't worry. Oh, and don't look up." Putting her other hand on her hip, Domi snapped her fingers.

Zeke shut his eyes just as an incredibly bright light flashed. Heat washed over his skin, and force slammed him against the concrete risers. Overhead, the metal stadium seat let out a pained shriek and buckled. Heavy, meaty thumps sounded as the muscular people bounced away down the risers, dropping into the bottom of the seating.

Zeke peeked up. A gaping hole remained where the glass

had been. Glass shards scattered inward, blown away by Domi's blast.

Domi grinned. "Let's see our announcers now!"

"What a play, John, what a play!" an old white man with a flabby body and a full head of white hair said, clapping. Despite the headset dangling half off his head, his voice still boomed across the stadium.

*So, that's Ron. Which means the other one is John,* Zeke noted to himself, glancing at the man beside the first.

A man with salt and pepper hair grinned back at Zeke, only slightly less overweight, rotund belly overhanging his belt. He stood, shoving his chair back. "Looks like we're up, Ron. I think it's time we got off the bench and showed these kids what's what!"

"Couldn't have said it better myself," John agreed, heaving himself upright. He cracked his knuckles and bared his teeth in a bright smile.

"Couple of old men think they're hot shit?" Domi muttered to Zeke and Mia.

"Are they really just old men?" Zeke muttered back.

Ron knelt. Latching his fingers under the edge of the desk, he threw it at the three of them.

Zeke dropped. The desk whizzed overhead, passing with such speed and force that his hair ruffled on his head. Allen hunkered, closing his inner eyelids against the wind.

On either side of him, Mia and Domi stared, eyes wide.

*Thump.* A full twenty seconds after the throw, the desk struck the field below, almost crossing the field's center line.

Sweat crept down Zeke's back. *Come to think of it, they didn't flinch from Domi's huge explosion. I don't think the glass even cut their skin.* Zeke's eyes darted over their faces and necks.

John raised his hand and wiped a handful of stray glass off

his collar nonchalantly. Not a single scratch marred his flabby, pale flesh.

Domi licked her lips. "I take it back."

The twin juggernauts stepped over the rim of the window. Zeke scrambled back a step, desperately looking through his skills. *Something...anything...*

Behind them, metal seats clashed as the muscular men and women charged up them once more, sandwiching them in from behind.

"What will our underdogs do now, Ron?"

"Hard to say, John. I can't see a way out of this for them."

"Mother *fuck you!*" Domi shouted, throwing both of her hands at the announcers. Her hands snapped in a massive *CLAP.* A huge blast of force, light, and fire washed over them, enough to give the men and women running up the stairs pause.

John waved a hand in front of his face, coughing gently from the smoke. Ron checked his cufflinks.

"Oh, fuck," Domi whispered.

### [Roll With Me]
### [Team Spirit]
*All stats boosted when facing a stronger opponent.*

"No kidding," Zeke grumbled at the System.

Zeke's eyes landed on one of his skills. His eyes flickered past the announcers, into the room behind them, toward a screen in the upper left corner. The screen showed him, Mia, and Domi from behind, with the muscular people hurtling toward them. He caught his breath. *This one? Can I...?*

John knelt, taking up a running stance. Ron lifted his fists and bounced in place, his eyes shining with a boxer's determination.

*No more time to waste!* Baring his both claws, Zeke activated his skill for the first time.

## [Electric Leap]

The world stretched all around him, leaving only him stable, as if the world were taffy and he was the hook candy-makers pulled taffy on. Zeke's vision blurred at the edges. At the end of the long taffy-puller world, a bright light strobed slowly, passing across the digital screen at the back of the announcer's booth.

Almost dreamlike, he extended both his hands toward the frozen, distended bodies of the announcers and stepped forward. The single step sent him across the entire room to the screen. Behind him, four red lines appeared on their flesh, the cuts only superficial, but cuts, nonetheless.

Zeke struck the screen, and the world snapped back to normal. He fell from the screen, hurtling toward the floor.

*Oh, shit!*

## [Flexible Body] [Catlike Reflexes] [Perfect Landing] [Strong Legs]

He landed on his feet. The shock of landing rolled through his legs, dispelling the jolt painlessly.

*Oh. Well. I guess...I guess I do have a lot of skills for landing well.*

Ron surged forward, raising his fists at Domi. He stumbled a little, thrown off-balance by Zeke's passing.

She caught his hands. Explosions burst in her palms, sending his arms flying backward.

John sprinted at Mia, running slightly off-kilter from Zeke's attack.

Armor glowed around Mia's body, and the glowing sword

appeared in her hands. She leaped to meet him, sweeping her sword at his right leg.

From behind the announcers, Zeke glanced left and right. Ron glanced up, meeting his eyes.

*All right. Not him, then. Time for a sneak attack!* He hurtled toward John.

John leaped into the air, dodging the sword strike. His feet passed over Mia. He landed behind her, then whirled, spinning a low kick at Mia.

Mia danced away, popping up onto the next step.

*Uh oh.* Zeke backpedaled, barely dodging Mia. He landed beside John. John grabbed for him.

Mia struck at John's wrist. Although he couldn't see her from the angle he stood at, he snatched his hand away.

*Huh? How did he—* Zeke looked over his shoulder. On the screen, an overhead camera showed him, Domi, and Mia from above and slightly behind.

*Can he see what's on the screen? That's cheating!*

Mia chased after John. The two of them danced over the stairs, dueling back and forth. To the side, Domi chased Ron off with explosions, while Ron dodged his way closer to her, moving with the same kind of prescience as John, able to see her attacks before he would be able to see them, as though he could see her every move from above. The muscular men and women drew close to Domi and Mia. Mia slapped one of them off with the side of her sword, while Domi swept her hand, and a streak of explosions forced them back.

Zeke backed away. He peered overhead. *If there's a camera, then...*

"Zeke! A little help?" Domi shouted.

Ron landed a heavy blow to her gut. Domi grunted and crumpled. Ron closed in, grabbing Domi by the shoulders.

Pressing her lips together, Mia deflected another attack

from John, backing away again. He darted in and landed a roundhouse kick. Mia went flying. She tumbled to the ground, rolling toward the muscular men and women.

"Allen, go!" Zeke shouted.

Allen leaped off his head and charged at John.

Zeke's eyes locked onto a black blob high overhead. He rubbed his hands together and bounced in place, shaking out his arms as he warmed up arms and legs both. *Here goes nothing. If they have that eye in the sky, this fight is theirs. We're fighting the odds and them both. I have to take it out.*

*Either this works...or we're all fucked.*

### [Electric Leap]

# 66

## LEAP OF FAITH

The tunnel opened around him again. The rest of the world slowed to nothing. The sky streaked to a white blob. Swallowed in its blaze, the black dot of the camera overhead vanished.

Zeke turned his head. Everywhere he looked, tunnels stretched off, the world zooming away from whatever point he focused on. Some were more distant than others, their pull so weak he instinctively knew he couldn't use those routes.

*Hmm. If I level this skill up, I'll be unstoppable.*

He turned back to the camera. Taking a deep breath, he pushed off. His foot stepped on air, and he failed to gain any more traction. Nonetheless, a force pulled him forward, toward something invisible, high in the sky.

A black blot appeared at the end of the tunnel. He closed in on it, moving faster and faster.

Zeke opened his mouth, claws bared.

The black blot flew at him. He struck it, and the world snapped back to normal. High over the brutal concrete steps of the stadium's seating, Zeke began to fall.

### [Catlike Reflexes] [Claw Fighter]

Lashing out with both hands, he snagged the camera and held on tight. The camera dropped under his added weight, dangling low on its wire. The engines that moved it around the field groaned, clicking and grumbling.

Black metal seared into Zeke's hands. His claws snagged cracks in the case and held on. He gritted his teeth against the pain. *Come on, come on—*

### [Resilient Regeneration]

The pain faded. Taking a deep breath, Zeke stared at the camera. It stared back at him, huge lens reflecting his face.

Down below and high overhead, his face filled up the screens. The announcers paused, startled.

"Looks like there's a bug in our camera. Let's see if we can clear the view," John joked, slapping Mia's blade away with an open palm.

"I wonder what his dismount strategy is?" Ron returned. He backed away, dodging as Domi unleashed an onslaught of attacks.

Zeke pressed his hands against the side, ignoring the pain. *It's a gamble, but a gamble I'm willing to try!*

### [Crystal Burst]

Crystals surged out of the side of the camera. The lens instantly occluded over with thick growths, crystals jutting thickly out of the camera's lens. Zeke's stomach grumbled, but he put it to the back of his mind.

*I was worried the crystals wouldn't grow without the ground* there to grow out of, but I forgot that the camera's lens would count as crystal!

Hmm... Is it that the crystals need a starter crystal to grow off, not that they refuse to grow out of anything but the ground? The ground has a good deal of quartz in it, so there should almost always be something to grow from. On the other hand, people don't generally have large crystals inside of them.

Interesting! It's good to remember that I don't know everything about my skills. I can always learn more!

### Defeated Member of the Stadium Apocalypse!
### Level + 1.00
### Level: 30.19 > 31.19
### Please assign your stat point.

No skills? Wait...I didn't Devour it! Dammit! Missed opportunity... Sighing, Zeke called up his stats. Hmm...my arms are getting tired. I need more STR.

### STR: 5 > 6
### CON: 10
### DEX: 3
### SPR: 10

The camera creaked, dipping lower on the wire. Zeke turned up, checking the screen. Did I destroy it?

On the screen, Domi and Mia once again fought the announcers. He bit his lip. Guess there's another camera.

As he watched, a group of the beefy people circled around Mia, trying to box her in. "Mia! Behind!" Zeke shouted.

"Got it!" Mia called back. She jumped back. In midair, golden light burst from her, and the beefy people paused for a moment, long enough for Mia to scurry up the stairs and away from them.

Even as Mia escaped danger, a platoon of the huge men and women made a run at Domi.

"Domi, watch out, from the left!" Zeke shouted.

Domi turned. Rather than run from them, she ran at them, charging into their midst. With inhuman speed and skill, she dodged left, right, avoiding their swings and grabs by inches.

*Huh. Guess Domi invested into DEX,* Zeke thought to himself.

Behind her, the announcer fought his way into the crowd. One of the beefy boys blocked his way. Growling, he grabbed the man and threw him. The man flew through the air for a solid twenty seconds and struck the very bottom of the stadium steps with a meaty thump and a loud *CRACK.* He started to rise, then laid still.

*Hah. Own goal.* Zeke smirked, shaking his head.

From the tunnels, a group of people in paramedic gear ran out with a stretcher and loaded the man onto it. They fussed over him for a few seconds, and abruptly, he sat back up. Pushing the paramedics away, he hopped off the stretcher and ran back up the stands. The paramedics *hup-hupp*ed back into the tunnels and vanished.

Pursing his lips, Zeke narrowed his eyes at them. *Of-fucking-course there's paramedics at a stadium. Fuck! And they have magical healing powers, too? It's not fair.*

*Damn. Domains are a huge advantage. The System obviously wants us to take them. Maybe I should. Maybe I can control it.*

Zeke shook his head hard, dismissing the thought. *Don't fall for the System's tricks. I'm not taking anything on until the System explains exactly what I'm getting out of it. Especially something I know as little about as a Domain.*

Dangling from his camera, he looked around. *All right. Clearly I didn't get all the cameras. I can play eye-in-the-sky for the girls...but it would be better if I destroyed the enemy's cameras, first. There's gotta be another one somewhere...*

Not too far from him, a second camera pointed at the stadium stairs. Digging his claws in, Zeke clambered on top of his crystal-ridden camera. The wire bounced and groaned, displeased with his actions. *Just...a little more.*

With one last loud groan from the camera, Zeke climbed on top of it. It shook under him, trembling, clearly on the verge of giving out. He narrowed his eyes at the other camera and took a deep breath. *I'm not going to fall. I'm going to make it. I'm fine! Don't look down, just don't look down...*

### [Electric Leap]

The world blurred around him. Tunnels stretched off in all directions, some strong, others faint. He wobbled slightly, the camera still wiggling under him, just in slow motion now.

*Fuck. Which way was the other camera?* He looked left, then slightly more left. Two almost-equivalently powerful tunnels stretched off in almost the same direction. He bit his lip.

*Eeny, meeny, miney, moe...* Pushing off the camera, Zeke hurtled down the left most of the tunnels.

# 67
## AT THE END OF THE TUNNEL

A small blot loomed at the tunnel's end. Zeke sucked in a breath. *Oooh, that's not good.*

Zeke struck something light. He grabbed onto it with both hands, only to immediately plunge out of the air. Four wildly spinning rotors sliced into his forearms. A small, long-armed black body stretched out in a square formation, a rotor at the end of each arm.

*A drone? Damn! I guess it makes sense, but—* Falling from the sky, Zeke snapped the fragile plastic in half. The rotors stopped spinning.

*Can I eat this?*

*There's one way to find out.* Zeke put the broken end of the drone in his mouth and bit down.

**[Devour]**
**Defeated a Member of the Stadium Apocalypse!**
**Level + 0.41**
**Level:** 31.19 > 31.60

**Please choose a skill.**

**Skills**
**Flying Proficiency (Minor)**
**Rotors (Small)**
**Digital Broadcast (Weak)**
**Lights (Small)**

Zeke pressed his lips together. *All those skills suck. But— Shit, I'm gonna die! First, let's get outta here!* As the floor closed in on him, he looked up at the camera again.

### [Electric Leap]

Again, he entered the world of tunnels. He took a step, but nothing happened. His legs kicked uselessly in the air.

*Huh? Oh...do I actually need to push off something? Fuck.*

*Or wait. Maybe it works like zero-G. It's worth a shot, anyway.* Looking at the tiny blot of the camera, Zeke clenched his hands on the drone. Crystals burst up over the drone's body.

His stomach grumbled again. *Guess that drone wasn't enough to fill me up. To be fair, it was small. And this Electric Leap skill seems to take a lot of energy.*

*Focus, Zeke. I have to move!*

*Make the drone more massive, and then...* He threw the crystalized drone behind him. His body moved forward, and the pull of the tunnel took over, drawing him toward the camera.

*Whew. I almost turned into red paste.* Zeke relaxed slightly, only to bare his claws a moment later and hold his breath again, staring wide-eyed at the camera. *But if I don't make this grab, I'll be paste anyway! I don't have a second thing to throw. I have to make it!*

The camera appeared before him. He snapped his arms around it and hugged it for dear life. Again, the wire sagged. Hanging onto it, Zeke took a moment to take in the field. *I don't see any more cameras, and I've already killed the surprise drone. I think this one is it!*

Taking a moment, he glanced over the drone's skills again, then chose Digital Broadcast. *I don't really want any of the other skills. At least this way I can rank up a skill I have.*

## [Digital Broadcast] (Weak) +1

Overhead, the screen filled with a close-up shot of Zeke's ruined shirt and his bloodstained body beneath. Across the arena, blurry close shots of Zeke's chest filled every screen.

Mia lunged forward, pushing John back. He stumbled, and for the first time, mis-stepped. His heel slipped off the riser, and he fell backward.

Pushing her advantage, Mia sliced down at him.

John's eyes widened. He slapped his hands together and caught Mia's blade. Grimacing, he tensed for impact.

His back hit the step. A heavy, meaty blow echoed through the stadium.

"Hey, can tech fix that camera?" John asked through gritted teeth. His muscles bulged as Mia pressed the blade downward, her expression resolute.

Across the stairs, Domi ducked into the milling muscular men and vanished. Ron flailed wildly, pushing the muscular people left and right. "Damn, but she can bob and weave! This is a level of athletic skill we haven't seen in a long time, John! Tech, I'd really love that camera right now!"

Out of the tunnels, a group of men and women in white jerseys with blue lightning bolts emblazoned on their backs hup-hupped onto the field, the same as the medics had. They looked up at Zeke, then froze. One furrowed their brows. Another reached to a mic and spoke into it, turning their head away so the camera couldn't catch their lips.

*Ah, dammit. I can't read their lips, either!* Zeke thought, mildly annoyed. He pushed his palms hard into the camera's sides. *But first...*

### [Crystal Burst]

Crystals pushed at the camera's enclosure, bulging the metal cage outward. With a snap and a mighty crack, they burst through. Zeke glanced down. *Can I eat this?*

Deep in the broken-open camera, a little ball glistened. Zeke wrapped his right arm tight around the camera and reached for it. He yoinked it out and gulped it down. *Here goes!*

### [Devour]
**You have defeated a Member of the Stadium Apocalypse!**
**Level + 0.23**
**Level:** 31.60 > 31.83

**Please choose a skill.**

### Skills

### Digital Broadcast (Weak)

### Eyes in the Sky (Weak)
*See the world from directly above you. Lose the ability to see from your own perspective while skill is active. Low detail, high SPR cost.*

### Guidewire (Lesser)
*Move more skillfully on wires.*

Zeke pressed his lips together. *Man, I really am cutting my*

*Levels by Devouring things. The System warned me, but I wasn't ready. Why did Domi level up so slowly compared to me, then?*

Images flashed through his head. Over and over, Domi fought with him up until the end, only for him to jump in and deal the fatal blow.

*Ah. Okay. I understand now. I've been a piggish teammate, always taking the kill...*

*Well, whatever! I need to be the final one to survive. I don't know if Domi is happy to remain my subordinate, or if she's 'sufficiently subordinated,' whatever that means. Plus, since it takes more kills for me to level, I need the kill more than she does.* Zeke nodded to himself. A second later, he sighed. *I'm just convincing myself.*

*All right. Let's look at these skills. Digital Broadcast is a good fallback, but it's not my first pick. Eyes in the Sky...that sounds fantastic. If I get another awareness skill later, it's a good target for fuse fodder, too. Guidewire is too specific, honestly. When am I going to move on wires? So...yeah. This time, I think, the choice is obvious. Eyes in the Sky it is!*

Clutching the camera, he looked down. The girls dueled the announcers before him. Mia pushed her sword ever closer to John, while Domi continued to avoid Ron, weaving through the crowd. From above, he watched bright orange light build up in her eyes as she tapped furiously on her phone.

*As I thought! Those cameras were key to the announcers' upper hand. Now that they're gone, we can fight on even footing with the announcers.*

*So...how do I get down?*

# 68

## FROM ABOVE, TO BELOW

Grasping tight to the camera's crystal-studded casing, Zeke looked down at the risers below him. *Yeah...not liking my odds there.*

The camera creaked. The metal casing snapped, and the part Zeke held onto popped, dropping a few inches. Startled, Zeke grappled at it. He wrapped both arms around the camera, holding on for a better grip.

The wire groaned, barely supporting his weight.

*Can't stay up here forever...not that I want to. Could try Perfect Landing. Pretty sure I'd still have broken legs from this high, though. Flexible Body would help, but I don't know that it would help enough to matter. I don't think I should rely on my physical skills this time.*

*Which leaves Electric Leap.*

Zeke's stomach grumbled, letting out the long, low rumble of a truly empty stomach. He scowled. *After my mishap with the drone, I'm not as excited about Electric Leap, and it uses a lot of energy— I mean, I just ate the apocalypse member's core, but I don't want to become pasta sauce, either.*

He took a deep breath. His eyes latched onto the screens in

the announcer's booth, barely visible from where he hung. *One last jump.*

### [Electric Leap]

The tunnels stretched off into infinity. This time, though, each tunnel wavered, trembling at the edges. Zeke's strength waned, his stamina fleeing through his stomach. His entire body ached for food, for sustenance.

*Damn, this skill uses a lot of stamina.*

He pushed off the camera, launching himself toward the tunnel pointing most toward the announcer booth's screens. The world zoomed by. He caught glimpses of the stadium flying by around him, the floor hurtling up.

*Screens, here I come!*

Zeke struck the screen and dropped. He twisted his body instinctively, putting his hands and feet toward the floor.

### [Perfect Landing]

With a *thump*, Zeke landed on all fours in the announcer's booth. He looked around. *Domi...Mia...*

*BAM!*

Bright light and fiery heat exploded forth in all directions. Muscular men and women flew back. Rob rolled head over heels into the booth, thumping to a halt beside Zeke. Brows furrowed, he rubbed his head and started to climb to his feet.

Before he could, Zeke jumped on top of him and slammed him back down. He knelt right into Rob's face and whistled as loudly as he could.

### [Whistle Blast]
### [Whistle Blast] (Weak) +1!

Rob flinched back. His body went still.

Zeke slashed at the man's throat with his claws. His hands ached, claws glancing off Rob's flabby flesh.

*Damn! This guy is sturdy!*

*Oh, well, nothing for it.* Grabbing the man's head and pulling it back to bare Rob's throat, he opened his jaws and bit down on the soft flesh.

### [Strong Jaw] [Devour]

His jaws clenched. He dug his teeth in. Twisting his head, he tore at Rob's flesh. The soft flesh resisted his teeth, rebounding back from his bite like fat, indenting without breaking or tearing.

Growling, Zeke bit harder. His teeth barely pierced Rob's neck. *Dammit, Whistle Blast isn't going to last much longer! Come on, come on!*

### Would you like to learn Lvl 30 Skill [Absorb]?

*Can I take it without a Domain?* Zeke wondered, narrowing his eyes in suspicion.

### Yes.

*Then, yes!*

### Lvl 30 Skill [Absorb] learned!

Under Zeke, Rob started twitching again.

*I don't have any time. I still don't know how to control Absorb perfectly, but I don't have a choice! I need to end this here!*

## [Absorb]

Under his jaw, Rob's flesh withered. It lost its soft, rebounding, fatty quality, growing thin and weak instead. Rob grew smaller, his body folding in on itself. He stared at Zeke in horror as the strength fled him.

Zeke's jaws snapped shut. He tore Rob's throat out. Grimacing, with some effort, he swallowed. Under him, Rob grabbed for his throat weakly. His arms scrabbled a few times, then went limp. He kicked one last time and died.

**Member of the Stadium Apocalypse defeated!**
**Level + 1.28**
**Level:** 31.83 > 33.11

**Please assign your stat point.**
**Please choose a skill.**

**Skills**

**Thick Flesh (Condition) (Weak)**
**Can't**
**Can't**
**Disabled – Absorb Failed**
**Announcer's Voice (Poor)**
**Teamwork (Lesser)**

*Thick Flesh is the obvious pick from how hard it was to break through his...but what's that 'disabled' mean?*

**You only have one chance to learn each skill. When you use Absorb, it automatically attempts to absorb one of the**

**opponent's skill (can be used once per opponent). If it fails, the skill is Disabled and cannot be learned with Devour.**

"Can I turn that off?" Zeke asked. *A low chance of automatically absorbing a second skill is nice, but disabling a skill if it fails is annoying.*

**No.**

*Huh. I guess that's a punishment for relying on Absorb too much, then. Is the System attempting to balance things here? Guess I can't ding it for trying. I mean, to start out with, Devour is kind of overpowered.* Zeke picked Thick Flesh. *I'll fuse it with Hardness later.*

**[Thick Flesh] (Condition) (Weak)**

Zeke wiped his mouth. Blood smeared the back of his hand.

"Yo, Zeke! Come help ya girl!" Domi shouted from outside, gesturing him toward Mia. Atop her head, Allen dropped a sick pushup, extending his dewlap for maximum authority.

Zeke waved back. "I'm coming!"

Domi nodded and ran toward Mia, leaving him behind.

Zeke chased after her. Out of the announcer's booth, and into the sun. The moment he stepped outside, the remaining muscular men and women rounded on him, faces distorted with hatred.

Lifting his fingers to his mouth, Zeke whistled.

**[Whistle Blast]**

Half the men and women froze in place, stunned, while the rest shoved them out of the way and chased after Zeke. Zeke turned and fled, following Domi.

*If Rob wasn't the apocalypse's core, maybe John is! Or maybe it's something else entirely.* Zeke took a deep breath. His eyes panned over the entire stadium. *It is called the Stadium Apocalypse.*

*But it would make sense if one of the announcers decided to make Stadium his concept! I have to believe in that. If not, how on earth am I supposed to Devour an entire stadium?*

**Absorb can be used at a short range not just melee.**

"Are you encouraging me to use Absorb, or aren't you," Zeke muttered to himself. He stopped and turned to face the muscular men and women. *Whatever. It's a new skill. Might as well try it out!* Zeke pointed his hand toward the group of people.

**[Absorb]**

# 69
## NICE

Z eke's vision flickered. A white circle spread out from his feet, stretching evenly in all directions. It reached the first of the muscular men and paused.

The man ran into the circle. His flesh instantly began to wither. Gritting his teeth, he pushed through, reaching for Zeke. The further he got, the more his body withered, until, as his hand brushed Zeke, he crumbled away to dust.

As he did, Zeke's stomach stopped complaining, and his stamina returned by a tiny margin. Zeke took a deep breath. *Whew. Finally, a skill that doesn't drain me!*

**Skill absorb failed.**

*Oh, well. Must be a ten percent chance, or something. It's failed every time so far.*

A muscular woman charged into his field, and another man. Both of them charged at Zeke like the first. Compared to the first, their bodies withered at half-speed. They closed in on him and swung. Zeke danced backward, dodging their blows. *Huh. So, there's a certain flat rate of absorption, and the more people who enter the field, the more the absorption rate on each one drops, because I get one rate of absorption to split across everyone inside the field.*

Two more muscular men entered the circle, and the withering rate on the first two dropped even lower, while the new entrants barely visibly withered. Zeke turned and fled, allowing them all to remain just barely within the field, without allowing anyone else to enter. *I understand. This isn't a sure-kill skill, or even a skill that should be relied on to kill. Instead, it's more like a slow area of effect debuff that I can cast in a large area around me and slow down my opponents while buffing myself with the energy I absorb from them. It's not a Devour-style mainline skill, but it's certainly the essential sort of buff/debuff skill I've lowkey needed for a while.*

*All in all...nice! I wonder if all level thirty skills are buffs and debuffs? Or maybe they're just more skills specific to your Concept and, well, Hunger obviously lends itself to buffs and debuffs. I'll have to ask Domi later, see if she's willing to share.*

*Though...maybe this skill is nothing special to Domi? After all, normal apocalypses seem to get skills as they level, rather than— well, obviously no one else can absorb the skills from other apocalypses, not that I've noticed, anyway.*

*Hmm. I'll have to ask her. Level thirty is obviously a special level, from getting a Domain alone. I'd expect she'd get something else special, as well.*

*And, of course, I still have to pin the System down and get it to tell me what the alternative to having a Domain is.*

More muscular men closed in on him. Ahead of him, Domi and Mia sparred John. Zeke glanced back, then gritted his teeth. *I'll sneak attack John, even if it means kiting these men over there! If John is the apocalypse, it's my win! If he isn't...if he isn't, then we'd have to deal with the muscular people anyway.*

He glanced over at Domi and nodded at her. Her eyes widened. She opened her mouth.

Zeke held a finger up to his lips. *Don't alert John!*

Domi opened her eyes wide. She shook her head.

*It's now or never. If I don't sneak up on John, we'll be here all day!* Zeke closed in on John from behind.

### Skill absorb failed.
### Skill absorb succeeded! Gained Skill: Teamwork
### [Team Spirit] (Minor) +1 > +2

*Huh. I guess if it's an AOE, the low chance of skill absorb makes more sense. It's not a nerf, it's a reasonable choice for balance!* Zeke nodded to himself.

Mia saw Zeke coming and struck out with her sword, forcing John back. John jumped toward Zeke, completely unaware of his presence. Zeke jumped forward, opening his mouth.

### [Strong Jaw] [Absorb] [Devour]

Mia's eyes widened. Her skin paled and her form grew thinner. She ran backward, fleeing Zeke.

*Oh, fuck! I forgot. It's an AOE, but that means I can do splash damage without meaning to. Sorry, sorry! I didn't mean to!* Zeke grabbed John by his shoulders and dug his teeth in as the man's flesh resisted his bite.

John reached over his shoulders. His hands latched onto Zeke and dug in, bruising his arms.

Domi glanced at Mia, then threw her hands out. Explosions burst in John's face, blinding him. He released Zeke to cover his eyes, and Zeke went back to digging his teeth in.

*Dammit. What more do I need?*

*I have a stat point to spend.*
*Well...why not?*

**STR:** 6 > 7

Instantly, his strength grew by a small margin. Zeke's teeth bit into John's weakening flesh, and blood spurted into his mouth. Strength boosted by the point in STR and Strong Jaw, Zeke clenched his mouth shut.

John stiffened, then went still. His body slumped.

**Defeated Member of the Stadium Apocalypse!**

"Fuck," Zeke muttered.

**Level + 1.20**
**Level:** 33.11 > 34.31

**Please assign your stat points.**
**Please choose a skill.**

**Skills**

**Thick Flesh (Condition) (Weak)**
**Can't**
**Can't**

**Instant Review (Lesser)**
*Play back an event that just happened to provide better commentary for it. Warning: It takes as long to play the event as it took for the event to occur in the first place. You will be immobile for the duration of the playback.*

### Disabled – Absorb Failed
### Teamwork (Lesser)

*Huh, looks like the skill I missed out on earlier was Instant Review. Kind of a useless skill, in my opinion. Could be useful to review enemies' attacks, but not if I have to do it right after I see the attack, and not if it takes real time to replay. Can't pick up Announcer's Voice this time, but... Eh. Didn't really want to.*

*Guess I'll just double up on Thick Flesh and see if I can get Hardness and Thick Flesh a couple levels when I fuse them.*

### Thick Flesh (Condition) (Weak) +1

The muscular men and women drew close to them, raising their fists. Dancing away from Mia and Domi, Zeke activated **[Absorb]** again. "Domi, do you have any big, splashy attacks?"

"I mean, yeah? Are any of my attacks not big and splashy?" Domi asked rhetorically.

"I mean...AOEs. Big zone-attack spells!" Zeke shouted, dodging away from a fist. It brushed past his chest. The off-center blow still sent him stumbling back.

*Damn. I need more points in DEX, too. I need to dodge at least half as well as Domi.*

*Good thing I have two unassigned stat points.*

### DEX: 3 > 5

*Whew! Was my DEX still 3? Damn! No wonder I'm struggling to dodge anything! I can't forget any stats if I want to make it to the top.*

*I still think SPR and CON are the most important stats, but I can't neglect my physical stats, either.*

"AOEs? Yeah, I got a few," Domi said. She rubbed her hands together. Bright orange and white sparks built up in between them, bouncing away down the stairs like molten sparks from a steel refinery.

Zeke glanced behind him. "Ready?"

Domi nodded. "Whenever you are."

Dropping Absorb, Zeke ran at her. The muscular men and women instantly sped up without the debuff, chasing after him. He dodged left and right, dancing over the stairs toward her. "Here we come!"

# 70
## KITING THE BADDIES

Zeke charged at Domi. Sparks burst from Domi's hands, bouncing over the stairs, bright as stars. The over-muscled men and women hurtled at Domi, leaving Zeke behind to go after the stationary target.

"Yeah, that's right. Come to Domi." Domi pressed her hands together, balling the sparks up tight. The sparks glowed even brighter, a thousand of them compressed in the space between her palms, tighter and tighter, like a time-lapse photo of a sparkler whirling in real-time.

The first muscular woman reached her and drew back her fist.

Domi yanked her hands apart.

For a moment, the ball of orange sparks continued to swirl, self-contained, a tiny ball of near-infinite brightness. In the next, it burst apart. Sparks zipped off in all directions. Everywhere a spark landed exploded, as if each was a tiny grenade, small, but more than capable of ripping a body apart. Explosions ripped through the metal seating and cut craters in the concrete steps. Thousands or more of them landed among the muscular people.

Blood, gore, bones, and organs went flying, mulched by the uncountable exploding sparks. As if someone had set off a box of fireworks all at once, nonstop *booms* rattled the stadium, cracking off one after another. Gunpowder and hot aluminum filled the air, a stifling, metallic smell that stuck in Zeke's nose.

Not far to the side, Zeke sprinted away from Domi and her spark grenades, running even faster than before. *Holy shit! What a damn skill! Domi's going to kill us all!*

Ahead of him, Mia raced down the stairs. She glanced back, then paused to waved him on.

"I'm coming, I'm coming! You run, I'll catch up!" Zeke shouted back, struggling to be heard over the nonstop boom and crackle of the sparks. He sped down the stairs, faster than before.

Mia nodded and charged ahead. She leaped the fence and raced onto the field, among the ordinary people. Waving her hand and sword, she shooed them away. "Get back. Back away from the steps!"

The ordinary people glanced at her, then looked at the sparks. Rather than attack her, as Zeke expected, they turned and fled, following her command.

*Huh. Must be a Hero skill,* Zeke noted, following Mia. He glanced over his shoulder.

Domi laughed maniacally, watching her sparks fly in every which direction. They bounced wildly, but always bounced away from her, never near her. Some bounced once or twice, exploding each time they made contact with something before they finally flickered out. The few muscular men and women remaining charged her blindly, unable to feel the pain or unable to stop themselves anyway. They charged into a field of fiery death. The sparks chewed them up and spat them out, absolutely unrecognizable as once-living beings.

Zeke licked his lips. *That's a terrifying skill. I hope that's her level thirty skill. If she's got something even more powerful than that hidden up her sleeve, we're in real trouble.*

*Or, well, everyone that isn't allied with us is in trouble. I think Domi... I don't think she's going to betray us soon, in any case. If she's going to betray us at all.*

*Us. Who is 'us?' Me and Mia?*

*Man, speaking of potential betrayals...Mia's the Hero. Her job is to save ordinary people... but is that the full extent of her job? Or is her job also to destroy the Apocalypses?*

*She's the Hero. What does the Hero do? Defeat the villain. When it comes to the world scale, to the grand scale of the innocents of earth...who's the villain?*

*Easy. The apocalypses are. It's literally our job to destroy the world. Whether I like it or not, that's certainly the System's goal.*

Zeke looked at Mia. For a second, his eyes turned cold. *How high level is she? One, five? And she's already strong enough to hold her own with a high-level member of a powerful apocalypse. How long before she can overpower me and Domi?*

*Should I just—*

He clapped his hands to his cheeks. *What the hell am I thinking? This is Mia. Mia! My childhood friend! Kill her? Who am I, Ryan? Honestly!*

*Is this what happened to Ryan? The System ate away at his mind, slowly, over time. Except he's stuck in this time loop. When everyone else resets, he remains, mind slowly eroding, The longer he spends stuck in the loop, the worse it attacks his mind.*

*It's affecting me this badly, and I've only experienced a few days of being an apocalypse. How long has he been looping, stuck in these hellish days, over and over? How long until there's nothing left of the Ryan I knew?*

*How much is left of the Ryan I know right now?*

Mia ran over to Zeke. "Any idea where the apocalypse core is?"

Zeke glanced down, embarrassed of his own thoughts. Rubbing his face, he took a deep breath. *It's okay. I'm not going to hurt her. It was just an intrusive thought.* With some effort, he smiled, distracted, then looked around, using the time to catch his bearings and register what she'd said.

Ordinary people milled about on the field. No one attacked Mia or Zeke, and Domi's spark grenades chased down the last of the distorted super muscular people. Zeke licked his lips and frowned. "Who's left? If no one we fought was the apocalypse, then..."

He looked into the mass of people. *Is it one of them? Are they playing it cool, pretending to be ordinary people? I mean, I could do that. Domi could. Not all apocalypses look...well, like anything but ordinary people.*

*Ugh. I guess I can look at them one by one and think that they're the Stadium Apocalypse until the System agrees with me, but...there's gotta be a better way. Something faster...*

Zeke froze. His eyes caught a flash of color in the middle of the milling people. He stifled a chuckle, shaking his head. *Really? Jeez... How did I not notice?*

"What?" Mia asked.

He pointed. "Look, right there."

Mia squinted. "I don't..."

Her eyes widened. She clasped a hand over her mouth but failed to hide her smile.

Panting slightly, skin dripping with sweat, Domi wandered over and slung an arm over Mia. "What? What'd I miss?"

Mia lifted her hand, pointing. "Er, it's..."

Domi stared, then laughed aloud. "Damn!"

# 71
## MASCOT TROUBLES

In the middle of the mob of people, a sad-looking robin mascot lurked, head down, black and orange feathers filthy, big bright eyes distinctly distant and traumatized. As it felt the gazes of all three on it, it looked up, startled. Their eyes met the embroidered eyes of the mascot.

**Stadium Apocalypse**
**Danger Rating:** B

Domi, Zeke, and Mia charged him as one. The mascot turned and fled, running across the field.

"Get back here!" Domi shouted.

Zeke cut the corner. *I'll cut him off!*

Mia ran the other direction, cutting him off from the opposite side. The three of them closed in.

"I don't want to! I didn't want to! I'm sorry!" the mascot shouted over his shoulder.

"How many people have you killed already?" Zeke shouted at him, remembering the corpses outside the field.

"I had to. I had no choice!" the mascot cried, sobbing. He

flapped his little arm-wings as he ran, orange-and-black fabric fluttering after him, his silly bird tail flapping, his orange bird-legs pumping.

"You had a choice!" Mia snapped.

Domi pointed. An explosion singed the robin mascot's fabricy butt. "Haha, fuck off, Robbie the Robin! I always thought you were a creepy motherfucker! Time to die!"

Robbie the Robin jumped into the air, patting his butt with both hands. "Stop! I didn't mean to hurt anyone!"

"It's too late for that," Mia snarled.

"Come back here, I wanna explode you myself," Domi shouted.

Zeke licked his lips. *Everyone's doing it, come on, Zeke! A one liner, anything!* "Uh, get back here and...uh, I'm hungry for chicken!"

Domi glanced over her shoulder. She shook her head at Zeke.

Mia sighed loudly.

"Oh, come on. It wasn't that much worse than 'explode you myself,'" Zeke argued.

"Except I wasn't trying," Domi said, clicking her tongue.

Zeke sighed. "Oh, all right."

Ahead of them, Robbie the Robin turned around. He gasped for breath, barely managing to run on. "I-I don't want to, but I won't die!"

He turned around and spread his wings, standing stock still.

A sword appeared in Mia's hand. Domi's eyes glowed orange.

Zeke hesitated. *What's he trying to do? He wouldn't stop for no reason...*

A wave of force burst out from Robbie the Robin's body, forcing Zeke and the girls back. Robbie's robin body expanded rapidly, growing from human-mascot-size to car size to giant size. He grew and grew, looming over them, as tall as a two-story building. His fabric skin stretched up to the heavens, rolls and rolls of fabric bearing down on them. His huge wings flapped, and wind gusted, blowing Domi and Mia's hair straight back.

"Holy shit," Domi muttered.

"How do we fight that?" Mia backed away, lifting her sword. Compared to the enormous Robbie the Robbin, her sword seemed as big as a toothpick.

Zeke's eyes widened. He rubbed his hands together, already salivating. *That skill...is it a skill that will allow me to become huge? Could I become a Zeke-kaiju? I want it, I want it so bad!* Eyes shining with a maniacal light, he breathed, "We have to kill him."

"The question is, how," Domi agreed.

Zeke stared up at the massive mascot. He licked his lips and pulled up his skills, looking over them.

**Skills**
**Manipulate Aerosols (Medium) +1**
**Pick Up (Weak)**
**Osmosis (Weak) +1**
**Subordinate Link (Weak)**
**Create Drug (Weak) +1**
**Crystal Burst (Poor)**
**Engulf (Poor)**
**Create Coffee (Strong)**
**Whistle Blast (Weak)**
**Digital Broadcast (Weak) +1**
**Electric Leap (Poor)**
**Eyes in the Sky (Weak)**

**Passive**

**Resilient Regeneration (Lesser) +7**
**Team Spirit (Minor) +1**
**Disguise (Minor)**
**Watertight (Minor)**
**Caffeine Rush (Average)**
**Growth (Lesser) +2**
**Heat Resistance (Lesser) +9**
**Strong Jaw (Minor)**
**Flexible Body (Average)**
**Roll With Me (Minor)**
**Strong Legs (Minor)**
**Catlike Reflexes (Lesser)**
**Claw Fighter (Lesser)**
**Perfect Landing (Lesser)**
**Steel Stomach (Minor)**

**Condition**
**Hardness (Lesser) (Condition)**
**Claws (Large) (Condition)**
**Thick Flesh (Condition) (Weak) +1**
**MOTORCYCLE**

*Hmm. If I use that...and that, and use it with Domi's ability, and then with Mia...* Zeke nodded to himself. He looked at Domi. "Can you put explosives under something?"

"Uh...sure?" Domi drew out her phone.

"Mia, that sword is made of light. Can you make it any bigger?" Zeke asked.

Mia looked at her hand. "I don't know. I haven't tried."

Zeke shrugged. "Give it a shot."

Closing her eyes, Mia focused. The sword grew twice as long, then three times as long. She opened her eyes and waved the sword around, trying it out. "Huh. It's pretty heavy, but...I'll, uh, put a few points into STR."

"You have STR?" Zeke asked, startled. *Heroes operate on the same system as apocalypses do?*

"Yeah? All the things you and Domi were talking about. STR, CON, DEX, SPR, right?"

"Huh." *That sounds like a confirmation. Then...do other things have the same system as apocalypses, too? Like Survivors.*

*Cockroaches all have the System? Forget apocalypses, humanity is fucked. It's time for cockroaches to take over!*

### Heroes and Survivors do not have the same level of authority with the System.

*Thanks for that reassurance,* Zeke thought, rolling his eyes. *I guess that's better than humanity being destroyed by cockroaches, regardless of what we do.*

He took a deep breath and leaned in. "All right. So, here's what we're going to do..."

Robbie the Robin stepped forward. His huge foot loomed over them.

"Split!" Mia shouted.

The three of them shot off in different directions. Robbie's foot smashed down on the field, sending bits of turf flying up where he stepped.

Zeke ran out in front of Robbie's foot. He slammed his foot down on the court and rubbed it into the ground.

### [Crystal Burst]

Crystals grew out of the ground in front of Zeke, a patch nearly as large as Robbie's foot.

Robbie stared down at the crystals and laughed. He shook

his head. His voice rumbled out, echoing through the stadium. "Is this your idea of a trap?"

"Domi!" Zeke shouted.

Domi poked her phone and stuck it in her pocket. "Ready!"

Explosions threw the crystals into the sky. Domi clapped her hands again. A blast of orange energy threw the crystals toward Robbie's leg. The crystals dug holes in the fabric, piercing out the other side.

Robbie stumbled. His pierced leg crumpled, folding in on itself.

Zeke turned, throwing his hand out. "Mia, now!"

Mia charged out, raising her sword. She swept it at Robbie's good leg.

"That little prick?" Robbie laughed.

"Talking big now that you're big, huh," Zeke muttered, mostly to himself.

As Mia swept the sword, the blade expanded. Two, three times its length. Sweat burst on Mia's brow, but she pushed through. The glowing blade carved through Robbie's fabric leg.

Robbie screamed. He swayed, then toppled over backward, sawed-off leg bared to the world.

Zeke blinked after Mia. "Huh?" *One swing? Damn, Mia's stronger than I thought.*

Domi leaned in, raising a hand to her eyes. "It's empty?"

"Wait, really?" Zeke peered closer at the suit instead of staring after Mia.

The mascot suit hung open like a sagging tent, nothing inside the fabric bird.

Taken aback, Zeke frowned. *How am I supposed to devour... nothing?*

# 72
## RISE AGAIN, BIRD KAIJU!

Staring at the empty fabric of the bird suit's leg, Zeke abruptly slapped his cheeks. *This is no time to stare! Go, go, go!*

**[Caffeine Rush] [Strong Legs]**

Using all the speed buffs he had, Zeke sprinted toward the hollow leg. As Robbie sat up and rubbed his head, he darted into the empty trouser leg and ran up it, further into the bird suit. *At the end of the day, it doesn't fundamentally change our plan. Get inside the suit, climb up to a critical point, disable it! Just...it might take a little longer to find that critical point, now.*

*Humans are obvious. Climb to the neck, bite the jugular. Or, I wasn't excited about it, but the femoral artery was also an option. And just biting randomly would surely piss him off if nothing else. But...what's the killing point in a giant empty bird suit? Where can I bite to take this behemoth down?*

All around Zeke, the fabric wall began to go from horizontal to vertical. Startled, Zeke extended his claws and caught onto the surface of the fabric. "Allen! Give me your climb ability!"

No response. Zeke turned his head, patting it against his arm.

No Allen.

*Huh? Where'd he go? Did he run away—*

An image flashed through his head. Allen, atop Domi's head, doing a pushup.

Zeke's eyes widened. *That's right! He went to Domi when I used Absorb. And...it seems like he's too far away for me to borrow his skills now!*

The giant bird mascot suit lumbered to its feet. It limped off-balance, stumbling along on its stubbed leg. Holding tight to the inside wall, Zeke swayed along as it walked.

*I can't just hang here forever. I need to keep moving. Somewhere in here, probably, I should be able to kill this bird suit!*

Zeke looked down, then pushed at his shoes. One fell away, and he extended his claws. Claws pressed out from his toes as well as his fingertips.

*Okay. I think I can do this.* Kicking off his other shoe, Zeke set his toe-claws into the cloth. He lifted his leg and pushed. One push at a time, he climbed up the inside of the suit. *It's way easier to climb when I use my legs and arms. Arms only, it's the most insane pullup workout ever. Using legs and feet, it's more like crawling. Upright crawling.*

*Farewell, my shoes. Good thing I grabbed all those shoes on the first day.*

Up, up, up. He crawled up the orange of the mascot's legs to the black of its underbelly, back to the orange of its belly. There, he paused and looked up, taking in the enormous cavity of the mascot suit's chest.

Nothing. Bare cloth, as far as the eye could see.

Zeke frowned. *Really? I was half expecting a cockpit and a human pilot, mecha style, but it seems like...it's just empty?*

*Is this just a giant cloth suit?*

*Wait, hold on.*

All the bodily alteration skills he'd seen flashed through his head. His claws. The Growth skill. The wings and rotors skills. He frowned. *All those skills indicated that the skill could not be undone. And the way this Apocalypse reacted...I don't think it's an inanimate object who turned into an Apocalypse. It feels more like a person.*

*Could it be? Did this person...the person who played Robbie the Robin, did they take an alteration skill that turned them into the suit itself?*

**Correct.**

Zeke blinked. He pressed his lips together, surprised. *Huh. Damn. Guess that's a reminder to be cautious about body-alteration skills.*

*But if it's really just cloth through-and-through...shouldn't Domi be able to light it on fire? Or...well, I guess if I was a cloth monster, the first thing I'd do is invest into fireproofness. I'm not going to drop this advantageous position over a potential chance to light a fire!*

He looked upward, where a dark void spanned overhead. The mascot's porous cloth body let in light, but the structured head created a dome of darkness, except for where light shone through its eyeholes.

*If I knock its head off, what then? Does it die?*

...

*Ha, not being useful now, huh, System? Guess that means there's only one way to find out.* Digging his claws into the cloth, he hauled himself upward, scaling toward the head.

Outside the mascot costume, Domi threw out her hands. A roiling mass of sparks flew toward the giant costume. The sparks bounced and burned, tearing holes in its body, but it stomped on anyway.

"Can he not feel pain?" Domi snarled, running backward.

"I don't know. It doesn't seem like it!" Mia returned. She darted in, raising her sword.

The bird mascot raised its arms and flapped, just once. A huge blast of wind bowled Domi and Mia head-over-heels down the field. They went tumbling into the ordinary people, who continued to mill about in the field's center.

"Huh? What are you guys doing? Run!" Domi shouted.

The people stared at her with glassy eyes.

"But we're here to watch the game."

"Rain or shine, we'll stay 'til the end."

"I want to see my team win."

Domi wrinkled her nose. "They're the worst kind of fans."

"They've been brainwashed. Wake up!" Mia shouted. Gold light flew from her mouth and washed over the fans.

The first few rows of people looked up, suddenly alert and bright-eyed, but a few seconds later, they lapsed back into their glassy-eyed state. Mia growled and ran her hair back, frustrated, her chest heaving, her legs heavy. She looked at Domi.

Domi wiped her face with her shirt, mopping the sweat away. Her hair hung limp around her head, half-pasted to her skull from the sweat. She nodded at Mia, managing half a smile.

"We can't keep going like this. We need a break," Mia said, breathing so hard she had to pause to swallow her spit halfway through the sentence. *It feels like I've been running wind sprints all morning. I can't keep this up!*

"Fuck this. I'm killing them all," Robbie the Robin grumbled. He stomped toward the gathered crowd. "Fuck the Audience skill. I'll get more of a buff from their levels!"

"Zeke! Hurry it up in there!" Domi shouted.

Mia turned to the people. She gritted her teeth. "System, do I have a skill that can help them? Anything? Anything at all?"

**It is up to you to solve these problems.**

Mia scowled. She looked at the people in front of her, then looked at her sword. "Domi, can you hold him back?"

"Uh...for a minute, maybe?" Domi said.

"Long enough." Mia turned toward the mob of people. She raised her sword. The blade extended, reaching three feet, five feet, ten feet. Holding it out at waist height, she looked at the crowd. *A little more.* Putting both hands on the blade, she pushed out. Another two feet. Three. Five. *Fifteen feet? That'll have to be enough!*

Domi stared. She blinked. "Mia?"

Holding her sword out to her side, Mia ran at the mass of onlookers.

# 73
## BLOODSTAINED FIELD

"Wait, hold on. If we're going to kill them before the creepy mascot does, I want some of the kills!" Domi shouted, chasing after Mia.

Focused on her blade, Mia ignored Domi. She closed the gap and struck, hands guided by the System.

At the very last second, she twisted her hands. Instead of striking them with the sharp end of the blade, she struck with the flat. The people stumbled back. Mia ground to a halt, her momentum broken.

"Ohh, okay. Hold steady!" Domi charged at Mia's sword. She smashed both hands into it and pushed. The people wobbled another few steps away from Robbie.

Robbie loomed over them. He raised his lone remaining foot. A shadow fell over Mia, Domi, and half the crowd.

Mia gritted her teeth. She pushed harder, digging her toes in. *Did I not put enough points in STR? I don't have any more points to put into STR! Dammit! Was it all for nothing?*

Standing at the middle of the sword's length, Domi turned around and put her back to the blade's flat. She threw her hands out. Explosions burst out from her palms, throwing her into the sword and pushing the sword onward.

"Let's go!" Domi shouted.

Mia pushed with all her might. The sword began to move. The people stumbled back, slowly moving out from under the shadow.

The foot dropped toward them, plummeting down.

*Not fast enough!* "Domi, let go!"

"Got it!" Domi jumped away.

Facing the foot, black cloth outlined against the black sky, Mia took a deep breath, then swung her sword, slicing the foot apart.

The fabric fell, draping over the people. Robbie's leg flailed in the air, and he flopped down to his mid-leg, barely able to stay standing.

"Do we even need Zeke?" Domi wondered aloud, looking at the flailing Robbie.

Mia fell back, panting heavily. The sword returned to its usual size, then vanished entirely. Her shining armor vanished as well.

"Mia?" Domi asked, concerned.

Mia waved her hand. She wiped sweat away from her brow. "I'm...fine. A little tired."

"Shit. Guess we need Zeke, after all," Domi muttered, looking up at the mascot costume.

Robbie grimaced down at them. He fell to all fours, reaching out a bird arm to grab for the people.

"No!" Forcibly summoning her sword, Mia ran at his arm as he grabbed. Even as she did, she stumbled. The sword vanished.

Domi threw her hand out. A big blast forced Robbie's hand back. "Zeke! Hurry it up in there!"

From the mascot suit's chest, Zeke's voice sounded out, albeit muffled. "I'm trying!"

"What is that? Where is he?" Robbie asked, looking down, his beak pressed against his rounded chest.

Zeke stilled. He glanced around, then scurried up Robbie's chest as fast as he could. *Into the head!*

"Hey! Stop that!" Robbie slapped at his own chest.

The fabric jumped all around Zeke. He clung on with his finger- and toe-claws, gripping tight to the fabric. *Shit! He's going for me!* The second the fabric settled, he scrambled even faster.

"Hey, birdbrain," Domi shouted. She pitched back, throwing something at him. A ball of orange energy flew toward the mascot's face.

Robbie the Robin raised a hand to block the attack. The orange ball burst through his fabric hand and exploded in his face, busting a hole in the suit's eye.

Inside, Zeke shielded his eyes as the light shone in. Squinting against it, he peered up at the black sky through the hole in the suit. Light illuminated the dome of the helmet.

A small lump in the fabric at the rear of the helmet caught his eye. It pulsated slowly, in a even rhythm.

Zeke stared. *Is that...is that the kill point? It's worth a shot!* Turning around, he faced the back wall of the suit and jumped. His arms and legs pedaled through the air. The cloth loomed.

### [Perfect Landing]

Zeke latched on with all four limbs and went back to climbing, his eyes locked on the pulsating lump.

Outside, Robbie the Robin reached over his shoulders, scratching ineffectually at his back with his mitten bird hands. "Stop it! Get out!"

"Distract him!" Zeke shouted.

Mia took a deep breath. She shook her head, then raised her

sword and ran at the giant mascot. Domi threw balls of explosives left and right, blowing apart pieces of his cottony body.

"Stop it! Stop! All of you!" Robbie the Robin whined, overwhelmed.

*Not the most mentally adept man-slash-mascot*, Zeke thought to himself.

The lump loomed. Zeke licked his lips. He dug his claws into the fabric and pulled it back.

A brain and heart laid tangled together in the fabric. Blood looped around them in thick veins, organs strewn about in a random pattern. Unhesitatingly, Zeke opened his mouth.

### [Devour]

The heart went down easy, slipping down his throat. Zeke swallowed, though he hardly had to.

Robbie the Robin screamed. He grabbed his chest, then tipped backward. The helmet struck the ground and bounced away, while the cloth body deflated.

**Defeated the Stadium Apocalypse!**
**Regeneration + 300%**
**Regeneration rate:** 306.1%
**Level + 3.28**
**Level:** 34.31 > 37.59

**Please assign your stat points.**
**Please choose three skills.**

**Skills**
**Gigantification (Medium)**

*Grow large, temporarily. For a span of 2 minutes, you can be much larger than your usual size.*

### Fabric Body (Lesser) (Condition)
### Mental Manipulation (Minor)

### Body Booster (Lesser)
*Alter others bodies to make them stronger, weaker, larger, or smaller. With more ranks in this skill, you can manipulate the people more strongly. 50% chance of failure.*
Share Steroids (Lesser)
*Pump a subordinate's STR. Subordinate's SPR drops proportionately.*
**Can't**

### Audience (Minor)
*Capture an audience and compel them to remain. SPR opposes. For as long as they remain, gain +1 to all stats for every ten audience members.*

### Can't
### Can't
### Subordinate Link (Weak)
### Wind Manipulation (Strong)

Zeke glanced down the list. *Okay. Gigantification I absolutely need. That's the first body alteration skill that doesn't change me forever or require me to know how to alter my whole body to use it. Well, okay. The second, considering Flexible Body. But, still. Gigantification. Need it.*

*Fabric Body, miss me with that. I don't need to become a mascot. Mental Manipulation...ugh. It's a hugely useful skill, but I mean, isn't that classic evil, manipulating other peoples' minds? I don't want to be evil. But it's so damn powerful.*

*Body Booster and Share Steroids... There're enough downsides to both of them that they aren't worth it. 50% failure rate on Body Booster? No thanks. Audience is an interesting skill, but...I mean, that basically means forcing ordinary people to stand around in the danger zone. Most apocalypses are going to dive straight for them and kill them, which makes them more powerful, while I have to not only have an Audience but defend them, too. Ugh. I hate to skip it. It could be an incredibly powerful skill. Still...the downsides are...ugh.*

*Subordinate Link...I could use some ranks in that, but it's not an incredibly compelling skill, and I already have it. Ooh, and Wind Manipulation? Fuse that into Aerosol Manipulation, and I'll have a seriously powerful manipulation skill.*

*Hmm...okay. I think I'm going with Gigantification, Wind Manipulation, and Mental... No, no, don't be evil! And...ugh. I already have Subordinate Link. I-I'm going for Audience!*

### Gained skills [Gigantification] [Wind Manipulation] [Audience]

Climbing out of the helmet, Zeke walked over to Mia and Domi. "Anyone need regeneration?"

"I'm good," Domi said.

Mia waved, out of breath but unhurt aside from some scrapes and scratches.

Zeke held his hand out toward Domi. Allen hopped off her head and scurried up Zeke's arm to his head, settling into his usual place once more.

In the middle of the field, the people who'd been wandering in circles suddenly jolted awake. They looked around them, startled. Some stared up at the giant mascot costume while some turned and ran, fleeing out into the city. Zeke watched them go, then sighed. He looked at the girls. "Should we go... figure that out?"

Mia nodded. She trooped on over, shoulders sloped from exhaustion.

"Might as well," Domi said, shrugging.

# 74
## FIGURING IT OUT

The three of them walked over to the people. As they approached, the mob flinched backward. An old man and a middle-aged woman strode forward to meet them.

Zeke nodded. "Good afternoon."

The woman nodded back at him. "What just happened?"

"Ma'am, this is the Apocalypse," Zeke informed her.

"The...Apocalypse? I don't see any horsemen," the woman said, staring around her.

Zeke coughed. "It's...more like *an* apocalypse than *the* Apocalypse. We're still working on figuring out that one. In any case, the city isn't safe. This is probably the safest place to stay. I recommend hunkering down here."

"That's what the police said, but then..." The old man trailed off, not needing to fill in the rest.

Zeke shook his head. "Think of it as having already been cleared. It's not likely that another apocalypse will set up here."

"*Another* apocalypse? There are people missing children. Missing family members. Lone kids! And you're going on about some apocalypse nonsense?" the woman demanded.

The old man nodded. "Son, be clear with us. What happened? Some kind of mass hallucination? A terrorist attack? We need to know to stay safe."

Zeke threw up his hands. *It's Mia all over again.*

"It's like crazy video game stuff happening in real life!" one of the teenagers shouted, rushing over. She nodded at Zeke and the girls. "They're the superheroes who saved us!"

"Yes, thank you, Millie," the old man said dismissively.

"What if they're dangerous? Go back," the woman insisted.

Domi raised a brow. "She's got it the most right of everyone here."

Zeke gestured for Millie to come closer. "Yeah. Hey, listen. You get it, right?"

Millie nodded. "I think I get it."

"Right now, this is like...a safe zone. Or not a safe zone, but like..." Zeke put a hand on his chin. *How to describe it?*

"Like a capture point that's been captured, and no one can capture it again?" Millie offered.

"Yeah. Like that. It's unlikely that people are going to come back here, right? But that's only as long as they don't know you're here," Zeke said, nodding.

"Because they can use us to level up," Millie agreed.

"Right, exactly. And there's an infection mechanic and everything, it's real nasty," Zeke said. *Damn. It's nice to talk to someone who's on top of this!*

"Infection? Nasty. Is that what happened to us here?" Millie guessed.

"More or less," Zeke said, nodding. "You get anywhere near something big and scary like what happened here, there's a pretty good chance you wind up...like you were, or worse."

Millie nodded. "Yeah. I guess it makes sense. Whew. I'm just hoping my brother's okay. He was at the elementary school just down the road... they locked it down, but..."

Zeke winced. He looked at the floor. "Yeah. I hope he's okay."

"Mmm. I know everything's nuts, but...as long as he's alive..."

"Just focus on yourself, on keeping yourself alive," Zeke said, putting a hand on her shoulder. *I don't know. He could be alive. The cartoon apocalypse didn't... It... Maybe he ran away? Maybe he was a different apocalypse? I don't know.*

Millie frowned. "All right. Stay alive. Got it. Ugh. Wish I could be a superhero." She gazed at Zeke hopefully.

Zeke laughed under his breath, startled into laughing. "I don't have the power to grant that. All you can do is survive. But so long as you hunker here and don't go out much, it's pretty safe. Understand?"

"Yep!" Millie said.

The middle-aged woman frowned. "What is this nonsense? Explain what's going on in plain English."

Mia took a deep breath. She looked at Zeke, then gestured for the middle-aged woman and old man to follow her. Zeke watched her go. *I should follow her...but no. I'll let her try on her own.*

---

When they were a few steps away, Mia stopped. She took a deep breath, looking at each of them in the eyes. *Zeke isn't the only one in charge. I need to do my part.* "Listen. I know this all sounds crazy. I didn't believe it at first, either. But trust me, you either start believing in everything—all of this—real fast or find your-self chewed up by it. It's been a few days. It might not have felt that way to you." *I know it felt like no time passed in the coffee shop.* "But if you're careless, you will die. You need to listen to every-thing Zeke tells you, and start running with it, right now."

"And who do you think you are, young lady?" the old man asked, twisting his lip skeptically.

Mia looked at him. Eyes dead, heart dead, she stared at him. *A few days ago, that would have cut me. My heart would have jumped, rage in my veins, my adrenaline surging. But now?*

She snorted and turned away, giving him a last look over her shoulder. "Someone who's trying to save your life."

"Are you really? You haven't told us anything! Where's the police? Where's the military?" the woman demanded.

"Ma'am, no one knows. We're all trapped in here," Mia said flatly.

"Trapped? What do you mean? Who put a ceiling over the stadium?" the woman asked.

Domi patted Mia on the shoulder. "I can take over from here," she offered, taking out her cellphone. She pulled up a few videos and stepped over to the woman and man's side. Her spine straightened, her shoulders squared, and her voice changed, suddenly more high-pitched and polite. "If you'll look here..."

Mia blinked. *Is that Domi? What happened?*

---

Seeing Domi take over, Zeke walked to Mia's side. He snorted, nodding at Domi. "She was a museum tour guide, remember? I told you, right?"

"Oh, right," Mia said, nodding.

Taking a look over the massed people, Zeke gritted his teeth. "I don't like this. I don't know what to do about it, but I don't like it. Leaving them here works for now, but not for forever. This is too many people. It's far too tempting for any apocalypse.

"We can't leave them alone here forever but taking them

with us is the same as painting a massive target on our backs. Not to mention supplies, logistics... We can't keep this many people alive for long, but we can't exactly turn them loose, either, without giving another apocalypse a huge advantage."

His stomach grumbled. Zeke chuckled. "Guess I could eat them all, but..."

Mia gave him a sharp look. "Don't joke about that."

"Sorry, sorry," Zeke said. He rubbed his forehead, frowning at himself. *What on earth was I thinking? Why would I even joke about that?*

*My Concept is eating at me. Maybe Ryan was right.*

Mia took a deep breath. She gazed at the people, then turned to Zeke. "What if we use that to our advantage?"

"What do you mean?" Zeke asked.

"The longer we drag this out, the more powerful everything else gets, right? We're on a constant race against time," Mia said.

"Right. We can't really rest. Have to keep moving all the time, or fall behind," Zeke agreed.

Mia nodded. "So why don't we hide them here overnight, then, tomorrow morning, make it incredibly obvious there's a bunch of humans left here. Drag all the apocalypses here. Have one last knock-down drag-out fight...but on our terms. We set the stage. We prepare the field."

"Use tonight to give ourselves a homefield advantage, then call everyone here to take them out all at once," Zeke mused thoughtfully. *Since we both rejected Domains, Domi and I start at a disadvantage in every fight if we go to the apocalypses. On the other hand, if we force the apocalypses to come to us...they abandon their Domains and, on top of that, we get to set the pace and manipulate the field to our advantage.*

Zeke nodded, slowly. "You know what? I think you're onto something."

Putting her phone away, Domi wandered over, tossing them a nod. "What's the plan?"

"We stay here tonight," Zeke said, gesturing her closer. "Listen..."

# 75

## A GOOD NIGHT'S REST

Zeke took in the VIP booth from its entrance. He nodded to himself. *Not bad, not bad. I'll have a good sleep tonight!*

Pushing past him, the old man cleared his throat and spat into a corner. "Wish I was home."

Zeke sighed. *It'd be perfect if I didn't have to share it with all the survivors.* He crossed to the window, gazing over the field.

The giant mascot's carpet-like corpse slumped over the field. Singe marks scarred the perfect grass, a gross approximation of the usual neat white lines and numbers. Here and there, bloody splotches marked where the corpses of the Stadium Apocalypse's members laid. Below them, the blown-out announcer's booth spat glass over the wrecked stadium seating, the stoic aluminum seats warped and bent.

From the other side of the stadium, Mia waved at him. Zeke waved back, a little sad. *It makes sense to separate the men and women for the night's rest, but...I would like to strategize with Mia and Domi a bit more.*

Domi appeared at the window. She waved as well, then

pointed up. Wrapping an arm around Mia and pointed up again.

*Oh, I get it. Meet us up top. Reasonable.* Zeke nodded. He moved away from the window. *But first, I should give them some time to get settled. Which means...it's time to fuse some skills! Let's look at that skill list.*

**Level:** 37.59
**STR:** 7
**CON:** 10
**DEX:** 5
**SPR:** 10
**Regeneration rate:** +6.1%

**Skills**
**Manipulate Aerosols (Medium) +1**
**Pick Up (Weak)**
**Osmosis (Weak) +1**
**Subordinate Link (Weak)**
**Create Drug (Weak) +1**
**Crystal Burst (Poor)**
**Engulf (Poor)**
**Create Coffee (Strong)**
**Whistle Blast (Weak)**
**Digital Broadcast (Weak) +1**
**Electric Leap (Poor)**
**Eyes in the Sky (Weak)**
**Gigantification (Medium)**
**Manipulate Wind (Strong)**

**Passive**
**Resilient Regeneration (Lesser) +7**
**Team Spirit (Minor) +2**

**Disguise (Minor)**
**Watertight (Minor)**
**Caffeine Rush (Average)**
**Growth (Lesser) +2**
**Heat Resistance (Lesser) +9**
**Strong Jaw (Minor)**
**Flexible Body (Average)**
**Roll With Me (Minor)**
**Strong Legs (Minor)**
**Catlike Reflexes (Lesser)**
**Claw Fighter (Lesser)**
**Perfect Landing (Lesser)**
**Steel Stomach (Minor)**
**Audience (Minor)**

**Condition**
**Hardness (Lesser) (Condition)**
**Claws (Large) (Condition)**
**Thick Flesh (Condition) (Weak) +1**
**MOTORCYCLE**

**Lvl 0:** Devour
**Lvl 30:** Absorb

*Hmm, I've never seen my level-based skills before. I guess now that I have two, it's worthwhile to put them on the list.* Zeke glanced over the list, then nodded. *All right. Let's start with the obvious.*

## [Manipulate Aerosols] (Medium) +1 [Manipulate Wind] (Strong)

Trumpets blared.

**Skill fusion succeeded!**
**Gained skill:** [Manipulate Aerosols] (Strong) +6

Zeke pursed his lips. *I guess I shouldn't be surprised. I'm pretty sure that was a fusion between Manipulate Steam and Manipulate Wind in the first place. But... whatever! Instead of having a +1 Medium skill, I now have a +6 Strong skill. I'll have to experiment with it and figure out exactly what that means.*

Sitting in one of the plush stadium seats, Zeke put a hand on his chin. *Maybe Team Spirit and Roll With Me? They're both fusions in the first place, but they're very similar skills. They both give me a boost when I'm around other people.*

**[Team Spirit] (Minor) +2 [Roll With Me] (Minor)**

A flat tone played.

**Skill fusion succeeded.**
**Gained skill:** [Roll With Us] (Lesser)

*Gain a small bonus to all stats if you fight alongside a friend or fight a stronger opponent. Gain a movement speed bonus when moving in a team.*

Zeke pressed his lips together. *Not the most incredible skill ever. It's pretty much just the previous two skills pasted together.*

*All right, all right. It's been boring fusions so far. Let's go for something more exciting. Hmm...*

**[Gigantification] (Medium) [Growth] (Lesser) +2**

*Here we go!*

### [Modest Gigantification] (Medium) +2

Zeke blinked. *Modest...huh? How is any form of gigantification modest? Did it just get smaller and less giant or something?*

***Your clothes and items grow with you when you use Gigantification. Cost grows with the number of items made [Giant].***

Zeke's eyes widened. His mouth made an O shape. *I understand. Modest, as in I'm not putting it all out there and I remain clothed in my giant form! Excellent, excellent. I didn't even know I needed it, but I absolutely needed that skill!*

*Hmm, what else? Oh, what about this?*

### [Catlike Reflexes] (Lesser) [Eyes in the Sky] (Weak)

*Maybe I can get a kind of pre-awareness sense, like a low-level, er, super perceptive sense! Right? Reflexes and eyes in the sky, what else do I need? That's the simple description!*

Zeke held his breath. He waited. A long silence passed. Biting his lip, he glanced at the skills. *Is it not working? Are they totally incompatible? I guess—*

Triumphant music played, longer and more upbeat than any other skill fusion. Zeke stared. *What am I going to get? Something totally new?*

### [Hunger Awareness] (Lesser) +2

*Eh. I'm already aware when I'm hungry, thanks.*

***Your senses and reflexes are tied to your hunger. Sense coming attacks with hunger pangs and feel awareness of the room***

*around you in your stomach. The hungrier you get, the more*
*powerful your senses and reflexes become.*

Zeke stared. *Well. Okay. I'll take it! It's not exactly what I want,*
*but it's a great skill!*

*One more. There's something I've been wondering. Does it have*
*to be two skills?*

**No. You can fuse multiple skills at once.**

*Oh. Then...what about this?*

### [Strong Legs] (Minor) [Strong Jaw] (Minor) [Claw Fighter] (Lesser) [Steel Stomach] (Minor)

*Going for a general bodily build bonus. One skill that gives me a*
*big, whole-body bonus!*

Zeke looked at the list of skills. He bit his lip. *That's a lot to*
*wager, though. Ugh. I feel like Strong Legs and Strong Jaw go*
*together, but what about Claw Fighter or Steel Stomach? One of*
*those goes with Strong Jaw or Strong Legs, but not both. It's like how*
*peanut butter and chocolate go together, and peanut butter and jelly*
*go together, but peanut butter, chocolate, and jelly would make a*
*strange sandwich.*

He stared at the list again, then removed Claw Fighter. *Of*
*the skills I'm fusing, Claw Fighter is the one I need the most in actual*
*life and death situations. I'll try fusing the three buff skills first, then*
*consider if Claw Fighter meshes with whatever comes out. But*
*instead, how about this...?*

### [Strong Legs] [Strong Jaw] [Steel Stomach] [Thick Flesh]

*After all, Thick Flesh, though it's a condition, is also a body-*

*buffing skill! It's reasonable to include.* He pushed the skills together. *Skill fusion, go!*

A jaunty riff played. Zeke clenched his fist. *Hell yeah! It worked! What'd I get, what'd I get?*

Someone gripped his shoulder, hard. A low voice growled, "Zeke..."

# 76
## SKILLS FOR THE SKILL GODS

Startled, Zeke went stiff. He turned, slowly.

Two figures stood over him, faces cast in shadow by the VIP lights burning bright overhead.

Zeke swallowed. "Hello."

Domi tossed her hair. "I told you to come over *forever* ago."

"Oh. I thought...you meant in a little bit," Zeke mumbled, cowed. *Whoops.*

Mia rolled her eyes.

"Uh, one second." Turning back ahead of him, Zeke peered at his System. *What did I get? What did a 4x fusion get me?*

### [Tough Body] (Lesser) +4
*Your entire body is tougher and stronger, inside and out. Gain a low-level bonus to STR and CON. 10% resistance to stab, bludgeon, damage, poison, decay, fire, etc.*

*Whoa, nice! Full-body buff and ten percent resistance to almost everything...* Zeke's eyes rested on the etc., and he raised his brows. *System? Care to explain?*

**There are a great many types of damage. The System cannot predict them all, nor predict how all will interact with this skill.**

Zeke snorted. *Even the System doesn't know the limits of the System, huh?*

*Wait...why not?*

**The System does not choose Concepts. Concepts are decided by the Chosen. Therefore, the System cannot predict all possible interactions.**

*But you know what everyone's Concepts are, right? I mean, you're the one who approves them...right?*

...

"Zeke? Earth to Zeke," Domi said, waving a hand in front of his face.

Zeke startled back to reality. "Uh, yeah! Yeah. What were we talking about?"

Mia sighed. She pointed up. "Let's go up to the top of the box. I think we should talk now, before the morning."

Zeke nodded. "Right, right. Our lureeee..." He glanced around him. *Probably shouldn't say that aloud. Er, er—* "er, interesting plan. Right. Let's go."

"Smooth." Domi rolled her eyes sarcastically. She gave him a look. "You ever get your level thirty bonus from the System, by the way?"

"Not yet," Zeke said.

Domi raised her brows. "Do you think it *has* a non-Domain level thirty bonus?"

Zeke clicked his tongue. *You know...that is a good point.*

"If there isn't one, then we just fucked ourselves good," Domi muttered, half to herself.

"I'm sure there is one. Probably?" Zeke said.

"There better be," Domi said, her voice deepening.

Zeke put his hands up "We can always ask the System for a Domain later. But I think we should push it for something else first."

"No, I agree." Domi sighed. She pointed up. "We should finish this up top."

"Right, right." Zeke shoved himself upright and dusted down his clothes. He nodded at the girls. "After you."

Out into the night. Darkness closed around them. A cool wind blew, bringing with it the distant scent of ash. They stood at the top of the stadium, only the top of the box reaching higher. From here, the city spread out beneath them. Only a few lights shone across the city, most of them streetlights. The distant fire they'd been closer to during their fight with the Cat Man raged so close to the dome's limits that they lit the inside of the black dome with their reddish light.

Zeke stared for a moment, captivated, and simultaneously empty. *So few people left. There were so many apocalypses that no humans stood a chance. Outside of the people held as a captive audience by the Stadium Apocalypse, how many people are left?*

He glanced at Mia. *She hasn't said anything. I'll have to assume there's almost none.*

*We're in the endgame, now. This city can't last much longer. We need to make our final moves and win, or else we'll be destroyed.*

Domi pointed at a fire ladder on the outside of the box. Retracted in on itself, the ladder hung out of any of their reach. A small explosion lit up the lock holding it shut, and the latter rattled down to them. She grabbed it and climbed, and Zeke and Mia followed.

Atop the box, Domi yawned and stretched, then sat down

on the edge, staring out into the field, legs dangling off the box's front edge. Zeke joined her, while Mia sat on his far side. Zeke glanced at her, then scooted a little closer, subtly.

Mia glanced at him. Zeke glanced back. *Should...should I say something?*

"So, do we want to figure out the plan, or jointly bully the System into giving us our level thirty bonus first?" Domi asked.

"I'm leaning level thirty bonus," Zeke said.

Mia sighed. "I wish..."

"What level are you?" Domi asked, leaning in front of Zeke to see Mia.

"Only level twenty-some," Mia said, shaking her head.

Domi raised her eyebrows. "Damn! Over level twenty already? Is there a catch-up mechanic?"

"Probably just getting more levels for fighting higher-level bosses at a lower level," Zeke suggested, shrugging.

"That is how games work," Domi allowed. She turned back around, staring into the night. "Hey! System! Where's our bonus, huh?"

**Calculating...**

Domi rolled her eyes. "You've had enough time to calculate. Spit it out already!"

**...**

"Come on. You've been holding out on us for long enough. Don't we deserve something?" Zeke tried.

**You can choose your Domain.**

"Choose implies there's another choice." Domi shook her head, not taking any of the System's bullshit.

•••

"Is it because you can't think of anything?" Zeke guessed.

Silence. Not even the three dots it usually spat out.

Domi clicked her tongue.

Zeke sighed. *But, on the other hand...doesn't that mean we can suggest something? What do I want? What would be super useful against other Apocalypses?*

*In this situation, where I'm surrounded by insane, massive monsters...what can I do to defeat them? What would give me an edge?*

Zeke slapped his fist on his palm. He sat up. "Oh! I know!"

"What?" Domi asked.

"Transformation. A transformation! If we're the heroes, and they're the monsters, right, then the hero gets a sleek hero transformation while the monsters become big, terrifying, and bloated with their Domains. It makes sense, right?" Zeke enthused.

"Someone's been watching too many movies," Domi muttered.

Mia spread her hands. "What else are we supposed to base this situation on? The real life time we were almost eaten by a man with cat ears? The last time cartoons hopped out of a television and attacked?"

"I know, I know, it's just...how cheesy," Domi said, shaking her head.

"What? Do you have something better?" Zeke asked.

Domi put her hands up. "Whoa, whoa. I didn't say that."

"Everyone's a critic," Zeke muttered to himself.

### Calculating... Transformation...

A new menu opened before Zeke's eyes. A small box, it bore no description, just the text: **Hunger Apocalypse: Transformation** and a small button labeled **OK**.

Zeke looked at the button, then at Domi and Mia. Domi stared back at him, expression just as uncertain. *What's this skill going to do? How much is it going to alter the world around us? If it's anything like our Domains, it might uncontrollably start trying to kill anything around us, and right now...that's Domi and Mia, or myself and Mia.*

"Mia, you stay here. Domi, why don't we head down to the field? Mia can watch from overhead and let us know how it looks," Zeke suggested.

"That's a good idea. I'll take left side," Domi agreed.

Mia looked left and right. "Uh, okay. Good luck?"

"Yeah." Zeke jogged for the ladder, Domi right behind them.

Down the stairs, out onto the field. Cool night air rushed around Zeke, the twisted metal stairs clanging underfoot as he jumped from slat to slat. Domi split off, sprinting to the opposite extreme, her slender body vanishing into the thin light on the field.

Zeke's feet whispered through grass. Late night dew flecked his shoes and ankles. He swooped by the empty cloth body, the huge empty head laying on its side, cavernous and dark. A faint smell of meat mixed with the grass and distant ash, a moment of unpleasantness as he ran by.

To the far end of the field. Zeke took a deep breath, settling himself. Darkness hung around him like a cloak, obscuring the shape of him. Though lights lit the stands and boxes, the field itself lay dark. None of the massive blocks of stadium lights that loomed high in the sky beamed down on the field.

*Okay. Here goes.* Zeke lifted his finger and pressed **OK**.

# 77
## TRANSFORMATION TIME

Bright light burst out all around him. A blast of energy flew up from his feet, sending his clothes flying. Wind whirled around him, strong enough to send his body left and right. Grimacing, Zeke protected his face with his arms. *What the—?*

From the opposite side of the field, explosions burst out. A fanfare of tiny fireworks lit the night around Domi, flashbangs and mortars that flashed, then vanished. Light strobed the field around her.

Squinting at Domi from across the field, Zeke shook his head. *Well, damn. Guess stealth isn't really an option with the transformation sequence.*

In the next moment, a blast of hunger slammed into his stomach. Zeke's mind went blank, and he stumbled back. *So hungry. So empty.* His body ached. His heart pounded. Saliva dripped down his face. Zeke dropped to his knees, his limbs weakening.

*Holy shit. The cost is no joke! This transformation is destroying whatever reserves I had.* He braced himself on the field on one arm, swaying in the wind that buffeted him like a leaf. *If it doesn't end soon, I'm dead.*

His body twisted. Black, bone-like armor pressed through his skin, curling around his limbs. The armor grew over his clothes and body, completely cloaking him. His limbs grew exaggeratedly slender, his body hollowing visibly. Long, bony fingers became near-skeletal claws. Slender black cloth-like tendrils swooped from his shoulder blades and snapped on the wind behind him.

The final bone spurs solidified into place on his elongated limbs. Black crawled down over his face, forming into a helmet over his head. Zeke's jaw, palms, and feet all itched ferociously. He turned his palm over to find a mouth growing there, teeth sharp as blades. The edge of the mouth lined up with the gap between his middle and fourth finger and, when he turned his hand back over, the mouth gaped on both the front and back of it. Curious, he touched his face. His mouth extended to the joint, sharp teeth all the way from the front to the back, cheeks and lips gone entirely.

*I'm a monster. This is an apocalypse's transformation, for sure. Black armor, teeth everywhere, mouths on my hands and—* He turned his foot over to check the bottom, only for his entire foot to split in two between the third and fourth toes, opening left-right. A blackened tongue licked out, and the mouth snapped shut. Zeke tasted grass, and a tiny amount of satiation reached his brain.

*Huh. So, they're functional mouths, and probably able to use devour. I'm not going to think about how they connect to my stomach. I'm probably better off not knowing.* He lifted his hand-mouths and opened and shut them a few times, disgusted but also somewhat intrigued. Sharp, piranha-like needly teeth lined the mouth, ready to tear anything to bits. Long black tongues scythed out and licked the back of his hands and his palms, sandpapery rough like a cat's tongue.

*Damn. I'm not sure if I'm disgusting or cool as hell.*

Closing his hand and opening it again, forcing the mouth to close, he took a deep breath. *Well. Transform. So, what can this form of mine do?*

*All right, here we go.* He clenched his fist and punched the ground.

His fist smashed into the ground. Mud flew up. His hand mouth opened and gobbled up a mouthful of mud and turf.

Zeke pulled his hand away. A nearly foot-deep hole opened in the earth where he'd struck. He raised his eyebrows and nodded. "Not bad."

**Transform:** Substantial boost to all stats. Armor + 500%. Gained skills: Extra Mouths, Extra Limbs, Multi-Devour, Hunger (Condition). 2:03 Remaining.

Pushing off the ground, he darted to the other side of the field. "Domi! What'd you get?"

"What is this, Christmas morning?" Domi snarked back.

The two of them caught sight of one another. Zeke stared. Domi blinked.

"What the motherfuck are you supposed to be?" she asked, horrified.

"Uh...I don't know. Hunger?" Zeke asked, not sure himself.

"Are you— Are your feet eating the field?" Domi asked.

Zeke lifted his left foot and shook it, then lifted his right foot and shook it. Little bits of chewed grass flew away. "So, *that's* why I've been tasting grass for a while now."

"Oh, *now* you notice," Domi muttered, giving his feet a suspicious look.

Zeke looked over Domi. He took a deep breath, hesitated, then spat it out all at once. "Domi...are you *alive*?"

Domi lifted her hands. She pressed her lips together, then shrugged. "I feel alive."

She floated in front of him. Her entire body glowed, made of a translucent, ultra-heated plasma that burned bright orange, blaring the rest of the night to pitch black. Whisps of orange plasma flared up at her shoulders and face, her hair burning up into the sky.

Even standing close to her, even with his armor, the heat beat at Zeke, pounding against his face, drying out his many mouths. His left hand's mouth licked and smacked its lips, sealing them against the heat. Her plasmid body wore no clothes, but neither did it have any details, the bright orange as smooth as a doll.

"Well. Damn," Zeke muttered.

Domi nodded at the ground. "Your feet are eating the grass again."

Zeke looked at his feet. They gnawed at the grass under them, chewing away like a cow chewing cud. He kicked them again and stepped backward, away from the gnawed grass. "Hey! Stop it!"

His feet ignored him, eagerly gobbling at the new grass.

"And what about you? That garb... 'I looked, and behold, a black horse; and he who sat on it had a pair of scales in his hand,'" Domi quoted.

"Huh?" Zeke tilted his head.

Domi nodded at him. "The Four Horsemen of the Apocalypse. Famine rides a black horse. And you're...what, Hunger? Yeah, Hunger. Black armor...Famine...black horse..." She spread her hands and quirked a glowing brow.

Zeke frowned. "If I'm a horseman, then what's my horse, huh?"

Giving him a look, Domi nodded toward the entrance of the Stadium. "The motorcycle, obviously."

"Right, right. So, what are you? War? War rides a red horse, orange, red…" Zeke said, nodding back.

"Eh…seems a bit of a push. By that rule, Mia wears gold, gold is like yellow, so that makes her Pestilence, right?" Domi said.

Zeke frowned. "Mia is the least like Pestilence. If she's any of them, with that big sword of hers…then she's Death, right? 'There was a pale horse, and its rider's name was Death.'"

They both stood there in silence for a few moments, neither of them knowing what to say.

All at once, Domi clapped her hands. An explosion blasted out from the clap, nearly bowling Zeke over. He grabbed a handful of the field and managed to hold on, though the mascot costume and head went tumbling.

Guilty, Domi ducked a little and ran a hand through her hair. "Ah. Sorry. Anyway, I was going to say…no point getting all worked up about this. Mia's a Hero, anyway."

"Yeah, yeah," Zeke said, nodding.

Another awkward silence. Zeke rubbed the back of his neck, standing there in black armor, the little tendrils lashing and licking at the air. Domi stared at the sky, flickering gently.

"Can we cancel these transformations early?" Domi muttered, breaking the silence for a second time.

Even as she said it, the orange light abruptly vanished. Zeke quickly looked away but, even as he did, he caught a glimpse of Domi's jeans and shirt. He turned back, relieved, a tiny twinge of disappointment in his heart.

*Hey, hey. She's a friend. Now isn't the time for that.*

"All right. I guess I'll cancel mine, too?" Zeke muttered.

**Cancel Transformation?**

**Warning:** You cannot re-enter Transformation for as long as you were in Transformed state.

"Yes," Zeke said. *Interesting. I'll have to keep an eye on my Transformation time. It's not something I should instantly activate, but something I should save for the most critical moment, when I'm sure I can win before my time runs out. After all, a few minutes can be an eternity in battle.*

His body shifted again. The dark armor vanished, subsuming back under his skin. The mouths all closed over, vanishing from jaw to lips. His torn and bloodied clothes returned. He drooped to the ground again, his stomach grumbling aloud.

*I need food.*

A large bag of nacho chips in clear, industrial packaging puffed down beside him, the date stamped on the side still good. Zeke looked over, then up at Domi.

She grinned. "There ya go. No need to eat pigeons this time."

"Thanks," Zeke gasped. He dragged the bag over and yanked it open. Shoving them in his mouth by the handfuls, he crunched them down. Pulling the bag all the way open, he poured the last of the chips in. He peered around the inside of the bag, then reached in, all the way up to his elbow, and scooped up the last crumbs on his fingertips.

His stomach grumbled. Zeke put a hand to it.

*I'm still hungry? A whole industrial-sized bag of tortilla chips, and it barely did anything to fill me up.*

*This can't just be my imagination. I think...I think I really need more food to sustain myself now.*

*It's been a few days. How much food will I require in a week? A month? A year?*

A moth flapped by. Thoughtlessly, Zeke snatched it out of

the air and ate it. His stomach quieted, filling up as much from the moth as it had from the whole bag of chips.

Zeke pressed his lips together. *Do I seriously do better from eating live animals than actual food? What's wrong with me?*

"Right, so I gave you the chips so you'd stop eating moths and things," Domi said, giving him a look from the corner of her eye.

"Where'd you pull them from, anyway?" Zeke asked. He nodded at her. "Since you were a humanoid lump of plasma a few moments ago."

She turned, revealing a brand-new backpack lying off to the side behind her. Robbie the Robin's cartoonish face smiled up at him from the black fabric. "Went on a walk around the stadium and broke into...er, scavenged a few shops. I've got more if you had asked instead of snatching bugs out of the air."

"I'm good," Zeke said reflexively, then froze. "Er, actually..."

Domi snorted. She walked over to the bag and dug through it, tossing him another bag of chips and a black T-shirt with *Robbie Robins* written on it in a cursive script and a picture of the Robins' mascot's cheerful face plastered on the front. "Here. And to replace that grimy old T-shirt of yours, too."

"Ah...thanks," Zeke said awkwardly. He yanked off his old shirt and pulled on the new one. *It does feel way better, though. That old shirt was pretty rough.*

"Whoa! Guys! What *was* that?" Mia asked, running toward them.

"Oh, that's right, you were watching. So? What did you think?" Domi asked, waggling her brows at Mia.

"Insane. What *was* that? You guys like, became superheroes! Monster-heroes! Totally makes up for not having a Domain," Mia said, nodding.

Domi nodded back. "Especially if we can lure the rest of the apocalypses out of their Domains."

Zeke took a deep breath, pausing in the middle of shoveling chips into his mouth. *Right. Our plan to lure them here...transforming is only the first step of our strategy.* "So...what's our next step?"

Mia looked from Zeke to Domi. "I have an idea."

# 78
## AN IDEA

Morning light played over Zeke's face, gently tracing down his eyelids. He twitched, swatting at it. "G'goff. I'm sleepin'."

"What?" an unfamiliar voice asked.

Zeke jolted awake. A strange ceiling unfolded before him, with big glass windows that filled an entire wall. He sat up, looking around. *Where am I? Where is this? What's—*

*Right.* Running a hand through his hair in a vain attempt to straighten it, Zeke sat up out of the VIP chair he'd slept in. He yawned, somehow still tired, and weirdly achy to boot. *Ugh. Chairs are not beds, noted.*

Getting up, he stretched. Across the way, Domi came to the window and waved to him. Sleepily, he waved back.

*Time to get going.*

Zeke waved his hands. "Hey, everyone. Stay in the stadium. Scavenge the vendors for food. Me and the girls are going to go out and find more resources, more food and water. It's essential that you all stay inside the stadium and don't go out, understand?"

A few sleepy yeses and agreements sounded out through the room.

*All right, good enough.* He clapped his hands together, slapped his cheeks, then headed out into the world.

Mia and Domi waited for him on the field. Mia waved as he got close, beaming. He nodded back, a grin splitting his face. *Mia's here, Domi's here, everyone's safe, and everything is good!*

*But if we don't make a move soon, someone will realize we're here, and when that happens...we're fucked. That's why we have to make our move now.*

"Everyone have backpacks?" Domi asked.

Zeke and Mia gave her a thumbs up.

Domi nodded back. "Excellent. Let's get to the motorcycle."

As they walked, Zeke nodded to the girls. "We're almost certainly going to be attacked by the pigeons as soon as we walk outside. I'll handle them—"

"Pigeon-eater," Domi muttered under her breath.

"—so you two focus on grabbing food, while I stay outside and handle the pigeon. Deal?"

"Ugh, you get to stay outside and eat pigeons while I have to go inside and work *so hard* to pick up all the food I can grab. I've got the hard job," Mia said, grinning.

Zeke rolled his eyes. He shoved Mia lightly. "Yeah, yeah."

"We're mostly doing this for Zeke, so focus on calorie content, not nutrition," Domi returned. She hopped onto the motorcycle and nodded to the other two.

Mia slid on behind Domi. Zeke threw his leg over the cycle and perched up on the back. He looked at Domi. "But don't forsake nutrition. We don't know how long we're going to be fighting once we kick this off. The ordinary humans in the stadium might need food."

Zeke briefly cast a look over the bodies scattered around the stadium entrance. His stomach grumbled faintly, and he quickly tore his eyes away. *Don't think about it. Don't think about it.*

Domi hummed distractedly. Her eyes glowed orange, and her knuckles whitened on the grips. The engine roared to life underneath them, and the motorcycle bucked, blasting down the street.

Wings flapped. Gray feathers blocked out the sun, the prismatic, oily sheen almost a rainbow from the massed forces. Hundreds, no, thousands of pigeons dropped down on them, leaping off the electric wires en masse. Claws flashed. Big round eyes reflected the motorcycle.

*Kill the evil one!*

"Uh, Zeke, you...you have that handled?" Mia asked nervously.

Zeke swallowed. "Maybe?"

The first pigeon darted in, beak parted, eyes glittering with bloodlust.

Zeke stood up on the motorcycle. Steadying himself on Mia's shoulder, he snatched the pigeon and stuffed it into his mouth.

### [Devour]
### You are fighting a [Mob] enemy. Rewards are deferred until the end of the battle.

Even as he swallowed the pigeon, a wave of gray feathers smashed into him. Catching him around the shoulders, they pushed him backward. Zeke swayed back, barely holding onto the bike.

*At this rate...at this rate—*

"Zeke! You okay?" Domi shouted.

*They aren't bothering Domi?* Zeke looked down. Mia looked up at him, concerned. *Or Mia. Just me.*

*Well, then.*

He jumped off the motorcycle, letting the pigeons carry him backward. They immediately flew away, unable to actually support his weight. "You guys go ahead. I'm going to deal with these featherballs!"

"You sure?" Domi asked.

"As I can be," Zeke said, backing away.

"We'll be right back. Ten minutes! Hold out that long," Mia shouted as they sped away.

Zeke gave a thumbs-up to her retreating back, only for a pigeon to barrel into it. Tiny claws dug thin lines into his hand.

"Ow, shit." Zeke glanced up at the whirlwind of birds overhead. He barely had time to take them in before another pigeon smashed into his jaw, knocking his head to the side. Zeke scowled, stumbling back. A gray blur of pigeons swooped low, striking him in the nuts.

"Fuck!" Zeke fell back, covering his crotch. Even as he did, pigeons flew in from all directions, pummeling him, biting, clawing.

*All right, enough. Domi and Mia have gotten away by now.*

### [Absorb]

All the pigeons swirling around him instantly dropped to the ground. Their wings flapped weakly, bright eyes closing. One burst into dust, then another and another, and Zeke's stomach steadily filled.

Zeke stood up straight, suddenly full of energy. He stared up at the pigeons swirling overhead and flipped them the bird. "Fuck off, birdbrains."

A fresh wave of pigeons swooped in. Zeke arched his palms, baring his claws.

### [Claw Fighter]

Left, right, left. Blood and feathers flew. Zeke danced around the pigeons, swiping at any that dared to draw close. One flew at his throat. He ducked his head and bit it out of the air, chewing as he fought. As they grew close, [Absorb] slowed the pigeons, making it easier for him to kill them and snatch them out of the air. Out of hunger's sake, he swallowed down a dozen of them. Between that and [Absorb], his hunger barely grew throughout the fight.

*Living things really do satiate me more. That's going to be a problem,* Zeke noted distantly through the bloodlust.

His stomach suddenly ached.

### [Hunger Awareness]

*Ah! A big attack!* Zeke dropped to the ground.

Black lines swooped at him, snapping and crackling. The air around him charged with static. The lines swung through the place he'd stood seconds ago, vanishing up into the mess of pigeons once more without harming them.

*What the hell?* Zeke looked up.

Overhead, the black electric lines clustered so thickly as to resemble a spider's web. Electricity crackled from the bared ends of the black-rubber-coated wires, copper snarling at the sky. Pigeon swarms carried the broken cables high, preparing to drop them on Zeke once more.

"Holy shit, the electric lines are an apocalypse, too?" Zeke asked, startled.

**Electric Line Apocalypse**
**Danger Rating: S**
**Level: ???**
**Allied with: Pigeon Apocalypse**

*Damn, making me guess the whole name that time. Not feeling generous, System?* Zeke wondered.

•••

*Or...is there also an Electric Apocalypse?*

•••

Zeke narrowed his eyes at the System. "Responses like that are why no one trusts you."

**The System is an automatic machine. It does not require trust.**

The electric lines swung down at Zeke again. He dodged to the side, only for the lines to reach after him, seeking like a cheap first-person-shooter hack.

**[Caffeine Rush] [Tough Body]**

Zeke arched himself backward, swaying his body away. The first cable missed, swinging over him, then back, electricity brushing over his skin and shivering on his clothes. The second one struck his chest.

His whole body jolted. His muscles tensed. His heart leaped in his chest, and for a moment, his thoughts went blank. The electricity snapped through his body, connecting his chest to the floor. Everything dimmed to that, a single line of white-hot pain snarling through his flesh, burning him on the way through.

**Thanks to the 10% electric resist of [Tough Body], you survived! Congratulations!**
**Resisted [Paralysis]!**

Zeke staggered back. He put a hand to his chest, and it came away damp with blood and some strange clear fluid, his flesh burned where the cable had touched. His heel burned when he put weight on it. *I pretty much got struck by lightning just now. If not for Tough Body, I easily could have died.*

Looking upward, he searched through the pigeons for the wires. Their flapping wings cluttered the air, feathers fluttering down, blocking his view. He backed away, only for his stomach to pang again with the warning kind of hunger. Instantly, Zeke dropped to the floor. Cables flew at him from behind, a new set of black electric wires. The second they swung to a halt, a team of pigeons lifted them into the sky again, vanishing behind their brethren.

*I can't let this battle drag on. They'll wear me down and finish me with those cables.*

*Damn. For birdbrains, they're actually pretty smart.*

Zeke took a deep breath. He threw his hand out at the pigeons. "I didn't want to use this, but you leave me no choice!"

**No one is listening.**

"I know, that's exactly why I said it," Zeke muttered back. He lifted his hand over the **Transform** button.

A storm of pigeons dropped out of the sky, flapping around

his face to blind him. Zeke waved his hand, frustrated. *Dammit, just let me—*

Wires swung at him from every direction, hissing and crackling as they fell.

*Shit!* Zeke tensed, smacking the birds away from his face. *I can't...see!*

# 79
## MOB BATTLE

"System!" Zeke shouted. He hunkered on the floor, making himself as tiny as possible.

The electric lines swooshed down, barely passing over Zeke. Little bolts of lightning grounded along the line of his back. Each one surged painfully down his spine, twitching his muscles. They tensed involuntarily, sending pain deep into his back.

**Initiating Transformation.**
**Transformed:** Hunger
**Time remaining:** 2:41

Zeke's body twisted. He rose from the floor, shifting from hunkering to a runner's pose as the black armor formed over his body. The helm closed on his head, and he darted forward, through the wall of pigeons.

Out into the sun. The asphalt burned against his bare feet, his foot-tongues hissing at the pain. He whirled, turning to face the pigeons.

Electric wires crisscrossed the sky behind him, thick as a

spider's web. Hundreds of pigeons sat on each wire, while more flapped around in a massive, feathery gray whirlwind. Zeke licked his lips, drawing a slow breath.

*I was trapped in there, huh? Whew. No wonder I was getting overwhelmed.*

The pigeons whirled around to face him. A stream of gray-feathered bodies darted toward him, almost an appendage.

Zeke laughed lightly. "I'm not letting you take the initiative twice." Opening his newly enlarged mouth, he charged at the pigeon column.

*Devour!* Zeke thought.

### [Multi-Devour]

His hands lifted on their own, hand-mouths gaping. Pigeons poured into his mouth and hand-mouths both, vanishing down into his throat one after another. For the first time in a long time, Zeke began to feel full.

*Damn! Not bad. I just need to eat literally hundreds of pigeons at once, and I'm fine!*

Feathers tickled his throat. The pigeons shifted in his stomach, struggling and clawing. Zeke pulled a face. *Oh, I don't like that.*

### [Tough Body]

The pain abated. The birds slowed, no longer able to move as well. The lowest ones stopped moving entirely. He clenched his stomach muscles, and the birds inside of him went still.

The pigeons pulled back, retracting their column. Zeke swallowed and licked his lips. Coughing a little, he turned his head and spat up a mouthful of feathers. *Ugh, yuck. I do not want to think about all the pigeons inside of me.*

A tendril on his back lashed out on its own and twisted around a pigeon flying at Zeke from behind. Squawking in surprise, the pigeon dropped the knife it had been carrying.

## [Extra Limbs]

Zeke looked at the tendrils. *They count as limbs? Huh. I was wondering about that 'extra limb' skill I got in this form. Guess that explains it.* Reaching out, he closed his hand.

The tendril snapped the pigeon's neck. Zeke opened his hand, and the tendril dropped the pigeon's limp body. *Pretty intuitive to use, too.*

*Ah! I should have devoured it for the skills!*

*Wait, am I even getting skills for devouring right now? The System said rewards are deferred until the end. Knowing the System, it's probably gonna use that to screw me, somehow.*

**The System is not interested in sexual intercourse.**

"Thanks. Fuck," Zeke muttered, wrinkling his nose. *Ugh. I didn't need that image in my head.*

Overhead, the pigeons whirled into a column and darted at Zeke again. Tendrils flying, mouths wide, Zeke rushed to meet them.

Blood and feathers flew. Zeke bit left and right. Tendrils lashed out, snatching pigeons out of the air and snapping their necks. Brittle bones shattered. Gray bodies hit the ground all around him. Pigeon blood dripped from his jaw and hands. His stomach filled, and he started spitting the pigeons to the side rather than swallowing. [Absorb] dissolved the bodies too close to him into ashy dust. Feathers and dust splashed around as he fought the pigeons, madly slapping and biting at their tiny bodies.

Another pillar of pigeons lunged at him. Zeke turned, smacking the remnants of the second pillar side to face the new one.

His stomach panged.

Zeke's eyes widened. In the midst of the new pigeon pillar, flashes of black wire appeared. He threw himself to the side.

The pigeons dropped the wire. It swung toward Zeke. Zeke backpedaled, dodging away.

## [Hunger Awareness]

Even as he dodged, pre-warned to their attacks by his hunger pangs, a new group of pigeons darted down, grabbed the wire, and thrust it at Zeke. He kept backing away, but the pigeons' wings glowed red. They hurtled toward him, twice as fast as before.

*Shit! I can't—*

*No way out of this. I have to go for it!* Throwing his hands out, Zeke activated his skills. *Maximum power. All the skill I can muster! All my SPR, in this moment!*

Zeke's hands latched onto the end of the live wire.

## [Multi-Devour] [Absorb]

Electricity coursed through his hands. It sparked up his arms, dancing around his blackened, armored skin, burning through his limbs. Zeke gritted his teeth and held on, not that he could let go if he wanted to. His arms tensed, hands unable to release the wire. The tension crept up his body, freezing his whole form in place.

*Absorb! Absorb it all! If you're energy, then I'll [Absorb] it! If you're wire, then I'll [Devour] it!*

His hand mouths clenched down, biting through rubber

and metal. The pain and tension alleviated for a moment, but Zeke immediately wound his hands up the wire, drawing more of it toward him. *I'll eat you. I'll eat you whole!*

Pigeons dove at him from all directions. Biting and clawing, they swirled around him. Wings battered at his face. They nipped at his armor, fighting the black bits.

The tendrils on Zeke's back darted forth. Unbothered by the electricity freezing the rest of Zeke's body, they snatched one pigeon after another out of the air. With near-mechanical efficiency, they caught pigeons, snapped their necks, and dropped them to the ground. Pigeons piled up behind Zeke.

The wires fought him. Thrashing in his hands, they struggled to break free of his grasp. Zeke wound his hands up the wires, slowly choking them away. Spitting one word at a time, he snarled, "You...aren't...getting...*away!*"

The birds mobbed him. One wriggled in under his helm and pecked at his eyes. Closing them against the pigeon, Zeke scowled. "Now, that's just unfair."

### [Manipulate Aerosols]

A powerful blast of steam issued from the top of his helm, ejecting the pigeon. Startled, it squawked and fluttered its wings, barely catching itself before it hit the ground.

Zeke grinned. "Again!"

### [Manipulate Aerosols]

Pressurized steam shot out of every crack and cranny in his armor. It blasted the birds directly in the face. They fluttered back or let out surprised *coos*. A few of the less lucky ones caught a beakful of pressurized steam and fell to the ground, twitching in pain. Zeke rubbed his toe in the ground.

## [Crystal Burst]

Clear crystals thrust through the downed pigeons, stained ruby red by their blood. They fluttered their wings once or twice more, then fell still, heads tipped back, black eyes empty and dead.

Screaming in anger, the pigeons flew at Zeke as one.

Zeke laughed. "Come at me!" He opened his mouth. *I was just getting a bit peckish!*

Overhead, a shadow appeared at the top of the nearest electrical post. A familiar figure looked down at Zeke, blond hair blowing in the wind.

Zeke's eyes widened. He bared his teeth. "Ryan!"

"It's time for you to die," Ryan replied. He leaped off the electrical post, dagger materializing in his hand as he plunged directly toward Zeke's back.

Zeke tried to release the electrical wires, but his hands refused to un-tense. He tried to lift his feet, but the electricity coursing through him glued them to the floor. *Fuck! Damn you, Ryan! If it's a dead run, then give the fuck up already!*

Ryan closed in, blue eyes flat. Zeke saw himself reflected in those eyes, saw his monstrous appearance, saw his death already playing out in Ryan's vision. "Farewell, Zeke."

# 80
## FAREWELL

*S*hit, shit, shit, shit, shit!

Ryan closed in. Zeke tensed, or would have, if the electricity flowing through him didn't already lock his muscles tense. His eyes widened. *I'm going to—*

*Haaa, is that what you thought?* He grinned.

It was Ryan's turn to widen his eyes. He threw the dagger at Zeke.

Too late. Zeke's body flashed away.

**[Electric Leap]**

He reappeared atop the electric pole where Ryan had been moments ago. Zeke crouched on the pole and stuck his tongue out at Ryan.

An almost forearm-length black tongue emerged from his mouth. Zeke stared at it. *That's mine? Gross.*

Ryan landed neatly and picked up his dagger. Turning, he scowled up at Zeke. "You're a monster."

"Fuck off and die," Zeke responded, swallowing his tongue back. *Let's just put that away for now and not think about it.*

"Finally facing the truth? Finally admitting you're a monster?"

Zeke spread his hands. "Look, my man, I don't know how to explain this to you, but you've been trying to kill me since this thing kicked off— No, since *before* it kicked off. I've been incredibly patient, and I've only knocked you out a few times, even though you've almost killed me every time we've met. Now I'm the monster for finally deciding to let you die?"

"Have you seen yourself?" Ryan parried.

Zeke shrugged. "Yeah, yeah. I look like a monster, I get it. I'm not running around trying to m—"

A gray tornado of birds rushed at him, holding an electric wire in their gnarled claws.

### [Electric Leap]

"—murder my friends," Zeke finished from the opposite electric pole.

A message popped up in the corner of his eye.

### Absorbed [Electric Resist] (Minor)!

*Thought my rewards were paused because of the battle type or something.*

### Skill granted early due to pause in Mob Battle.

*Ah, got it. Good one to pick up mid-fight.*

### Absorbed [Resilience]!
### Absorbed [Steel Stomach]!
### Absorbed [Wings] (Tiny) (Condition)!

"Hold up, I don't need that last one," Zeke said, as his shoulders itched, and tiny wings pushed through his back.

**You cannot reject skills. If you don't like a skill, try fusing it!**

*Knew there had to be a drawback to Absorb's skill pickup chance. Oh, well. Nice to pick up a few levels on all the other skills.*

"In any case, you're a [Hero], aren't you? What... Time Hero, or something?" Zeke guessed, looking down at Ryan.

**Time Hero**
**Danger Rating:** S
**Level:** ?????????????????????????????????????????????????????????????????????

*Whoa, what's with that level? I've never seen so many question marks.*

**Level:** ERROR

*Yeah, still not liking that.* Zeke sucked a breath. He looked at Ryan. "Are you a Hero, though?"

Ryan flipped his dagger, narrowing his eyes at Zeke. "What do you mean?"

"You can turn back time, right?" Zeke asked.

Ryan inclined his head.

"Then...of all of us apocalypses, aren't you the only one who's successfully destroyed the world?" Zeke asked.

"What?" Ryan asked.

"Every time you turn back time, what happens to that world? That reality? Does it melt away? Does it end abruptly?

Did it never happen? No matter what...didn't you destroy a world every time you turned back time?"

Ryan stared. His jaw gaped. A second later, his mouth shut, and he rolled his eyes. "That's the most ridiculous thing I've ever—"

**Time Hero** popped up again. Both Zeke and Ryan stared at it, surprised. The words trembled. Letters scrolled by like icons in a slot machine. One after another, the letters stopped rolling, revealing new words underneath.

**Ouroboros Apocalypse**
**Danger Rating:** SSS+
**Level:** N/A

Zeke laughed aloud. "Who's the monster now? Ryan!"

Ryan slashed at the message box. "I'm not an Apocalypse! I'm not, I'm—"

**You have destroyed the world multiple times. You are the worthiest apocalypse.**

"So...Ryan, Ouroboros Apocalypse. What do you have to say for yourself? Between the two of us, only one of us has destroyed the world," Zeke gloated. The pigeons closed in on him. He glanced across at the opposite pole and activated **[Electric Leap]** again, reappearing across the street from his original spot.

"Not true." Ryan threw his dagger at Zeke.

Zeke vanished, appearing on yet another electric pole. *This isn't bad. Electric Leap is overpowered against the Electric Line Apocalypse.* His stomach grumbled. He turned, looking at the rush of pigeons, and licked his lips. *And here we go. Instant fuel!* As the pigeons flapped at him, he snatched them out of the air and closed his hands around them, letting the hand-mouths **[Devour]** them. Left and right, until the pigeons fell back, retreating before his **[Claw Fighter]** skill.

His belly bulged. Zeke put a hand on his stomach. *I don't taste the dusty feathers and iron pigeon blood as much when my hands eat them. The only problem is that the volume I can eat is much lower.*

Ryan raised his hand, and the dagger reappeared in his palm. He took a deep breath, his chest heaving. "I-I don't care. I'll kill you, then turn back time. Next time, next time—"

"Next time, you'll turn back time again. And again. And again. You've defeated yourself, Ryan. By pursuing perfection, you have single-handedly doomed the world to stagnate, never to move past the end of this sequence," Zeke declared, pointing down at Ryan.

"What would you know?" Ryan scowled. He shook his head. "You have no idea. No idea! All the time I've spent, all the endless iterations—"

"I don't, but, Ryan...you just admitted yourself. It's endless. You can't fix this. You have to accept what's happened and move on, just like the rest of us," Zeke said.

Ryan's face contorted. He vanished.

Zeke scratched his back. A mass of pigeons loomed overhead, darting down on him. "Well. I guess...I just..."

### [Electric Leap]

A dagger flew at him the second he reappeared on the opposite pole. Startled, Zeke jumped back. Ryan leaped after him, raising the dagger even as they fell.

Zeke grabbed Ryan's arm. The two of them struggled. They plunged, hurtling toward the ground.

*Maybe I can tank the blow—* Zeke glanced down.

A nest of electrical wires twisted on the ground like snakes. Pigeons grabbed them by their ends, yanking them up toward Zeke and Ryan.

*Nope. I will not survive that. Electric Leap!*

**You cannot use this skill while you are [Grappled].**

"Now you tell me!" Zeke complained. *Oh, shit. Oh, shit. Guess I'm relying on Electrical Resistance this time!*

Ryan's face twisted into a grimace of a smile. He tightened his grip on Zeke, foregoing the dagger to fully pin Zeke. "Farewell, Zeke. I'll see you again soon."

"Fuck!" Zeke shouted.

The pigeons cooed. Big black eyes stared down at him, wishing him nothing but death. From below, the electrical lines crackled, waiting.

# 81

## ETERNITY'S END

Digging his fingers into Zeke's armor, Ryan laughed. "Finally! This fucking...useless run—"

"I'm still alive," Zeke snarled. *And I'm not going to die here!* His eyes flashed.

**[Modest Gigantification]**

"Target it to my back!" Zeke shouted.

The tiny gray wings on his back grew, suddenly bursting out to dozens of times their original size. Zeke flapped them once, twice, and surged upward, up away from the electrical wires and away from the pigeons.

Still holding onto him, Ryan's face changed from triumphant to terrified, and his grab went from a killing hold to desperation. "What the fuck? When did you get wings?"

"Only noticed now? I've had them the whole time," Zeke taunted. He looked at Ryan. *Hold on. I can solve Ryan right now. He won't ever pose a problem to me again, and all I have to do is—*

Ryan let go, but Zeke grabbed on. His tendrils darted out, yanking Ryan's left arm away from his body. The gesture pulled his shoulder down, revealing his neck. Opening his mouth, Zeke darted in.

For a moment, Ryan tensed but, in the next, he relaxed. Eyes half-closed, he snorted under his breath. "Fucking awful. This whole run."

*If he's saying that, then as I suspected, killing him restarts the loop. Well, fuck that!* Zeke paused, climbing another few flaps into the air.

Ryan looked at him. "What are you waiting for? You won. Go. Do it."

"Not...quite yet..."

### Skills granted early thanks to pause in Mob Battle.
### Absorbed [Resilience]!

Even as the skills continued to pop up, Zeke canceled Absorb and bit down. Rather than on Ryan's neck, though, he bit Ryan's shoulder. Twisting his head, he ground his teeth shut. Muscle tore. Blood splattered. Ryan screamed, instinctively kicking and punching Zeke with all his might. The blows bounced off Zeke's armor.

With one last twist, he tore the arm free. Tipping his head back, he chewed, crunching bone, and swallowed the arm down.

"Fuck! *Fuck!* Why? Just kill me! Just kill me and be done with it!" Ryan snarled.

"Do you think I'm stupid? No," Zeke said. Extending his black tongue, he slurped down the last of the blood.

"Kill me!" Ryan demanded, punching Zeke's chest with his good arm.

Ignoring him, Zeke looked up. "Hey, System. That's enough of a bite, right? For me to get one skill."

Ryan tensed. His eyes widened. "No! *No!*"

**Yes.**
**Ouroboros Apocalypse**
**Skills**
**Regression**
**Time Teleport**
**Can't**
**Can't**
**Speedster**
**Active Hunter**
**Dead Man's Switch**

...

Ignoring the rest of the skills as they scrolled by, Zeke slammed his finger down on Regression. "This one. Give me this one!"

### Regression (Lesser)
*Turn back time to the moment before the apocalypses began.*

"What?" Ryan asked, startled. He looked at Zeke, his eyes wide. "You can't do that. You're not allowed to do that! System! You've never allowed that before!"

...

*Typical System.* Zeke shook his head.

"Dammit. Should've just killed the run from the start." Ryan twisted in Zeke's grip, struggling to escape.

"Are you sure about that?" Zeke asked.

"You have Regression. This run is fucked beyond all belief. It's time to start over," Ryan grumbled.

"I'll just follow you. You can't reset this, Ryan. I'll go with you and have even more of a head start on winning this time than I did last time. If you turn back time, you're giving *me* the advantage," Zeke reasoned.

Ryan stilled. He scowled, twisting his nose in distaste. "So? What do you want?"

Spreading his wings, Zeke floated there for a moment, over the city. In the distance, part of it burned. Closer to them, a building abruptly collapsed, spilling its contents into the street. "I want to see where this goes. I want to end this apocalypse battle. I want to go home, go to sleep, and pretend like none of this ever happened."

Ryan shook his head. "That's not how this works. That's not what happens. After this, it just gets worse. There's no escaping it."

"Did you see that?" Zeke asked.

"See what?" Ryan returned.

Zeke nodded at the black dome, visible from this high up. "See the outside. Escape this dome. Did you ever find out what comes next?"

Ryan opened his mouth, then shut it. He scowled deeper.

"You didn't, right? Only one can escape, but you never beat me. So... what do you say? Let's see tomorrow together." Zeke looked down at him, quirking his brow.

*I'd just kill him, but that Dead Man's Switch skill scares me. If it works the way it sounds like it does, then that means killing Ryan is the same as a Game Over. In other words, if I gank him here, that's it for this 'run,' for this reality. Now that I have Regression, I can chase him, but I'd rather not relive everything that's happened. Sure, there's things I could do better...but that's exactly it. That's the trap Ryan's been living in. There's always something to do better, to fix, to perfect. There's no end to it. I'd just become the second Ouroboros Apocalypse.*

*Besides, I'm the only one who can chase him. Mia, Domi...liter-*

*ally everyone else but me and Ryan would be dead. It's not worth it. Not even once.*

"So?" Zeke asked. *We could use everyone we can get for our plan. Ryan's a capable fighter. Not sure if he'll still be with a traumatic injury, but...what the hell, we're all apocalypses here. I'm sure he can figure out a way to heal his arm.*

Ryan gave him a look. "You just *ate* my arm."

Zeke gestured, flapping his wings to gain air as the pigeons rushed up toward them. "You've almost killed me five times, I think we're even."

"Five attempted murders equals an arm?" Ryan snarked, quirking a brow.

Zeke nodded ferociously. "At *least*."

Ryan looked at the ground. He took a deep breath.

"So?" Zeke asked.

Ryan tensed. His arm closed over, rapidly sealing up. The instant it closed over, he thrashed wildly, kicking and fighting with all his might. He slashed at Zeke's chest with his good hand. The dagger scraped over Zeke's armor, bouncing off the ridges harmlessly except for a few scratch lines.

Zeke grappled at him, more bothered by the twisting than the slashes. *It's like trying to hold a wet fish in your bare hands!* "Hey, whoa!"

Feathers beat all around Zeke. Seizing his moment of distraction, the pigeons mobbed his face. Tiny claws darted at his face. Beaks pecked at him. Frustrated, Zeke took one hand off Ryan to beat them away. "Get back!"

With one last wrench, Ryan twisted free. He fell, dropping toward the unforgiving road below.

"Shit!" *The Dead Man's Switch!* Zeke lunged after him, folding his wings back in a dive.

Asphalt rushed up. Zeke beat his wings, propelling himself faster. He reached out to Ryan. "Come on!"

With a smirk, Ryan vanished.

Eyes wide, Zeke spread his wings, catching as much wind as he could. Too late. He slammed into the floor and tumbled, bouncing over the asphalt.

*Dismiss Modest Gigantification!*

The wings shrunk as he tumbled, escaping the worst of the damage. His black armor scraped over the asphalt, scuffing its surface. Only faint pain broke through the armor's protection, and that immediately diminished as **[Resilient Regeneration]** took over.

As he rolled to a halt, Zeke slammed his hand down, digging his claws into the asphalt. He immediately jerked to a halt as pain shot through his entire hand, sharp, hot, acid pain, enough to break through even **[Resilient Regeneration].** Removing his hand from the asphalt, he held it to his chest and jumped in pain, head tipped back.

*Ow, ow, ow, fuck, fuck, fuck! I didn't expect that. Shit! In the movies, they always leave cool claw marks behind as they slow to a smooth halt! Dammit, ow!*

The heavy sound of flapping wings swooped down on him. Zeke looked up. Pigeons swooped down on him, once more rushing at him.

He spread his stance, opening his mouth and hand-mouths. "All right, motherfuckers. Round two—"

**Transformation time remaining:** 0:14.

"What? No way! It hasn't been that long!" Zeke shouted, startled.

**Transformation time remaining:** 0:13.

"Fuck!" Zeke charged the pigeons. The pigeons formed a

huge pigeon with their small, feathery bodies and clashed with him.

*At least they're cooperating.* Zeke bit down on the huge pigeons, hands chewing into the giant pigeon's body.

The giant pigeon instantly burst apart. He chased it down, [Devour]ing left and right.

Behind him, an engine revved. "Get out of the way!"

Zeke dove to the side. Domi flashed by with a whoop, motorcycle gleaming in the sun. She leaped off the motorcycle, sending it leaping riderless into the mess of pigeons and electrical wires. Running to a halt, she spun around and snapped her fingers with a flourish.

The motorcycle exploded in a fountain of blood and feathers. Bits of rubber and metal flew off, shattering nearby windows.

"My motorcycle!" Zeke shouted, aghast.

"Just make a new one," Domi said, shrugging.

"Just make a new—" Zeke stared at her, all his mouths open, hands splayed to fully express his disbelief.

Abruptly, Zeke's transformation wore off. The armor melted away, and the mouths sealed shut. A wave of exhaustion and hunger washed over him. Zeke dropped to his knees, barely catching himself with his arm.

"Zeke! Here, quickly." Mia ran up beside him and stuffed a bag of cookies in his hand.

Zeke tore the bag open and tipped all the cookies into his mouth at once, barely chewing or tasting them on the way down. They stuck in his throat. Zeke coughed, smacking his chest.

"Here, here." Mia shoved a sports drink at him.

Grabbing it, Zeke twisted it open and dumped it back. With the extra liquid, the dry cookies slid down his throat. He swallowed, ducking his head against the pain.

"You okay?" Mia asked.

Zeke nodded and gave her a thumbs up, coughing a few more times to clear the last of it. "Whew. Thanks."

His stomach grumbled. Embarrassed, Zeke scratched the back of his head. *Ah, well...food isn't doing much for me anymore.*

Mia frowned at him. "Do you need more?"

"Nah, I just..." Zeke gestured vaguely at the battle, then ran without explaining himself. *I can't tell the Hero, Mia, that I need to eat living things to stay full nowadays.*

Electrical wires lashed at Domi. She snapped her fingers and burst into orange plasma. The electrical lines landed on her. Electricity sparked over her body and vanished into her plasmid form.

Zeke ran up and grabbed a pigeon, quickly **[Devour]**ing it. "You need help?"

"I need you to back the hell up so I can finish this bitch," Domi responded.

Zeke flashed a thumbs-up and retreated, running back toward Mia. "Get down, get down!"

"Around the corner!" Mia shouted.

Behind them, Domi's light burst up to nova brightness, then supernova. She tensed, balling herself up.

Zeke jumped around the corner. Mia followed him, putting her back to the wall.

*BAM!*

# 82
## EXPLOSIONS AND OTHER FUN THINGS

A wave of flame crested over the wall and surged down the street. Black soot blasted the wall. Zeke wrapped his arms around Mia, shielding her from the force of the blast. It struck them a moment later. Even bouncing around the corner, it still slammed into Zeke's back with enough force to send him stumbling forward. He pressed a hand against the wall and braced his legs, and barely kept himself from bumping into Mia.

The explosion passed. Zeke drew a breath. *Whew. Domi isn't fucking around.*

Mia glanced back. Her big brown eyes met his for a moment, only to glance down the next, shaded by heavy lashes. "Thanks."

Zeke nodded. "You think Domi did it?"

"I think she got close," Mia said, snorting.

"Yeah, that's a good point," Zeke allowed. *I still want to Devour the apocalypses, after all. It'd be better if she didn't kill them entirely.*

He ran back out into the road. Mia chased after him, right on his heels.

Domi stood in the midst of the smoking ruins of the electrical wires and pigeons. Blood painted the walls, burned black closer to Domi. Feathers floated down all around her, dancing on the updrafts from her explosion. Her body flickered, the plasma growing dark, then fading out entirely to reveal Domi beneath.

Drawing close, Zeke nudged a charred pigeon to the side. "Are they dead?"

"The pigeons? I'd say yeah, if I had to guess." Domi gestured at the blackened corpses around her, some of them little more than ash.

"The apocalypses," Zeke returned, rolling his eyes.

Domi shrugged. "Damned if I know."

The tangled wires overhead trembled. Pigeons once more accumulated on the wires.

Zeke gritted his teeth. "It's endless."

"We're just fighting the ends, we're not fighting the source," Mia muttered.

Shaking his head, Zeke sighed. "There're too many pigeons. We can't kill them all." *Not at this rate. We'd need to basically destroy the whole city, and...*

"Let's use our brains, then. You and Domi got Transformations. Most people get Domains. The pigeon and electrical lines... they seem at least level thirty, right? Who..." Mia paused. "*What* ever is leading them should have some defining characteristic. Either a Domain, or...something else."

"But what? That could be anything. The System gives Domains and Transformations, sure, but is that all? Remember the T-rex? It was followed by a bunch of smaller dinosaurs, or something. That wasn't a Domain or a Transformation," Zeke pointed out.

Domi looked overhead, arching her head back. "The proliferation of electrical wires and pigeons could be their Level 30 bonus itself, then, is what you're saying."

Zeke looked up.

Thousands of black wires crisscrossed down the road to the left and right. In places, they almost blacked out the sky. Pigeons lurked atop the wires, watching them with big dark eyes. Every wire was laden with pigeons. Bird poop crusted the road beneath the wires, drawing parallel lines of white-and-black splatter under the electric wires.

He grimaced. "Yep."

"But even so, the T-rex is much bigger than the other dinosaurs, right?" Mia said.

"Are you suggesting we're going to fight a giant pigeon?" Domi queried.

Mia spread her hands. "I mean...maybe?"

"Wait, hold on. Electric wires come from somewhere, right?" Zeke said.

Domi rolled her eyes. "Yeah, the power plant, which is way off outside the dome."

"No, no, the thing that's in the city...or near it. A-a-a, um, a substation! A substation. Isn't that probably the heart of the Electric Line Apocalypse?" Zeke suggested.

Domi and Mia exchanged a look. Mia shrugged. "It's worth a try."

"It does make a certain kind of sense," Domi admitted.

"So...does anyone know where the substation is?" Zeke asked, grimacing a little.

Fixing him with a look, Domi pulled out her phone.

"Oh. Right," Zeke muttered. *Mine got destroyed immediately by the Coffee Apocalypse. I keep forgetting everyone else has their phones.*

"Where does that go when you become plasma?" Mia asked.

"Where does anything go when I become plasma?" Domi returned carelessly.

Mia shrugged. "Fair."

Turning her phone around, Domi showed them a route on her map app. "There's a substation inside the dome! It's about two minutes, driving."

"Driving, what a great idea! Too bad someone blew up our motorcycle," Zeke said, shaking his head regretfully.

Domi grinned at him. "Good thing someone can make motorcycles on demand."

"Do you even know how much that costs me? How hard it is?" Zeke complained.

"Don't be stingy, come on." Domi gestured, spreading her arms at the ground as if to manifest a motorcycle.

"Do you want to waste all that food we gathered just now?" Zeke shook his head. "It isn't as easy as you think. Everything I do makes me hungry."

"Right, so what's the difference?"

"That's not what I—"

"Uh, guys," Mia said.

Zeke and Domi both turned.

She gestured at the cars parked haphazardly on the street all around them. "Just...pick one?"

Domi looked at Zeke. Zeke looked at Domi.

"Yeah, I guess." Domi sighed regretfully, shaking her head.

"If you're going to be so broken up about it, maybe don't blow up the motorcycle, next time," Zeke pointed out.

On his head, Allen dropped into a single pushup.

Domi raised her brows. "Maybe make a motorcycle with fuel in it next time, if you're gonna get snitty about it."

"Guys, guys. Come on. Let's go find a car." Mia waved her hand between the two of them, interrupting their gazes.

"Yeah, yeah." Domi turned away, heading toward the nearest car.

Zeke rolled his eyes at her back, then turned for a different car.

Shaking her head at Domi and Zeke, Mia wandered off for a car of her own.

It only took a few minutes to find a car with keys. Domi hopped behind the steering wheel, and they set off. Every now and again, Domi glanced at her phone, turning left and right. Under her breath, she grumbled to herself, "Fuck the one-way streets. I do what I like."

Zeke tensed, then shrugged internally. *Who else is driving right now, after all?*

As they drove, the electrical wires grew thicker overhead. The pigeons, too, massed, flapping in a dark whirl of gray feathers. Pigeon poop splattered over the hood of the car and dotted the windshield. Domi flipped on the windshield wipers to wipe the worst of it clean and leaned forward, squinting through the gaps. The electric wires grew thicker, twisting and twining together like vines in a jungle. Ahead, the wires became so thick the car could no longer fit through.

Domi put the car in park and looked at her passengers. She thumbed toward the door. "We walk from here."

"No kidding," Zeke agreed under his breath. He opened the door, only for the door to jam on the electric wires. Raising his leg, he kicked it the rest of the way open, then squeezed out.

Here, the electric wires were so snarled and tight that few birds sat inside it. They regarded the trio with blank gazes and pecked the ground, hopping off down the road.

Silence hung over the space. Aside from a low buzz that emanated from the wires, nothing made a sound. Even the pigeons moved silently, not even daring to ruffle their feathers. Behind them, the car quietly pinged and creaked as it cooled down, the only sound besides the dull hum. The scent of ozone and hot rubber mingled in the air, mixed with the dry-sweet smell of asphalt.

Zeke swallowed, his throat suddenly dry. The hairs on the back of his neck stood up, and his hands clenched subconsciously. *Something's watching me. I know it—*

*BAM!*

Zeke and Mia jumped, whirling toward the sound.

Domi stood there, one hand on her shut car door. Mia and Zeke both stared at her, eyes wide. She put her hands up. "Sorry, sorry..."

Mia gestured at the tight net of electric wires ahead of them. "Should we...I don't know, crawl through?"

"We could try exploding the car again," Zeke suggested.

"Again?" Mia asked, squinting at Zeke.

Zeke waved his hand. "Tell you later. They already know we're here. Might as well make a flashy entrance."

"Explode the car?" Domi chuckled. Opening the door again, she reached in and adjusted a lever. That done, she walked around to the back of the car. Rubbing her hands in anticipation, she flashed a devilish grin. "I've got an even better idea. Stand back and watch the master at work!"

Her eyes glowed orange. Waves of fiery force built up around her hands. As she rubbed her hands together, the waves grew larger and larger. Bright light lit the cavernous wire-knit space. Heat simmered around her, shuddering off the back of the car.

Zeke and Mia made eye contact. Without another word, they whirled and sprinted in the opposite direction.

# 83
## BLAST THROUGH!

Domi chuckled, her eyes burning with orange light. Waves of force, light, and pressure thudded against the wires around her as she built up more and more energy. The energy grew into a ball in front of her, growing larger and larger with each passing moment.

"You're good, Domi! Blast off whenever!" Zeke shouted, then ducked back around the corner. Dropping to the ground, he covered his ears and tensed, bracing for impact. Beside him, Mia did the same.

"Go!" Domi threw the ball, then sprinted away herself. The ball impacted the back of the car and stuck there. It hesitated a few moments, whirling in the air, pushing into the car.

Domi threw herself around the corner and hunkered next to Zeke. Covering one ear with her hand, she snapped with the other.

*BOOM!*

The explosion thudded in Zeke's chest. He slammed into the wall and bounced away. Heat washed over him, as if he'd opened a preheated oven on a summer's day, but a thousand times more intense. He raised his hands to protect his face as his hair crisped. Ash washed over him.

Around the corner, the ball ignited. All at once, it blasted off, propelling the car forward with incredible force. The car smashed into the wires going well over a hundred miles an hour and broke through effortlessly. Wires snapped all around it, breaking away like paper. Bits of wire and rubber shrapnel flew. Still the car tunneled deeper. Deeper and deeper until, with a heavy *thud*, it smashed into a wooden pole and wrapped itself around it, full of force but unable to break any further.

The three of them peeked around the corner. A deep tunnel carved through the wires, but more wires blocked the way ahead. Mia pursed her lips. Zeke sighed.

Domi scowled. "Who put that damn pole there? Come on. That's ridiculous."

The pole creaked. Wood cracked, then snapped. It toppled backward, slowly, taking the wires with it. One at a time, they broke off, and with each broken wire, the pole fell farther. The last wires burst free. The pole fell, smashing into a chain-link fence, and bore the fence to the ground.

Beyond it, the substation awaited them, all matte stainless steel, coils, wires, and crackling electricity. Black wires blocked out the sky over the substation, so thick as to become a wall of rubber. They knitted together into a miniature copy of the dome that coated the city, protecting the substation from any attacks from above.

In the heart of the substation, a hugely bloated pigeon at least as tall as Zeke and equally wide sat atop an enormous nest full of regular-sized pigeon eggs. Feeling their eyes on them, the pigeon cooed, big eyes even wider than usual. One of the eggs beneath it trembled, then cracked. A baby pigeon broke its way free. It wobbled out, wet and weak.

"The miracle of life," Mia said, tilting her head adorably.

In the space of a few seconds, the pigeon grew from a tiny baby to a fledgling, from a fledgling to an adult. Shaking its wings, it let out a ferocious war coo and leaped from the nest.

Behind it, all the other eggs began trembling. Cracks darted through their shells.

Zeke licked his lips. "That isn't good."

"No kidding." Domi snorted.

"But, hey, focus on the positive! We found the apocalypses!" Mia said, beaming.

"No denying that," Domi agreed.

Zeke stepped out from behind the corner. *System? What's the timeout?*

**Time until Transform:** 0:15.

He nodded. "My transform's nearly up again. Domi?"

"Yeah, I'm good to go," Domi said, nodding.

"I'm ready whenever you are," Mia said.

Zeke stepped forward. "Let's go."

The three of them charged forward, into the substation.

Broken wires thrashed at the air, whipping at them. Domi jumped forward and grabbed them bare-handed. Electricity coursed into her, lighting her skin from the inside out. Rather than a grimace of pain, though, she grinned. The white-blue energy condensed into a ball that hovered over her chest, growing larger with each moment.

The wires struggled, twisting and fighting to escape. She pulled, yanking them out of their bindings instead. Explosions burst out along the cables' lengths. They struggled, but weakly. Domi pulled again, harder. They plopped to the ground like dead snakes, still kicking in their death throes.

The orb of blue-white energy glowed bright on Domi's chest, about the size of a cantaloupe. It whirled, throbbing with power. Running a few steps ahead of the others, Domi spread her arms wide, then clapped. The white-blue energy coursed down her arms and flew forth in a bright beam. The beam slammed into the heart of the substation, then exploded. White-blue electricity arced through the air.

Bits of metal flew. Machines broke apart. A cloud of smoke welled up. From within the cloud, the giant pigeon cooed in fear, flapping its wings, yet unable to shift its enormous body.

Zeke and Mia stumbled back, raising their hands against the blast. Domi spread her arms wide and soaked it in, laughing aloud.

"Did that do it?" Zeke wondered aloud. *Too bad. I wanted to Devour them.*

Slowly, the smoke cleared, blowing away on a faint breeze that wriggled through the wires.. A shimmering barrier of electricity hummed in the air, protecting one of the transformers inside the substation along with the giant pigeon and its overlarge nest.

"It gives itself away," Domi chuckled darkly.

"Then it's time for us to take it down." Mia raised a hand. The translucent gold armor and sword appeared once more. She charged forward, hurtling toward the barrier.

Wires shot at her, striking like vipers. Jumping up beside her, Zeke snatched them out of the air before they could bite. The electricity crackled over him instead, burning black marks in his flesh.

**[Tough Body] +6**
**[Tough Body] +7**
**[Tough Body] +8**

Domi ran up alongside him, protecting Mia from the wires

on the other side. Explosions blasted them back. The wires thrashed as if in frustration.

Pigeons hurtled toward them. Zeke surged ahead. Claws emerged from his fingertips. "Leave this to me!"

## [Claw Fighter]

Blood and feathers danced down. Pigeon bodies vanished down Zeke's gullet one after another. A few hit the ground, thumping in little puffs of dust and pigeon dander.

Together, they raced toward the barrier. Electricity crackled around the barrier, dancing in white bolts that grounded themselves on the other machines and burst the bits of metal shrapnel away from the central transformer.

Wires as thick as Zeke's calves reared up around the barrier. Hissing and dancing, they struck the air, inviting them to try. Hundreds of smaller wires wriggled on the ground, racing toward Zeke and the others.

Freshly born pigeons flew from the nest, growing even as they flew. A vicious light glittered in those dark eyes, their claws as sharp as daggers.

"Here we go!" Gritting his teeth, Zeke led the charge.

# 84
## DEATH OF AN ALLIANCE

The thick wires thrashed. The little ones writhed on the floor. Pigeons flapped through the air, charging at them.

Zeke slammed his hand down on the **Transform** button. Between one step and the next, his body warped. Black armor wrapped his body. Tendrils exploded from his shoulder blades. The helm clanged down over his head. Black claws curled from his fingers and toes, permanently out unlike his usual white retractable claws. His limbs elongated, and his body grew slender, the bulge of his stomach from the pigeons he'd eaten instantly vanishing. Mouths opened at his hands and feet, and the mouth on his face grew wider, opening to his jaw joint.

Opposite him, Domi lit alight, transforming from flesh to orange glowing plasma. She ran for the transformer, while Zeke hurtled to meet the pigeons.

**[Caffeine Rush] [Roll With Us]**

Both of them sped up under Zeke's buffs, Zeke speeding further ahead than Domi under the power of both buffs at once.

Mia followed close behind, letting out an excited yelp as Roll With Us lent power to her limbs.

From out of the tangled wires that lined their path, strange forms lunged. Flesh singed black, their eyes blind, bones poking out of the ends of their burned hands, the remains of people intercepted them. They clawed at the trio mindlessly, reaching out with sooty, bony hands to tear them down. Their bodies cracked and crumbled as they moved. Barely holding together, they nonetheless stumbled forth to stop Zeke, Domi, and Mia.

"What—" Mia stepped back, startled.

"They're already dead!" Zeke snapped. Grabbing the closest one, he opened his mouth and chomped on its whole head. It fell apart like charcoal in his mouth, dry and bitter, instantly sucking every drop of moisture from his mouth. He turned and spat, grimacing. *Yuck. No one wants a mouthful of charcoal.* "Compared to the Cartoon Apocalypse or the Stadium Apocalypse—"

"I know, but still..." Mia murmured. She stepped forward, cutting one of the charcoal figures down. Ash crumbled beneath her blade, the shining sword slicing cleanly through the bone. As the figure struck the ground, she ducked a little, apologetically.

Zeke kicked a few aside, watching them fall to pieces under the force. They fell silently, unable to even scream. "They're... There's not much left of them. Better to put them out of their misery."

Mia grunted but didn't say anything.

"I think the pigeon just ate all the people it encountered," Domi said, breaking the silence. She pointed at the nest ahead of them.

Lifting his head as he kicked another one of the charred people back, Zeke squinted. *Is she talking about those rocks under the—*

*Oh. Oh, those are bones.*

Bleached bones littered the ground beneath the pigeon's nest. Some were stained with speckles from the pigeons' poop, while scraps of blood and viscera still clung to others. Others laid clean, picked to the last scrap of flesh by hungry pigeons. Beak marks cut into the bones where pigeons had gnawed on them, searching for any sustenance.

*Man-eating pigeons. Is this what the world's come to?*

Pigeons and charcoal people charged at them. Zeke fought them back hand and foot, chomping at everything that came close. Rubber and ash mixed on his tongues, mingling with the acid-salt flavor of pigeon blood. He pushed slowly toward the nest while Domi charged the barrier, smashing into it bodily. Mia ran the middle line, fighting away any pigeons that went for Domi or charcoal figures and wires that went for Zeke.

Electricity crackled over Domi's orange skin. She dug her hands into the crackling barrier. Her hand burrowed through. Eyes widening, Domi grinned. A ball of orange flame flickered in her palm, growing and growing as the glow of her body faded. She jerked her hand back, leaving the ball of energy behind.

"Mia, get back," Domi called.

"Got it!" Mia shouted. She fell back. With a flourish of her hand, the sword turned into a tower shield. She thumped it down and crouched behind it.

"Uh, what about me?" Zeke asked, concerned.

Domi snapped her fingers.

An explosion roared out. Zeke raised his arms as bits of red-hot shrapnel pierced past him. A particularly fast piece clipped his helm and knocked out a piece of his visor. He stumbled back, putting a hand to his forehead. "Ow!"

Atop the nest, the fat pigeon's eyes gleamed. It leaped out of the nest, revealing strangely powerful long chicken legs, and charged Zeke.

Zeke stood upright, grinning at the pigeon. "Fooled you."

The pigeon backpedaled. Its chicken claws skittered over the bones, which rolled under its feet, providing little traction.

*Why don't I speed that up a little?* Zeke pointed at the bones.

### [Manipulate Aerosols]

Mist coated the bones, slicking them. The giant pigeon lost traction on the slippery bones and fell backward with an ugly squawk. Zeke darted in. The pigeon swung at him with its powerful wings. He caught them with his hands. His hands flew backward, almost entirely thrown away. Zeke stumbled back. *Wow! It's strong!*

*But edible.*

His feet dug into the ground, foot-mouths taking big bites of the dirt underfoot for extra traction. Ignoring the flavor of filthy dirt, Zeke raced in again. The pigeon swung its massive wings at him. This time, he ducked them, speeding past toward its chest instead.

With a startled coo, the pigeon struggled, flapping its wings to get back to its feet, but its massive weight worked against it. Aside from plopping out another half-dozen eggs, it did nothing but flail on the ground.

### [Devour]

Eggs crushed underfoot. Zeke's jaws closed around its throat. He tore. Bright scarlet blood spilled over the ground. The pigeon beat at his back with his wings and clawed with its feet, but its blows skittered off his armor. Big eyes stared into his in panic. Its chest heaved, gasping for breath that wouldn't come.

"Sorry, but this could only end one way," Zeke said. He wiped the blood off his mouth and smiled, his bared teeth still stained crimson. "Winner, winner, chicken dinner."

All around him, the remaining pigeons shook their heads. They blinked around. Those in the sky dropped for a few seconds before realizing they were flying, and belatedly flapping their wings again. One of the pigeons crash-landed in a puff of dust, then paused and looked around, innocently blinking at Zeke as it clambered back upright.

**Defeated:** Pigeon Apocalypse!
**Remaining:** Electric Line Apocalypse

"Zeke!" Mia shouted.

Zeke whirled.

Thousands of slender wires burst out of the transformer box, ensnaring Domi. Domi flared bright, burning them away, but more grew from the box the next moment. Mia whirled, slashing the wires away, but too slow. The thin wires drew Domi ever closer to the box. Uncontrollable energy crackled from the box, so bright it hurt to look at. Lightning bolts shot from the box and grounded on the earth all around Domi and Mia, crackling with miniature thunder every time they struck.

Domi grimaced in pain. She pulled back, only for the wires to pull her closer. The wires pulled at her body. Her plasma body flickered, darkening one moment, only to brighten the next. The wires in direct contact with her melted as she burned bright, but as she darkened, they latched on again. "Zeke...Mia... someone!"

Zeke gritted his teeth. *I can't stop now!* He charged toward Domi, baring his claws.

# 85
## BOYS AND BOXES

The electric wires pulled Domi slowly closer. Bits of molten wire and rubber fell to the ground around her as she flashed brightly, and she backed up half a step, but the rest of the wires were there a moment later to reel her back in as her body darkened.

"It's draining my power!" she shouted.

"Turn back, turn back!" Zeke called, closing in.

"She can't! They'll cut her to pieces!" Mia said, holding up her arm. Fresh blood rolled from a deep gash on her mid-forearm to past her wrist, thick and dark.

*Dammit, that's no good!*

Zeke reached the box. Without hesitating, he slashed at the wires with his claws.

His hand bounced off. All bunched together, the wires proved stronger than any one single wire, too strong for him to cut through even transformed.

On the other side, Mia dueled the leg-thick cables. She darted forward and slashed one down, only to fall back as two more surged in, attempting a pincer maneuver. A third one snaked low for Domi's ankles, but Mia jumped in, sweeping her sword, and sliced it back. "This stupid...thing!"

Zeke stepped back, taking in the whole situation. *The box is trying to devour Domi. It's using the thick cables to keep Mia back, and the thin wires on their own. I can't cut them all at once. I can chew through it, surely, but it might be too late. I need a weak point.*

His eyes traveled downward. Below the box, a sturdy metal post vanished into the ground, wires rapped around it, almost growing into it.

*Not very weak-looking, but I'll take it.* Zeke dropped to the ground and bit at it. With all his strength, he gnawed away at the wires and post.

Electricity sparked in his mouth, tingling in his jaw and teeth. His tongue numbed immediately. He lifted his hands. They split apart to chew the wires. Yet again, rubber and metallic copper filled his mouths.

*After this, I'm treating myself to something that tastes good. Even if it's useless to feed me, I'm still eating it!*

A cable snapped. One of the thick cables dueling Mia flopped to the ground, lifeless, and a handful of the wires entangling Domi went dead.

*It's working!* Zeke kept gnawing, focusing on the next wire.

The thick wires turned about and flew at Zeke instead of Domi. With a yelp, Mia chased them. One closed in on Zeke, hurtling toward his face.

Zeke braced for impact. *This is going to hurt—!*

Mia threw her sword. It impaled the cable, piercing it into the ground beside Zeke. The cable twitched, fighting against the impalement. Mia stomped it down. Rubber and metal burst under her foot as the cable evaporated.

Zeke stared. He looked slowly up at Mia.

Mia grinned. "Hero's Stomp. Cool, right?"

Atop Zeke's head, Allen did a pushup in admiration, extending his dewlap and all.

*That's right. I almost forgot!* "Allen! Lend me your strength!"

**[Subordinate Link]**
**Subordinate Allen has shared his STR.**
**STR:** 7 > 22
**[Subordinate Link] (Weak) > [Subordinate Link] (Weak) +1**
**[Tough Body]**

Instantly, Zeke's strength surged. His jaws clamped tighter. The wires shredded beneath his teeth. The metal pole resisted his bite, but only for a moment. Zeke put his molars on it and clenched, squeezing shut with all his might. The metal cracked, then shattered.

The box toppled backward, away from Domi. She pulled free of the wires. They grasped at the air instead, thrashing madly. Even as Zeke watched, their thrashing slowed.

*Before it dies—* Zeke charged after it. He thrust his arm into the thin wires, reaching, searching. *Come on. Where's the core?*

A smooth orb met his fingertips. Zeke gripped it and pulled, yanking the orb free. The box stilled completely the second the orb separated from it. Formed from thin wires, it undulated gently, beating almost like a heart. Electricity flickered over it. Without hesitating, Zeke **[Devour]**ed the orb.

**Congratulations! You've defeated the Electric Line**
**Apocalypse.**
**Congratulations! You've vanquished the Pigeon-Line**
**Alliance.**

Zeke stood. He dismissed his transformation. "All right! That should get us ready for the battle."

"I hope," Mia said, nodding.

"Let's see those levels!" Domi cheered, dismissing her own transformation.

**Level + 6.50**
**Level:** 37.59 > 44.09
**Regeneration + 300**
**Regeneration rate:** 307.4%


**Please assign your stat points.**
**Please choose your skills.**


**Pigeon Apocalypse**
**Giant (Condition) (Lesser)**
**Progeny (Average)**
**Rapid Egg Laying (Average)**
**Resilience (Average)**
**Steel Stomach (Strong)**
**Can't**
**Can't**


**Shared Vision (Average)**
*Share vision amongst yourself and all of your subordinates.*


**Nest (Lesser)**
*Create a shelter wherever you land.*

Zeke scanned the list, blanching at the mention of egg laying. *That one could have been a 'Can't,' System. Men can't lay eggs.*

**Neither can human women. However, body modification is allowed.**

*Yeah, I don't think I'm going for that particular modification,* Zeke thought, shuddering. *Rather than body modification, that's pure body horror.*

**Electric Line Apocalypse**
**Manipulate Wire (Medium)**
**Electrify (Medium)**
**Can't**
**Absorb (Medium)**

**Cutting Edge (Lesser)**
*Put a sharp edge on any metal object.*

**Can't**

**Grid (Medium)**
*Connect to a greater source of power and transfer its power through yourself.*

**Conduct (Medium)**
*Easily move power through yourself without harming yourself.*

Looking over the lists again, Zeke put a hand on his chin. *I'm not really that excited about any of these skills. I already picked up a few levels in Resilient Regeneration from the pigeons, so it's not like I need to much more of that and, er, most of the pigeon's skills are kind of questionable. Of the skills...I guess Resilience, Shared Vision, and Nest make the most sense?*

**Gained [Resilient Regeneration] (Average) > [Resilient Regeneration] (Average) +9, [Shared Vision] (Average), [Nest] (Lesser).**

*As for the Electric Line Apocalypse...well, these skills are a little more interesting. Manipulate Wire could be incredibly useful in an urban environment, though it is kind of useless in the wilderness. Electrify...it's a good combo with Manipulate Wire, plus, so long as I have a metal weapon, it's going to be overpowered. Cutting Edge is the third piece of the Manipulate Wire combo, but of the three, it's the one I could ignore the most.*

*Wire-fighting combo aside, there's Absorb, Grid, and Conduct. If I'm going to use Electrify, I should probably take a skill that keeps electricity from hurting me. Absorb would probably combine well with Osmosis, though that's a skill I've never used. Grid...kind of sounds like a more powerful version of Absorb? And, honestly, same with Conduct. It sounds like a weaker form of Grid.*

*There're probably subtle differences in usage between the three. I could imagine Absorb probably allows me to store power, while Conduct might allow me to pass any sort of power through myself, not just 'power from a greater source.' But then, it's not as if I'm an electric substation. I'm a human. Almost any power I run into will qualify as 'power from a greater source.'*

*Hmm...so I think the pick here is Manipulate Wire, Electrify, and Grid.*

**Gained [Manipulate Wire] (Medium), [Electrify] (Medium), [Grid] (Medium).**

*As for skill points...I got, what, six levels? Let's do this:*

**STR:** 7 > 8
**DEX:** 5 > 8
**SPR:** 10 > 12

*I'd like to keep pumping my SPR and ignore the rest of my stats, but given the battle we're about to undertake, I'm going to need strength and dexterity to survive. Still, I don't want to neglect my good stats in order to fix up my weak points, so let's not completely ignore SPR.*

*Which leaves my stats looking like this:*

**Level:** 44.09
**STR:** 8
**CON:** 10
**DEX:** 8
**SPR:** 12
**Regeneration rate:** +7.4%

**Skills**
**Manipulate Aerosols (Strong) +6**
**Pick Up (Weak)**
**Osmosis (Weak) +1**
**Subordinate Link (Weak) +1**
**Create Drug (Weak) +1**
**Crystal Burst (Poor) +2**
**Engulf (Poor)**
**Create Coffee (Strong)**
**Whistle Blast (Weak)Digital Broadcast (Weak) +1**
**Electric Leap (Poor)**
**Modest Gigantification (Medium) +2Nest**
**(Lesser)Manipulate Wire (Medium)**
**Electrify (Medium)Grid (Medium)**
**Regression (Lesser)**

**Passive**
**Resilient Regeneration (Average) +9**
**Disguise (Minor)**
**Watertight (Minor)**

**Caffeine Rush (Average)**
**Heat Resistance (Lesser) +9**
**Flexible Body (Average)**
**Roll With Us (Lesser)**
**Hunger Awareness (Lesser) +2**
**Claw Fighter (Lesser) +3**
**Perfect Landing (Lesser)**
**Tough Body (Lesser) +8 Audience (Minor) Shared Vision (Average)**

**Condition**
**Hardness (Lesser) (Condition)**
**Claws (Large) (Condition) +1**
**Wings (Tiny) (Condition) +2**
**MOTORCYCLE**
**Lvl 0:** Devour
**Lvl 30:** Absorb

**Transform:** Substantial boost to all stats. Armor + 500%. Gained skills: Extra Mouths, Extra Limbs, Multi-Devour, Hunger (Condition).

Zeke took a deep breath. He ran his hair back. *Damn, that's a lot of skills. I really need to sit down and go through them, take some time to really fuse them down to something manageable. Even if I lose a few skills, at this point, it's a sacrifice I have to make just to keep my skills to a sane level.*

He nodded at the others. "You guys all leveled?"

Domi gave him a thumbs-up.

"I hit level thirty!" Mia said, excited.

"Don't pick Domain!" Zeke snapped quickly.

Mia blinked. "Domain? I didn't get a choice for anything like that."

*Oh, right. She's a Hero.* Zeke waved his hand. "Right, right. Ignore me."

"So...are we ready for tonight?" Domi asked.

Zeke took a deep breath. He made eye contact with Mia.

Mia looked back into his eyes. She nodded slowly.

"Let's do this," Zeke said, slapping his fist into his palm.

# 86

## THE PLAN

Back at the stadium, the three of them stood in the middle of the field. All the people they'd rescued stood before them, some confused, some chattering, a few yawning from boredom. As the last few stragglers picked their way down the stadium seating to the field, Zeke licked his lips and clenched his fists. He looked at Mia.

Mia nodded at him. Quietly, she murmured, "You've got this."

"And if you don't, we're right here to pick up the slack," Domi said, laughing.

"Why aren't you the one taking point? Ms. Tour Guide," Zeke asked, looking at her.

Domi spread her hands. "It's your plan. I can't sell it as well as you can."

"Isn't it Mia's plan?" Zeke asked.

"It's *our* plan," Mia said, nodding.

Zeke crossed his arms and squinted at her. "You just don't want to lead the public speaking."

"You've seen through my devious plan!" Mia gasped, putting her hands over her mouth.

Zeke pursed his lips at her, then turned. What seemed like a hundred eyes gazed at him, though there were only a few dozen people on the field. Adults, children, elderly, men, and women, all of them gazed at him.

He took a deep breath. His eyes shut.

*Here goes.*

"Um, hi," Zeke started.

He closed his eyes again, barely resisting the urge to put his palm on his face. *Oh, come on. "Um, hi?" What an opener! Am I ten years old, giving my first presentation?*

*Reset, reset.*

He opened his eyes.

The people gazed up at him, confused, waiting. The old man and the middle-aged woman from earlier scowled at him while the girl smiled expectantly.

*They want to hear what I have to say. So, let's say it.*

"I'm sure you've all noticed that the world's gone nuts. It's an apocalypse. It's...the end of the world. You saw me and Domi on the field last night...you were all subordinated by the Stadium Apocalypse. If you remember, we took that bird down together."

Zeke looked up, meeting their eyes. For a second, the words vanished from his mind. Everything went blank. The world vanished.

*Focus. Beyond them. Keep going.*

His eyes latched onto a point beyond all their heads, so he gazed at them without actually meeting anyone's eyes. His words returned. He caught his breath.

"There's only one way out of this." He pointed up at the black dome. "One of us has to win. Or...one team. Me, Domi, Mia..." *and Allen,* he added silently.

"Resources are not infinite. It's dangerous to go out and find more. Out there, the apocalypses...you ordinary people are nothing but levels to them. Nothing but a buff, a quick bite to make them even stronger."

"You're talking nonsense!" the middle-aged woman shouted.

The old man harrumphed. "Even if all that madness is true, so what? We'll stay here and wait them out."

Zeke nodded. "We could hunker here. We could batten down the hatches and try to survive while the other apocalypses grow stronger and stronger, while we slowly run out of resources. Eventually, one of them will break in, and then what? Then we're fighting on their terms. Then we're at the mercy of their timing.

"They can wait. They can wait, while we grow weaker and weaker, while our food runs down. They can attack at night, while we're sleeping. There's only three of us. We can't keep watch forever. And even if the three of us go out, we're on their home turf, where they have the homefield advantage. We're constantly on our back foot, constantly struggling to keep up.

"Or..."

Zeke took another deep breath. He lowered his eyes, meeting the crowds' gaze. "Or we set the time."

The girl frowned. "What does that mean?"

"We let them know. Tell everyone you're here. Broadcast it across the entire city. The other apocalypses...to them, you guys are...like drugs. Steroids. There's no way they can resist. They come, they *all* come, because only one apocalypse can cash in. The first one to get here, the first one to fight us off, will have the prize: you."

The crowd glanced at one another. A few of them shook their heads. One or two backed away, eyes wide, terrified.

Zeke stepped forward. "But we won't let that happen. We'll defend you. Because we're the ones in control. This way, we set the time. We set the place. They fight on our home turf, not theirs. We'll keep you safe, and destroy all the other apocalypses, and we'll all get out of this together."

Murmurs. A few of the crowd members glanced at one another.

"So, we're bait," the middle-aged woman said.

Zeke nodded. "I'm not going to lie. Yes. You are bait."

"But if you beat all of them, we survive, the dome goes away, and we all go home? This is over?" she asked.

Zeke nodded again. "Yes. This nightmare comes to an end."

"Why you? You looked like monsters to me. Same as that bird thing!" the old man challenged them.

"We don't want to destroy the world. The others...they're called Apocalypses for a reason. If they win, that's it. That's it, for the whole world. W- we're like you guys. We just want to go home. Go to school, go to work. Play video games. Get back to our ordinary lives," Zeke said, spreading his hands.

The old man squinted. "How can we trust you?"

Zeke spread his hands. "We haven't killed you. We haven't subordinated you. If you want to leave, then you can leave right now. I won't stop you. None of us will."

"Right. If anyone doesn't want to be used as bait, if you'd rather try your hand at surviving on your own, go ahead and leave," Domi said, stepping up beside Zeke. She made intense eye contact with the old man and the middle-aged woman. "We won't stop you. But the second you leave this stadium, you leave our protection. That's it. You're on your own."

"And...outside...almost everyone is dead," Mia said softly. She looked up, meeting the crowd's eyes. "So few people are alive. This...this is the largest group of living people remaining, who haven't been corrupted or subordinated past saving."

The middle-aged woman crossed her arms. "So, our options are stay and be used as bait or leave and die?"

"Stay and be protected," Zeke adjusted, nodding.

"Protected, but used as bait," she pointed out.

"Yes," Zeke said.

She harrumphed. "Just so everyone knows! This is ridiculous."

"It is. This whole situation is ridiculous. But we want to end it. We want to end this and go back to our ordinary lives. If you want to help...stay and help, then...then we will protect you to the end," Zeke pledged.

The girl raised her hand. Zeke pointed at her.

"Hi! Hello. Uhm, will we be here? What if you...like, hid us somewhere else and just *said* we were here?"

Mia nodded at Zeke, moving to the front. "There's only three of us. We can't spare someone to protect you elsewhere. You would potentially be in more danger if you were hidden somewhere else."

"Only if they find us," the girl argued.

Mia shook her head. "There are skills. Skills to locate people. Smell them, sense them...display them on a mini-map. If we try to hide you away, they'll find you. It's safest to keep you here, exactly where we say you are. That way we can protect you openly. If we try to hide you, one of the apocalypses will find you, and all it takes is one apocalypse to kill all of you...or worse."

"Worse?" the girl asked.

"Worse," Zeke confirmed.

Silence fell, but only for a moment. The crowd began to talk. Some people argued back and forth. One or two shouted at the three of them, standing on their tiptoes to catch their attention. The sound grew louder and louder, swelling to fill the stadium.

Intimidated, Zeke took a step back. *How can I answer all these questions? I don't even know where to start.*

Domi strode out in front of Mia and Zeke, clapping her hands for attention. "All right, everyone, ladies and gentlemen and everything in between. If you want to stay, head on back up into the boxes. We'll send out the notice bright and early in the morning. If you want to leave, you have until dawn. At dawn, we send out the notice, and all the apocalypses will close in on us. If you aren't staying, remember, we aren't protecting you, so you'll want to be far, far away when the sun rises. Thank you, thank you, and please have a nice day."

With that, she nodded at Zeke and Mia. Quietly, in her inside voice, she said, "Let's leave them to it."

"Shouldn't we stay? Answer questions?" Mia asked.

"What questions can we answer in a way that will satisfy anyone here? We've said our part. If we hang around, we'll get abused, but we won't help. Now is the time to abscond and let them make up their own minds." With a nod, she headed toward the box.

Mia and Zeke shared a long look. Zeke opened his mouth. "Mia..." *If I don't say it now, when will I?*

"I-I don't know either. But I think Domi has the right idea. I'll see you in the morning? We need to get to sleep now if we're going to send the message at dawn." Mia smiled, absolutely exhausted.

Zeke shut his mouth. *It's not the time.* He nodded. "I'll see you in the morning."

The two of them parted, leaving the crowd on the stadium field.

# 87

## THOSE WHO REMAIN

Zeke awoke with a start. He blinked, bleary-eyed, around the dark room. *That beeping, who—*

He looked down. His wristwatch beeped insistently.

Sighing, Zeke turned off the alarm. He lay there in the chair for another few seconds, exhausted still. The chill dark of pre-dawn hung close around him, the heat of his own body in the chair's fabric barely warding it off.

*Up and at 'em.*

He shoved himself to his feet and stretched, looking around, then headed for the door. Climbing up to the top of the box, he found Mia there waiting for him, staring out into the horizon. Not even the smallest glimmer of light shone on the ground, the light as dark as the dome itself.

She glanced over her shoulder, then patted the ground beside her. Zeke walked over and sat, staring out at the dome with her.

Zeke sat there in silence. He put his hands in his lap, stealing a glance at Mia. Her chestnut hair ruffled with sleep, her clothes rumpled from wear, she still looked beautiful. He smiled quietly.

*If I had to be here with anyone, at least I'm here with Mia.*

"It's crazy," she whispered.

"Yeah?" Zeke asked, a little too quickly.

Mia looked at him. She lowered her head. "A few days ago, we were going to school. Now..." Turning, she looked at her hands. She closed them, curling her fingers over pale palms. "We hold the fate of dozens of people in our hands."

"More than that. If we don't win, that's the world, right? I mean, aside from us, they aren't going to stop at conquering the city. World's next." Zeke shrugged.

They sat in silence for a few beats. Mia clenched her hands tighter, knuckles white in the dim light.

Zeke sighed. "Not that it matters too much. We'll be dead." *I have Regression. If I have the chance, and it's hopeless, I—*

*I shouldn't. I'm just becoming Ryan.*

*But if the other option is to die, then...*

Mia looked at him. "You're not helping."

Zeke spread his hands. "I'm doing my best."

More silence. A cool breeze blew. In the distance, the first rays of light glowed at the edges of the tall buildings.

"Yooooo," Domi said slowly.

Both of them turned.

Half-ducking, she gave them an awkward salute. "Wasn't going to interrupt you, but it looks like that moment's over?"

"Moment?" Mia asked, frowning.

Zeke winced. *It was only me, huh?* Hiding his pain, he stood. "Let's go see who's left."

They walked down onto the field, where they could see both of the boxes from one place. About half the people remained. At the sight of the trio, they headed down onto the field.

Watching the crowd gather, Zeke scanned them for the troublemakers. The girl waved at him. In the back of the group, the old man scowled. The middle-aged lady was nowhere in sight.

*Guess we couldn't please everyone.*

Domi waved at the group. "If you'll follow me, we're headed into the home lockers. Buried under a tunnel of steel and concrete, they're as safe as you're going to get around here. Right this way, right this way."

Zeke nodded and smiled as Domi led them away. In a few moments, he and Mia stood alone on the field.

Mia clapped her hands together. She sighed. "It's kind of spooky. All alone on the field this early in the morning."

"Yeah, I know," Zeke agreed. He looked at her. "It'll all be over soon."

"One way or another." Mia's hands tightened nervously on her shirt.

Zeke reached out, hesitated, then put a hand on her shoulder. "We'll be okay. We can do this."

She gave him a nervous smile. "Wish I had that confidence."

"I mean, it's not my confidence. Ryan's the one who's confident I can destroy the whole world." Zeke grinned at her.

Mia snorted. She shook her head. "I guess you have a point."

"Hey, you guys flirting again?" Domi asked, jogging out of the locker room.

Zeke stepped away from Mia quickly, dropping his hand. "No."

"Flirting?" Mia squinted at Domi.

*Ouch, my heart.* Zeke pressed his lips together in something half a smile, half a grimace. He waved his hand. "Let's get back to the box. I should go ahead and send out that notice, but I don't want to get ambushed on the field."

The three of them wandered back up to the box. The

motions now familiar, Zeke grabbed the ladder and climbed up onto the top of the box.

At the top of the box, Mia tilted her head at him. "So...how are you going to do that? Send the message, I mean. You said you could, but..."

Zeke winked. "Watch and learn." For the first time, he activated the skill.

### [Digital Broadcast]

In his head, a message box appeared, along with a few simple formatting options. Zeke almost laughed aloud. *Really? It looks like a forum message box from a forum made at the dawn of the internet.*

*Well, what did I expect? Full in-depth graphic controls? The ability to attach images?* Holding out his hands, Zeke began to type.

Across the city, screens flickered to life. Words appeared, scrolling across the screens one letter at a time.

**T**
**Th**
**Thr**

Zeke quickly backspaced.

**The**

"Type faster," Domi muttered under her breath, watching the words form on her phone.

"Shut up. I can't see the keyboard," Zeke grumbled. *I can touch-type, but being completely blind from the keyboard is rough. I'm lucky I hit the T the first time!*

Ever so slowly, the words appeared.

**The last living people in the city are gathered in the Robins' Stadium.**
**Come and get them if you want them.**
**Let's end this. All of us.**

Domi put her phone away. "All right! Could be a little less wordy, but it gets the point across. Let's finish this battle royale with a bang."

"If you're so good at it, you write the dang message," Zeke complained. His stomach grumbled.

Domi tossed him a can of soda. Zeke caught it, the cool bottle slick with perspiration. "Drink it up. Let's all be topped up. Today's gonna be a long one."

"That's right. What do you guys need to do? To be at the top of your game," Zeke asked, looking at them. *Like how I have to eat all the time...do they have that kind of thing, too?*

Mia squinted at him. "I-I just have to rest?"

Domi frowned. "We didn't all pick dumbass Concepts like Hunger, you know."

Zeke gritted his teeth, sucking a breath between them. *Right...yeah. Fair.*

Cracking the can with a pop and fizz, he downed it, chugging the whole thing down all at once. Zeke tossed the can away and burped, loud enough to echo in the stadium. "Let's go."

"Gross," Mia grumbled.

"Litterer," Domi added on, grinning mischievously.

"Can't win with you guys." Zeke rolled his eyes, shaking his head.

The sun rose. Sunlight spilled over the building, illuminating them brighter and brighter. The city lay still, utterly empty, almost beautiful in its stillness.

"Soooo...who do you think is going to show up first?" Domi asked.

"Cat Man," Mia said, without hesitation.

"Really? I think he's one to hole up and try to wait it out with that Nine Lives skill of his," Domi commented.

"It could make him even more brash on the other hand," Zeke offered in Mia's defense. He shrugged. "I think it's gonna be the T-rex."

"Dinosaurs can't read," Domi countered.

Zeke turned and looked at her. He crossed his arms. "All right, then, who do you think it's going to be?"

She lifted her hand and pointed across the stadium at the top of the enormous light fixtures. "Who else?"

Following her finger, Zeke blinked, then stared. "Ryan?"

Ryan perched at the top of the lights, crouching down in the wire box behind the bulbs themselves. Their eyes met, and Ryan vanished.

"He's coming!" Zeke shouted.

Domi backed away. Mia drew her arm back, as if to call a sword to hand. Zeke extended his claws. Staring expectantly toward the lights, they waited.

Ryan's voice came from behind them. "You're all insane."

The three of them whirled. Ryan stood at the opposite end of the box, up against the edge. His dagger glimmered in one hand. He shifted slightly, revealing a second, uninjured arm.

*Ha. He could grow it back. Knew it.*

*It's a good lesson to remember. If I don't finish an enemy, I can expect them to come back fully healed and raring for revenge.*

"What do you want?" Zeke asked. He eyed the transform button, ready to activate it at any moment.

Ryan looked at the dagger. He tossed it up, caught it out of the air, and threw it.

"Watch out!" Mia shoved Zeke back. A gold shield materialized on her arm.

The dagger cut into the surface of the roof at Mia's feet. Ryan put his hands up. "I'm not here to fight. I'm here to help."

Zeke eyed him, suspicious. *I'd love if that was true, but...he was hellbent on murdering me the last hundred times we saw one another.* "You've decided?"

Ryan shrugged. "If I'm going to see this out, I might as well give you the best chance possible."

"Really? You're not going to kill me anymore?" Zeke asked.

Pursing his lips, Ryan gave him a look. "Can I?"

*I do have Regression as well. If he tries... even if I don't have Dead Man's Switch, I still have a chance to pop Regression before he kills me and end up in exactly the scenario Ryan wants to avoid: me, back in time, with even more of an advantage than he thinks I already have.* Zeke spread his hands. "Fair enough."

Mia relaxed, dismissing her shield. Domi stood upright, crossing her arms.

Ryan snorted. He held his hand out, and the dagger flew into his palm. Spinning it with a flourish, he slid it into an invisible sheath, and it vanished. He looked at Zeke. "I'll warn you. Regression only works until the dome melts, and I get a final warning. If it isn't working out..."

"If we're all dead, fine." Zeke waved his hand. *If we're not the last one left, then...might as well.*

Domi glanced at Zeke and nodded meaningfully at Ryan. "Hey, you wanna subordinate him? If he's gonna be on our side..."

"Oh. Right." Zeke looked at Ryan. "If you want to get out of this with us, you kind of have to—"

"I'll be your subordinate," Ryan agreed.

**Ryan has chosen to become your subordinate.**
**New Subordinate:** Ouroboros Apocalypse
**Subordinates:** Anole, Explosion, Ouroboros

Zeke put his hand on his chin. "A, E, O...I just need I and U to complete the set."

Domi squinted at him. "What?"

"Never mind, never mind. Hey, System! Can Mia escape without being my Subordinate?" Zeke asked.

**Heroes do not follow the same rules as Apocalypses.**

Zeke nodded. *Well, that's useful.*

*As easily as Ryan agreed to become my subordinate, I'm going to go ahead and guess he doesn't remain my subordinate if he regresses. That's fine, though. We aren't turning back time. Not this time.*

Ryan looked down at the field below. "Did you prepare?"

"We've got a few traps set up," Zeke said, nodding at the tunnels from the entryway into the field.

"I've never seen this before. If nothing else, this run is unique," Ryan muttered, half under his breath.

"Not too surprising, when you only had ten or a hundred runs," Mia joked.

In the near distance, something huge roared, the sound rattling through the surrounding buildings.

All four of them looked up.

"Look sharp. Here they come," Ryan murmured.

# 88
## HERE THEY COME

Zeke stood on his tiptoes, peering into the streets. "Is it the T-rex? Was I right after all?"

"We already got the first apocalypse. It was Ryan," Domi returned.

Narrowing his eyes at her, Zeke shook his head. "That doesn't count. He didn't attack."

"Still counts," Domi said, shrugging.

Mia shook her head. "I'm with Zeke on this one. Ryan didn't count."

Ryan looked around at the three of them. "Didn't count for what?"

"First apocalypse to show up after we put out bait," Domi explained.

Ryan crossed his arms. "Doesn't count."

"There you have it. Doesn't count," Zeke said helplessly.

"The vote was rigged. I demand a recount," Domi grumbled.

In the near distance, the roar came again, loud enough to drown out their conversation. Overhead, the lights trembled. The stadium's seats keened, resonating with the blast of sound.

Zeke took a deep breath. *This is going to be a marathon fight. I can't pop my transform right away. We'll have to take it slow, rely on our traps, and kill as many as we can.*

*I'm not expecting all the apocalypses to take our bait. We'll probably have to wander the city and do cleanup afterward. In other words, the last thing we can do is fight recklessly. The 300% regeneration we'll get from defeating apocalypses will go a long way to sustain us but, even then, there's four of us. Considering that I can share and dole out regeneration, it could be worse, but still...we have to defeat four apocalypses for all of us to heal up. Not to mention that we don't regain energy when we regenerate. We need to play it safe.*

Thunder rolled down the street toward them. Sharp clatters and clacks mixed into the low grumble. With one last roar, the T-rex skeleton burst into view. Following it, a herd of smaller T-rex skeletons surged forward, dry bones and dagger-like teeth bared as they rushed for the stadium.

"Ha. I was right," Zeke said quietly. He swallowed, his mouth dry. Subconsciously, he tensed a fist. *That's a lot of T-rexes.*

*I can do this. I have to.*

The T-rexes closed in. The first little one threw itself toward the makeshift barrier of cars lined up in front of the stadium's entrance. Two, three, five, ten, little T-rexes charged at the cars, biting them and clawing their way over.

"Wait for it...wait for it..." Domi muttered to herself, her hand held out, fingers ready to snap.

The enormous T-rex stomped forward. Letting out a low snort through its bony nostrils, it lifted an enormous claw to slam down on the cars.

"Now!" Domi threw her hand out and snapped her fingers.

With a rattling *boom*, the cars exploded. Flaming shrapnel burst up at the small T-rexes, sending their bones flying.

Screeching in horror, the ones closest to the explosion burst into splinters.

The large T-rex stumbled backward, battered by the blast and the fragments. It turned its head against the blast, protecting it with its ribcage.

"Damn, didn't get the biggun," Domi muttered.

"Still, one trap pretty much wiped out a whole apocalypse," Zeke pointed out, shrugging.

Twisting her lips, Domi nodded. "Fair."

Straightening, the T-rex shook its head. It looked around it, sniffing at the ground. Its nose bumped against the fallen skeleton of one of the little T-rexes. It let out a low, mournful murmur. Another fallen skeleton, another. The T-rex's mournful murmur grew louder and louder, turning from a murmur to a wail.

"Hey, uh...you think...those little T-rexes were like...its babies, or something?" Domi suggested, backing away.

Mia bit her lip. She shook her head. "No... Its babies? I hope not. That's too sad."

"Get ready. It's never happy when we kill the little ones," Ryan muttered.

Down below, the T-rex threw back its head and let out a roar full of despair. Green light glowed over its bones, forming the illusory shape of organs, muscles, then skin. A ghostly green T-rex stared at them, pale bones still visible through its mantle of glowing flesh.

Zeke's eyes widened. "Oh, fuck. It's pissed."

"Be on your toes. It looks dumb, but it usually invests a good chunk of points into SPR. Don't underestimate it," Ryan warned.

Even as he spoke, the T-rex leaped at the stadium. The green glow around its stubby arms shone bright, and the glow around the arms grew longer. Long claws at least three times as long as the T-rex's usual arms wrapped around the top of one of the stadium's girders. Its claws kicked, then dug into the metal and concrete walls. Roaring, the T-rex hauled itself up the outside of the stadium one push at a time.

Zeke jumped off the box and sprinted over to the wall. Mia, Domi, and Ryan followed. Climbing up to the back wall, he looked down at the T-rex, then pressed his toe on the top of the wall.

## [Crystal Burst]

Crystals burst out of the wall, burrowing into the T-rex's transparent flesh. Ignoring them, the T-rex continued to climb. The spectral flesh tore beneath the crystals but repaired itself moments later.

"It isn't real flesh. The only thing that counts are its bones," Zeke said.

Domi held out her hand. A burning ball of orange light grew in her palm. Its outside lay placid but, inside it, energy raged, growing brighter and stronger by the moment. "If that's the case, then we'll just have to blow them away."

The T-rex's eyes latched onto the ball of light. A flicker of recognition and fear burned in its eyes, then hatred. It threw itself upward, leaping toward the group of them.

Zeke took a step back. "Domi..."

"These things can't be hurried. They take time to cook," Domi grumbled. She pressed her other palm to the ball, putting more and more energy into it.

Mia held out her hand, summoning her sword. She bounced in place, jiggling the jitters off. "Come on, come on..."

The T-rex reached a ghostly hand upward. The claws dug in bare feet below the surface of the stadium.

"A little longer..." Domi muttered.

Zeke quickly threw his hand out over the edge. *I need to stall it!*

### [Manipulate Aerosols]

A blast of steam struck the T-rex in the face. It flinched back, hesitating just a moment.

### [Manipulate Wires]

A new sensation burst in Zeke's mind. He closed his eyes, focusing. Dozens of new fingers wiggled in his mind. He flexed them, and they curled, bursting free of their bindings. Throwing out his hand, he called the wires to life.

Wires burst through the stadium's glass façade and curled around the T-rex's legs. Zeke clenched his hand, and they tightened, binding it in place.

The T-rex looked down. It kicked its leg, but the wires clung tight. Bracing one leg on the concrete, it lifted the other and scraped at the wires.

Zeke grinned. *Now!*

### [Electrify]

Electricity coursed through the wires. The T-rex stiffened, shuddering. It clawed at its caught leg with greater urgency, baring its teeth at the wires yet unable to bend far enough to snap the wires away.

"Haha, gotcha," Zeke gloated.

His stomach grumbled. He put a hand to it. *I'm hungry, but I'm not starving yet. I still have some fuel in the tank!*

The T-rex glared at him. Digging its off-foot into the concrete, it kicked harder, pulling away from the stadium with all its might. Wires snapped. Bits of rubber and metal flew off into the air, raining down on the burned-out cars below.

Domi raised her hand. "Here we—"

In the distance, a bolt of fire lifted out of the flaming part of the city and surged toward them, hurtling through the sky toward them. Startled, Domi turned.

The T-rex jumped upward. A green glowing claw latched onto the top of the stadium, right at their feet. It pulled, and its heavy body shifted upward.

"Throw it!" Zeke shouted.

Whirling, Domi raised her hand again. As she did, the floor jolted. All of them staggered. Domi flailed with her off-hand, barely holding her balance.

Zeke rushed to her side and grabbed onto her shoulder. "Don't drop it!"

"Not trying to!" Domi spread her feet and bent her knees, lowering her center of gravity.

The T-rex latched onto the stadium with all four limbs and hung on for dear life as the metal creaked and the concrete complained. Dust flew off the pillars, and the broken glass from where the wires had broken through rained down on the cars and street. The shaking grew more intense.

"Is there an Earthquake Apocalypse?" Mia guessed, looking around.

Distantly, a mournful whistle played. A heavy rushing sound blasted through the air.

"That sounds like a train. Tornados are supposed to sound like trains. A Tornado Apocalypse?" Domi asked, peering into the sky.

The center of the field trembled. The dirt liquefied, then burst up into the sky. A subway car pierced through the field and charged into the sky, hurtling upward on steel tracks that formed beneath it as it drove.

Zeke stared, then laughed. "Nope. It's just a train!"

The subway train flew straight up out of the earth, lights blaring. It tooted its horn menacingly. Clattering over the tracks, it looped around in the air and charged down toward them.

**Subway Apocalypse**
**Danger Rating:** S+

# 89
## CHUGGA, CHUGGA

Domi looked back and forth between the T-rex, the train, and the fast-approaching bolt of fire. The orange ball of energy shimmered in her hand, barely stable. Glancing at Zeke, she shouted, "Which one do I hit?"

Zeke gritted his teeth. The train hurtled down from above. The fireball closed in, no longer in the distance, but rapidly approaching. On the opposite side, the T-rex latched on with a second claw, heaving itself up toward the edge. A bony nose with hand-length teeth peeked over the surface.

"The T-rex, hit the T-rex!" Zeke shouted. *The T-rex is SSS rank, it's closer and, according to Ryan, it's smart. We need to gank it right out of the gate before it gets the chance to fight us seriously on even footing.*

*Right now, the T-rex is relatively immobile, too, compared to that fireball, flying freely, and the train, making its own tracks. The T-rex can climb, but it's still stuck climbing, unable to dodge except left and right... assuming it can even throw its weight around that well.*

*I don't know how capable the subway or the fireball are, but if we can kill the T-rex here and finish off one apocalypse, it's better to kill it outright rather than to weaken one of the fresh apocalypses with all their strength and potentially end up fighting three apocalypses at once!*

"All right, you're the boss!" Whirling around, Domi spiked her explosive ball down on the T-rex's nose.

"Not at our feet!" Ryan shouted. He vanished, reappearing halfway down the seating.

Zeke stared at the ball. In his eyes, it moved in slow motion, descending toward the T-rex's rising nose. His eyes met Mia's, horror flashing between them. As one, they whirled and scrambled down the stadium seating, jumping from seat to seat, aluminum clattering underfoot.

The orange ball struck the T-rex with a boom like the conclusion of a fireworks show going off all at once. Force blasted out. Domi yelped, lifted off her feet by the blast. Zeke flew forward. The aluminum seats rushed up. He threw out his hands.

### [Perfect Landing]

He caught himself on all fours, the seat inches from his nose. Slowly, Zeke pushed himself upright, ears ringing, the world's sound faded away, his body trembling internally. Blinking, he looked around.

The T-rex dropped back over the edge, its nose and half its skull caved in, beige bone stained black with soot. Domi dropped down toward the seats, arm thrown out. A blast fired from her palm and threw her upright, and she landed on her feet. In the distance, Ryan stood up, rubbing numbed ears.

*Mia. Where's Mia?* Zeke turned, the world still silenced.

The subway train bore down on him and Mia both. Its lights beamed at them. Distantly, its horn blared.

Zeke ran for Mia. "Watch out!"

Mia looked up. She threw her hand out, as if she could fend off the enormous subway car.

"Run!" Zeke shouted.

Brilliant gold light shone from Mia. It swirled around Mia's body as she hovered in midair. The light twisted around her body, forming physical, solid armor, unlike the glittering, translucent armor she'd worn before. A heavy sword appeared in her hand, as real as the armor.

"Manifest," Mia whispered, closing her hand around the sword. She spun it around, leaving a skein of golden threads behind the blade as it spun, then leaped off the bleachers at the subway.

Zeke stared, wide-eyed. *Manifest? Is that like me and Domi's Transform? But she didn't transform...so Manifest creates gear of sorts, I guess. Almost like the halfway between Transform, that changes yourself, and Domain, that changes the world around you. Instead of changing you or the world, it creates new gear in the world that you can equip.*

*Hmm. Might be worth asking the System for if we get a second bonus at 60 or something.*

Mia stepped on the air. A golden disc appeared beneath her foot, and she leaped off it. She swept the sword at the subway car, growing longer as it flew forth.

The subway car jerked upward, dodging away at the last second. Its steel rails curved upward, pulling away at Mia. Her sword bit into its undercarriage. Bits of metal flew off. Black oil gushed out like blood.

Undeterred, Mia whirled around and sliced horizontally. The sword cut through the steel rails and the coupling between two of the cars. The trailing cars fell backward. The railing crumpled in on itself. Falling backward, the whole rear half tumbled down toward the field below.

The subway train started to tumble. As it fell, steel supports burst out of the underside of its rails and slammed into the stadium's seating. It caught itself and wheeled around, rushing toward Mia once more. New cars materialized behind it. Wheels clattered, the horn blew, and the steel beast rushed toward Mia.

Zeke's eyes flashed. *It needs the rails to support it? Ha, why don't I help?* He slammed his foot down and rubbed his toe on the aluminum bench.

### [Crystal Burst]

Crystals surged out of the steel rails, the steel itself twisting and weakening. The subway's rails hit the crystals, and it leaped off the track, hurtling down toward the seating.

"Mia, now!" Zeke shouted.

Mia closed the distance. Her sword swept out, already angling at the subway's cabin. It slashed through the subway's walls, separating the roof from the subway's base.

The roof caught the wind and flew off. Inside, brilliant crimson painted the subway's walls, while the maimed remnants of bodies tumbled down into the field.

Zeke pulled a face. *I guess that's where it got all its levels. Everyone riding it... Thank goodness I wasn't on the subway when the apocalypses kicked off.*

Twisting around, the subway rushed past Mia. She stared, confused. "Huh?"

Wheels clacking over the rails, its internal seating whistling in the wind, the subway threw itself at Zeke.

Zeke jumped up on his toes, lifting his hand. His claws extended. He grinned. "Realized I can just keep throwing crystals on your rails, huh?"

In response, the subway sounded its horn. Lights blared. The full weight of it rushed down at Zeke.

"Zeke, run!" Mia called, terrified.

He held his ground. Lowering his center of balance, he tensed his legs. "I've got this, Mia!"

### [Electric Leap]

The world slowed. Dark tunnels burrowed off in all directions. At the end of one, the subway barreled down on him, so close that even the long tunnel couldn't hide its face. Zeke jumped himself toward it, baring his claws.

### [Tough Body] [Flexible Body] [Hardness]

"Here we go!"

He burst into the light. The subway rushed by inches below him. Lashing out with his claws, he caught onto the passing seats and held on tight. Force jerked through his arms, and the subway carried him off. It shook itself, fighting to throw off the pest on its back.

He scrambled, searching for a grip with his feet. *Come on!* His sneakers kicked at the seats, unable to find a hold. Tossed left and right, he barely resisted being thrown entirely free.

Unable to shake him free, the subway hurtled straight upward, climbing at speed, faster than any roller coaster ever could. Wind rushed by. As it rose, the train tipped back, back, back, only held on its tracks by its momentum. The sky swung out over them, and dozens of feet gaped between Zeke and the concrete seating below.

Zeke's claws slipped in the upholstered seats. His weight swung outward, down, away from the seats. Panicking a little, he muttered, "Fuck, fuck, fuck," as he scrambled for a grip.

*This isn't working.* Zeke glanced down. Raising one foot, he kicked off the other shoe, then pulled his remaining shoe off with his toes. He flexed his toes, revealing claws, then swung his legs down. His claws dug into the upholstery, and he clung on with hands and feet, dried blood flaking off into the air.

Still rushing upward, the train turned upside down. The ground yawned below, eager to snap Zeke up. Zeke held on for dear life, digging his claws in deep. For a moment, they seemed to hover there, pausing at the apogee of the train's rise.

Zeke caught his breath, taking a moment to orient himself. He latched onto the first passenger cabin, directly behind the conductor's car. No one sat in the conductor's seat, the chair just as bloody as the rest. Bits and pieces of the passengers and their lives bounced past him, a bit of bone flying off into the air, chased by an empty candy wrapper.

*Good. I'm close to the controls.* Zeke smiled.

The train finished the loop. Frustrated, it blasted downward again, zooming directly into the field, its entire body vertical.

*I can't hold on here forever. It'll shake me off sooner or later! So long as I'm here, I'll do as much damage as I can!*

Zeke lifted one hand and pointed it at the conductor's box, up at the front of the train.

### [Manipulate Wires]

The control box trembled, then tore itself apart. Wires burst out, lashing at the air like snakes.

The subway stuttered. Its lights flickered out, and its engines cut out. It fell out of the sky, dead in the air.

Zeke jumped forward. He bounded from chair to chair. The gap between the passengers and the conductor loomed. Digging his claws into the last passenger seat, he cleared the gap in one great leap and dug his claws into the conductor's chair.

The subway's headlights lit again. Its engine kicked on. Once more, it roared down at the field.

"Where the hell is your core?" Zeke gestured with one claw, and the control column split to its root, wires unrooting themselves to give him a better look inside. *If it's not in the head, here... in the engine, the heart? Or...it's an inanimate object, after all. Could be anywhere.*

An image replayed in his head. Mia swiping at the train's underside. The train, rearing back to avoid her.

Zeke's eyes widened. He turned over his shoulder. "Mia!"

"Coming!" Mia shouted. She sprinted after the train, gold discs materializing under her feet as she ran.

The grassy field loomed up. Zeke scowled. *Fuck. She's not going to make it!*

An explosion rocked the field. The train stuttered, shaking on its tracks.

Zeke dug his toes in. *Right! Slow it down!*

### [Crystal Burst] [Manipulate Wires] [Whistle Blast]

Crystals jabbed out of the rails, not enough to derail it, just enough to provide friction. Zeke pressed his foot into the cushions. More crystals dug out of the train's rails, thickening on the steel. The train's wheels skidded over the rails. Sparks sprayed. The train jolted as it slowed. Zeke flew forward. The fabric shredded under his claws. His fingers latched onto the metal frame beneath, and he kept himself from flying away.

In his mind's eye, every wire in the train lit up, even the wires in the wall. Zeke yanked his arm down, clawing at the air. All the wires jolted, yanking themselves free of their solder.

The subway train's lights flickered again. Without any

engines to power it, and the rails thick with friction, the train ground slower.

### [Whistle Blast] Stun failed!

*Oh well. Two out of three isn't bad.* "Mia!" Zeke shouted.
Mia closed in. Biting her lip, she raised her sword.
Zeke held his breath. *Come on, Mia! You can make it! Go!*

# 90
## STRIKE THE HEART

The train fell. Mia dropped alongside it, running vertically downward after the train. Gold discs appeared beneath her feet with each step, her feet landing as firmly as though she ran on solid ground. She chased after the underbelly of the train, watching Zeke.

"Strike where you struck the first time, but deeper! Cut it through!" Zeke shouted.

"I'll hit you!" she called back.

Zeke shook his head. "Don't worry about me!"

The train jolted. Zeke whirled. Its nose bumped along the last few inches of crystalized tracks. No more tracks materialized in front of it.

*Oh, shit! I forgot! Without the train...a-awake...there's nothing to make the rails! Fuck!*

The front of the train rolled off the tracks, and the whole thing groaned and sped up as it entered free fall.

Turning back around, he gestured Mia on. "Hurry!"

Mia gritted her teeth. She leaped off the golden disc and struck at the train, sweeping her sword in a wide arc.

The train jerked. Its lights cut back on, blinking a few times.

Coughing, the engine caught again and *vroomed* to life. Heaving, it curved its rails back in on itself in a loop-the-loop and barely dodged Mia's slice. It rattled away, slowly gaining speed.

Zeke frowned. *How? I cut those wires! System, let me see again! Let me see what happened!*

### [Manipulate Wires]

Once more, the wires appeared in his vision. He watched the wires reconnect themselves, healing the damage he'd done to them. Scowling, Zeke reached for the wires again, but this time, they slipped through his grasp like sand between his fingers.

### Subway Apocalypse's SPR opposes!

"Eh? But it didn't the first time?" Zeke muttered.

### High SPR equals a higher chance of opposing. There is still a percentage-based chance of success or failure.

"So, if I tried again, it might work? Do the percentages get rerolled every time I use the skill?" Zeke asked.

### There is a short cooldown between each use.

Zeke scowled. *Unlucky. But then...what about this?* He lifted one hand to his mouth.

### [Whistle Blast]
### Stun inflicted!

The train jerked in place. The rails fell away again, and the engine stalled.

Zeke jumped away from the train. "Mia, now!"

A silver blade pierced the floor of the engine car. It cut through, striking from the rear of the train to its front. The train fell away in two pieces, lights darkening for the final time.

Shimmering in between the halves, an orb slowly spun in place.

Zeke activated **[Modest Gigantification]**, focusing the skill on his wings once more. They burst out of his back, and he flapped once, diving toward the orb. Like with the motorcycle, the orb faded, turning soap-bubble delicate. Thrusting out his head, Zeke snatched the orb out of the air with his teeth and swallowed.

**[Devour]**
**Level + 2.45**
**Level:** 44.09 > 46.54
**Please assign your stat points.**

"SPR, put them in SPR!" Zeke shouted.

**SPR:** 12 > 15

**Devourer is allowed ONE (1) skill.**
**Skills**
**Lay Rail (Average)**
**Momentum (Lesser)**
**Can't**
**Flash Lights (Average)**
**Impossible Arc (Lesser)**
**Pierce Through (Minor)**
**Transport (Average)**

### Can't
### Toll (Average)
### TR

*Yes! Come on! Give me TRAIN as a skill!*

Static burst before his eyes. His vision blacked out for a moment.

*Eh? Why this time?*

The world flickered in, bits coming in from the left and the right. The System menu was nowhere to be seen. Rails flew at him. Zeke desperately flapped his wings and flew backward. The tips of his wings scraped the rails.

"Hey, System! Where'd the skills go?" Zeke asked.

The rails quivered, then toppled, clattering down on the field.

Zeke beat his wings desperately. He flipped around in midair and sprinted away, flying with more speed than he'd ever mustered before. Rails smashed down all around him, piercing into the grassy field.

### [Hunger Awareness]

Hunger panged over and over, alerting him to the tumbling rails at the last second. He swept left and right, dodging the rails by inches. "Mia!"

"Zeke, in front!"

Zeke looked up. A blast of fire surged toward his face. At the same instant, his Hunger Awareness panged.

*A bit late there.* He flared his wings, preparing to back away.

Again, Hunger Awareness flared up. Zeke whipped his head around.

Rails plunged down at him, hurtling toward his back.

*Shiiiiiit!* Zeke closed his wings and dropped.

Fire blasted into his chest. One of the rails whooshed by, ruffling his feathers. The other slammed into his ribs with a horrible *crack*. Zeke fell to the side, grabbing his ribs.

A flaming human form materialized in front of him, one hand thrust forth in a claw to grab. Body cloaked in orange-red-yellow flames, the figure flickered and danced, as fluid as the flames themselves. The flames obscured their gender, age, and appearance. Only the vague outline of a human figure and an almost smiley-face-like expression remained, and even those burned back and forth, not solid but ever-changing, bright enough to sear into his pupils.

The claws flew toward Zeke.

*I can't wait any longer.* Zeke closed his eyes.

## [Transform]

Black armor covered Zeke's body as his form went slender, stomach hollowing, limbs desiccating to the bone. His lips pulled to the jaw, revealing a mouthful of fangs. Mouths opened at his hands and feet, and tendrils lashed out from the back of his head and shoulders.

Bony armor materialized over his wings, coating the upper part of the limb in black layers. His feathers stretched out beneath the armor, gray and shiny as ever.

Belatedly, a menu flashed in.

**Skills**
**Lay Rail (Medium)**
**Momentum (Minor)**
**Can't**
**Flash Lights (Medium)**
**Impossible Arc (Minor)**
**Pierce Through (Lesser)**

### Transport (Average)
### Can't
### Toll (Average)

*No TRAIN? What a pity. Then again... I don't think there's enough food in the world for me to manifest a whole train, given how much energy a motorcycle takes.* Without hesitating, his eyes landed on Pierce Through. *That one.*

### [Pierce Through] (Lesser)

The flaming hand closed on his shoulder. Red-orange fire sizzled against his armor, but Zeke barely felt the heat.

The flaming figure looked at his hand, their inferno-white eyes wide, then back up at Zeke. They pushed it harder into his shoulder. Nothing happened. Zeke's armor barely even charred.

Fear flashed across their face for a moment. They backed away.

Before they could release him, Zeke snatched the burning hand. He looked up at the flaming figure and grinned.

"Hey."

The figure jerked away, struggling against Zeke's hold.

Zeke tightened his hold. He formed his other hand into a blade, claws all pressed together into a single weapon. "Perfect timing. I just got this new skill. Help me test it out."

He jabbed his hand into the flaming figure's solar plexus.

### [Pierce Through]

Fiery flesh parted with ease. His hand surged through an even hotter center, hot enough to burn against his armored skin, then slammed out the other side. White-hot material splattered from the figure's core. Where the white goo struck the field below, it left black burn marks and set the grass aflame.

"Damn. Bet it's hard for you to find a girlfriend," Zeke muttered, eyeing the scorched field with trepidation. He looked at his arm, still jabbed in the flaming figure. *I...should probably retract that before I lose it.*

He yanked his arm back. Before it left the figure's body, the figure slammed both hands down on Zeke's arm, holding it inside them. White-hot eyes met Zeke's. The figure grinned, mouth releasing heat like an oven as it parted.

Zeke yanked again, fighting its grip. The figure latched on tighter. Fingerprints scorched into Zeke's armor, smearing as the figure changed its grip.

Searing heat accumulated on his arm. The armor began to melt. Black globs dripped down to his elbow, sinking in tarlike clumps to the floor. At the thinnest point, the armor dripped away entirely, revealing thin, stringy flesh. The smell of barbecue filled the air as Zeke's flesh charred instantly.

Intense pain blasted into his brain. Zeke clenched his teeth, tensing against it. Even with Resilient Regeneration dulling it, his vision still whited out at the corners. Every thought left his brain, except for one: *Let go! Let go of me!*

He yanked with all his might, fighting the flaming figure. Lifting a leg, he planted it on the figure's chest. Flame burst around his foot, flaring and cracking as it burned away the dust on his sole. He kicked with all his might, pulling away with his upper half at the same time.

The flaming figure stumbled back. Zeke's arm emerged from their stomach, burned to the bones. He tried to clench his hand, but nothing happened. It refused to move.

Zeke raised his eyebrows, looking at the bare bones. *All the tendons are burned away, after all.* As he watched, the skin and armor sloughed off his hand.

*I should probably be panicking,* Zeke thought. He took a deep breath, then shook his head. *Panic comes later.* Lifting the arm to his jaw, he opened his mouth.

"I'm gonna make this a habit," he muttered to himself, then bit down on his arm. Tossing his head back, he quickly chomped it down, swallowing it with a satisfied sigh. *It does taste like barbecue. Actually, not bad!*

The flaming figure stared at Zeke, frozen in place.

Zeke blinked back. "What?"

The flaming figure mimed eating its arm.

It was Zeke's turn to freeze. *I just ate my arm. What the hell? What's wrong with me?*

*I mean. It did taste good, though. And I was hungry. Like... Hungry-hungry. Deserves-a-capital-H hungry.*

Zeke smacked his lips. "Well, okay. I can't explain that. But, I mean, you're on fire. Right? Let's not pretend like this makes sense."

The flaming figure shrugged, then nodded. Raising its hands, it rushed at him.

Throwing his good hand out, Zeke braced himself and narrowed his eyes. "Let's finish this."

# 91
## FINISH THIS

Zeke and the fiery figure rushed at one another. Flames streaked behind the flaming figure, each foot leaving scorched footsteps in the grass.

Thrusting his hand out, Zeke activated his new skill. *Now is the time to test it out!*

Startled, the flaming figure flinched back.

### [Grid]

Nothing happened. Zeke looked at his palm, then at the flaming figure.

The flaming figure looked at Zeke's palm, then up at his face. Their white-hot smile stretched wider. With a ferocious sizzle, they leaped at him.

Zeke spun about on his heel and sprinted off in the opposite direction, racing over the field. Vaulting a fallen rail, he shouted, "Hey, System! What went wrong?"

Behind him, the flaming figure stepped on the rail as it chased after him. The metal glowed red hot beneath its foot.

**You must connect to the energy source to use [Grid]. [Grid] is incompatible with a wireless connection.**

*Oh. That makes sense.* Zeke glanced over his shoulder at the fiery figure, then up, at the train wreckage lying in chunks across the field. He gestured, making a grabbing motion at the nearest passenger car. *Good thing I only shredded the wires in the engine car.*

### [Manipulate Wires]

Wires leapt forth from the car and slithered across the ground toward him. The fiery figure paused, confused, as the wires wrapped around Zeke's wrist.

Snapping his wrist, Zeke operated Manipulate Wires. They flew forth, zipping toward the fiery figure.

The flaming figure grabbed the wires out of the air. The second their hand touched them, the plastic coating the wires melted away. The metal beneath turned red-hot, melting more of the plastic. The figure wrapped the wires around their wrist and pulled.

Zeke stumbled toward them. He dug his feet in and fought back, refusing to take another step in the figure's direction. *Nope. I'm using these against you, you aren't using them against me!*

"Hey, System, they're connected, right?" Zeke called. Without waiting for an answer, he activated his skill.

### [Grid]

Instantly, energy surged into his arm. The armor trembled, standing on end. The energy rushed through his arm into his core and invigorated his entire body.

**Regeneration +50.49%**
**Regeneration + 101.3%**
**Regeneration + 154.23%**
**Temporary Stat Up! +20...+30...+50!**
**[Resilient Regeneration]**

Zeke's missing arm itched. Bone pushed out of the stump. Flesh coated it, then skin, then armor, the forearm growing into a wrist, the wrist growing into a palm, the palm sprouting fingers. As the last of the arm reformed, Zeke yanked the wires toward him. The flaming figure fell toward him, their body dimming as they dropped. The flames dancing over their form guttered, revealing a charcoal-black body beneath.

Revolted, Zeke drew back. *The System did keep warning me not to change my body if I didn't know what I was doing. Is this a side effect of that?*

**Yes.**

*Damn! Wait, hold on. Transform?*

**Transform is taking the place of your Domain. As a courtesy, the System manages your physical changes for you.**

Zeke blinked. *The System is helping me?*

*Wait, hold on. That shouldn't be a surprise. It wants us to become the most powerful apocalypses we can be. It's just...it usually leaves us to our own devices to make our own mistakes. Why help now?*

**Managing a Domain is an all-encompassing task. The System usually assists with managing Domains. As your**

**Transformation has replaced your Domain, the System will assist you with managing your Transformation.**

"Is that what you call it? Like how I couldn't stop my Domain from expanding in the 'Free Trial' or whatever?" Zeke retorted.

**That would have made you a powerful Apocalypse.**

*Right, that's right. The System's all too happy to help, so long as you dance along to its tune. If you don't want to destroy the world, though...* "Right, right. I remember now."

At the far end of the wires, the flaming figure struggled weakly. Only a few flames flickered over their blackened body. They grabbed the wires, blackened hands crackling as they tensed.

Zeke yanked the wires, jerking them toward him. His other hand formed a blade. The figure stumbled toward him, and he plunged his hand into their chest.

### [Pierce Through]

Charcoal flew. The figure gripped his hand again but, this time, it pushed instead of pulling, shoving him away.

"I don't think so." Beefed up on the boost from Grid, Zeke ignored the push entirely. He scrabbled blindly in the figure's charred ribcage, searching for a core.

His fingertips touched a hard, hot orb, so hot that it scorched his fingertips through the armor. Zeke flinched back instinctively, then shoved his arm deeper all at once. His fingers carved through the charcoal chest. He snatched the orb and yanked his hand free, backing away from the apocalypse. Flame flickered off the orb as it burned merrily like a lump of coal.

The figure staggered a step. It reached out to him, to the burning orb he held, then toppled onto its face. It shattered when it hit the floor, dissolving into black ash.

### Fire Apocalypse Defeated!

The orb faded out, no longer burning, and its ashen glow darkened. Tossing the orb into his mouth, Zeke swallowed it quickly.

### [Devour]

The orb singed his tongue, the roof of his mouth, and his tongue. It burned all the way down, only cooling as it struck his stomach.

*Oof. That was rough.* Zeke rubbed his jaw and swallowed a few times. His mouth quickly healed, the high regeneration rate still working in his favor.

### Regeneration +300%
**Regeneration rate:** +454.23% (Temp. 3:01 remaining)
### Level + 3.25
### Level: 49.79

### Please assign your stat points.
### Please choose three skills.

### Skills
### Burn (Average)
*Your fire attacks have a 50% chance of inflicting Burn (Condition).*

### Can't
### Manipulate Flame (Weak)

### Can't

### Spread (Average)
*Enhance the speed at which something you manipulate covers an*
*area. Expands area covered by 20%.*

### Firestarter (Minor)
### Heat (Average)
### Can't
### Charred Armor (Lesser)
### Fire Flight (Average)

Zeke let out a sigh, stumbling back a step or two almost on reflex. His body trembled. Electricity coursed over his body, energizing his every move. *Three stat points to allot, three skills to choose.*

*But...I have all this power from Grid. It would be a waste not to use it. Let's use this first, then choose my skills!*

He gazed up at the top of the stadium. Explosions burst out as Domi fought back something hidden behind the wall. Instinctively, Zeke reached out to the electricity flickering around his body and drew it into himself. His stomach quieted, not sated, but his energy needs met.

He looked at his hand, then clenched it. *I'm so strong right now. Let's go punch that T-rex a good one!*

Activating Modest Gigantification for his wings, he flapped once and took to the air, hurtling toward Domi. The wind streamed past, ruffling his hair and feathers alike. He swooped by the burned-out wreckage of the subway, darting around the rails, then zooming up over the seats and toward the stadium's upper edge.

An enormous roar shook the stadium, halting Zeke in his

tracks. He beat his wings against it, struggling not to fall backward, and clasped his hands against his ears. *What on earth?*

From the other side of the stadium wall, a beige bony wall rose. Higher and higher, piercing toward the heavens, dark eye holes staring into infinity, bony nose cavities snuffling. Huge teeth became even more enormous, and the elongated, originally stubby forearms dangled out over the stadium.

*Holy shit!* Zeke's eyes widened.

Down below, a cavalcade of cats large and small charged onto the field. From the rear, a cloud of wasps surged toward the stadium.

*One wave finishes, and the next begins!* Zeke hesitated, looking down at the new apocalypses.

"Go! I'll take the Cat Man," Mia shouted at him. She raced over the field, a lone warrior running to meet the wave of cats.

"Got it!" Zeke called back. Beating his wings again, he burst over to join Domi and Ryan on the stadium wall.

The skeletal T-rex loomed over them, casting a shadow over the entire field. The stadium wall barely reached its hips. It threw back its head and roared again, then lifted an enormous bony leg high, pulling it up to its body like a bird, and slammed it down toward the stadium wall where Domi and Ryan stood.

Domi looked up, her eyes wide. Ryan's form flickered.

"Domi! Ryan!" Zeke reached out, flying toward them with all his might.

## 92
# DINOSAUR ATTACK

The claw smashed down toward Domi and Ryan. Domi sprinted to the right. Explosions blasted off behind her, pushing her forward in bursts. Ryan flickered away to the left, barely appearing for a split second before he reappeared a dozen paces further down the stadium.

Zeke flared his wings, backflapping away from the claw. A wall of ancient bone whooshed past him, the dagger-sharp claw barely missing his face. The claw slammed down on the stadium. Metal snapped and keened, screaming out as it broke. Concrete cracked. Chunks rained down on the road and tumbled into the field. The step-seats crumbled in on themselves. White concrete dust filled the air, clouding up into the sky, filling the stadium with a sandy, dry scent.

"That's...not where the locker rooms are, right?" Zeke muttered to himself, pursing his lips.

"How the hell are we going to deal with that?" Domi shouted at Zeke. Using both arms, she gestured at the enormous T-rex towering over them.

The T-rex growled. The entire stadium shook. Zeke fell back in the air, barely remaining airborne.

Zeke licked his lips. "System, how long does my transform have left?"

**While [Supercharged] (Condition) thanks to [Grid], Transform timer stops.**

He grinned. "Excellent. Can I take that energy and put it all into Modest Gigantification?"

**Yes. Would you like to do that?**

"Do it."

The energy flickering over Zeke's body all poured into it. His flesh burned, aching as it grew. His legs expanded, stretching out to the ground below. His wings vanished as the rest of his body grew larger.

"You can cancel the wings being large entirely," Zeke said.

**Understood.**

As he stretched upward, Zeke looked at his armored, clawed hands. He flexed them, closing, then opening them. *I'm pretty sure I should collapse in on myself if I actually grew this large. I wouldn't even know where to start with keeping my body whole.*

*You know what? Letting the System handle my Transformed body's integrity* is *a worthwhile benefit.*

His growth halted abruptly. Zeke frowned, still looking up at the enormous T-rex. "Er, System?" *I've upgraded from ant to toddler but, er, I'd rather be the same size!*

**You've run out of energy.**

Zeke glanced up at the T-rex. *I'm child size, take pity!*

With a growl, the T-rex stomped toward him. It opened its mouth, baring massive teeth.

"Hey, Zeke? Why'd you stop there?" Domi asked.

"I ran out of energy!" Zeke shouted back. He ran away from the T-rex, running into the stadium. *Wait, shit! That's where the survivors are!* Whirling about, he ran toward the T-rex.

The T-rex bent down and opened its mouth.

Zeke sprinted toward it, gritting his teeth. "I'm not the one who gets eaten, dammit!"

"Zeke! What are you doing?" Mia shouted. She kicked a giant cat halfway across the field and sprinted at the T-rex, almost keeping pace with Zeke.

"Can you stall it?" he shouted, reaching out toward the stadium.

### [Manipulate Wires] [Grid]

Mia ran forward, even as wires peeled off the stadium and flew toward Zeke. His stomach grumbled immediately, and his knees weakened. Vision blackening, he dropped to one knee to avoid blacking out.

"What the..."

### Your skills have a greater reach while [Giant] (Condition) but require more energy to use.

*Luckily, I should have access to infinite energy now!* Zeke grabbed the wires tight, using his claws to shred the coating. *Go! Grid!*

Energy poured into him. His arm tingled and ached, but [Resilient Regeneration] quickly pushed the pain into the background. Zeke's body grew once more. The lights on the stadium flickered, then went out. All around the stadium, the buildings went dark. Streetlights went out. Sparks burst from the thickly layered electric wires.

The T-rex didn't hesitate. It stomped toward him, mouth open, adjusting its maw upward as Zeke grew.

Zeke braced for impact, tightening his grip on the wires. He stood shoulder-height to the T-rex, not yet its size. *I need to grow bigger. I'll take the hit!*

"Zeke!" Mia leaped forward, swinging her sword. As she swung it, it grew longer, a blade of light emerging from the physical sword. It sliced into the dinosaur's ankle and carved a deep crescent into its bone.

The T-rex growled and kept charging.

Explosions burst around its ankle, a thousand spiraling sparks dancing around its foot. From the top of the stadium, Domi pressed her hands together, cooking a second spark grenade. She nodded up at Zeke. "I've got you, Zeke!"

The T-rex flinched. It turned, growling at Domi instead.

Ryan appeared on the T-rex's forehead. He drove his knife down. The T-rex whirled, tossing Ryan into the air. Ryan vanished, and the T-rex froze.

"Huh?" Zeke muttered.

"I Paused it. Go!" Ryan shouted from atop a nearby light fixture.

Zeke nodded. The electricity stopped tingling in his hand. He looked at the wires, then around him. It was hard to tell in the daylight, but from what he could see, all the lights were off in every direction.

*Whoops. Caused a brown-out by drawing too much electricity. I guess that's as big as I'm going to get.* He stood at the T-rex's jaw, its heavy head above him but not unreachable. Zeke nodded. *Good enough.*

*And for one last thing...* He turned to the list of new skills.

**Skills**
**Burn (Average)**
**Can't**
**Manipulate Flame (Weak)**
**Can't**
**Spread (Average)**
**Firestarter (Minor)**
**Heat (Average)**
**Can't**
**Charred Armor (Lesser)**
**Fire Flight (Average)**

*I'll go with Burn, Manipulate Flame, and Spread. Spread can work with Manipulate Aerosols, too. It's got good synergy with my current set, as well as with the new skill Manipulate Flame. Firestarter seems like a worse version of Manipulate Flame. Heat could be useful, but then, I don't want to overheat myself. Charred Armor...I don't know if that's a skill they intentionally gained or something they inflicted upon themselves by burning themselves. As for Fire Flight, it sounds like I'd have to set myself on fire to use that, and...no real interest in self-immolation.*

**Gained Skills Burn (Average), Manipulate Flame (Weak), Spread (Average)**

Zeke cracked his knuckles. He pulled back his fist and punched the T-rex in the face.

The T-rex fell backward like a bad asset in a video game. Its whole body frozen in its initial pose, it tumbled to the ground heavily, digging a hole in the grass field. Zeke kicked it, propelling it out of the stadium entirely. The T-rex's body crashed into the office buildings opposite the stadium in a shattering crash of broken glass and breaking supports. A few office chairs slipped down from the collapsed floors and bounced down onto its massive body.

"You guys take the little guys, I'll take care of this!" he called.

"Yeah no worries, you got this," Domi said, giving him a thumbs-up from the top of the crushed stadium. She glanced down, then scowled. "Hey! I see you. Get back here!" She threw the spark grenade toward the ground, where it burst into a thousand bouncing grenades, battering a humanoid metallic figure back and forth.

Ryan snorted from atop the lights. He turned, then vanished again, reappearing beside Mia. The two of them forged into the tide of cats, while the Cat Man, perched proudly atop one of the large cats, stood in the background, directing the battle. The cloud of wasps darted around the three of them, alternatively swooping at the cats and Mia or Ryan.

"Domi!" Mia shouted.

"Coming!" Domi pointed at the swarm of wasps. An explosion burst out from inside, breaking it apart. Thousands of tiny wasp bodies hit the field but, moments later, it reformed and swarmed at the group again.

Zeke stomped over the stadium. Each step felt heavy and slow, though he covered massive ground with each step. His stomach growled loudly, demanding his attention.

*Fuck, I use so much energy in this form... and I imagine it isn't easy to fill a stomach this large. I can't use this carelessly.*

He looked down at the T-rex and raised his fist, a maniacal grin on his bare-toothed jaw. "But I *can* use it to crush you!"

# 93
## MAN VS. MONSTER

Zeke punched the T-rex again.

As his fist plunged toward the T-rex, the T-rex snapped back into motion. Whirling its head to meet him, it opened its jaw wide. Zeke's fist swooped inside.

Zeke's eyes widened. He snatched his arm back, but too slow. *Oh, fuck, not again—*

Enormous teeth closed around Zeke's arm.

**[Harden] [Tough Body]**

The T-rex's teeth glanced off his armor and bounced open. Zeke retracted his arm seconds before the T-rex snapped its jaws shut again, tighter this time. Deep tooth marks scarred his slender arm, the armor broken off where it had bitten him. Bright red blood spilled out, splashing down onto the T-rex. Zeke grabbed his arm and backed away.

**[Resilient Regeneration]**

The wound closed, but slowly. Zeke frowned. *My 400%-plus regeneration rate is that slow?*

**You are very large. Those wounds are equivalent in size to your entire ordinary body getting slashed in half several times.**

Zeke bared his teeth. *Fair enough.*

The T-rex bucked, throwing him backward. Zeke reached out behind him, barely catching himself before he slammed into the rubble of the stadium wall. Clambering to its feet, the T-rex chased after him, charging directly with its mouth open.

Zeke threw his hands up. As the T-rex slammed its jaws down on him, he snatched each end of its jaw, hooking his hands through the holes in the skull. The T-rex pushed against him with its whole weight. Its elongated claws scratched at his arms, tearing long scratches in his arms' armor. Clawed feet tore at his stomach, grating over his stomach plates.

"Get...off!" Zeke threw the T-rex away from him with all his might. He crawled to his feet, spreading out his hands as he did.

**[Manipulate Aerosols]**

*Not water this time. Something a little more...spicy.*

Zeke's hand-mouths opened, releasing a thin mist into the air. The mist issued from his foot-mouths as well, though it meant his foot-tongues dragged along the asphalt and tumbled over the burned-out cars underfoot. A thick, floral scent filled the air, aggressively artificial. Turning his head, Zeke coughed slightly. *Whew, that's noxious.*

**[Spread]**

The mist thickened, growing wider around Zeke. Instantly, his stomach emptied, going from normal hunger to *very* hungry. He backed down the road away from the stadium, leaving mist behind him the whole way. "Hey, ugly! Over here!"

Shaking its head, the T-rex climbed to its feet. It glared at Zeke and hissed. Turning its head, it regarded him with one eye socket.

"Yeah, you. Come here!" Zeke shouted.

Growling low in its throat, the T-rex charged toward Zeke. Its feet slammed craters into the road. Windows shattered every time its feet landed from the shockwave of their impact. Cars bounced into the air, smashing back to earth behind it. Its long, bony tail swept into the passing buildings, smashing broad swathes of their façades away.

"Right...this...way," Zeke murmured to himself, continuing to back away. The mist grew ever deeper. Ankle height, then mid-calf.

Zeke's stomach protested loudly. He swallowed, forcing himself not to think about it. *Not now. Hold out for just a little longer!*

The T-rex roared. It sped up, closing the last distance between them.

Zeke's eyes glittered. He jumped back, pointing at the mist at the same time.

### [Manipulate Flame]

A ball of fire sparked into the center of the mist. The hair-spray mist sparked alight. It wrapped around the T-rex's feet. Its bones charred, burned in an instant.

### [Burn]

Even as the short-lived blaze burned out, the T-rex's feet caught on fire. It roared, rushing toward Zeke even faster.

As it closed in, Zeke rushed to meet it.

### [Caffeine Rush]

The whole world slowed around Zeke. The T-rex turned slowly, ducking its head to bite at him. Zeke crouched low. Its teeth cut past Zeke's shoulder, slicing at his armor and tendrils.

*And...now!*

Zeke shoved upward with all his weight, throwing the T-rex backward. The T-rex flailed, then fell back, into the ashes of the burning hairspray.

Pinning it with a foot on its chest, Zeke turned toward its burned and cut ankle. He opened his mouth. *This time with ice!*

### [Create Coffee]

Iced coffee spilled out of his mouth and his hand mouths, spewing down over the T-rex's heated ankle. The ancient bone snapped, cracking audibly as it suddenly changed in temperature. Raising his foot, Zeke stomped on the T-rex's ankle. With an earth-shattering *CRACK,* it broke through. The T-rex's foot fell to the ground.

Panting, Zeke wiped his mouth, coming away with a surprising amount of drool. He glared down at the T-rex. "Just die already."

**Warning:** the Condition [Supercharged] is about to wear off! **You are only able to use your [Giant] form because of your [Supercharged] stat bonus. If [Supercharged] wears off while you have the [Giant] Condition, you will be [Paralyzed] or worse.**

**Time remaining:** 0:15

Zeke's eyes widened. "Fuck!" He stomped the T-rex's chest a few times. Bones cracked under his heel. *Its core. Where is its core? If I can find it, I can kill it. Now, before I shrink...please!*

**Time remaining:** 0:10

Dropping to his knees, Zeke pinned the T-rex's elongated arms to the floor. He fished in its hollow rib cage, groping blindly between the slats of its ribs. *I don't think it's in the head. The heart, then? Come on, come on!*

**Time remaining:** 0:05

The T-rex fought against him. It bucked under him, momentarily lifting Zeke into the air. Zeke pressed it back down, scraping his claws along the inside of its ribs, searching for something, anything. *A lump in the bone, a bauble, anything! I can't run out of time like this. I can't beat the T-rex if I'm tiny and have no idea where its core is!*

**Time remaining:** 0:03

His huge fingertips scraped over a strange bump. Zeke froze. He craned his neck, peering into the T-rex's ribcage.

The T-rex bit at his head. Giant teeth bore down on the top of his helmet.

Time remaining: 0:00

"Make me small again!" Zeke shouted.

Instantly, he shrunk. His body collapsed into itself. Zeke

grabbed the T-rex's rib bone and held on tight, even as his hand grew smaller and smaller. When his hand could no longer fit around the rib, he tightened his grip on the edge of the bone, anchoring himself to the T-rex.

The T-rex heaved itself upright. Zeke swung outward as it stood. The long claws scraped toward him, jittering over the T-rex's rib cage. One of the claws swooped toward him, scratching over the very top of the rib bone he clung to.

Zeke tensed. *Oh, fuck!* He grabbed onto the rib bone with both hands and swung his legs up. His feet slammed against the claw. Still about the size of a van, he managed to barely hold the claw off.

The T-rex pushed harder against him. His legs bent inward, even as he grew smaller. Inevitably, the claw pressed him back.

"Help...someone help!" Zeke shouted.

### [Subordinate Link]

Time ticked by so slowly it hurt. Zeke gritted his teeth. Sweat dripped down his face and back. The claw slowly compressed him. His hands slipped, sliding over the top of the bone. He glanced over his shoulder at the edge of the rib.

### Subordinate Allen is willing to share his STR.

"Do it!" Zeke snapped, no time to waste.

### STR: 8 > 23

Strength surged through his limbs. He kicked the claw away, and it bounced off the ribcage entirely. Hanging there, Zeke laughed breathlessly, diminishing in size from van to human. "Yeah, shows you right, you giant bone—"

The T-rex's other claw careened toward him.

Eyes widening, Zeke grabbed the rib bone tight and threw himself over it, sliding his body through the enormous gap in the dinosaur's rib bones. "Allen! Can I have your climb skill?"

**Subordinates can only share one skill or stat at a time.**

"That's fine! Give me climb!"

## [Subordinate Link]
## [Lizard's Climb] (Medium) (Temp)

Zeke braced his feet on the bone. They stuck, clinging to the steep wall, toes splayed, foot tongues idly licking the bone. He yanked his hands over the edge of the bone and pressed them to the bone as well, then ducked his head down over the edge as the claw hurtled toward him.

# 94

## BONE CLIMBING

Pulling his hands and head down, Zeke hunkered on the inside of the rib bone, his knees pulled up to his chin, his head ducked down between them. The claw scraped over the top of the bone, spilling sparks and bone dust as it passed. The off-white dust settled onto his head and flecked his tendrils, and then the claw was gone.

Zeke peeked from behind the rib and looked around, glancing left and right. *Where is that lump I felt? I don't know that it's the answer, but it's a good place to start!*

A dozen feet along the curvature of the ribcage, a strange bony outcropping caught his eye. Zeke scurried toward it on all fours. On his head, Allen leaned forward, curious.

The T-rex roared in its frustration. A rush of wind hurtled past Zeke. It caught under his chest and pulled him away from the rib bone. Startled, Zeke wrapped his arms over the upper edge of the bone, clinging tight. *Its weird no-voice-box roaring still involves wind in its chest? It's almost like a ghost is possessing this skeleton, behaving like the T-rex would have, all its instinctive muscle movements and organ functions.*

*Actually, come to think of it, how on earth is an ancient skeleton even... How did it wake up? The T-rex that made this skeleton died millions of years ago. Assuming ghosts are real, that ghost should have long since left this mortal plane! No way it stuck around that long. So...what's powering this T-rex?*

Zeke shook his head. *I'm being stupid. A coffee machine came to life. I don't know what the System did, exactly but, obviously, anything can gain awareness. Even a T-rex's skeleton.*

*Still, if that's the case, why did it make tiny T-rex skeletons instead of growing a Domain by default?*

The T-rex beat at its ribcage with its claws. One of the claws thumped the rib Zeke clung to, and he gripped it tighter, jolted back to reality. *Now isn't the time to get philosophical! Now is the time to finish things!*

Pushing on, he climbed along the T-rex's rib again, one arm hooked around the top of the rib to keep from getting shaken off entirely. Slowly, he scooted toward the bony outcropping.

The T-rex's claw hooked over the edge of the rib. Cutting through the center of the rib, it keened as it swooped toward him.

*Shit! Gotta go!* Zeke scrambled up to the top of the rib and reached to the next. His hands stuck to the upper rib and, kicking off the lower rib, he hauled himself up. The claw cut through the space he'd been moments before, leaving a thin white line in the bone.

Behind it, the bony outcropping crumbled a little, revealing a shiny metal object.

*Huh? Metal? Oh, well. I'll figure it out when I get there!* Zeke sped up. Throwing caution to the wind, he sprint-crawled along the inside of the rib, hurtling toward the object. In a few moments, he reached the space over it, then jumped down.

As he jumped, the T-rex lunged forward. Its ribs flew away from him, the back half of its ribcage rapidly closing in on Zeke.

## [Modest Gigantism]

The tiny wings on Zeke's back grew large once more. Flapping them, he swooped after the front ribcage, only for the T-rex to abruptly stop. The bone wall of its ribs flew at Zeke. He flared his wings and reached his arms out, bracing for impact.

*Bam!*

His hands and knees slammed into the T-rex's rib. Shockwaves flew up his wrists and femurs. Zeke winced. *Oof. That hurt even through Resilient Regeneration.*

A loud growl issued from his stomach. Zeke's vision blurred, and his grip on the T-rex slipped. Shaking his head, he forced himself onward. *No time. Keep moving!*

The bone lump lay just ahead. The metal thing stuck out of it, a square plaque of some sort. Zeke pulled.

Nothing.

Growling under his breath, Zeke pulled harder, bracing his feet against the bone and pulling back with all his might. The plaque shifted once, twice, then burst free all at once. Behind it, something off-white fell out. Zeke lunged, barely catching it before it fell.

The T-rex froze. Its head drooped, and it slumped toward the ground.

Zeke looked down. In his left hand, a bronze plaque read, *Most of Milly's bones are recreations! This small fragment of her rib is one of the few pieces of real fossil on display.*

He turned. A tiny fragment of parchment-colored stone lay in his other hand, barely recognizable from its strange layers as a bone.

Startled, Zeke blinked. He drew it close, peering at it. "I'm... I'm holding a piece of a T-rex. A real piece of a T-rex! Millions of years old..."

**Would you like to [Devour] the Dinosaur Apocalypse's core?**

*Huh? Oh. It makes sense, doesn't it?* Zeke stared at the bone, frowning. *But then...doesn't that mean...that the T-rex apocalypse's core was the actual fossil? Then, maybe—*

*It's not the time for philosophy!* Zeke threw his head back and shoved the fossil into his mouth.

**[Devour]**
**You defeated the Dinosaur Apocalypse!**
**Level +10.31**
**Level:** 49.79 > 60.10

**Please assign your stat points.**
**Level 60 reached! Please wait. Level 60 bonus loading.**

**Please choose three skills.**

**Skills**
**Grow (Strong)**
**Giant (Condition) (Lesser)**
**Claws (Large)**
**Can't**
**Charge (Medium)**
**Bite (Medium)**
**Strong Jaw (Strong)**

**Roar (Medium)**
*You emit a powerful roar, which can be used as a sonic attack. 30% chance of inflicting Stun.*

**Can't**
**Stomp (Medium)**

Zeke let out a breath. He glanced down, then hopped from rib to rib, rushing to the bottom of the ribcage. There, he dropped to the ground and walked out through a hole in the skeleton's hips.

Turning back, Zeke looked up at the massive skeleton. *A female T-rex, who created a group of smaller T-rexes. Was she re-creating her family? That's almost sad.*

He slapped his cheeks. *Focus, Zeke. Let's not get sentimental over a million-year-dead creature the System kind-of revived. Skills. Pick skills.*

*Hmm. I already have Grow, and it hasn't helped me much. Ended up fusing it away. Giant...I don't want to be big all the time. I already have claws. Charge could be useful, but if the T-rex is any example, it's a very no-nuance straight-forward attack. If I'm facing anyone with SPR or intelligence, they'll be able to see through the attack very quickly. Bite...that one's a no-brainer yes. I can always use skills to give me more jaw powers. Strong Jaw I fused away, but I could use a +1 on Tough Body. Roar sounds useful. I can always use more Stun chance. Stomp might be worth it? I do have foot-mouths. It might have synergy with using them.*

*Okay, let's go with this set.*

**Learned [Bite] (Medium), [Roar] (Medium), and [Stomp] (Medium)!**

*As for stat points...*

**STR:** 8 > 10
**CON:** 10 > 12
**DEX:** 8 > 10
**SPR:** 15 > 20

Zeke took a deep breath. He looked up at the stadium, the

crumbled wall, tangled with twisted metal, the concrete block rubble still tumbling down here and there. *Let's end this.*

**Three non-allied Apocalypses remain.**

# 95
## FINISH THIS

Z eke looked up, startled. "Really?"

**Confirmed. You are not the only Apocalypse busy killing other apocalypses.**

*Then this is really it.* Zeke stepped forward, flapping his wings. A great rush of wind swirled around him, and he lifted into the air, leaving dust and trash whirling behind him.

He landed at the top of the stadium. Down below, Mia and Ryan dueled the Cat Man, while an exhausted, soot-stained Domi, Transform long since worn off, fired off explosions into the cloud of wasps. Zeke stepped forward, preparing to reenter battle.

His armor shifted, then vanished, melting into his limbs. His limbs plumped, and his cheeks regrew, while the mouths on his hands and feet closed over.

**Transform wore off! Cannot use Transform for another 5:45.**

Zeke startled. "Wait, what?" *Transform timing out I get, but that crazy cooldown? Isn't it the time I was in Transform? But the timer stopped while I was [Supercharged], so it shouldn't—*

**The countdown timer stopped while you were [Supercharged], but the cooldown counter continues to count up.**

"Could've used that information ahead of time," Zeke muttered. *Though, what would I have done differently? I needed every second of that time.*

Looking down at the battle, he took a deep breath.

### [Roar]

A blast of sound rolled over the field, nearly as fierce as the T-rex's cries. Down below, the Cat Man and several of the cats froze. About a third of the wasps fell out of the air, where Domi quickly blasted them into oblivion.

"Listen to me!" Zeke shouted, stepping to the edge of the field. He looked down at the gathered apocalypses. "We're the last men standing. Subordinate to me or die!"

*I don't really want the Cat Man as my subordinate, but since he has [Nine Lives], he's a pain in the ass to kill. Better to subordinate him so we can get out of here, then turn him over to law enforcement or something once we're out.*

Cat Man paused. A thoughtful expression passed over his face.

The wasps whirled around and flew toward Zeke in a buzzing mass, all of them zipping toward him at once.

Zeke lifted his hand. He waited, holding his breath. *Closer. Closer.*

The wasps shot toward him, wings as loud as an airliner's

turbine, stingers glittering in the sunlight.

*Now.*

### [Manipulate Flame]

A blast of flame shot from his palm and engulfed the wasp swarm. The wasps not immediately immolated beat their wings furiously, pulling a desperate about-face. Zeke stepped forward, pushing out with his palm.

### [Spread]

Like wildfire, the flames spread from wasp to wasp. They tumbled out of the sky, charcoal-black corpses as thick as dirt underfoot.

Domi pulled out her cellphone, quickly tapping away. She clicked a button, then shoved it back in her pocket.

A semicircle of explosions rattled the air around the wasps, herding them toward the flames. The wasps jerked away from the noise, only to bump into their flaming colleagues. The flame devoured them all, and no more wasps buzzed in the air.

**Subordinate defeated Wasp Apocalypse! Sharing levels... Levels shared between all subordinates! +0.02 Levels. Level: 60.12**

Isaac the Cat Man looked at the tumbling wasps, then at his cats. The cats looked back at him. A few sat down and curled their tails around them. One of the large cats even laid out flat on its side, closing its eyes to slits.

He put his hands up. "I subordinate myself."

**Gained Subordinate:** Cat Man Apocalypse!

"The last one...Domi, where did it go? The one you were fighting?" Zeke asked, wiping his face in exhaustion.

She shook her head. "I destroyed that thing, dude. Steel Apocalypse or something? It's dead. Got the System message and everything."

*Huh. I didn't get a 'subordinate defeated' message for that. Was I too far away?* Zeke frowned, then froze. He looked around. "There were three remaining. Where's the third one?"

"Huh?" Domi asked.

"Three Apocalypses Remaining. Is it hiding somewhere in the city?" Zeke turned. From atop the stadium, he could see to the limits of the black shield. The enormity of the city spread before him. From the burned-out husk to the south, the glittering office buildings downtown, the cultural center to the right where the crushed remains of the museum and the empty husk of the elementary school stood, the hugeness of it weighed upon his shoulders.

*And somewhere, anywhere, in there, is a single apocalypse. One lone apocalypse we have to find and destroy to escape.*

Domi jolted. She reached into her pocket and fumbled her phone back out. It buzzed, receiving a call. She looked at Zeke. "What the hell?"

"Answer it!" Zeke encouraged her, miming holding it up to his ear.

She rolled his eyes at him. "I'm not stupid. I know what you do with a phone." Lifting it to her ear, she paused. Her eyes bored into Zeke's. "If it's the Robocall Apocalypse and this makes me go insane or something, that's on you."

Zeke raised an eyebrow, amused.

Grinning back, Domi put it to her ear. "Hello?"

Her grin vanished. Brows creasing, she frowned, expression growing more serious by the moment. "Uh huh... Yeah, okay.

So...right. You can see? You saw it all? Uh, okay. Yeah." Her eyes widened. She paused, then lowered the phone.

"What?" Zeke asked.

"It's an apocalypse. They'd like to become your subordinate."

Zeke frowned. "What apocalypse? Wait, the apocalypse called you?"

**Gained Subordinate:** Apartment Apocalypse!

"Apartment?" Zeke squinted, confused. He put a hand on his chin, then shook his head. *They subordinated themselves to me without a fight. I-I guess I should be grateful.*

Ryan and Mia climbed up the seats to Zeke's side. Mia gazed out at the city while Ryan faced inward, a wary eye on Isaac.

"So...is this it?" Mia asked.

Zeke spread his hands. "They have to be sufficiently subordinated, whatever that means."

She sighed. "How long do you think we have to wait before that happens?"

"I have no idea," Zeke replied.

"It's almost over!" Domi shouted. She stretched up to the sky, then down to her feet. Casually, she wiped a streak of soot off her face. "I want to go home and have a shower. I feel gross."

"What do you think the rest of the world is like?" Mia asked.

"Huh? Normal, right? This was the Apocalypse Incubator. We're the ones who were supposed to break out and end the world," Zeke explained.

Mia shook her head. "Do you really think that's it? We're the only incubator, and that's the end of the fight?"

"I..." Zeke paused. *The System couldn't be...but then, why wouldn't it?* He shook his head. "Let's worry about that once we get out. No point talking about hypotheticals."

"Yeah." Closing her mouth, Mia nodded, but her eyes gazed into the horizon, past the black wall that enclosed them.

Ryan took a deep breath. He looked at Zeke. "You did it."

"I did?" Zeke asked.

"I'm...I'm not going to turn back time. It's not perfect." Ryan turned, following Mia's gaze to that point beyond the horizon. "But you're right, it's never going to be. All I'm doing is dancing in the palm of the System's hand."

Zeke smiled. "Good."

Ryan clenched his fist. "There's a part of me that still wants to, but..."

"But?" Zeke asked.

Snorting, Ryan punched him on the shoulder. "But you're not a monster spawning near-infinite hunger zombies, so I'll give it a try."

"Oh, thanks," Zeke muttered, shaking his head at Ryan. *Was I really that bad?*

*How could I not be? If I had my Domain, and the System was whispering into my mind, shaping my thoughts, and something horrible had happened...something like, I don't know, my best friend trying to kill me and Mia dying...then, then I could see it all falling apart.*

He offered Ryan his hand. "No more trying to kill each other?"

Ryan looked at his hand, then took it. "No more trying to kill each other."

"Aww, bromance." Domi tilted her head and grinned, putting her hands against her face.

"All right, enough of that." Zeke glanced over his shoulder at Isaac. "Hey, you subordinated yet?"

Isaac flipped him the middle finger.

"That doesn't look very subordinated," Zeke said, shaking his head.

Down on the field, Isaac bent, giving him an overly dramatic bow.

Zeke nodded. "That's more like it."

"Zeke!" Mia grabbed his sleeve and pointed.

Zeke turned.

Across from them, light shone on the horizon. At its very base, the black dome cracked open. The crack climbed upward, splitting it in two from the ground up to the sky. The moment the two pieces separated entirely, they folded open, falling back into the earth.

Blue sky beamed down on them, the sun glowing overhead. Green earth rolled out to infinity, streaked with roads and spotted with strip malls, subdivisions, and gas stations.

As the last of the dome faded away, emergency vehicles rolled into the city, sirens blaring. Fire fighters, policemen, ambulances, all rushing in as fast as they could.

Mia sniffed. Tears welled up in her eyes. She grabbed Zeke, holding on with all her might, the gesture more cling for hope than hug. "We did it. We did it!"

"We did it," Zeke confirmed, a grin on his face. He hugged her back, patting her gently.

"Group hug!" Domi called, glomming on to the hug.

Ryan scoffed. "Yeah. We did it." He turned back to the horizon and swallowed. Blood leaked between his fingers where he clenched one hand too hard, far too hard.

"Hey. Come on in," Zeke said, gesturing to Ryan.

"No, no..."

Mia released Zeke. She grabbed Ryan, then dragged him into the hug. "Group. Hug."

"Oh...okay, okay," Ryan grumbled. Reluctantly, he joined in.

Zeke laughed. "We did it. We really did it."

"Um, excuse me..."

Zeke turned.

Down on the field below, the middle-aged woman looked up at him, careful to keep her distance from Isaac. "Uhm, we noticed that it got quiet, and now the sirens... Is it..."

Zeke pointed upward. "It's over. We're safe."

The woman's eyes widened. Nodding, she rushed back into the locker room.

Isaac watched her go, an almost predatory light in his gaze.

"Hey. Cat Man. Bad boy," Zeke called.

Narrowing his eyes at Zeke, Isaac flashed another middle finger his way.

Sighing deeply, Zeke turned back around. *It's over. It's all over now. I don't need to worry about the System, or Apocalypses, or anything ever agai—*

**Congratulations, Survivors!**
**WELCOME TO THE APOCALYPSE BATTLEGROUND.**
**EXPAND YOUR DOMAIN.**
**DEFEND YOUR CITY.**

Zeke froze. "Uh...did anyone else get that?"

Mia leaned forward, squinting. She pointed. "Zeke, look. There."

Zeke squinted as well.

In the distance, a black dome arced, blocking out a section of the horizon.

Pressing his lips together, Zeke closed his eyes. When he opened them, the black dome remained as solid as the earth underfoot.

He sighed. *We've got our work cut out for us.*

---

**The story will continue in Apocalypse City!**

# THANK YOU FOR READING
## APOCALYPSE ME

We hope you enjoyed it as much as we enjoyed bringing it to you. We just wanted to take a moment to encourage you to review the book. Follow this link: Apocalypse Me to be directed to the book's Amazon product page to leave your review.

Every review helps further the author's reach and, ultimately, helps them continue writing fantastic books for us all to enjoy.

---

**ALSO IN SERIES:**
Apocalypse Me
Apocalypse City

*Check out the entire series here! (Tap or scan)*

---

Want to discuss our books with other readers and even the authors? Join our Discord server today and be a part of the Aethon community.

Facebook | Instagram | Twitter | Website

You can also join our non-spam mailing list by visiting www.subscribepage.com/AethonReadersGroup and never miss out on future releases. You'll also receive three full books completely Free as our thanks to you.

**Looking for more great LitRPG?**

*The Young Gods Tournament awaits. Only the victors will break through to the worlds beyond the heavens. In an unfair world where a single monster can wipe out an entire village, Thomas is not one of the chosen few. He wasn't gifted with immense power from the moment of his birth, nor does he have a powerful backer to defend him. By the laws of the world, it's near impossible for him to rise to the top. But where the god's themselves have failed him, Thomas will push on and gain the strength to protect his friends, and his home, from the ever rising dangers of the world. There is only one true opportunity to break through the shackles of his life — The Young God's Tournament. After surviving a deadly ambush, he'll use every ounce of his strength as he faces off against his rival Prospects, a continent-wide conspiracy, and the ever looming threat from the once-slumbering Empire. Western Cultivation melds with LitRPG as a single man rises against an unfair world in this new series from bestseller Cale Plamann (*Blessed Time, Viceroy's Pride*), together with Alex Beaumont.*

Get Young Gods Tournament Now!

*The King is dead. His heir too young to rule. Who will claim the crown?* The noble houses gather to choose a new Lord Protector, sparking old rivalries. If they can't agree, civil war looms. That is if foreign kingdoms don't smell blood in the water and invade first. Lord Vale wants to take up the mantle, spurred by his ambitious brother Konstans. Lord Isarn likewise seeks this power. He is aided – or thwarted – by the return of his brother, the knight and war hero Athelstan, whose squire, Brand, hopes to restore his family's fortunes no matter the cost. Through all of this, an enigmatic traveler makes plans with jarls, scribes, and priests for his own mysterious purpose. Only one thing is for certain. War is inevitable. **Power-hungry lords scheme and warriors fight for glory in this epic fantasy tale from D.E. Olesen, which was one of the Top 10 highest rated Royal Road web-serials ever written. Equal parts** Game of Thrones **and** Vikings, **the series digs deep into every level of a struggle of power, from lords to serfs. From political intrigue to the bonds between family. Join the fight for the soul of Adalmearc!**

Get Eagle's Flight Now!

**The Connected System has come to Earth, bringing with it the apocalypse...** *In an instant, life as it was known is gone, replaced by a System called The Connection. It doesn't come quietly as earthquakes rock the planet, the chosen survivors falling unconscious as the Connection takes their bodies and Adapts them. Lochlan Brady and his family were on their way home from a camping weekend when the Connection appears. He awakens with a new Adapted body, finding his wife missing. Now Loch must survive and thrive in this new world with his two teenage daughters, Harper and Piper. All Loch wants to do is protect his daughters and find his wife. A chance encounter with creatures straight out of myth will force the family to quickly confront the reality of their new lives, the changed world and give Loch a jump in power. But with that power will come responsibility and more danger. Along with the attention of some of the most powerful beings in The Connected System.*

Get Warbreaker's Rise Now!

---

**For all our LitRPG books, visit our website.**

Made in the USA
Monee, IL
22 June 2025

19801248R00364